PRAISE FOR *THE LAST BUSH PILOTS*

"TOP 100 BREAKTHROUGH NOVELS"—Amazon.com
"You won't put it down while the midnight sun still shines!"
—*Airways* Magazine
"Suspense and drama in spades. Romantic entanglements and a covert mission help this aviation tale take off."—Kirkus Reviews
"I flew through *The Last Bush Pilots* in one sitting, keeping my seatbelt securely fastened.!"—John Wegg, Editor, *Airways* Magazine

"The author paints pictures with words that are every bit as beautiful and moving as anything ever drawn or photographed."—Aviationguy.com

"As an Alaskan bush pilot, reading *The Last Bush Pilots* was like a glance in a mirror."
—CloudDancer, Airline Pilot, Author, *CloudDancer's Alaskan Chronicles.*

PRAISE FOR *There I Wuz! Adventures from 3 Decades in the Sky-V's 1-4*

"When we come across an aviator with a gift for storytelling, those adventures jump off the page. Eric Auxier is such an author, and *There I Wuz!* is the book."
—Karlene Petitt, Airline Pilot; CNN Correspondent; Author, *Flight to Success*
"I freaking love this series!"—Steve Thorne, pilot-videographer, flightchops.com
"Captain Eric Auxier is not just a pilot, he is an aviation author, ambassador and legend. He opens the bullet-proof cockpit door and welcomes us into the most technically-advanced, risk-laden, yet safest profession."—Captain Richard de Crespigny, author, QF32

PRAISE FOR CODE NAME: DODGER Young Adult FLY/SPY Thriller Series

*Series rated a **PERFECT** 4 out of 4 star rating by the Online Book Club!*

Mission 1: Operation Rubber Soul—"Flawless execution of the plot line, with a multi-dimensional protagonist that sets this book apart from the rest."
—*Online Book Club Official Review*

Mission 2: Cartel Kidnapping—"**4/4 STARS!** Reluctant and avid readers who enjoy teenage fast-paced spy adventures will love reading this book."
—*Online Book Club Official Review*

Mission 3: Jihiadi Hijacking—"**4/4 STARS!** Superb on so many levels. A highly detailed, entertaining, and character-driven spy thriller!"
—*Online Book Club Official Review*

"An engaging espionage tale that aims to enlighten readers!"—*Kirkus Review*

Mission 4: Yakuza Dynasty—"**4/4 STARS!** One of the best books I've ever read! More twists and turns than many mysteries. Amazing that this level of action, intrigue and humor could last an entire book. Absolutely in the same league as the Harry Potter series!"
—*Online Book Club Official Review*

ALSO BY ERIC AUXIER

There I Wuz! Adventures From 3 Decades in the Sky

Volumes 1-4

CODE NAME: DODGER Missions 1-4

ADVENTURES OF CAP'N AUX

(Capnaux.com)

THE LAST BUSH PILOTS

Eric Auxier

First edition paperback November 1, 2012.
First edition eBook November 1, 2012.
First edition hardcover November 1, 2021.

Published by EALiterary Press.

Courage is the price that
Life extracts for granting peace.
The soul that knows it not
Knows no release from little things:
Knows not the livid loneliness of fear,
Nor mountain heights, where bitter joy can hear
The sound of wings.

— Amelia Earhart

STEVE RAY WILSON, 1965-2007

Dedicated to the memory of my good friend Steve Wilson, a career Alaska bush pilot. Steve, you taught me so much about flying the bush, and about the simple joys in life.
You will be sorely missed.

PREFACE

People will inevitably ask me just how much of this book is true. While this novel is entirely fictional, many larger-than-life characters and "tall tales" are inspired by real people and events I encountered while flying the Alaska bush in the summer of'87.

For example, in Chapter 3, *Eagle & Salmon*, the scene where an eagle with a salmon in its talons flies inches over the boys' heads while they're chatting on the Juneau Airport ramp, happened to me. It remains one of the most breathtaking scenes in my life. And in Chapter 22, *The Sky Fell*, DC faces the bush pilot's ultimate fear. That experience also happened to me, and proved to be a watershed moment in my flying career. Readers of my blog at capnaux.com will recall the true story in my post, *The Sky Fell*. Moreover, the way both pilots handle their emergency landings come from hours plying the Southeast Alaska skies, contemplating exactly just what I would do if faced with those situations.

In another incident that inspired a subplot for this book, I did indeed fly three orphaned bear cubs. As in the novel, a poacher killed their momma sow. While those real-life cubs found homes in zoos in the Lower Forty-Eight, I wanted to spin a fun yarn exacting poetic justice on said poacher; hence, the Doyle brothers in the book. And, by the way, bear cubs really do *stink to high heaven!*

Some minor facts have been altered to serve the story. For example, Etolin Island, not Pleasant Island, contains the Roosevelt Elk herd. I also have to confess that real-life credit for Ralph Olaphsen's genius "volcanic" April First hoax goes to one Oliver "Porky" Bickar.

A major theme that shapes this book is Alaska; the land, the people, their way of life. But Alaska's dominating trait, in this book and in real life, is the weather. In *The Last Bush Pilots*, Mother Nature is personified as the Ultimate Adversary, and modern day bush pilots would do well to think of Her as such. She dominates every decision we make, from how much fuel to take, what route to fly, even whether to launch or not. To that end, the most accurate scenes in this book, I believe, are the ones that take place in the air.*

While firsthand experience and painstaking research went into this novel, it could only take me so far. I would like to thank several key friends and advisors, who have helped make this book what it is today.

First of all to my mother and father, for believing in me from Day One, and supporting all my hare-brained decisions, from learning to fly, to moving to Alaska, to soloing a hang glider at age 15.

Also a huge thank you to my brother, Allen and his wife, Mari, two decades-long residents of Alaska. Another kudos to my friend and fellow bush pilot, Kevin Hufford, who to this day flies the Southeast Alaska skies in his intrepid Beaver amphibian. Thanks also to Cristina and Donald Gregory for their insight into Tlingit life and customs. Thank you also to fellow airline pilot and Alaska hunting guru Mark Marshall, as well as another fellow airline pilot , Captain Gary B.—now retired and back flying the Alaskan skies, where his heart is. Captain Gary is better known as "CloudDancer," of *CloudDancer's Alaskan Chronicles* (clouddancer.org). Check him out for some wild "There I Wuz" tall tales!

Special thanks to the Red Dog Saloon and to Heritage Coffee Company, for allowing me to use their names in the novel. Very real places that I enjoyed frequenting during my Alaska adventure. While several scenes figure prominently in both establishments, the events and descriptions therein are entirely fictional. Nevertheless, my pilot buddies and I spent many a memorable time in both locales.

And finally, a big Thank You to Mother Nature and Alaska Herself, for granting me to survive my brief, rich, unforgettable *cheechacko* life. I may have only spent a scant summer season in that magical land called Alaska, but the lessons and impressions, both on the ground and in the sky, have stuck with me for life.

And inspired this novel. Enjoy!

Eric Auxier
Phoenix, Arizona
October 24, 2021

A note about the safety of air travel: while an author must inevitably take poetic license by embellishing the hazards to "up the drama," flying in a general aviation airplane is still* ***ten times safer than driving**.*

TABLE OF CONTENTS

JNU VFR SE*CTIONAL CHART*
(Do not use for air navigation)

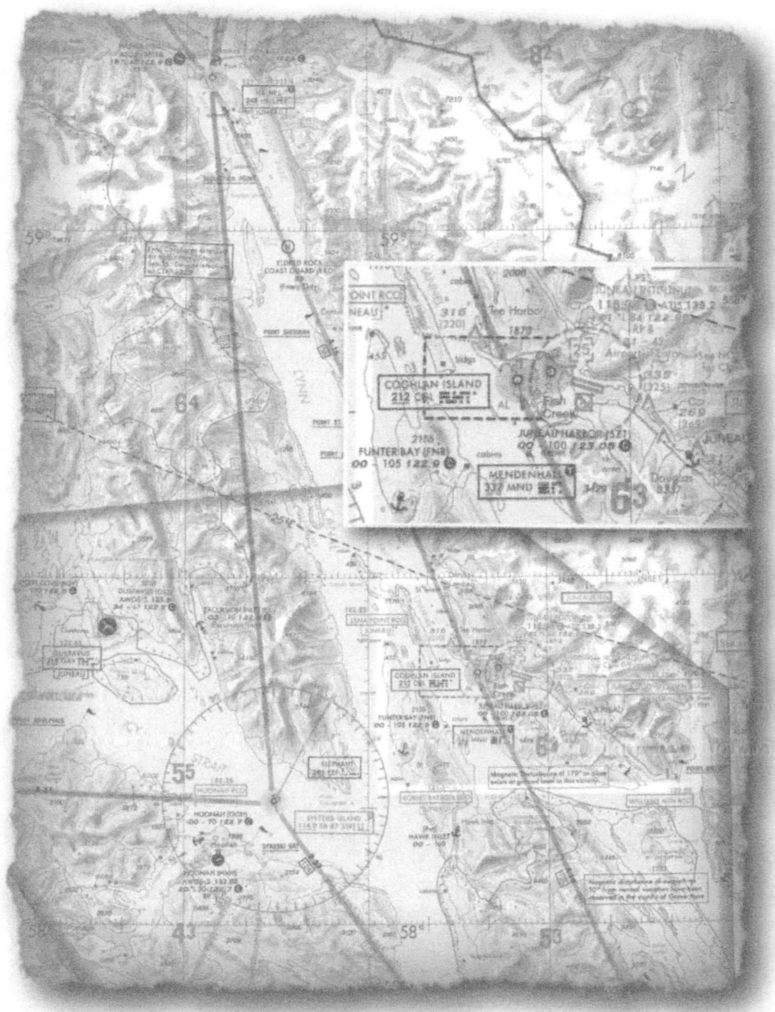

Inset: JNU (Juneau Airport),** harbor, city;* ***To North: *Juneau Icefield, Haines, Skagway, Davidson Glacier;* ***To South:*** *Kake, Sitka, Admiralty Island Wilderness;* ***To West:*** *Hoonah, Gustavus, Glacier Bay Nat'l Park, Pelican, Elfin Cove*

THE LAST BUSH PILOTS

PROLOGUE: A Crash in the Wilderness

(Southeast Alaska, late 1980s)

“Mayday, mayday, I’m going down!"

The frantic radio call rang in DC Alva’s earphones. Instantly he recognized the pilot’s voice: his best friend Allen Foley.

"Engine failure, south of Davidson Glacier,” Allen’s transmission continued. Then fell silent.

DC’s guts churned. The glacier, the young pilot knew, was miles from civilization—and help. Worse, flying visually beneath the clouds as all Alaska bush pilots did, Allen would have mere seconds to save the plane.

Shoving the throttle full forward, DC banked his floatplane hard left, north up the coastline toward the crash site. The engine surged. The manifold pressure needle straddled red line. He crowded the rugged slopes of the Chilkat Range. Pine trees dense as shag carpet loomed below. *Taku* winds tumbled like whitewater over the cliffs and pummeled his craft. Left hand gripped tight about the control yoke and right hand working the throttle, he fought to keep the aircraft upright.

With trembling voice, DC relayed the distress call to headquarters. "SEAS Base, this is *Sitka Shrike*," he radioed, using the company's designated call sign for his plane. "*Gastineau King* just called, 'Mayday.' Engine's failed. South of Davidson. I'm enroute now."

Another crash, DC thought. One was seven times more likely to be struck by lightning, for God's sake. But once again, lightning had struck too close. The question burning in the back of his mind always was, Who next? Only in his darkest nightmares had he imagined . . .

Allen would be down by now. Images flashed through DC's mind of the man dying beneath a smoldering wreck. Instinctively he shoved again on the throttle, already firewalled.

"*Shrike* to *King*, do you read?" DC called. No reply. "*King*, this is *Shrike*, come in!" Static.

DC leaned over the controls and squinted through the plexiglass. Drizzle cut his view up the channel to a myopic three miles. Each visual cue, each bulge in the land or curve in the shore, floated toward him through the misty curtain like ghosts in a fog-shrouded graveyard.

"Coastline. Got to keep the coastline in sight," DC mumbled, not realizing he'd voiced the thought aloud. The leaden sky pressed down on him like the slab roof of a tomb. And it might as well be made of cement, he thought: fly into it, or penetrate the blinding rain ahead, and splat across the first mountain that came along. The moist air pressed through the cabin's filters and cooled his cheeks. He shivered, more from fear than chill. The drizzle turned to rain and formed a wall around him. The drops pelted his windshield. With each moment, the terrain popped through the curtain ever closer—visibility dropping fast. Less than a mile, he figured.

"Dammit," he cursed, throttling back. For Allen, every minute lost was a mile closer to death. But in this weather, speed was DC's first enemy. Any worse, and he would have to turn back or land.

The de Havilland Beaver floatplane slowed. As the airspeed trickled down, DC lowered a section of flaps to compensate. The trailing edge of the wings extended downward, adding lift.

He eyed the waves near shore. Chop the size of Volkswagens.

DC grimaced. Even landing with engine power, he could dig a float or catch a wing and flip.

Allen, flying a fixed-gear wheel plane, had even less hope. High tide covered the soft beach. Ocean waves slammed against a rocky shoreline, backed by a forest wall. Nowhere could he have glided to safety.

"*Shrike* to *King*, do you read?" DC called, for the hundredth time it seemed. "*King*, come in. At least key the mike, dammit." No reply. "SEAS Base, what about rescue?"

"Coast Guard chopper's launched from Sitka, ETA one hour," the dispatcher's voice crackled.

"Can you make it through?" another pilot asked.

He eyed the wall of water ahead. "I—I'm not sure."

"Negative, *Shrike*," his Chief Pilot's voice cut in. "Weather's too solid. Seas are too rough for you, DC. Turn back."

But he couldn't shake the image of the dying man from his mind. He pressed on, squeezed between cloud and ground.

An hour passed—or a minute, he couldn't tell.

The drenched air formed fog; all turned murky. Forest, beach, even the air itself retreated into shadows of twilight. The saturated atmosphere phased between the elements of cloud and sky, water and air.

"Holy—" his voice trailed off. His gut churned. He'd heard of the phenomenon but had never seen it; never believed it could happen.

The sky fell.

The cloud base dropped, sucking the air below into its fold.

DC pushed forward on the yoke. The plane dove. He led the plummeting ceiling by a mere wingspan. The altimeter needle spun through five hundred feet.

Below the legal limit, he thought. But FAA rules were the least of his worries.

Four hundred . . three hundred . . the needle spiraled downward.

A glance out the side window: treetops whizzed by, inches below his floats. A startled eagle took wing.

"*Shrike*, I say again. Turn back immediately," his Chief Pilot ordered.

But his life's in my hands, he thought.

His hands. He looked at them, tight and trembling about the controls.

Flying through this weather was hazardous at best.

Flying through this weather could mean two accidents.

Flying through this weather would take all the training and all the experience he'd strived to gain while flying the Alaska bush—which, he realized now, was pitifully little.

If he crashed, his dream of flying for the airlines would crash too.

If he survived.

DC swallowed hard.

And made the toughest decision of his life.

CHAPTER 1: Grand Canyon Tours

(3 months earlier)

"You're too young to fly!" the thick lady tourist exclaimed in thick New York accent.

DC suppressed the urge to roll his eyes. Running a subconscious hand through his blond locks, he replied with a hint of sarcasm, "Last time I checked, Ma'am, silver hair wasn't a requirement for a pilot's license."

She crossed her arms. "Well, you still look like a frat boy."

"We're kind of nervous," her husband cut in, chuckling with embarrassment. "This is our first time in a small airplane."

"Me too," DC replied.

The couple glanced at each other. The three other tourist-passengers, a young Japanese couple and solo German, looked to him with alarm.

With jaded hazel eyes, Daniel Christopher Alva stared evenly at them for a long moment, then said, "That's a joke."

The five relaxed, but only slightly.

DC smiled and added,"Look, I've been flying for seven years, and have flown Grand Canyon tours for nearly two." *And have heard that* stupid *line about six hundred times*, he didn't add. "Well, if there are no more questions, the Canyon awaits," DC exclaimed with false enthusiasm.

He led them across the Scottsdale Airport ramp. Ducking beneath the high wing of his company's Cessna 210, he straddled the right main wheel of the single-engine prop plane. He opened the door and helped each tourist squeeze into the tiny cabin. All passengers aboard, DC ran around and hopped into the left front pilot's seat.

Like a seasoned flight attendant, he glided through the passenger briefing, adding a few personal touches of his own.

"Folks, here's the two exit doors; seat belt on at all times. During the flight, if you have to smoke, please feel free to step outside." A few nervous chuckles trickled from the crowd. "Next to the emergency briefing cards in the seat backs are little bags we call Sic Sacs. If you use them, they're yours to keep."

With a smirk, Mr. New York asked, "Where're the parachutes?"

DC cringed. *On every flight, I swear!* "Only one for me, so you'd better behave," he shot back. That earned him a few laughs.

Strapping in, DC reached over the lap of his "copilot"—the German in the right seat—and slammed shut the cabin door.

Out his side window, DC yelled, "Clear prop!" After a moment's pause, he cranked the ignition. With a rumble, the Continental piston engine fired up.

Several minutes later, after taxiing out and performing his required flight checks, DC pulled the plane onto Runway Three for takeoff.

"Whee," cried Mrs. New York from the back as DC powered up. Upon reaching flying speed, he pulled back on the control yoke.

The plane nosed skyward, fighting the pull of gravity. Out of the corner of his eye, DC spied the German's white knuckles gripping the armrest. Banking north, he settled the craft into a cruising climb across the desert. While the passengers stared wide-eyed at the scenery, DC scanned between the airspace outside, and the artificial horizon, airspeed, compass and altimeter inside.

For the next forty minutes, DC played pilot, navigator, radioman and tour guide. His hands, feet and mouth worked in the busy, synchronized patterns of a one-man band, playing the familiar tune with a competent ease of experience measured in hundreds of hours. He babbled away, rattling off each highlight along the route. The low pass over the landmarks, the Old West anecdotes, the same jokes he strained hard to deliver fresh, all orchestrated to maximize the flight's tip.

Approaching the south rim of "*the Ditch*," as the tour pilots jokingly called the canyon, DC eased the craft back down from cruising altitude. He leveled off 500 feet above Coconino National Forest.

"Folks," he announced over the intercom, "watch closely below out your side windows; I'll bet you see some mule or white tail deer down there." He glanced in back. Each passenger's nose pressed against the plexiglass, eyes staring at the ground racing by below. A mischievous grin spread across DC's face.

"Geronimo!" he cried.

The plane launched over the South Rim. The ground fell away.

Over his headset, he heard the collective gasp of five awestruck tourists.

Scanning for other aircraft, DC keyed his transmitter and calmly announced his position to the other tour planes. "Grand Airways Cessna Six Two Six reporting over Vishnu Temple, nine thousand five hundred feet, westbound."

Similar reports from other aircraft constantly sounded off in his headphones, as flights from around the region all converged on the Grand Canyon. Dozens of aircraft, flying at airspeeds nearing two hundred miles an hour, virtually shrank the planet's largest canyon to the size of a terrarium buzzing with flies.

For the next thirty minutes, the eager tourists gazed, gaped and rubbernecked through the windows at the spectacle below. With sparkling eyes, each tourist gazed upon a vermillion rainbow of sandstone, limestone and shale. The red prism of rock stretched in horizontal bands for miles up the canyon, as if some eccentric topographer had painted contour stripes for clarity. Above the north rim, cumulus clouds dropped thin veils of *virga*—wisps of evaporating rain. The ghost of a true rainbow peeked through the mist.

For thirty minutes, DC's brain switched to autopilot and fought the fatigue of boredom.

A glint of sunlight on metal caught his eye; an airliner, contrail streaking far above, arced north toward Seattle, or Portland. To him, the trail seemed an unattainable white rainbow, beckoning him, taunting him, tormenting his ambitions. Laughing at the limits of his feeble craft.

Some day, DC thought. *Some day*.

But not while stuck in this rut. Seven years, he'd worked toward his goal. Seven years of full time college, flight school *and* two jobs to pay for it all, and for what? To fly a plane smaller than a minivan. Hell, not even Dad believed he could make it to the big boys from here. Not without going military.

DC gritted his teeth. He had to prove him wrong. Had to show the old man his investment paid off. But how?

It was the classic paradox of aviation. No job without the experience, and no flight time without the job. The hurdle plagued every step up the civil aviation ladder, from single-engines to twins, turboprop commuters to jet airliners.

His hands tightened about the controls in frustration. He *knew* he could do it, if given the chance. But with three airlines down the tubes in recent years, pilots were like pigeons: a dime a gaggle and willing to fly for scraps. He needed a niche.

Allen Foley's words echoed in his head, spoken every Spring as flying season approached. "Go north, young man, go north!" And with that, Allen would throw on his backpack and head for Alaska.

Not a month earlier, he'd done it yet again.

Too risky, DC thought with dismay. What if he didn't get a job? What if he wasn't good enough? What if he crashed, got killed, or blacklisted from the airlines with an accident, or some other screw-up? Too many *What ifs*. Yeah, way too many.

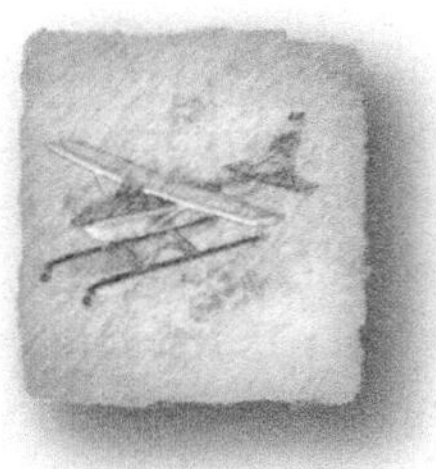

The phone rang. DC stirred. A glance at the clock: 7 a.m. He grumbled. His only day off, and for once no flight student was waiting for him at the airport for a sunrise takeoff.

He glanced to his left. The sheets lay tossed back on Stephanie's side of the bed. He heard the gentle hiss of the shower. Getting ready for her eight a.m. Biology at Arizona State, he realized.

The phone continued its assault on his ears. He rolled over and groped for the receiver.

"Hello," he croaked. A long pause. "Hello?" he repeated, just as the other party spoke, and the two cut each other off. He paused again in the confusion. Finally, he heard a reply.

"DC?"

"Uh, yeah, who's this?"

Another rude pause.

"DC, it's Allen. Wake up, dumbshit. Man, if we were back at ASU, you'd still be dreaming through Thompson's Meteorology."

"Allen?" he asked. "Why do you keep pausing when you—"

"Sorry about the time delay on this phone line. It's the satellite link. Geez, you'd think I was halfway to the moon." He chuckled. "I guess we kind of are up here in Alaska. Listen, DC, I won't talk long. Calls to the 'Outside' cost a fortune."

DC sat up. A tingle of excitement ran up his spine at the mention of the "A" word. "Alaska?" he asked.

"Yep. And I've already done a Hoonah round trip, so it's time you got your lazy ass out of bed, and up here."

"Hoonah, what the hell's that?"

"Hoonah's a Tlingit Indian village, twenty minutes as the Cessna flies, west of Juneau. Southeast Alaska panhandle. You know, the Inside Passage."

DC slowly shook the cobwebs out of his head. "Wait, did you say, get up there?"

"Damn straight, buddy. I'm flying for Southeast Alaska Seaplanes —'SEAS', we call it. Flying mostly their wheelplane Cessnas, but once in awhile I bag a float trip in a de Havilland Beaver, too. Fly a few months up here and they'll check you out as well. How's that sound?"

"Umm . . . "

"Here's the clincher: if you're one of the lucky few they pick to fly in the winter season, you'll fly twins."

DC perked up. "Oh?"

"That's right, bud—multiengine time, on a silver platter. Our ticket to the major airlines. Or at least the commuters."

DC chewed his lip.

"Look, DC," Allen continued. "You fly your butt off all day and hate it. How'd you like to fly your butt off all day, *love* it, and clear three times what you make now?"

"Well—yeah, of course." To DC, it sounded like the lottery.

"I talked to Dusty Tucker. He's our Chief Pilot. We need another plane driver! I'm talkin' right now. Next flight out."

"Are you kidding? My boss would kill me."

"He knows the business, he'll get over it. All you gotta do is show up, prove to Dusty you can land an airplane halfway decent—which I know for you takes enormous effort and blind luck—and you're a bonafide Alaska bush pilot. You'll leave ten times the pilot you are today. *If* you ever leave. Our first step to the majors, señor!"

DC's heart pounded at the thought. Then he remembered the old paradox. "Wait, I thought all those guys up there wanted Alaska flight time. You know I got nothing but this clear blue desert skies shit."

"I'm getting you in on the back course approach, buddy. They're going on my recommendation. The season's started, and one pilot just quit. Lost his nerve. *She* beat him out."

"She?" DC asked.

"You know, Mother Nature. The weather. *Alaska.* Home of the Friendly five hundred foot overcast and Cheery one mile visibility. Where 'Continued VFR flight into deteriorating weather' is not just an adventure, it's a job."

"*Continued VFR flight into deteriorating weather.*" A common phrase from FAA accident reports he'd read during college. Flying VFR, Visual Flight Rules, and then stumbling blindly into clouds. While IFR pilots had the equipment and training to safely fly through clouds on Instrument Flight Rules, a VFR pilot could easily get vertigo and spin in. Or hit a mountain hidden by clouds. *Cumulogranite*, pilots called it with a grim tongue in cheek.

DC recalled his brush with *cumulogranite* two years earlier.

Fresh out of college and eager to please his new employer, he'd misjudged the intensity of a front passing through Northern Arizona and pressed on. Too late, he realized his mistake. With sweat streaming down his sides, he dodged the clouds, all the while trying to appear nonchalant to the passengers. But a glance in back told him he wasn't fooling anyone. The family of four was white with fear, the mother weeping silent tears. Fighting off panic, he spotted a "sucker hole" in the cloud deck and dove through. Luckily, he made it to an emergency strip. Barely.

DC had learned a valuable lesson on that flight: Never screw with Mother Nature.

And a tiny seed of fear had been firmly planted in his gut, slowly growing with each weather encounter. Those beautiful cotton balls that beckoned to him as a child, had risen in his subconscious and mutated into sky-borne dragons of water and air.

Allen's voice jarred him back to the present. "Listen, DC, you're getting nowhere down there."

DC stared at the closed bathroom door. "Well, yeah, I guess so."

"Think about it, DC. But don't think too long. This is your big chance."

"I know."

"Remember our battle cry: 'Go for the gusto, or stay the fuck at home'!"

Yours not mine, DC thought but didn't say. "Uh, yeah, right. Thanks."

He hung up. Sitting back, he glanced between the bathroom door and the phone. He reached for the receiver, but hesitated. He played idly with it for a moment, sliding it back and forth in its cradle.

"*To hell with it*," he said, and picked up and dialed.

The Southeast Alaska Seaplanes secretary cheerfully patched him through to Chief Pilot Dusty Tucker.

"Dusty," the man answered in a southern drawl.

"Uh, Mr. Tucker, my name's Daniel Alva, a friend of Allen Foley."

"Oh, yes, Daniel. 'DC', isn't it?"

"Yes, sir."

"Allen said you were dying to fly for us up here. What kind of time do you have?" In aviation, a pilot's experience was measured by flight hours and equipment flown.

"Twenty-two hundred," he replied proudly.

"Hmm. A good start, I guess. But no Alaska time, right?"

DC grimaced. "Sorry."

"Well, what kind of birds? Any Cessna Two-oh-Sevens?"

"Close to 207's. 210's. 172's when I'm teaching."

"Have your Single Engine Sea ticket?"

"Yes sir, but I've only got a few hours in float planes. Um, I understand you've got twins?"

"Well, yeah," the Chief Pilot replied. "But we're pushing it on the insurance with you as it is. Maybe come winter, if you prove yourself. We can only keep a few."

"I'm your man," he exclaimed, hoping he sounded more confident than he felt.

"We'll see. When can you be up here?"

At that moment, Stephanie stepped out of the bathroom, toweling her Arizona blonde hair. Beads of water dappled her breasts as she stood nude before him, in the unabashed comfort of long time intimacy.

He gazed upon the too-familiar but still appreciated curves of her body.

She cocked her head and with curious, pale green eyes returned his anxious stare.

He watched her expression droop as the revelation hit her: this was the phone call she'd been dreading.

DC cleared his throat.

"Two days," he replied, and hung up with his new boss.

CHAPTER 2: Allen David Foley

"You're too young to fly!" exclaimed the thick lady tourist in thick midwestern drawl.

Allen David Foley suppressed the urge to shake his head. Instead, with a twinkle in his pale blue eyes and an *aw-shucks* scratch of his cropped black hair, he deadpanned, "Well, ma'am, they say if I survive this flight, they'll give me my pilot's license."

The woman stared wide-eyed at Allen for a moment. An ear-piercing cackle followed as she caught on, sending to flight several resident jays of Juneau Airport.

Allen had paid his dues. Son of a deadbeat dad, he'd grown up in a less-than-admirable section of Fort Pierce, Florida. Slight but tough, smart but poor, he'd known all along what he wanted, to fly, but not how to get there. A book on Alaska checked out from his eighth grade library got the wheels churning. The next year he and his mother rid themselves of his drunk father and moved to Phoenix, Arizona. The library book went with them.

After high school, he strapped a pack on his back and hitched the Alaskan Highway to Anchorage, where he took a job offloading fish. Allen hauled in cash by the net load. His summer job paid for a year of college and flight training back in Phoenix.

There he met DC, and the two fast became friends.

Winter months found them both hard at work on their advanced flight ratings, and the Bachelor's degree required by the airlines. Every summer, while DC flight instructed and took summer courses, Allen shoveled salmon and halibut into a boat off the coast of Valdez or Anchorage or Ketchikan.

Upon graduation, Allen once again headed north. This time, in his light blue junker Ford truck. This time, on the car ferry up the Inside Passage.

This time, in search of a flying job.

Each prospective boss scanned Allen's log book. Each man shook his head, a look of sympathy creasing his brow. Insurance requirements, they explained. And the old paradox. Allen lamented the demise of the day, long before his time, that men, not numbers, ruled the Alaskan skies.

He scoured the charter companies in Haines, Skagway, Valdez, and finally Anchorage. His cash reserves dwindled. He sold his truck.

Nearly ready to return to the fish game, he happened to overhear a conversation in a bar in Palmer. Two grubby prospectors griped over their beers about driving back to their camp because the company pilot had quit.

"Goddamn wuss if you ask me," said the first.

"Why do you think he up and left so sudden?" asked the other.

"Hell, if you were a prissy-assed pilot, would you put up with—" The man fell silent when he noticed Allen's keen interest. "Whadda you lookin' at?" he groused.

"You guys need a pilot?" Allen asked.

The man laughed. "You? You're still in diapers, boy."

Allen flashed a lopsided grin. "Don't worry, I've got a note from my mother."

The two miners howled. Allen bought them a few rounds, and was in.

The indifferent supervisor of Point Julia Prospecting signed him up with hardly a thought, but Allen stopped him short. He asked just one question.

"So, why did the other pilot quit?"

The supervisor looked to his men with raised brow, then Allen. "*She* beat him out." His eyes narrowed. "I don't expect Her to beat you out."

Allen met his gaze. "She hasn't yet."

It wasn't float plane time, nor was it twin engine experience. But it was Alaska time. Allen flew hard, long days, shuffling loggers and supplies back and forth from the various camps in the company's decrepit Cessna 172RG. The pathetic rig reminded him of his Ford. No mechanics in the area would touch it without cash upfront; the shady company, he found, had long since lost its credit.

Daily, Allen resorted to his own 'bailing wire maintenance.' That, despite having no Airframe and Powerplant license.

"Just survive the summer," he repeated to himself daily. "Just one summer and I'm out of this shithole."

Paychecks, it turned out, came as sporadically as the maintenance. For an entire month, he never saw a dime. He bugged the foreman, called the secretary, hounded the shift bosses. All pointed to someone else.

Finally, he went on a one-man strike. He refused to fly until a check was cut. It finally was, with great haste and grumbling, and Allen was sent to Anchorage to pick up a new batch of miners.

As he taxied up to the terminal, the crew sauntered out to meet him. He cut the engine, hopped out, and walked toward them. They waved.

"You here for Mining Camp Six?" one asked.

"Yep. Here you go," he replied, tossing them the keys to the plane. He jabbed a thumb at the horizon. "Go northeast about sixty miles. Second mountain range on the left. Dirt strip near the river bank. Can't miss it!"

Waltzing past the stunned miners and into the terminal, he caught the next Alaska Airlines flight out.

Miraculously, the check cleared. Allen breathed a huge sigh of relief.

The next summer, he set his sights on the next goal: seaplanes. Over the years he'd bummed rides with scores of float pilots, racking up hundreds of hours and tips on the art of flying boats. But the rules still hounded him; since none of his flying buddies was a Certified Flight Instructor, he couldn't legally claim one minute in his log book.

Allen foresaw the coming season, another summer of Air Taxi operators turning him down for a float job. Finally, throwing up his hands in exasperation he exclaimed, "*To hell with it.*"

In his logbook, below the 'Single Engine Sea Hours' column, he scratched a '1' in front of the 15, and his total float time became 115.

With a smug smile he said, "There. A hundred instant hours of *Parker Pen* time. "

He received nearly a dozen invitations to interview. On his first, Chief Pilot Dusty Tucker of Southeast Alaskan Seaplanes, asked the inevitable question.

"Where'd you get your float time?"

Allen looked him dead in the eyes. "With a mining camp out of Palmer called Point Julia Prospecting," he replied, knowing full well the shady business had failed six months earlier.

Through luck of his own making, Allen snagged the float plane job.

The Juneau-Haines-Skagway run was one of Allen's favorites, and cargo was his favorite passenger. That way, he got to play with his winged toy, practice his latest trick, and scream to some old Talking Heads or Marley or Buffett, which always blasted through his Sony Walkman. Sometimes he wondered which scattered the crows on final approach first, the drone of his plane or the screech of his singing.

Allen flew the *Soapy Smith*, a company Cessna 207 wheelplane, on its regular run. The load was often light, since much of the mail, freight and tourists to the gold rush towns came by car or railroad over Chilkoot Pass.

For maximum performance, Allen had lightened the plane by removing all the seats but his own.

With a sly grin, he thumbed the mike switch on his yoke and said, "Juneau Tower, SEAS Cessna Eight Alpha Kilo ready for takeoff. Request Special VFR clearance westbound for Point Lena."

Over his heavy green David Clark headset came the air traffic controller's reply. "Eight Alpha Kilo, no inbound IFR aircraft at this time. Special VFR approved, remain a minimum of one mile visibility and clear of clouds. Wind two-five-zero at eight, Runway Two Six, cleared for takeoff."

Allen taxied onto the runway, lined up and pressed both feet to the toe brakes. With his right hand he pushed the throttle lever forward. The manifold pressure surged, and the propellers whined. The nose settled and the wings rocked in anticipation. Tweaking the throttle to maximum power, he released the brakes.

The plane lurched forward like an F-14 off a carrier.

Allen sank in his seat. The airspeed gauge sprang through liftoff speed. He pulled back on the control yoke and the nose lifted. Like a hand out a car window turned palm up, the wings caught a bigger bite of air and the Cessna leaped skyward. Allen held the nose high above the horizon, pegging the airspeed needle to the plane's best angle of climb speed. By the time he reached the end of the paved runway, his altimeter read 850 feet.

He frowned. His goal had been 1,000.

* * *

Sitting in silence beside Stephanie in the back of the booth, DC idly stirred his eggs and beans with a fork. Her traditional *Huevos Rancheros* plate remained untouched. Her breakfast burrito remained barely nibbled as well.

DC forced a tiny morsel into his mouth, chewed a moment, then pushed the plate away. "I thought one last meal at *Rosita's* on the way to the airport would be a good send off. But I see this is turning into the Last Supper."

She dropped her fork to the plate with a clatter. "Just tell me one thing. Why are you doing this?"

DC shrugged. "Like I told you, I gotta kick my career in gear."

"I know. I can't help but think that, once you're on the move, you'll never come back."

DC shook his head and said, "Hey, I'm no Allen Foley. But you know the nature of this business. I've got to go where the flying is."

She sat back and crossed her arms. "This is your way of breaking up, isn't it?"

DC let out an exasperated sigh. "We've been through this, Steph. It's only for the summer."

"Unless they keep you on. Or you find an Eskimo woman to keep you warm."

DC scowled. "Allen says Tom Zion's up there. Shall I kiss him for you?"

Stephanie raised a hand to slap him, but checked herself. "I guess I deserved that." She sighed. "Seems we do need some time away from each other—"

"Just a few months."

"—to sort things out." She choked on the last word. The sobs hit. She sniffled. "Dammit. I promised myself I wouldn't do this."

His eyes now filled with sympathy, DC slid closer and wrapped an arm around her. She leaned her head on his shoulder for a minute, then pulled away.

"OK," she said, "let's make sure I got this straight. We agree to date others for a while. At the end of the summer, we'll see how we feel about . . . everything."

"Just remember, you've got an open invitation to come visit. Any time, okay? "

Gently, she kicked him in the ankle. "I'd better, sailor. 'Cause don't think you can escape from my clutches that easily."

"I don't intend to," he replied, wondering if it was true.

* * *

Leveling off just below the cloud deck, Allen pulled the throttle and propeller controls back to cruise setting. The engine's high-pitched scream lowered a few octaves as the three "constant speed" propeller blades took a bigger, more efficient bite of air, the equivalent of shifting a car from first through fourth.

Like all planes, Allen's was nothing more than a ship submerged in the fluid called air. The forces of nature—thrust and friction, lift and gravity—forever played a game of tug-of-war, and it was his job to parley that struggle into a peaceful harmony. A sailor trimming his sails, Allen fine tuned the aircraft's controls, and the plane settled into a new equilibrium. Taut and clean, the craft cut through the ocean of air like a pirate's corsair.

Juneau Tower, the only controlled airport in the region, released him. Switching to company frequency, he checked in.

Keying the mike, he said, "SEAS base, *Soapy Smith*, at Point Lena for Haines and Skagway."

"*Smith* at Lena for Haines-Skag, roger," replied the company dispatcher. "Have a good flight, Allen."

"Oh, but I intend to."

"Hey, Allen," Will Steven's voice crackled over the radio.

Allen smiled. "Where are you, Will?"

"Commin' outta Glacier Bay."

"How's the weather there?" Allen asked.

It was by no means an idle question. Before each flight, Allen and the other pilots checked Juneau Flight Service Station's latest weather reports, but the exercise was largely futile. By the time each station's report was observed, recorded, processed, analyzed, collated and disseminated, the notoriously fickle climate along the Alaskan coast rendered the data literally as useful as yesterday's weather. The best report lay just beyond the pilot's windshield. As a result, airmen traded weather observations over the radio like truckers CB'ing the 10-20 of Smokies.

Will replied. "A little fuzzy here. Six hundred foot overcast, visibility two to four. Looks like pretty good weather up Lynn Canal for you, though. Broken layers, it looks like. Good visibility beneath. How 'bout Juneau?"

"Same. Twelve over, kinda drizzly, about three miles on the *viz*."

After exchanging a few more pleasantries, Allen turned the radio's volume down. He rigged his tape player up to the aircraft headset, pushed play, and he and Jimmy sang about changing latitudes.

* * *

DC's first impression of Alaska came at the boarding gate at Phoenix Sky Harbor Airport Terminal Two. Something, he realized, set this group apart from any other airline passengers he'd seen.

"Well, at least I picked the right costume," he whispered to Stephanie. Dressed in jeans, boots and a flannel shirt, he floated in an ocean of jeans, boots and red flannel shirts.

But something else, something subtle, set him apart as an outsider. Though he matched the standard profile that fit three quarters of the passengers—Caucasian or Native American males—the resemblance ended there. The Caucasians were just that, white. No tan adorned the otherwise weather-worn, bearded faces. Weather-worn too were their clothes, so much so that DC suddenly felt itchy in his brand new attire.

Stephanie ribbed him gently. "You look like a blue light special."

After confirming his seat with the gate agent, the two lovers' conversation took a serious turn. Both knew full well that this was it.

DC found himself utterly at a loss for words.

Stephanie put a finger to his mouth. Her lips followed.

DC was saved from a farewell speech by the gate agent's announcement.

"Ladies and gentlemen, now boarding Alaska Airlines' Flight 721 to Seattle, with continuing service to Juneau. All passengers are welcome aboard at this time."

The Alaskan passengers, veterans of air travel, fell in place like a drill team.

Stephanie looked away. "Well, they're playing your song."

DC hesitated. A pang of fear shot through him. Suddenly, Stephanie's warm side seemed far more enticing than the harsh, unknown world ahead. He cleared his throat. "Listen, Stephanie, it's not too late. I don't have to—"

She thumped his chest and pushed him gently toward the jetway. "You just don't forget me, flyboy."

* * *

Off to his left, the blue-white icefall of Meade Glacier sailed by.

Solo once again on the return leg to Juneau, Allen leveled off beneath the broken cloud base and sat back.

Shafts of light shone through the clouds ahead, reflecting off the ocean waves in a surreal checkerboard. Into a beam steamed the passenger ferry, inching its way up Chilkoot Inlet toward Skagway.

Allen smiled. The ship had left Juneau hours before him, and by the time it docked, he'd be sipping a Chinook beer at the Red Dog Saloon.

The cloud base rose. He climbed higher and leveled off eye to eye with the Sinclair Mountain ridgeline to his left. Waterfalls stretched in long, dainty strands down the sheer emerald face before plunging into the sea.

He banked right in a shallow, lazy turn, and aimed across the channel toward Eldred Rock lighthouse. The extra room between cloud and ridge allowed him a few minutes' play time. He glanced about the cabin for loose objects, then turned to eye the cargo in back. Still cinched tight. From his shirt pocket, Allen produced a pack of Marlboros. He fished out a cigarette and placed it gingerly on the dash board.

He scanned the horizon for other aircraft and, finding none, pushed over. Out the front window, water replaced sky. The shrill rush of air penetrated his headphones. The airspeed indicator shot upward. He eyed the needle as it pushed through the yellow arc toward red line.

Now!

He yanked back on the yoke. Blood drained from his face. He felt his innards sink as he pulled through two, three times the force of gravity. The airspeed slowed. Eyeing the cigarette, he shoved the yoke forward with his left hand, and with his right eased back on the throttle. The aircraft arced in a parabola, mimicking the trajectory of a spacecraft in orbit. Weightless, his body strained against the seatbelt. The Marlboro lifted magically off the dash board and floated toward him. He opened his mouth. The cigarette bounced off his shades and spun away.

He pulled up. The cigarette plunged to the floor.

"Damn," he mumbled.

* * *

From the passenger window of the Boeing 737, DC watched the receding terrain. For the first time in his life, the *Ditch* tour veteran beheld the entire Grand Canyon in one frame. Clouds puffed up along the North Rim, casting shadows over Vishnu and Shiva Temples. Though he'd seen it hundreds of times, it all seemed much smaller now. A thin smile spread across his lips as he spied a half dozen Grand Canyon tour planes, small as gnats, crawling across the terrain.

Soon the view gave way to unfamiliar territory to the north. A pang of homesickness hit, but no tears fell for love left behind. Even Stephanie already seemed like a remote memory. DC closed his eyes and inhaled deeply.

At seven miles a minute, Daniel Christopher Alva distanced himself from his old life.

CHAPTER 3: Eagle & Salmon

Past Seattle, the entire route was overcast.

DC frowned. Here was the perfect opportunity to inspect his new home, but all he could see was the green glow from the plane's starboard wingtip. Frustrated, he sat back and thumbed through the inflight magazine for the fourth time.

Though he had done well in college geography, for the life of him he couldn't picture what southeast Alaskan terrain was like. Mud? he wondered. Tundra? Rugged, perhaps, like the mountains of Nepal. Or was it one gigantic ice cube? An image of Eskimos and igloos flashed in his mind, and he chuckled the absurd thought away. Though he knew Alaska was far more modern and tame than that, he was prepared for the worst. On top of the carry-on at his feet, he'd stuffed a newly-purchased subzero parka. Packed in his checked baggage was his crispy new brown leather flight jacket, heavy duty long johns, and a pair of clod stompers, weighing, it seemed, about eighty pounds each.

The Last Bush Pilots

The Boeing 737's PA crackled to life. His ears pricked up, wishing he was at the helm of the airliner.

"Ladies and gentlemen, from the flight deck, this is your Captain speaking. We're now approaching ten thousand feet in our descent into Juneau. Typical day here, low overcast with broken clouds beneath, visibility restricted in light drizzle, temperature fifty-eight degrees."

DC cringed at the temperature. Though cold by Phoenix standards, it was hardly subzero. Red-faced, he discreetly toed his parka deeper beneath the seat in front of him.

As the jet's gear and flaps lowered, his pulse raised. He gazed out the window, straining for a glimpse of the future.

Through the grey mist, Mother Nature teased him with momentary flashes of earth and sea. For DC, the effect was a series of postcards imprinted in his mind, first of white-capped ocean, then thick green pine forest, then ocean, then forest, each closer than the moment before.

The plane passed through one last, low fog bank, then a mountain seemed to leap up out of the mist at him. DC flinched in surprise. He could almost count the pine needles on the treetops. The 737 banked sharp right, leveled, then touched gently down.

"Ha! A paved runway . . ." DC's voice trailed off as he realized he'd spoken the thought aloud.

The man next to him chuckled. "First time here?" he asked.

"Yeah," DC answered, embarrassed.

"Don't worry. You may not be able to drive a car to Juneau, but it's still civilization. We even got a McDonald's or two. Juneau's the state capital, you know."

DC didn't know. He eyed the ponytailed, dark skinned man sitting next to him. "Say, are you an, um, I don't know, an Eskimo?"

The man laughed aloud. "No, son, they're way up north. I'm a Native American Tlingit. You'll find a lot of us around here. And no, we don't live in igloos."

DC smiled. "Well I kind of figured that." He glanced at his watch. "I can't believe it's so bright outside. Eight thirty at night, and it looks like afternoon."

The Tlingit grinned. "Welcome to the land of the midnight sun."

Down a 60's-vintage portable stairway, the passengers shuffled off the plane to the ramp. Drizzle danced on DC's cheeks as he stepped down, and the desert-bred Phoenician shivered from the mild chill. Reluctantly, he donned his parka.

He inhaled a deep, long breath into his lungs. The air seemed magnificently fresh, almost sweet. The slight headache from his stuffy ride cleared instantly.

As the line of passengers filed into the terminal, DC paused to gaze at his new home. The weather teased him once again, blocking most of the scenery. Still, through the mist, he spied nothing but thick green pine forest in every direction. To the north, a steep hill climbed into the clouds. To the south he could barely make out a large river, and the outline of the opposite shore.

"*Alva!*" he heard a familiar voice call. DC spun around to find Allen trotting across the asphalt tarmac, grinning from ear to ear.

DC returned the expression. "Allen," he shouted.

"Hey, you old *cheechacko*," Allen said, sliding up. "Welcome to the great white north." They shook hands.

DC smirked. "Yeah right. I don't see a drop of snow. What did you call me?"

"*Cheechacko*. That's what the natives and the sourdoughs called the greenhorns back in the Gold Rush. Now that you're the new guy, maybe they'll stop calling *me* that. I was hoping I'd get here in time to catch you. I just got back from Skagway."

DC's jaw went slack. "You mean you really fly in this stuff?"

Allen raised his brows twice as if to say, *You got it*. "Far cry from 'Ceiling and Visibility Unlimited' Phoenix, huh?"

DC looked back along his jet's flight path. "We just flew through that gap in the mountain," he said with awe.

Allen laughed. "We call it *The Cut*."

DC shook his head in disbelief. "That's crazier than buzzing Zoroaster Saddle in my Cessna 210. And these guys do it in a *Boeing 737*!" He turned back to Allen. "I'm not sure if I'm up for your bush stuff."

"It may seem hairy at first, but you'll get used to it."

"Hey, you guys," a voice called. They looked up to see an airport "ramper" driving by in a tug loaded with baggage. "This is a secure area. You'll have to get inside."

Allen tapped the I.D. badge hanging from his shirt pocket and answered, "It's okay, I'm with SEAS. I'm escorting him."

"Oh, all right. But you'd better head back to the General Aviation ramp."

Allen pointed across the tarmac. "Come on. Let me show you around." They strolled away. Allen nodded to a Cessna ahead. "That's the bird I just flew in, the *Soapy Smith*."

DC looked upon a fleet of Cessna 207's, all painted a slick emerald green and gold. In the back row, several de Havilland Beaver "amphibians" towered above the others, each straddling two floats, each float sitting atop two wheels. The fleet's tails all donned the word *SEAS* in fancy black script superimposed over a gold silhouette of a grizzly swatting a salmon out of a stream.

They started across the ramp. DC pointed to the wheelplane. "Thought you were flying float planes."

"Occasionally. We got five of 'em docked over in the 'Pond,' paralleling the runway. But low frog on the totem pole is last to get the water jobs. That's you, now. The ravens at the top, the sourdoughs, get the floats and twins."

DC nodded, eyeing the amphibian planes with envy. "In seaplane training I never got to fly an actual amphib. Fun?"

"A freakin' blast. Retract the wheels, land on water. Lower the wheels, land on a dirt strip or a runway. Perfect for Alaska."

"Or forget to raise the wheels, land on water and crash," DC added.

With a smirk, Allen said, "There are two types of pilots . . ."

"Those that have, and those that will," DC finished.

At the buzz of an approaching plane, they turned their heads. "Speaking of sourdoughs, here comes one," Allen said.

A Beaver amphibian taxied around them and into a parking space. Its pilot cut the fuel, and the drone of the nine-cylinder radial engine died as the propeller spun to a stop. The two trotted over to help tie down the plane.

DC looked toward the plane, imagining just what a real, grizzled bush pilot would look like. No different than any other pilot, he thought with a chuckle. Nevertheless, an image flashed before his mind of a dashing, white scarf-and leather-clad Lindbergh, all muscle and swagger and jawline.

The door opened. Out jumped, not a pilot, but a huge black and white Alaskan Malamute. The dog howled and, tail wagging, bounded over to Allen.

"*Eluk!*" Allen exclaimed, kneeling to pet the canine. "DC, meet Eluk. That's Eskimo for 'friend'. He's Crash Whitakker's dog, but he flies with everybody."

"'Crash' *who*?" DC exclaimed. But before Allen could answer, the pilot jumped out.

DC blinked. Apart from the ratty leather jacket, his resemblance to DC's vision ended there. Scrawny, bespectacled and homely, the man looked more wino than hero. Stubble sprouted from his chin. Tangled black hair poked from beneath his baseball hat, which sported an image of Tweety Bird. But the eyes held an unmistakably intelligent gleam.

Allen said, "Ralph Olafsen, meet DC Alva, our new pilot."

Ralph hopped down and eyed the newcomer.

DC held out his hand and said formally, "It's nice to meet you, Mr. Olafsen. I'm looking forward to—"

"Have you heard the word of Jesus Christ our Lord and Savior?" Ralph interrupted. Instead of shaking hands, he thrust a pamphlet into DC's open hand.

DC cleared his throat. With a quizzical glance to Allen, he said, "Well, I, uh . . ."

Ralph spun and left.

DC looked to Allen. "Is he for real?"

Allen nodded to the pamphlet. "What's it say?"

The two read the cover: *Condoms, IUD or The Pill—Which Method Is Best For You?*

Over the page, Ralph had drawn a very explicit and exaggerated cartoon of two moose mating.

Inside the terminal, Allen led DC to the company's "pilot lounge"—a row of seats in the main lobby. There, DC met several other pilots, from grizzled and grey-bearded Sam, who looked like he'd be more at home panning gold, to young, skinny redheaded local Will Stevens. All shook his hand and welcomed him aboard.

That done, Allen escorted him into the office to meet his new boss. Allen knocked on his open office door and peeked in. DC tucked in his shirttail and straightened.

Chief Pilot Dusty Tucker was leaning back, feet propped on desk. DC's immediate impression was that of a *good ol' boy*; pleasant, sixtyish face, grey hair and bulging "captain's belly."

True to his profession, Dusty wore a classic brown leather pilot's jacket. Distressed and faded, DC saw, but nothing like the rag that had hung from Ralph's gaunt frame.

Dusty sat up and leaned over the desk to offer a hand.

"Howdy, DC, it's good to meet you. Heard a lot about you." The man's warm, soft Southern drawl completed the *good ol' boy* image. DC instantly relaxed.

"Nice to meet you, Sir."

"No need for '*sir*' cowpie around here, son. I'm Dusty, and we're all family."

DC grinned. "Okay, uh, Dusty."

DC turned to meet the man with whom Dusty had been conferring, and came face to face with his ideal image of the Alaskan bush pilot: rugged, tall, solid jawline, with sandy hair and penetrating blue eyes. But instead of the leather jacket, the forty-something man wore a sleeveless, pocketed tan fisherman's vest. *A pilot's pilot*, DC decided right then.

"I'm Jake Whitakker."

We call him'Crash'," Dusty interjected. "He's either the luckiest or the lousiest pilot on the staff. We can't figure out which."

"Both," Crash replied with a smile, shaking DC's hand. "We've been needing some fresh meat around here. Welcome aboard, DC."

Following Allen out, DC whispered to Allen, "'Crash'?"

"I'll explain later," Allen said. "But don't let them kid you. Crash is *the* best."

* * *

Asleep in his new home, the extra bedroom of Allen's apartment, excitement kept DC tossing and turning all night. Nevertheless, as he sat up to the 4:00 a.m. alarm clock on his first duty day, he felt strangely energetic.

Halfway through a warm shower, he realized its source: the sun. Sliding the bathroom window open, he gazed through the steam upon a fully lit world.

As he dried and dressed, the aroma of coffee filled his nostrils. Inhaling deeply, he shuffled into the kitchen to find Allen busy burning eggs and toast.

Allen looked up from his pan. "Okay, this is the first and last time you get my gourmet breakfast. After this you fend for yourself."

"Deal," DC said as he sat in the breakfast nook.

"How do you like your *java*?" he asked.

"Like my women."

"Sorry, we don't got any stupid coffee. Uh, Stephanie excluded from that insult, of course."

DC smirked. "Light and sweet, please."

Allen plopped a cup of coffee in front of him. "How are the Suns doing?" he asked.

"Boy, you are isolated up here," he replied, and took a sip. "Axed in the first round of the playoffs. They got good gunners, but their defense still sucks."

"Sounds like our team." Allen flipped the omelet over, breaking it in the process. Shrugging, he scrambled the mess. "Noticed you burned the midnight oil last night studying."

"Hmph. Didn't have to with your midnight sun. Just reviewing your Cessna 207 manual."

Allen waved a hand dismissively. "Don't worry too much about that around here. Skill is more important than the ability to sketch an electrical system, or rattle off every number in the book. 'Course, we do have one FAA inspector who's kind of a numbnuts."

DC nodded in understanding. "Every airport has one."

Allen slid into his seat, two sizzling plates in hand.

DC stared blankly at the grub. "Well, at least you're a coffee connoisseur."

"Everyone's a critic. Cheers." The two pilots clinked mugs, then attacked their plates.

Once done, Allen fished out and lit a Marlboro. DC frowned.

Allen said, "Sorry. Haven't quite kicked the habit. But it's a necessary substitute for the stuff I used to do in college. It's legal up here, you know."

"You serious?"

"Well, kind of. But the Feds might get a little upset when you flunk the piss test."

DC sat back and crossed his arms. “Don’t worry, I wasn’t planning on taking up the habit.”

In a cloud of smoke, Allen stamped his cigarette and the thought out. He jumped up and said, “We’d better make tracks. I’ve got a Kake turn in an hour.”

“Kake turn?”

“Kake’s another Tlingit village. A *turn* means you fly out, turn around and come back.”

With a clatter, the two bachelors threw their dishes in the sink, and headed out the apartment door for the fifteen minute walk to work.

Though still overcast, the weather had lifted from the day before. While Allen wore only a light windbreaker to fend off the chill breeze, DC zipped up his new leather jacket and thrust his frozen hands into the pockets.

“Any last advice before I’m fed to the lions?” DC asked.

Allen mulled it over. “Just load the plane right, do all the dirty work and fly smart. And don’t let *Her* beat you out.”

DC cocked his head to look sideways at his friend.

Allen explained. “Up here it’s a different type of flying, DC. Remember back in our cross country training at school, we’d climb through a hole in the clouds and get a ’VFR on top’ clearance?” DC nodded. “Well, here, if you climb on top, you’re screwed. There ain’t no ‘sucker hole’ to spiral back down through. The overcast is *always* solid. And, there’s hardly any radio navaids to follow; the land’s just too vast and mountainous. Everything here is done visually, because every cloud’s made of *cumulogranite.* So we fly *below* the overcast, and cut along the coastline and mountain passes.”

A shudder ran down his spine at the thought of being so boxed in. “Wh-what about the weather?” he asked. “I mean, how do you know when its gonna turn to shit?”

“You get to read it pretty well. But it can surprise you. The air is usually saturated with water, and fog’s always ready to pounce. The fog can turn to drizzle, the drizzle to rain, and the whole overcast drops in seconds.” Allen stopped. He stared in his friend’s eyes. “The sky falls.”

DC whistled softly. Suddenly, he regretted taking the job. How anyone survived such flying he couldn’t fathom. And now here he was, about to do just that.

Allen continued. “And the turbulence—*hooey*, the *Taku* winds! The air cools down over the glaciers then blasts out over the peaks, whipping the winds around here like a Cuisinart. Makes the summer desert thermals look like a kiddy ride."

DC's brows furled with concern as he looked to the claustrophobic clouds and fog, seeming to close around him.

Allen slapped him on the back. "Hey, don't worry. It's a fucking blast! It's your own personal E-ticket ride. You fly by the seat of your pants, always on the edge, with only your eyes and wits to guide you."

"Great," DC replied sarcastically.

"Oh, come on, you'll love it. It's the most amazing scenery on the planet. There's wildlife everywhere. Deer, black and brown bears, seals, eagles. And all kinds of whales."

The two crossed Glacier Highway and ambled down Shell Simmons Drive, paralleling the fence which marked the airport boundary. At a side gate, Allen punched his security code into a keypad and the two slipped onto the airport tarmac. They took a shortcut across the ramp to the terminal. They waved at Ralph, several parking spaces away, loading his Beaver amphibian with cargo. The scrawny pilot nodded back.

DC turned back and stared at the asphalt, lost in thought.

After a moment he asked, "How often does a plane crash?"

Allen's face darkened. "You don't want to talk about that around here. Too many people know too many who've augured in."

"I'm asking you."

Allen paused a moment. "Hmm. Well, in the summer season, in all of Southeast Alaska, I'd say about once a month. We had one a couple weeks ago, so I'd say you're safe for two weeks at least."

DC crossed his arms. "Hah, hah. I'm laughing. What happened?"

"The usual. *Cumulogranite.* Most of 'em buy it that way." Allen turned to him, hands spread in explanation. "Listen, you've got to remember the incredible amount of flying that goes on up here. Alaskans take a plane like people in the Lower Forty-Eight take a taxi. And you know as well as anyone, it's far safer than driving."

"Yeah," he said, and grew silent.

In the middle of the ramp, DC stopped and turned. Now, out in the open and with the clouds lifted, he could gaze for the first time upon spruce-packed Thunder Mountain, towering above Juneau Airport. A murky blanket of cloud swirled around the peaks, still obscuring portions of the ridgeline. Those mountains, so beautiful and alive, he thought, could swallow him up as easily as a grizzly chomping a salmon.

"Beautiful, isn't it?" Allen said.

DC shook his head. "Spectacular!"

A movement caught DC's eye. He turned to look. A black dot in the sky at first, the object grew larger, larger, until finally DC recognized it. Sucking in his breath, he pointed frantically.

"Allen! There's a, there's a—"

Overwhelmed, he couldn't finish.

Across the tarmac, inches above their heads, as resplendent in noble beauty as the land in which it lived, soared an enormous bald eagle. From beneath a snow white crown, its piercing black eyes and yellow beak glowered with a hunter's grim determination.

Its wings seemed to flap in slow, graceful motion, as if to glorify its stately beauty. In its talons hung a freshly caught salmon, still flopping in the last throes of life.

The raptor soared through the mist toward its nest atop Thunder Mountain. DC squinted as the wind-borne hunter shrank to a speck, then disappeared in a tapestry of crag, cloud and pinetop.

The two awestruck pilots stood in reverent silence.

Allen came back to reality first.

"*Welcome to Alaska*," he whispered.

DC blinked, licked his lips, and took a deep breath. "I'll take that as an omen."

At that moment, Ralph poked his head between them.

"Yeah," he said. "But are you the eagle, or the salmon?"

CHAPTER 4: Dusty Tucker

Dusty Tucker was a veteran of the war—*The* War, as those of his generation called it. He'd served his country proudly, dueling Nazi Messerschmitts in the skies of Europe in that Cadillac of fighters, the P-51 Mustang.

Late to The War, the newly minted fighter pilot was shot down on his second mission. A French farmer hid him for eight months until Germany surrendered. In gratitude and lust, Dusty married the man's beautiful, starry-eyed daughter Suzette and whisked her away to his little lonesome hometown in the Lone Star State.

Upon arriving Stateside with his new war bride, he found his family's cattle ranch, the one he'd been groomed to take over, greatly diminished in size and stature. Moreover, oil was fast becoming the ranch's new herd, and Dusty found little interest in rounding up crude and roping wells. Dad had other sons to work the black stuff.

The world had changed, the States had changed. He had changed.

Commercial aviation boomed. Like hundreds of his fellow dogfighters, he jumped on board.

Whisking Suzette to the big city of Dallas, they enjoyed the pay and prestige of his new profession. Flying a DC-3, then later a Lockheed Electra, for Trans Lone Star Airways, he plied the skies across Texas and beyond.

Suzette made him a comfortable nest and bore him two daughters, Betty Lousianne and Bobbi Suzette—Betty Lou and Bobbi Sue for short. Nothing could be more perfect.

Nevertheless, Dusty found himself curiously restless. Despite the challenge of dodging seasonal thunderstorms, there was little adventure in the game for him. He felt like nothing more than a glorified bus driver. He no longer belonged. Where the hell he did belong remained a mystery. Through the boredom, something called to him, pulled at his inner conscience during the long, droning hours from Dallas to Denver and back. And then, one day, eighteen thousand feet over Del Rio, a single word popped into his head: Alaska.

His soul cried out.

"Dusty, you're crazy," Chief Pilot Baxter pleaded. "You're on the leading edge of your career. I'm telling you, this is the Roaring Fifties. Commercial jets are just around the corner. This industry will take off, and you'll be on top. You'll be an airline captain flying from Dallas to *London* nonstop. Think of that!"

He did—with distaste. Make more dough than God, but at what cost? Missing his kids' childhoods, that's what. The way he saw it, he had to choose between a life providing *for* his family and a life *with* his family. He gazed out the window at the drab countryside.

"*To hell with it*," he said to the cacti.

That spring, Dusty once again pulled up roots and whisked his wife, accustomed now to her lover's whisking, to Bethel, Alaska, 400 miles west of Anchorage.

To him, the tiny Yupik Eskimo village was home.

His family was shell shocked.

He traded his Electra for a Cessna. With the help of family oil stock, and a little cash squirreled away by the shrewd former airline captain, Dusty put a down payment on a brand new, 6-passenger, single-engine Cessna 185 taildragger, complete with optional ski package. Tucker Air Taxi was born.

Like most in Alaska, his was a one-man airline. He had no ticket agents, no flight attendants, no baggage handlers. Everything that went on board, he loaded. Inflight meals consisted of thermos coffee and a baloney sandwich.

Through endless summer days and eternal winter nights, Dusty plied the vast skies between Eskimo villages, mining camps and trading posts. Up and down the Kuskokwim and Yukon Rivers he flew, between Aniak and McGrath, Galena and Fortuna Ledge, delivering mail, natives, trappers and prospectors, frozen fish and frozen government servants. Airfare depended on destination, client, and his disposition that day. Payment came sporadically, often in the form of gas, fish, or caribou steaks.

He eked out a modest living.

No satellites or TV forecasters beamed him the weather; Dusty was his own weatherman, and what he saw out the window was the forecast. There were often times that he took off into blue so pure it seemed sea and sky had traded places, that water and air were one friendly entity, only minutes later to conspire and force him down in a whiteout blizzard.

Few hangars existed to change a spark plug; Dusty was his own mechanic, and his garage was what he took with him. A survival kit always accompanied him as well, complete with food, blankets, medical supplies, and a Remington 12 Gauge shotgun. Little room was left for revenue payload.

No gas stations existed enroute; Dusty was his own fueler. He learned where the local pilots stashed their emergency 55 gallon drums of avgas; which dirt strips, which patches of permafrost, which river banks. He stashed his own along his bread and butter routes, and never hesitated to tell the others about it. When weather forced him to circle above the Arctic tundra, he would land, siphon some juice into the Cessna's wing tank, then sit back, light a pipe, chat with a passenger if he had one, and wait for the pass to clear. On the next run upriver, he always landed and replaced what fuel he borrowed.

No maps or electronic gizmos guided him; his navaid was his eyes. For Dusty, "IFR" meant,"I Follow Rivers." Each bend in the stream, each mountain pass, each pool in the tundra he strove to memorize. His one extravagance was an ADF, Automatic Direction Finder, which pointed like a bird dog to any of the government's few low frequency radio navigation stations scattered across the land. Far better, he found, were tuning into local village AM stations. But the beacons' low range, and fickleness in twilight or mountains, made it more useful as a companion than a compass.

With skill, quick thinking and luck, the *cheechacko* survived by learning the hard way: on his own. Far from being the first, he was still one of the few, and therefore greatly appreciated.

Being treated like a big halibut in a small auger hole never went to his head. Dusty knew better. He gleaned tips and tricks from the other pilots. But the natives, so long used to living off the harsh land, taught him volumes. More than once, as Dusty pushed for a pass through the mountains, his Eskimo passenger would tap him and shake his head, then point to a landing spot. After several futile attempts, Dusty learned to trust their judgement nearly ahead of his own.

Even better, Dusty found, was what the pilots jokingly called the "Eskimo ADF." While looking for a microdot of a landing strip amidst miles of featureless tundra, he could take a furtive glance at his local passengers, whose gaze always pointed like a bird dog at their destination. With a subtle change of course in that direction, he would nail the landing strip every time.

Every day taught him new lessons. Lessons, he found, that the fledgling Civil Aeronautics Bureau back in Washington never bothered to learn before slapping their rules willy-nilly upon the Alaskan skies. Far from Big Brother's arbitrary arm, Dusty and the other pilots simply chose to ignore much of them. Free to play by his own rules, Dusty had finally found his element.

He loved it. His wife tolerated it. His girls hated it.

For two years, the young women stoutly put up with cabin fever, six-month days and six-month nights, and frozen "honey buckets," the sarcastic euphemism for toilet pot. Finally, after a particularly brutal spell of 70-below wind chill, even Dusty's determination wore thin.

Sensing blood, the girls attacked.

"We're the only white kids in our grade at school," Betty Lousianne complained.

"So, it's a great chance to learn another culture," Dusty countered.

"We get teased and bullied every day," Bobbi Suzette added.

Dusty had no answer for that.

"How can we expect our girls to live in a tiny foreign village," Suzette asked in her seductive French accent, "where the sole excitement is betting on when the Kuskokwim River ice will break up?"

Bobbi Suzette began to cry. Betty Lousianne wrapped an arm around her and rocked. It had the desired effect.

Cocking his head sideways, Dusty looked at them. He turned his gaze out the window and into the darkness.

"Well, where would you have us live?" he asked.

"Anchorage!" they chorused.

Dusty held up his hands. “No way. Too big. Might as well have stayed in Dallas driving them fancy sky buses.”

It took great reserve for all three not to scream out how much they *wished* he was back driving “them fancy sky buses.” The three silently bit their lips.

With a resigned sigh, Dusty said, “*To hell with it.*”

That spring, after breakup, the Tuckers moved from the Interior to the Southeast Panhandle, to Alaska’s state capital, Juneau.

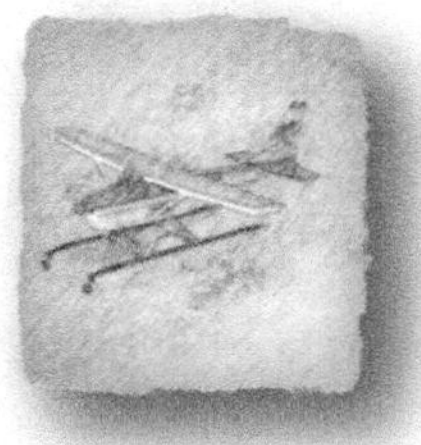

Sitting in the “copilot’s” seat to DC’s right, Dusty said, “Nice takeoff stall. Now show me a landing stall.”

DC hated checkrides. All pilots did. While it gave him a chance to “show his stuff,” each model airplane differed drastically, and DC found himself pressured to get a quick feel for his new bird. Though merely a warmup flight for his real test, DC still knew that, with every little move, he was being sized up by his new boss. He fought, as usual, to keep the butterflies from his stomach. At least, he thought with relief, the skies were mercifully clear today.

DC pulled back on the control yoke. The Cessna’s nose pitched higher. The rush of wind diminished as the aircraft slowed. DC lowered his flaps to compensate. At minimum flying speed, the stall warning horn blared in his ears. The plane shuddered as the wings lost their lift. He pulled back further. Out the front window, sky turned to forest as the plane suddenly dropped earthward. DC felt his guts leap to his throat. Used to the sensation from years of practice, he calmly eased the nose further over and shoved the throttle full forward. The engine screamed to life, and the sudden acceleration returned lift to the wings. Easing the nose back up, DC raised the flaps and leveled off.

Without warning, his boss reached down and cut off the fuel supply.

“Engine failure,” Dusty announced. The engine wound down, and the airplane became a makeshift glider.

Suddenly, the *cheechacko* became very busy. Simultaneously flying the plane and trying for an engine restart, he searched for a landing spot. But unlike the vast, relatively flat desert landscape in which he'd won his wings, this new land offered scant more than freezing ocean, thick pine forest and *cumulogranite*. Sweat trickling down his side, DC finally spotted a tiny sandbar hiding in the Lynn Canal, mercifully offering its services. Angling for the near end of the makeshift strip, he set up his approach.

"Good eye," Dusty said. "But beware. Sand bars appear and disappear at the whim of the tide, which cycles up to twenty feet every six hours."

"*Twenty feet in six hours*?" DC asked, shaking his head in disbelief.

Dusty nodded. "You might be able to land a broke airplane on a sandbar, only to be swept away before rescue."

DC whistled softly.

At a scant 300 feet, when it was obvious they would make the "field," Dusty switched the gas back on. The windmilling propeller suddenly sprang to life. "Okay, go around."

DC added full power and pitched up. They climbed skyward as he "cleaned up" the airplane, raising flaps a notch at a time.

Dusty said, "Let's head back to Juneau for touch and go's."

For another thirty minutes, DC practiced landings and takeoffs. Dusty constantly critiqued his performance, and suggested tips for improvement. By the time they finished, DC felt fairly comfortable with his new bird. But exhausted.

* * *

Back in the terminal, Dusty shook DC's hand. "Congratulations, son. You're our newest pilot."

DC's grin stretched ear to ear. "Thank you, sir—er, Dusty."

"We'll set you up for a checkride with Holly Innes. She's my Assistant Chief Pilot, and our designated check airman."

DC's brows raised a smidgen; a female Check Airman was new to him.

As they strolled through the SEAS office, Dusty rambled on. "After your checkout, we'll get you familiar with the main routes and the way we do things around here. Then a route check, and you're on your own." He studied the pilot/fleet scheduling board, a large white chalkboard covering the wall behind the dispatchers' desks. "But we've gotta squeeze you in when there's a plane available. I don't see any—ah, there. Tomorrow at seven a.m. Guess you'll have to watch yourself tonight at the Red Dog."

"Red Dog?" DC asked.

"Allen didn't tell you? The Red Dog Saloon, downtown. We have a little get-together once a week to let off some steam." Dusty looked left and right, then bent closer and whispered, "Somebody, I'm not namin' names, dubbed it, 'Drunk Pilot Night'."

"Ralph."

"Hehe. You learn fast, son." Dusty turned and led him to his office. Over his shoulder, he said, "Afraid I can't join you for long tonight. One-a my grandkids is playin' Wicked Witch of the North. Grade school production."

Dusty stopped by his secretary. "Delores, this young man is Daniel Christopher Alva, and he can fly a plane. Set him up with an I.D. card will ya?"

* * *

Paperwork finished, DC strutted up Shell Simmons Drive to the bus stop. Maybe, he thought, this bush stuff wasn't so tough after all.

He remembered the eagle—*his* eagle—perched somewhere atop Thunder Mountain. He gazed up at the green peaks. Still lost in a swirl of cloud. Nevertheless, he felt as if he could soar along the ridgeline with his feathered brother.

With a shriek of brakes and a pungent cloud of diesel, the bus pulled up. DC hopped on and took a window seat. Turning onto Egan drive, the coach trundled toward town. DC gazed out at the Gastineau Channel, the ocean inlet splitting Juneau from Douglas Island. Beneath the overcast, the waters appeared ominously black. Along the surface, wind-formed ripples hitchhiked along the larger ocean waves.

About ten knots of breeze, DC guessed, trying to think like an Alaskan float pilot. Or maybe less, or more; he couldn't remember that part from ground school.

Entering town, the bus slowed. DC peered out the window. Between the thick pines, Victorian style houses perched on stilts along the side of Mount Juneau. Their Gold Rush architecture, he saw, clashed with modern, glass-and-steel Alaska State government offices. DC crinkled his nose at the drab monstrosities.

Hopping off at Marine Park, he strolled along the breezy dock. He zipped up against the chill.

Much to his surprise, he spied a *Taku Air* floatplane loading dockside. Sitting on a snubbing post, he watched four chattering tourists board the aircraft. Their rotund pilot, chawing a lipful of tobacco, held a lady's arm as she awkwardly stepped aboard the bobbing plane.

"You sure this thing is safe?" she asked.

"Don't worry, I wound up the rubber band this morning," the pilot quipped.

"Where're the parachutes?" cracked her husband. DC rolled his eyes.

The pilot snapped his fingers. "Damn, knew I forgot something," he replied, to a chorus of laughs. DC snickered.

"How far are we above sea level?" another passenger asked.

The pilot spat into the water. Watching as the chaw hit, he said, "Oh, about five feet." DC stifled a laugh. Now that was a new one.

The Beaver fired up and taxied off, blowing a wet spray over him.

Turning away, DC strolled down South Franklin Street among the tourist shops, bars and restaurants.

Following Allen's directions, he found his buddy's favorite coffee house, Heritage Coffee Company, and ducked inside for a mug in his honor. Sitting at the counter along the window, he gazed out at the charming little town.

The sun broke through the overcast, bathing the shops in a bright yellow glow. Long used to the perpetual clear skies of Phoenix, DC rarely appreciated the sun. But here, he realized, each shaft of light became a blessing.

A movement along the street caught his eye. Into the sunbeam floated a striking young woman. Clad in no more than Levi shorts and sleeveless T-shirt, not even goosebumps had formed on her toffee-colored skin; an indigenous creature, fully adapted to her environment. DC suddenly felt overdressed in his jeans and jacket.

Stopping by the window, she peered in. Black hair cascaded, soft and straight, over her bare shoulders. Full lip bit as if in anticipation, her chocolate brown, almond-shaped eyes darted from patron to patron. *Like an island girl*, he thought, though obviously Native American.

She spotted him staring back. Embarrassed, he looked away, heartbeat kicking up a notch. Shyly, he looked back. She flashed him a smile and moved on.

For a moment he could think of nothing but the stunning vision. What struck him most was her eyes, so big and soft and beautiful. But behind that innocent front lurked the glint of—what? A wild animal, he decided. Like a brown bear, cute and cuddly up front, deadly beneath. To men and salmon alike.

Entranced, DC rose and stepped out. He looked up the street in time to see her turn the corner.

The sky darkened; the sun hid. He followed.

He trailed her up into the old town, each street smaller and steeper than the last. Road gave way to alley, alley to staircase, the long, meandering wooden steps dividing neighbor from neighbor. The path twisted and turned, like Japanese scroll paintings he'd seen of foggy mountain hamlets.

She trotted up the stairs. He struggled to keep the pace, but, unaccustomed to the steep terrain, slowly fell behind. Finally, she disappeared into the mist.

A distant horn honked; DC blinked. A screen door screeched shut somewhere. Children laughed at play. He found himself lost in a forest of Victorian lumber.

Here, closer up, the old homes seemed tired. Planks sagged, nails rusted and paint peeled, victims of Her relentless beauty.

CHAPTER 5: Jake "Crash" Whitakker

In the ego-filled world of Alaskan commercial pilots, Jake Whitakker was the undisputed king of flight. This was not consciously acknowledged by those around him, it was simply understood as fact. Many disagreed with his cowboy ways in the cockpit, especially FAA Inspector Bruner and his government cohorts back in Oklahoma City.

Nevertheless, Whitakker's airmanship remained unquestioned. And, as a hunting and fishing guide, Jake Whitakker had no equal.

Born in Kalispell, he spent much of his youth hunting the Montana wilds under his prospector daddy's muddy boots. With Mom gone long before his memory, young Jake learned to bring home the buck and skin it while Dad panned and sluiced his way across the Rockies, Canada, and finally Alaska. Squandering a healthy family inheritance, father and son traveled in an aging Piper Super Cub, which Jake soloed before his thirteenth birthday.

A year later, his flight-of-fancy life suddenly crashed and burned.

In a bar room shootout over a shady lady, Jake lost his one anchor: his friend, his mentor, his hero. His dad. For the first time in his life, Jake was alone. Abandoned by the one he loved.

Devastated, a wall went up around him.

Authorities sent the wild boy to a Catholic orphanage. Though Catholic on the birth certificate, he'd rarely set foot in a church. Like Tarzan coming to the city, he didn't fit in, didn't belong. And he didn't care. Weekly fistfights with the other boys and the nuns' daily knuckle rappings did little to temper his demeanor, for the seeds of his life had already been sown. Jake Whitakker was a renegade and mountain man, born and bred.

After high school, to finance his commercial flight training, he landed a summer job on a forest fire fighting crew. Each season he worked up the fireman's ladder, eventually landing in the copilot seat of a slurry bomber, a modified C-130. Flying troops and slurry over the burning brush, he and his crew squeezed the four-engine turboprop plane into and out of some of the shortest dirt strips in the country.

Once, during a low pass over a particularly hot fire, an underground fuel tank exploded, sending liquid fire and shrapnel flying into his path. He banked hard and climbed, but too late.

The number two engine disintegrated and his right wing caught fire. Before the captain and crew realized what had even happened, he calmly deadsticked the craft into a meadow, dumping the slurry as he did. The plane landed, wheels up, in a cloud of red dust. The fire retardant doused the flames, and though the plane was a total loss, the men escaped with few injuries and no burns.

The action earned him command of his own ship, and the dubious nickname of "Crash."

A small scar from that action graced his square chin cleft, complimenting his woodsman's good looks. And at six foot two of swaggering muscle, he was equally skilled at landing ladies.

During winter months he flew, backpacked and hunted the wilds of North America. His outdoor talents caught the eye of a U.S. Fish and Wildlife official, who talked him into taking on another role: Game Warden. Jake's contempt for poachers nearly equaled his passion for hunting, as only a man brought up firsthand to understand nature's delicate balance could. He added to the Department's arsenal a most effective weapon: a floatplane. With great mobility, efficiency and zeal, the man enforced his beat.

It was an idyllic, if ironic, existence for the wild man. But even along the Canadian border, civilization hounded him. Finally, a tough young Yupik Eskimo named Sophie, working a summer job for the forest service, caught his eye. Sparks flew as hot as the embers from his old job, melting the glacial ice around his heart. But when the season ended, despite Jake's frantic pleading, she returned to her native village of Akiachak, Alaska.

Abandoned yet again by the one he loved, Jake was crushed. He took a long hard look at his life, then looked at her photo. He recalled his youth in the vast Alaskan Interior. The land and Sophie beckoned.

"*To hell with it*," he said, and followed her to Alaska.

The love affair, so perfect in the Lower Forty Eight, was a train wreck. Only Eluk, the family's new Alaskan Malamute puppy, seemed to enjoy his presence. Including Sophie.

Sensing her slipping away, he begged her to marry him. She refused. More to the point, her family refused. While a *Gussik* husband might mean a step up in wealth, a pilot would never be around to help during the tough times. Moreover, Sophie's father had other plans for her, in the form of a tribal official in Bethel.

Jake left with his tail between his legs. With his tail wagging, Eluk followed. Except for the affection Jake felt for his new companion, the glacial wall around his heart refroze. He fled as far as possible, to the opposite corner of the state, from Sophie. But never again did he leave Alaska.

Joining an upstart air taxi firm in Juneau called Southeast Alaskan Seaplanes, Whitakker quickly gained a reputation as one of the region's premier hunting and flying guides.

But that was not the only fame he gained. While some said he invited the worst of luck, to pilots he enjoyed the best. Starting with his legendary slurry bomber crash, Jake survived no less than two accidents and three "incidents," as the National Transportation Safety Board called his minor crackups in typically dry government legalese. He walked away from them all. And, while eighty percent of all aviation crashes were attributed, rightly or wrongly, to "pilot error," only one was ever blamed on him.

The accident had occurred in Gastineau Channel. Summer tourist season had brought yet another luxury cruise ship into port, and while some passengers power-shopped downtown, the more adventurous signed up for the SEAS' glacier "flightseeing" tours.

Sunny skies and whitecaps promised a scenic but bumpy ride for Whitakker's passengers.

A barf bagger day for sure, Jake thought with a grim smile, as he flew his floatplane up the Gastineau Channel toward the cruise ship.

Jake's de Havilland Beaver led a squadron of cohorts, strung in trail from the airport. Like Navy pilots in a carrier pattern, each planned to touch down, glide up to the ship dock, load up and launch again, only seconds apart. All part of the show.

Slowing the Beaver to final approach speed, Whitakker scanned the channel for boat and plane traffic. Calculating wind, waves and channel current, he selected the prime touch down point which would slide his bird up to the dock with minimal work.

Off to one side, an inebriated boatload of partiers raced along the channel. Beer goggles firmly in place, the speedster blasted through the waves, happily oblivious to anything as strange as an air ship landing on water. With a playful laugh, his woman poured a Budweiser over his head. In retaliation, he swerved to plop her back down in her seat. The action sent him straight for Whitakker.

Out of the corner of his eye, Jake caught the motion. The boat he'd dismissed as nonthreatening was now heading straight for him.

Whitakker banked sharply right. At the same moment, a wind gust stalled his lower wing, which dropped further, catching the tip in a wave. The plane cartwheeled and flipped.

Suddenly Whitakker found himself upside down, looking through the windscreen at the murky green depths of the channel. He gasped as freezing water poured in. Releasing his harness, Jake "fell" to the ceiling, his head hitting hard and submerging in water. He fumbled to slide the window open and the water gushed in. Finally, when enough water filled the cabin to equalize the pressure, he popped open the door and swam out.

Disoriented, he eyed the bubbles rising about him, and swam with them to the surface. Lungs nearly bursting, he broke surface. He gasped for air, twice sucking in seawater as the rough waves slapped at him. He dragged himself onto the nearest float, now upside down.

Shocked, the drunks circled to rescue him. They pulled up in time to see a figure standing on the float and looking like a humiliated, rain-soaked cat. As they eased up along side, Whitakker turned to them, a look of murder in his eyes.

Thinking twice about rescue, the driver shifted into reverse. "Uh, hey there, buddy," he said, "I'll go for help."

The drunk hit the throttle, but the cat leaped, landing on him with all his weight.

By the time the others pulled Whitakker off him, the driver sported a broken nose, two missing teeth, and a gouge above his left eye that took eighteen stitches to close.

Assault charges were never pressed, but the incident bought him a one-month pilot license suspension for *Careless and Reckless Operation of an aircraft.*

And one month's free drinks at the Red Dog Saloon.

A brilliant sun shone from a partly cloudy sky, and a blanket of pure white snow sparkled in reply. The light danced in crystalline prisms across the Juneau Icefield, as if it were spun of glass. Island statues of rock, dappled in white, towered above the frigid blanket.

From DC's vantage point, in the copilot's seat of Jake Whitakker's floatplane, he felt he could see a thousand miles. Despite wearing his brand new Serengeti sunglasses, he had to squint at the shining panorama before him. Behind them, three other tourists gazed in awe. Cameras clicked and whirred.

Whitakker chuckled at the wide-eyed *cheechacko*. "Beautiful, isn't it?"

Overwhelmed by the scenery, all DC could do was nod.

At the end of the icefield, Jake closed in on a pine-topped ridge. He aimed for a cut in the rock along the ridgeline. The granite spires towered ever higher.

DC noticed a slight gleam in Whitakker's eye.

"*Bonzai!*" Jake exclaimed as they launched through the tiny niche.

The ground dropped away. A girl screamed in back. Suddenly, DC and the tourists aboard were faced with a raging waterfall. DC actually had to look *up* to see its crest. Even above the din of the engine, DC could swear he heard its thunder. A puff of moisture cooled his cheeks.

Whitakker banked away, out over the Taku River. Below, green islands of grass sailed by.

"Wait, I think I see something ahead," Jake announced, throttling back.

DC glanced at his cohort, then followed the man's gaze out the window. After a moment, DC spotted a tiny brown figure in the water. As the tour plane closed in, he realized with amazement that he was staring at an Alaskan moose.

Whitakker circled the beast to get a better look, careful to keep a respectful distance. Though it stood knee high in the river, DC could tell the animal was enormous.

Whitakker rolled out of the turn and headed for home. For ten reverent minutes the plane flew straight and level and silent, as DC and the other awestruck passengers contemplated the amazing world.

As Jake set up for a water landing back in Gastineau Channel, DC watched in quiet respect. Out the front window, he saw the gentle blue waves rise up to meet them. Suddenly, he felt the shoulder straps press his chest. Spray leapt up to the sides in a *whoosh!*, like the grand finale of a log ride. With a swan's grace, the plane settled in the water.

Whitakker idled the engine, lowered the water rudders, and deftly sailed the flying boat up to the small wooden dock floating next to the cruise ship.

With lines dangling from the wingtip, dock hands pulled the Beaver in and lashed it fast.

While the ecstatic tourists climbed out, spouting praises, DC remained in his seat, speechless. For the first time in a long time, he felt alive. Somehow, this magnificent land had pumped him with the stuff of spirit. And DC knew he was in love again. In love with flying. In love with life.

In love with Alaska.

* * *

Opening the apartment door, DC called, "Honey, I'm home."

Allen said, "And how was your day at the office, dear?"

"Pretty damn spectacular," he exclaimed. He looked across the room to find Allen pulling something from the oven. Inhaling deeply, DC added, "Man, you're becoming a regular Betty Crocker."

"Heh heh. You learn to become independent around here. But, like I said this morning, don't get used to it."

DC walked over and eyed his friend's creation. "And what's my little punkin' cooking for us today?"

"Moose roast," Allen replied.

"No shit?" DC exclaimed. He thought of the beast he'd seen earlier. An animal that size could feed a small family for a month. He looked at his friend. "Been out hunting in your spare time?"

Slicing a sample for each of them, Allen explained. "Flew Greg Mastis in from the bush today. He's an Alaska Department of Fish and Game guy. He'd been out hunting for a few weeks. Nice tip, eh?"

DC popped the piece in his mouth and chewed. Despite having a slightly gamey taste, the roast melted in his mouth. "Mmm. I'm beginning to like this job more and more."

Allen nodded agreement. "It does have its fringe benefits." While Allen served up the roast, DC grabbed two Coors from the refrigerator. The two sat at the small table and dug in.

"So, whaddya think?" Allen asked between bites.

Through a mouthful of moose, DC mushed, "This plashe is aweshome."

Allen grinned. "Thought you'd be impressed. But I'll warn you, these last two days were about the best we've seen for weeks. It's usually pretty hairy."

DC paused mid-chew. At his friend's dire words, the elation he'd felt all day disintegrated. "Thanks for reminding me," he said glumly.

"Stop worrying, man." Allen reached across the table and punched his friend on the shoulder. "You'll do fine. Besides, that's what's great about Alaska. No matter how many black marks on your record, you can always find a flying job."

DC gave a noncommittal shrug. "That may be okay for guys like Ralph and Crash. But you and me, our whole lives we've dreamed of flying the big irons. One screw up and we're blacklisted. And all the time and money we invested would be wasted. And, worse, my dad would say, 'I told you so'."

Allen stared at his plate for a long moment. "My drunk fuck of a dad, I'd love to walk up to him one day and say, 'See these stripes on my shoulders? That's what I did with my life, no thanks to you'."

"Yeah." After a reflective pause, DC brightened. "At least you got some hot babes running around here."

"Oh?"

"Yeah, I saw a beaute downtown yesterday. The kind you'd beg to have your children."

"Hah! Musta been a tourist."

DC shook his head. "Not this one. I think she was an Indian. What do you call them?"

"Tlingits," Allen answered. "And I wouldn't be calling them 'Indian.' You'll just sound like a dumb *cheechacko*." Allen gulped down his beer, a dark expression suddenly covering his face.

"Roger that," DC replied. "Oh, did I tell you? Donna Martinez bagged United."

Allen's jaw dropped. "Are you shittin' me? She just landed that commuter job a few months ago. Just a lowly turboprop First Officer."

With a laugh, DC said, "I'd give my right nut to be a 'lowly turboprop FO'."

"Me too. Damn this business. Good for her, I mean, but . . . damn this business."

The two remained silent for several more minutes. Finally, Allen looked DC in the eye. He pointed his finger at him for emphasis. "Just don't lose sight of why we're here, DC. Get a little quality Alaska time, and you can write your own ticket, too."

DC nodded. "Yeah, but a ticket to where? I mean, we're too white and male to make it to the big leagues from here, right? And at the end of the season, at least one of us is out of a job."

Allen shrugged. "Throw the backpack on and start somewhere else, I guess."

"Oh, great."

"Well, you have any ideas?"

DC felt his insides churn. "I don't know," he said finally. "Guess it all depends on if I survive up here—the checkride, I mean," he added quickly.

For a moment the two sat in silence, avoiding the great *What If* each one thought but dared not speak.

* * *

"Trip up," Dusty called, waving the flight manifest. "Float job. Crash, you're on."

Jake grabbed the paper from Dusty's hand and read. "Mack and Mike Doyle? Christ, not those psychos." Crumpling the paper in his hand, he followed Dusty into his office. "This was Marty's trip," he protested, dropping the wrinkled manifest on the Chief Pilot's desktop.

Walking around behind his desk, Dusty shrugged. "Marty's mechanicaled down in Tenakee Springs. Dinged his float. A customer thought he could help by grabbing the dock rope on the wing as Marty floated up. The plane pivoted around him and right into the dock."

Jake shook his head. "Why the hell didn't yell '*Stop!*'? He knows better."

"He did. Guy was a deaf mute." Dusty sighed. "Passengers just don't make good deck hands."

Jake leaned over the table. "You know, Dusty, you don't get out of the office enough. Why don't you fly 'em?"

Dusty looked at him with gleaming eyes that belied the sympathetic wrinkles on his forehead. "Nice try, Crash. But actually, they requested you. Always do. And since your Pelican turn canceled, you're back to your original date."

"Guys give me the creeps," Jake protested. "Besides, they hate my guts too."

"Match made in heaven," Dusty quipped. "Don't take it personally, they hate everyone."

Jake plopped down in a seat. "They're so damn rich, why don't they just buy their own plane? Save 'em the slither back to New Jersey come winter time. Hell, Mike's so shady, he claims year-round residency so he can get the local hunter's fee and skip on a guide. If he could, he'd scam a Permanent Fund dividend every year." Jake looked at his boss. "Look, I flew him last time. It's Ralph's turn."

Dusty sat behind his desk and leaned back. "You know, Jake, for a dashing bush pilot you sure whine a lot." Hands laced across his chest, he propped his feet on the desk. "Look, if you don't want the bonus, that's fine with me. But I'll bet you a Chinook you can't talk Ralph into it."

"You're on, my friend." Jake jumped up and stuck his head out the open office door. "Oh, Ralphy, Ralphy Olafsen," he called in a singsong voice.

Ralph, loitering suspiciously within earshot, walked in and replied, "Heads." Jake tossed a quarter and slapped it on the back of his hand. Ralph peered over Whitakker's shoulder. "Damn. Should've known not to mess with your luck."

"You Vikings never were very smart," Jake replied.

Cinching up his jeans and thrusting his pelvis forward, Ralph answered, "It don't take smarts to rape and pillage when you've got a big broadsword stuck in your pants."

Chuckling, Dusty said, "All right, I owe you a pint, Jake." To Ralph he said, "Weather's marginal down the channel, but I think you can make it."

"Ain't turned back this season yet," Ralph boasted.

Jake said, "See those Coke bottle glasses of his? He can't see past the prop, anyway."

"That's my secret," Ralph said. "To me, visibility's always two feet."

Still chuckling, Dusty stood and handed Ralph the trip manifest. "Sixty One is fueled and ready to go."

"'Sixty-One I-think-I-Can'?," Ralph replied, referring to the pilots' cynical nickname for the aged floatplane. Every airline fleet had its dog. Ralph sighed. "This trip's going downhill fast."

Eyeing the manifest, he said, "So, where do I pick up Tweedledum and Tweedledumber?"

Dusty laughed. "At their cabin. Drop off in Haines. Brown bear I'll bet," he ventured.

Jake said, "Not unless they're hiking way the hell up to Northway or Yakatat. Unit One's closed till September. Nope. Gotta be fishing at Chilkat Lake."

"Bastards could do that in their front yard," Ralph grumbled.

With a grin, Dusty said, "But then we all couldn't fleece them of their riches, now could we?"

"Hey Ralph," Jake called as the pilot walked out. Ralph stopped and turned. Jake said with a smirk, "Eluk's due for a ride."

A devious smile crept across Ralph's mug. "Oh, they're gonna love me."

The three pilots chuckled.

CHAPTER 6: Ralph Olafsen

Ralph Olafsen was a walking contradiction.

He was a hermit. And a joker. He was a soldier. And a peacenick. He was a creative artist who wasted his talent sketching unflattering caricatures of those he thought little of, or those he admired. People rarely knew into which category they fell.

A wallflower if given the chance, Ralph kept to himself. Any patron stepping into the Red Dog Saloon on Drunk Pilot Night would invariably spot the legendary Jake Whitakker first. And Ralph last. Even his faded, chocolate brown flight jacket, so often the proud trademark of the bush pilot, instead seemed to camouflage him in the dark tavern or the airport lounge. But if a pilot's skills were truly based on the distress of his leather, Ralph's tattered rag would proclaim him a sky god.

Ralph's flying career, however, had started quite by accident; he was drafted. If not for Viet Nam, he would have been happy making trinkets in Arkansas with his wife Misty. But the backwoods hillbilly with the A.S. degree in Arts took to Army helicopters like a salmon to stream.

Much to Misty's relief, Ralph missed a tour of'Nam by three short months. Instead, the Army sent him to Anchorage for a liaison tour of Elmendorf Air Force Base. There, he quickly won friends with weekly wilderness "recons" in his Sea King pontoon helicopter, fishing tackle and poles included. All on the taxpayer dime.

After his tour, despite the glut of ex-'Nam chopper pilots saturating the market, Ralph lucked into a distant cousin's logging operation in Arkansas. He quickly racked up time hauling machinery in and out of the hills in an old Sikorsky. A floatplane was added to the fleet, and Ralph took to it as naturally as his first whirlybird.

A corporation from Little Rock eventually bought out the mine. Treating him like a backwoods hick, the company's Chief Pilot tacked Ralph onto the bottom of the seniority list; he would only get to fly the worst of jobs. After eyeing the man for a moment, he tossed his company badge on the desk.

"*To hell with it*," he said, and marched out the door.

The counterculture couple packed up their van and headed for Alaska. The Last Frontier proved the perfect land to hone his skills as a pilot . . . and as a practical joker. And one incident in particular solidified his reputation for both.

It came to be called, The Great Mount Edgecombe Volcanic Eruption of April First.

Sitka Sheriff John McCabe valued his beauty sleep. But every summer morning, he was rudely shaken out of bed by the drone of Ralph's single engine Beaver, or the *whop-whop* of his whirlybird. In hot retaliation, McCabe accused Olafsen of everything from reckless flying to poaching. Though perhaps somewhat guilty of the former, Ralph was completely innocent of the latter, and the accusation incensed him.

In the early dawn twilight of April first, the very first day of the summer season, Sheriff McCabe was once again rudely shaken out of bed. But this time by a phone call. The harried voice of the desk sergeant snapped him to.

"Mount Edgecumbe's on fire, John," he cried. "The whole thing's erupting!"

"Impossible," McCabe replied with unmasked anger. "It's extinct."

"Take a look for yourself, then," the man answered.

He did. Shuffling out the front door in his emerald green pajamas and Martha's pink slippers, he looked west across Sitka Sound. And gasped in horror.

Mount Edgecombe, long dormant and dominating the skyline west of the city, highlighted in predawn twilight, belched an enormous cloud of black smoke.

"Jesus," he exclaimed, grabbing his keys and racing to his patrol car. He screeched away. "Prepare for an evacuation," he cried over the radio as he careened down Katlian Street. "Call the National Guard. And phone Ralph Olafsen. Tell him to get his chopper ready. We've got to see if this thing's gonna blow."

Over O'Connel Bridge and onto Japonski Island he raced, circling the airport perimeter and finally skidding up to the helipad.

Ralph was already strapped in the cockpit, sipping from his coffee mug, chopper blades spinning lazily. McCabe hopped in.

"Nice uniform, Chief," Ralph said.

"Shut up and move," he growled.

Ralph pulled the collective, the blades cut the air and the ship launched toward the rumbling menace. As they edged closer to the mouth of the volcano, McCabe fidgeted nervously in his seat. But Olafsen remained strangely calm.

He said over the intercom, "Relax, Chief. If this thing goes, we won't know what hit us. Well, except for the writhing in hellfire part as we plummet to our death."

McCabe shot him a scowl. "Move closer."

They did, enough to see over the rim. McCabe's eyes widened in surprise. His mouth dropped open.

"Well, looky there," Ralph said, "looks like someone decided to dump their old tires and burn 'em up. Nice they did it away from town, so's no one gets upset."

McCabe's eyes narrowed; the veins in his neck bulged against his pajama collar. Just as it looked like his head would explode, he shouted, "Take us back home!"

They landed at the helipad amidst a media melee. McCabe stared out the window in horror, realizing what was to come.

"Well, Chief, let's see. Half hour's flight time will be $125.00, special government rate. Shall I bill you, or the Department?"

"I owe you nothin'," McCabe spat, hopping out.

"Happy April Fool's Day, Chief," Ralph called as the Sheriff was mobbed by snickering reporters.

Cameras snapped away, and a half dozen microphones were thrust into McCabe's face, but all he could say was a clipped, "False alarm, no comment," before escaping.

The next day, the *Sitka Daily Sentinel* proudly sported a front page full color shot of McCabe in his "new uniform" of green and pink, the "volcano's" black smoke belching in the background.

Sheriff Erupts Over Volcanic Hoax, read the caption.

Every government agency, from the FAA to the EPA, investigated. But, aside from a two-hour discrepancy in the helicopter's flight log and two witnesses who heard a distant "*whop-whop* sound" on or about three a.m., no evidence was found.

Knowing when he was beat, and preferring to keep further shots of his "new uniform" out of the paper, Sheriff McCabe quickly and quietly squelched his own department's investigation. No charges were pressed.

Olafsen never once admitted guilt, but for months afterward he drank free in every bar in southeast Alaska.

Judging wind, wave and current, Ralph "sailed" the idling Beaver backward across the lake at a 45 degree angle to shoreline. At just the right moment, he cut the engine and hopped out onto the port float. As the craft drifted up to the rocky shoreline, he stepped off into ankle deep water and crouched under the horizontal stabilizer. Lifting the tail with his back, he walked backward up the beach, hauling the plane ashore and making sure the floats didn't grate on the rocks. Then a voice behind him grated on his nerves.

"Yo, where's Whitakker?"

Ralph turned to greet the greaseball walking toward him. Camouflage fatigues draped Mack Doyle's bulky frame, more fat than muscle. Pot belly spilled from beneath a black tee shirt that read, *Nuke the Gay Whales*. Gold chains jingled about his thick neck, as if he couldn't decide whether to firefight with the commies or disco with them. Behind him, little brother Mike, a smaller version of Mack and similarly dressed, dragged another load of gear from the cabin and dropped it on the beach.

"Nice to see you, too, Mr. Mack," Ralph replied. "Jake had a run to Angoon he couldn't pass up. Good tippers," he lied, just to needle the asshole.

Mack sat on a stump, sipped what was left of his coffee and watched contentedly as Ralph struggled alone to load the brothers' gear.

Eluk bounded out of the plane, ran down the float and jumped up on Doyle, spilling his morning coffee across his chest.

"Goddamn mutt," he cursed. "We don't pay good money to have your dog stinkin' up our shit, you know."

Ralph grabbed a load of supplies and tossed it in back. "Nope, I'm sure your shit stinks just fine already. Don't worry, you don't have to pay his fare."

Mike knelt, giggling, as Eluk ran over and licked his face. Upon spotting the *Lassie*-like scene, Mack Doyle shook his head in disgust. "Mike, get the rest of the goddamn gear," he barked.

"Uh, sure, Mack," Mike said, scurrying back to the cabin.

Ralph stepped off the plane and brushed his hands, having loaded the first pile of gear.

"Those too." Doyle pointed with his mug to three large aluminum game boxes. Eluk trotted over to them and sniffed, then wagged his tail excitedly.

Ralph raised a brow. "Going hunting?"

"No, no, fishing," Mack replied quickly. "A few pounds of cutthroat, Dolly Varden. Maybe an early run of coho. Just provisions in there now. But I expect we'll pull out our limit pretty quick, and use the lockers to haul 'em back."

"Chilkat Lake?"

After a pause, Mack answered, "If you must know, yes. Taking the RV up."

Mack stood and slung his rifle bag over his shoulder. Ralph tossed the lockers in back with the rest of the gear. He turned to his passenger and motioned with his hand. "I'll take that," he said.

Mack grabbed the shoulder strap tighter. "What, you think I'm gonna hijack my own plane, for chrissakes?"

"Well, you do kinda look like one'a them Iranian terrorists I seen on the wall in the Post Office."

"Oh, come on," Mack protested.

"You oughta know the law by now, Mister. Federal Aviation Regulation One Thirty-Five Dash Oh Five One Point Twelve states . . . "

Ralph bluffed his way through a fictitious rule, hoping it sounded good.

"Whitakker never bothers me with that shit," Mack groused.

While Alaska law actually required a firearm to be aboard a commercial bush plane, Federal Aviation Regulations banned them from the cabin. Like most pilots flying in the less remote areas, Ralph ignored the state rule and rarely bothered enforcing the federal. But the thought of the Doyle brothers riding shotgun in his cockpit didn't sit well. Besides, it gave him the chance to throw another barb Mack's way.

Ralph cocked his head sideways. "Mack, I haven't drunk enough beer yet today to get in a pissin' contest with you, so just accept it, okay? Look, you can hold the rounds in your pocket if it makes you feel warm and fuzzy. But the rifle goes in back."

With a great show of reluctance, Mack surrendered the weapon. Ralph unzipped the bag, checked that the clip was empty and laid it gently in back. "Why you bothering to take it, anyway? You're just going fishing, right?"

"You ever heard of bear attacks?"

"Ah, right. Never know when Smokey's gonna show up packing an uzi." Ralph held his hand, palm up, and motioned with his fingers. "Your brother's sidearm, too."

Mike, standing idly behind his big brother, swayed his head in an equally theatrical show of reluctance. "Aw, crap," he replied.

Little more was said during the hourlong flight to Haines, and that was fine by Ralph. He didn't know much about hunting and fishing, but he did know that those game lockers were just too damn big and bulky to carry the few legal pounds of fish.

* * *

"Eluk!" DC exclaimed, as he and Allen walked up to the entrance of the Red Dog Saloon.

The dog, playing sentry at the door, wagged and howled in greeting as they approached. The two pilots bent to pet him.

"Well, at least we know Crash is here," Allen said, fishing out a cigarette from his shirt pocket.

"I can't believe he's sitting here without a leash," DC commented.

"What do you expect? He's underage."

DC snorted. "Yeah, right. I mean, what about the cops? Isn't there a leash law or something?"

"Probably," Allen replied, lighting up. "But they know Eluk's no problem." Allen shot a grey cloud from his nostrils, then pointed to the dog with his stogie. "It's his job to guide Jake's drunk ass home, along with whatever lady friend he's snagged for the evening."

Cigarette dangling from his lips, Allen thrust open the swinging doors to the Red Dog Saloon and stepped in.

DC followed. A blast of heat and sweat and smoky sound hit him. As he and Allen elbowed their way to the bar, DC scanned the room. Every piece of furniture, from carved wood table to sawdusted floor, reminded him of a John Wayne western. He almost expected the place to be filled with prospectors, shady ladies and cowboys. But the six-shooters and gold dust and ten-gallon hats had long been replaced with pagers and credit cards and cameras.

Raised in Phoenix, DC was more than familiar with Old West tunes. To the best of his knowledge, Hendrix's *Hey Joe* was not one of them. The house band, however, was apparently oblivious to that. Happy hour, he saw, was the same everywhere. Yet in Alaska it seemed slightly askew, just like the rest of it he'd seen so far. An air of lawlessness, of true frontier, seemed to permeate the land, even here in midst of the state capital.

Allen shouted above the noise, "Let me be the first to buy you a drink. Two Chinooks," he called to the bartender. He and DC leaned against the bar and surveyed the crowd.

"Just like old times, eh?" Allen said.

DC replied, "Not quite the target-rich environment of the Mill Avenue bars back at ASU, I see."

"Oh, single so soon, are we?"

"Steph and I are—well, semi-broken up, I guess. We can date," he said lightly.

"Yeah, sure. Well, in Alaska it's about ten men to every woman. So good luck."

DC recalled his mystery woman. He still couldn't believe he'd actually followed her. He scanned the crowd further, hoping to spot her. The eclectic mix of patrons amazed him. Most, he saw, were tourists. He smiled at his sudden ability to distinguish a tourist from a local; then realized, with embarrassment, that his crisp flannels tagged him as a foreigner too.

The drinks arrived. The boys picked up their glasses.

"Here's to new horizons," Allen toasted.

DC took a swallow, then eyed appreciatively the amber liquid in his mug. "Mm, good. I gotta watch this stuff, though. I got a checkride tomorrow at seven. Some chick."

"Holly Innes is no 'chick'," Allen said. "She'll rip your head off if you fuck up."

With creased brows, DC looked at him. "That bad, huh?" Allen nodded. DC's thoughts turned to the few female pilots he'd known. In the testosterone-dominated field of aviation, he knew, women had always had a bad rap. He leaned forward. "How good is she? At flying, I mean?"

Allen gazed evenly at him. "I'll let you decide that for yourself."

Glancing around the room, he said, "Well, um, do you think she'll be here tonight? I wouldn't mind meeting her to kind of break the ice."

Allen shook his head. "Not a chance. She never joins in our reindeer games."

Through the dim, smoky light, the two scanned the crowd. Allen nudged DC. He followed Allen's gaze upstairs. Jake Whitakker leaned on the railing above them, prowling the crowd with his eyes.

The two *cheechackos* headed up the back stairs to mingle with the sourdoughs.

Pilots, mechanics, rampers and staff from the SEAS company bantered and babbled with each other, their spouses and friends. Four more pilots and mechanics played pool on the green felt table in back.

Dusty sat at the largest table. He stood and greeted DC, then introduced him to several others, all of whom welcomed him, and all of whose names, despite his best effort, he promptly forgot.

DC spotted Ralph Olafsen standing in a dark corner, quietly sipping a mixed drink.

He pointed him out to Allen, who replied, "He's like that. Go say hi."

"Think he'll remember me?"

"Sure."

Reluctantly, DC stepped toward him. Ralph caught his movement, and stared back as he approached. DC fought for something to say to get the ball rolling.

"So tell me, Ralph, how does a guy get to join your church?" he asked with a smirk.

He stared back, eyes lost behind a glint of glasses. DC shifted awkwardly, not knowing whether the man had heard him or not. He glanced back at Allen for reassurance, who stood with his back to him, engaged in another conversation. Turning back to Ralph, he said, "I was joking. Uh, you know, from yesterday. You gave me that pamphlet. My name's DC," he finished, holding out his hand.

"I don't see a drink," Ralph finally said.

"Huh?"

"You're holding your hand out, but it's empty. Rum and Coke."

"Oh, sure. But I'm afraid I can't join you. I've got a checkride tomorrow with Check Airman Holly Innes, so I can't drink much."

He put a palm on DC's head. "My son, to join the flock you must be anointed with holy water. Morgan's Dark, to be exact."

DC shifted uneasily to his other foot. "Uh, yeah, okay. One or two wouldn't hurt, I guess. I was just finishing this beer."

He stepped over to the upstairs bar behind them. "Two Morgan and Cokes, dark," he ordered. Charlie the bartender looked to him, then to Ralph, who pointed at DC's back, held up two fingers and mouthed, *Doubles. All night*.

Long clued into Ralph's antics, Charlie fixed the drinks.

DC fumbled for some bills in his pocket, but Charlie said, "I'll start a tab."

"Yeah, great," he said, grabbing the drinks and serving his new buddy.

Allen and Jake joined them.

Ralph raised his glass to DC and said formally, "Here's to your honor."

DC replied, "Thanks, I—"

"Once you're *on* 'er, don't get *off* 'er," Ralph finished.

Laughing, the four men clinked glasses.

"Mm. Smooth," DC commented, watching the ice swirl in his glass.

Ralph, Jake and Allen exchanged knowing glances.

"So, DC, how'd you get your time?" Jake asked.

"Oh, the way most of us get it nowadays. Flight instructing. Hah! Glad I'm done with that."

"Here's to no more flight instructing," Ralph toasted with a flair. Once again, the four clinked and drank.

"And charter flying. Mostly Grand Canyon tours. Sick of that, too."

"Here's to no more Grand Canyon tours," Ralph sang.

DC felt a heavy hand slap his back.

"Didn't think you had the balls to join us up here, DC," a voice said from behind. DC stiffened. The hair on his neck raised. The all too-familiar voice screeched in his ears like a jammed radio call.

"Hello, Tom," DC said coolly. He turned to face his old college rival. A young, starry-eyed girl hung on the man's arm.

"Allow me to introduce my new friend, Charlotte," Tom said.

"Charlene," the girl corrected him with a playful slap on his bulging bicep.

With a quick nod to Charlene, DC eyed Tom. Crossing his arms, he said, "I see you haven't changed."

Tom Zion slapped his belly. Well, I've had a few too many Chinooks up here, but otherwise I'm still the old football star of my youth. Hey, I don't see Stephanie here. She finally dump you?" DC turned his back to him, unable to answer. "Aw, come on DC, you're not still sore about that are you? Friends share everything, right?"

DC's fist tightened and raised, but Allen's hand on his arm stopped him.

"As always, Tom," Allen said, "your lack of tact is only surpassed by your poor stick."

Tom laughed. "I'm not sure what you call that, Foley—"

"Double-entendre."

"—but it was a good one. Listen, Dad might have got me on with Air Chinook up here, but you gotta be hot shit to keep the job. Anyway, I'm looking forward to competing with you two losers. If you can hack it, of course." He leaned forward and said in DC's ear, "By the way. After this summer, the old man's gettin' me a commuter job in California. Twin turboprops, man. A captain buddy of his at Delta owns a chunk of an airline. And from there, it's, 'Hello, majors'! How you gonna build your twin time?" DC tersely shook his head. "Well. Maybe I can put in a good word and get you on. I'd offer the same to your buddy Allen, but he's too much of a dick." After slapping DC's back, Tom walked away with a "See ya."

"Not if I see you first," DC muttered into his glass, then gulped.

Allen watched Zion walking away. "Well, Alaska has it's ugly qualities, too."

"My, oh my, I suddenly feel an Arctic breeze in here," Ralph commented.

"A long and unpleasant story," Allen answered.

"Well, maybe another time. For now, I need something to shake off this chill." Ralph tossed back the rest of his drink.

Another table opened up and Whitakker grabbed it. The pilots sat while Ralph ordered a round at the bar.

"Don't forget that double," Ralph said as Charlie poured.

"Fresh meat?" Charlie asked, motioning with his head to DC.

Ralph nodded. "Rite of passage. Checkride tomorrow."

He sat the drinks in front of Ralph. "*Hoo boy*. Now I know why I always take the ferry."

Ralph returned with the round.

Dusty moved over to their table. He said, "About time this old geezer got along, boys. The wicked witch of the north wouldn't be happy if I missed her show. How you fairin', DC?"

Tongue quickly loosening, DC sat back and shook his head in disbelief. "Man, I just can't believe I'm here. Alaska!"

"Here's to Alaska," Ralph toasted.

After a gulp, DC looked to the older pilots and said, "So tell me, oh exalted ones: what're the secrets to becoming a great Alaskan bush pilot?'

"Survive," Jake answered.

They laughed. Ralph leaned back in his chair, content to let the others do the talking.

"The age of the bush pilot is dead," Jake said flatly. Dusty nodded agreement.

DC looked to each of the pilots. "Oh, come on. You don't mean that."

"You're about fifty years too late, I'm afraid," Dusty said. "All the trails have been blazed. Carl Ben Eielson, Shel Simmons, Glacier pilot Bob Reeve, Mudhole Smith, Thrill-em Gillam, the Wien brothers . . . those were the real bush pilots. They flew Jennys and Stinsons and Bellancas held together by baling wire and their own guts, over terrain not even mapped yet. They made their own skis, plowed their own landing strips, and lit them at night with lanterns. You know what the first strip at Fairbanks was? A baseball diamond. That's the only place we had to land in some villages."

"Yeah, yeah, and you guys had to walk two miles to school, uphill both ways through snowstorms," DC said.

"Dusty speaks from experience," Allen said with a raised finger. "He's the closest of any of us to being an original bush pilot."

Dusty laughed. "Don't date me, son!"

Jake lamented, "Now we all fly out of a tower-controlled airport, off a paved runway, sometimes to another paved runway."

"Okay, so we're based in civilization," DC said. "You still do real bush stuff, don't you?"

Jake pursed his lips. "If you call buzzing Kake's gravel strip to chase the bears away, then, yeah, we do."

DC let out a short laugh, unsure as to whether the man was serious about the bears or not. A discreet nod from Allen assured him he was.

"You can still find it in bits and pieces," Dusty allowed. "But the frontier is dying. Entire villages used to come out shouting '*Tingoon!*' and cheering us as we landed, even when we were a week late with their mail. Now they grumble if you're an hour late."

"We're no longer bush pilots, we're 'Air Taxi Operators'," Jake complained. "We gotta have a license for making money, a license for the plane, for landing on the water, even an instrument pilot license, though we can't legally fly through clouds. We can't so much as change a spark plug without an A&P license. Even the engine parts got licenses. The same 25-cent bolt from the general store costs twelve bucks when it's got *FAA approved* stamped on it."

"Now I hear they're gonna license our piss," Ralph chimed in. "Have to urinate in a bottle and test it for heroin every time Inspector Bruner's in a sour mood."

"Stop it already," DC cried, "you're making me depressed."

They laughed.

Dusty put his hand on his shoulder and said, "DC, if I'd-a stayed in the airline business, I'd have already retired with a bank full of gold. But instead I work fourteen hour days to bring home chump change. Suzette and I will retire from this business with nothing. But do you think I regret it? Not one damn bit." The old man bent to his ear and whispered, "You're always a pioneer if you've never done it before. The adventure's still out there, son. You just gotta go find it."

DC sat in silence, letting the man's words soak in.

Dusty straightened. To the others he said, "You gentleman take care of this one. He's got an early show. G'night."

Ralph raised his glass. "Oh, we will, Chief. Promise. Hail to the Chief!"

DC, feeling happy again among his new friends, took a big gulp.

Ralph leaned forward. "Hey, *cheechacko*. You know what makes an airplane fly?" he asked.

DC smiled at the old joke. "Money," he answered.

"Yeah, yeah, that too. That and fuel." Ralph swirled the ice around his empty glass. "And right now I'm runnin' on fumes. Catch my stink?"

"Oh, sure. My turn I guess," DC said, standing. He swayed a moment, then ambled over to the bar and ordered another round. Charlie, sticking with Ralph's standing orders, doubled DC's. Returning to the table, DC noticed Allen staring down through the railing. He followed his gaze to the first floor. And sucked in his breath.

There she stood in the middle of the room, silhouetted from behind by the bright stage lights. But he could recognize that profile anywhere.

Setting the drinks down, he whispered to his buddy, "That's the girl I was telling you about."

Without turning, Allen said, "Not surprised."

"Who is she?"

"That, my friend, is Tonya, full blooded Tlingit native."

They watched as she made her way to the bar. A man walked up and kissed her on the cheek. DC slumped. But then another did the same. She worked her way through the crowd that way, seeming to be on intimate terms with every man she met.

"Popular gal," DC remarked.

"Oughta be. She's a waitress here."

Only then did DC notice her drink tray, tucked beneath an arm after having delivered a round. DC said, "We need to hang out here more often."

Looking sideways at him, Allen said, "I don't normally like to discourage people from chasing their dreams, *cheechacko*, but that's one bear that'll eat your heart for breakfast."

DC glanced at him. "Speaking from experience?"

Allen hesitated a moment before replying. "Um, well, not really. But she's a helluva flirt."

"I can see that. Well, here's to bear hunting." They drank.

Allen finished his gulp first. "If anyone could catch her, Crash could." Turning to the older pilot and pointing towards Tonya, he asked, "Ever meet that filly down there?"

Jake nodded. "Flown her and the family around a bit. Forget to where. She's a local, though. Big clan."

DC leaned forward. "Ever get to know her . . . better?"

Jake chuckled. "That's classified."

"He did," Allen said flatly.

Jake held up a hand. "To be honest, boys, no. Too young. And, more to the point, too many relatives with shotguns around."

Ralph goaded him on. "Never stopped you before."

"She's young enough to be my daughter," Jake protested.

"Could be, for all you know," he shot back. "C'mon, Crash, don't play virtuous knight with us. I've seen you rob the cradle more than once."

Inspecting the ice formations in his drink, Jake said, "Yeah, I do like 'em young. And old. And my age. But mostly I prefer blondes. Or brunettes. Or redheads."

"Breathing, preferably," Allen said.

"*And* attached," Ralph added.

Jake waggled a finger at his friend. "Hey, watch it." Draining the drink, he held up his glass. "Garçon, I'm dry."

"Got it," Allen said, jumping up.

Charlie fixed Allen the round, doubling DC's. Plopping the first drink in front of Allen, he said, "This one's a freebie. For pretty boy, Jake." Allen looked questioningly at him. He nodded to the end of the bar. "From her."

Allen rolled his eyes. "Here we go again." He served the drinks and sat. DC and the others thanked him. "Thank Blondie for yours, Crash," Allen said.

They all turned. A woman, dolled up in big city makeup and bleached hair, smiled back and raised her glass. A frilly white leather vest, white sweater and gold necklaces accented her healthy bust by Dow-Corning.

Nodding, Jake hoisted his drink in acknowledgement.

As they turned back, DC said, "Not bad."

"Lady I had on a tour today," Jake explained. "Guess I let slip where I'd be tonight. She tipped well enough, though."

"I'll bet she did," Ralph said. He turned to the boys. "Nary a night goes by a woman either buys him a drink or throws one in his face. Looks like a good night." Ralph lifted his glass. "Here's to a good night!"

The four drank to the toast. DC threw down half the drink in one gulp. The rum found its way straight to his head.

Leaning over, Allen shook DC's shoulders. To the others he said, "*Cheechacko* here sold his squaw to the Injuns back in Arizona. I say we give him first crack at the Princess. Otherwise, I'm afraid he's gonna come crawling into my bed tonight."

Jake shrugged. "Knock yourself out."

Chuckling nervously, DC raised a hand. "That's okay. You don't have to —"

"C'mon, DC," Allen whispered in his ear, giving him one more shake. "Impress your new buddies."

DC looked questioningly at him. Not even here a week, and already Allen was tempting him to play with matches. He thought about Steph and sat back. Certainly she was worth more to him than the likes of a one night stand.

Allen seemed to read his mind. "You're in Alaska now, Alva. Land of the lawless."

DC turned and looked unsteadily at the woman. She caught his gaze and smiled back. Through his rum goggles, the gal didn't look too many years older than him. He thought of Tom Zion and the girl he'd picked up that night. He couldn't let the little fuck beat him out again, could he? But then Tonya's alluring smile forced its way into his mind. If he was going to play with matches, might as well try for a forest fire. He turned back.

"Nah, one-a you guysh can—"

Ralph slapped a bill on the table and said, "Ten bucks says you can't get her to kiss you within five minutes." Two more tens followed from Jake and Allen.

DC eyed the money. Maybe a little flirting wouldn't hurt. Smiling broadly, he gulped the last of his drink and slammed the empty glass on the table. "Eashiesht money I'll ever make," he slurred.

He could work his way up to Tonya.

"That's the old Sun Devil spirit!" Allen cried.

Ralph held up his battered Micky Mouse wrist watch. He raised a finger. "Ready, set . . . *GO!*"

Grabbing a chair for support, DC stood. After steadying himself, he stumbled through the crowd toward the target. Halfway he hesitated, but with a magnetic smile the woman pulled him in.

"Hey, watch it, asshole," a female voice shouted as he trampled some toes. He paid no mind. All concentration was centered on shooting this approach, and with five minutes of fuel in the tanks, he had but one shot before crash and burn.

How to do it? he thought. The well-lubricated gears churned in his head as he approached. Finally, he stood close enough to smell her expensive perfume. Closer up, she looked older. Still pretty, but her overdone makeup and jewels made for way too much icing on the cake.

She stared back in silence, expression welcoming, yet waiting for his move.

Looking her square in the eye, he said, "Jake will shleep with you tonight if you kiss me."

She tilted her head back and laughed. Slinking a hand around his neck, she drew him close and whispered in his ear, "Well now, Honey, what makes you think I don't want you instead?"

Amidst a chorus of catcalls, she swooped the young buck over her lap and planted a deep, long, wet kiss on his lips.

That was the last thing DC remembered.

CHAPTER 7: Checkride-itis

Out of the mist, an eagle swooped in, snatching the salmon from the stream. The raptor flew away, talons shredding its prey into bloody strips. Before the bird could gain altitude, a grizzly swatted the fish away. Squawking, the two predators fought over the prize. Searing pain ripped through the victim as the foes tore it apart.

Something slapped his face. A staccato beep echoed in his head, in competition with the ringing in his ears.

"DC! Get the fuck up, man. And turn off your alarm."

DC groaned. His head pounded. His eyelids felt cemented shut. With great effort, he sat up and rubbed his eyes.

Standing over him, Allen said, "I was just on my way out. Turned off the radio and heard your alarm. Don't know how long it's been on."

"Sorry." DC fumbled with the electronic travel clock. Spotting his clothing scattered in clumps around the room, he recalled the night before, and the blonde.

He stammered, "Did I, uh . . ."

"Nope. Crash did."

"Oh. Good. I guess."

Allen walked out. "He was just playing with you," he called back. "But you impressed the hell out of 'em all. Set a record with that kiss. What did you say to her, anyway?"

His chuckle gave way to a dry cough. "Trade secret," he managed to say between chokes. Finally he cleared enough cobwebs from his head to read the clock: 6:30.

"*Shit!*" DC cried, jumping up. "That thing's been ringing for half an hour!"

"Well, while you're in the shower, guess I'll play mom again and fix you some breakfast," Allen said from the kitchen.

"No time," DC said, stumbling into his jeans. "My checkride's at seven." He made a beeline for the bathroom, nearly bowling over Allen in the hallway.

"Whoa, slow down, Ace," Allen said. "This is what I meant."

He handed DC a glass of orange juice and two aspirin.

"Hmph. Breakfast of champions."

"Our standard college fare."

"Thanks." DC popped the pills and threw down the juice. Between gulps he said, "I'm gonna kill that Ralph. He got me drunk for my ride."

Allen chuckled. "No one forced anything down your throat. Consider it your initiation."

"What ever happened to the FAA rule about 'Eight hours between the bottle and the throttle'?"

"Up here it's eight feet."

"Ya, right," DC replied. After a thirty-second wash-down over the bathroom sink, he threw the rest of his clothes on. Grabbing his jacket, he raced out the door.

"Good luck," Allen called after him. "Or maybe I should say, break a strut."

DC ran through the drizzle.

"Gonna have to get a damn bike," he mumbled, zipping up his jacket. Suddenly he slowed, realizing that he could not even see through the fog to the airport. When he looked back over his shoulders to the north, the clouds masking Thunder Mountain pressed lower than ever. Maybe, he thought with a tinge of hope, they would have to reschedule the checkride. But then he heard the buzz of a propeller plane taking off. Shaking his head in disbelief, he returned to his run.

He made it to the airport with minutes to spare, and used the time to freshen up in the restroom. Splashing some water on his face, he looked in the mirror. Bloodshot eyes, with dark grey bags sagging beneath the lids, looked back. He hoped his pale looks would go unnoticed in this land of untanned skin.

His mouth was parched, but whether from hangover or anxiety, he didn't know. Slurping some water from the bathroom faucet and running his wet fingers through his hair, he straightened and took one last look. He felt naked without a tie, always standard attire for FAA checkrides. But Allen had assured him that such formalities wouldn't be necessary here.

DC stepped into the SEAS' headquarters.

"Ms. Innes's office?" he asked a secretary. She pointed to a corner room. DC walked over, wondering what she might look like.

He envisioned an enormous, scowling German barmaid. The thought almost made him laugh, and he relaxed slightly.

He knocked on the half open door.

"Enter," a female voice called.

He poked his head in. "Ms. Innes?"

"Hello, DC, nice to meet you," she said in a neutral voice.

DC tried to conceal his surprise. She was much younger than he'd expected, somewhere in the early thirties. Thin, petite, but bearing an aura of authority that defied her slight frame. Her brunette hair was pulled back tight on her scalp and tied in a bun. Intense blue eyes hid behind serious glasses.

The term *librarian* came to his mind.

Standing, she extended a small hand over her desk. They shook hands and sat.

"Are you a runner?" DC asked, both out of curiosity and to start the conversation right. "I mean, you look so thin."

The compliment fell flat. Her lips tightened. "No time. It's easy to get your exercise around here, though, loading your own plane and running from one flight to the next." She eyed him closely, blue irises drilling into him. He swallowed self-consciously. "Are you fit to fly?" she asked him. "You look a little peaked."

He cleared his throat and straightened. "Oh, well, yeah." He tugged unconsciously at his neckline, at a tie that wasn't there. "I guess I'm a bit worn out from the big move," he answered lamely.

After a long pause in which he felt she was reading his mind, she said, "Let's reschedule this thing for another day."

He was tempted, but finally held up a hand. "No, I'm okay." Always best to get the torture over with.

"Well, let's get started then. I've got a busy schedule." From a drawer, she produced the FAR/AIM manual, the pilot's "bible." Out from another drawer came a Cessna 207 operator's manual. She slapped the books down and turned to the first page. "Let's start with limitations."

DC slumped. Everyone else in Alaska seemed to fly by the seat of their pants. Even on his warm-up ride the day before, Chief Pilot Dusty hadn't bothered to crack one manual. He realized, too late, that this check airman flew solely by the book.

"What's the gross weight of the Cessna 207?" she asked.

He struggled to recall the numbers, glanced at two nights before and in a fog of jet lag. He bit his lip. "Um, 3,600 pounds?"

Her brows lifted. She peered at him from above her reading glasses. "You sure?"

"Um."

"Correct. Show some confidence in your answers. What's '*Vee-ess-oh*'?"

He strained to recall *Vso*, the flaps down stall speed. From daily use, he'd known the numbers of his old Cessna 210 cold. But as similar as it was to the 207, no two airplane systems, procedures or numbers were ever the same. And now the old numbers jumbled with the new ones in his head.

A bead of sweat tickled its torturous way down his side. "Fifty-two knots. Or so." He held up a hand. "I'm sorry, I just haven't had much time to study. I only got here two nights ago."

Her lips twitched sideways in dismay. "Irrelevant. You've got to know it."

"Look, why memorize a number you can read right off the color-coded airspeed indicator, right?" He immediately regretted the comment.

She swept a hand over the book. "This is basic stuff, DC. As a Check Airman designated by the FAA, I have to use these numbers to see how familiar you are with your airplane. I've nothing else to go on." She sighed. "What did you do all day yesterday, anyway?" He started to answer, but she cut him off. "Well, let's see what you do know and go from there."

About the only thing he seemed capable of doing without a glitch was the weight and balance problem. DC quickly added her imaginary payload of passengers and freight and calculated the aircraft center of gravity. He sat back, smiling smugly.

She glanced at the worksheet, nodded without comment, then tossed it aside and grilled him on Federal Aviation Regulations. After an agonizing half hour, she slammed the rule book shut. Sitting back, she looked at him like a judge about to pass sentence. He stared at her in anticipation.

"Go preflight," she said finally.

Once outside, DC let out a sigh of relief. Phase One complete. But he knew the hardest part was yet to come.

Rain began to fall as he inspected his plane. As he stood on the wing strut and popped off the gas cap to check the fuel level, he eyed the clouds. Five hundred foot bases at best. Still too low. He gauged the visibility by looking across the channel. Two miles, at a guess.

A wave of claustrophobia swept over him. Worse weather than he'd ever experienced from the air. And these guys flew in it without blinking. Then again, he reminded himself, his estimate could be way off. The thought gave him little relief.

From the sump drain, he poured a cup of gas and held the sample at eye level. The fuel was fine, but his hand was not; it shook. The gas sloshed out over his fingers. He cursed, and slung the rest of the gas across the tarmac.

"Anything wrong?" Ms. Innes called from behind.

He closed his eyes, breathed deeply, then turned to face her. "No ma'am. Plane's fine."

"Good. Hop in."

He hesitated. "Um, this weather. You think it's good enough? I mean, for a checkride?"

She swept her gaze across the skies, then trained her eyes back on him. "Well, what do you think? Should we go?"

He remembered the Canyon trip that turned into disaster. His boss at that time had asked him that same question, his tone demanding a "Yes."

His fist tightened involuntarily around the gas cup.

"I . . . I'm not comfortable with it."

She looked past him, across the Gastineau Channel at Douglas Island. "Hmm. 'Bout an eleven hundred foot base, a good five-plus miles visibility."

He had to consciously keep his jaw from dropping. He'd been so far off from his guess about the weather, he might as well have been blind.

As she looked back at him, she smiled for the first time.

"Tanning weather around here." The smile quickly disappeared. "I can understand your apprehension, Daniel, coming from your background. Above all else, you must trust your own judgement. But if you can't fly in weather this good, then I'm afraid we can't use you."

Weather this good! he thought. Five miles of rain took a mere hundred seconds for his bird to punch through. This was a whole new perspective on flying. He forced a casual smile.

"All right, let's go," he said. They climbed aboard.

Strapping into the seat beside him, Innes said, "Treat me like I'm a passenger. Brief me."

Back home he could do it with his mind on autopilot. But his brain suddenly went on vacation. He coughed. "Well, um, here's the fire extinguisher, uh, fasten your seat belts for takeoff and landing. Oh, yeah, please read the emergency briefing cards in the seat pocket there." He stumbled through the rest.

He knew that, as a check airman on a formal commercial checkride, Ms. Innes could only tell him what maneuvers to perform, and was forbidden to help, hint or comment on anything. But her expression spoke volumes.

He sighed. "Sorry. I usually do better. I'm just nervous, okay?"

She turned to stare straight ahead. "Let's go."

Snapping on the battery master switch, he tuned the radio to the *ATIS*, the Automated Terminal Information Service.

The weatherman's recorded voice said, ". . . sky conditions twelve hundred overcast, visibility six miles."

Brow raised, he threw an appreciative glance at her. This Amelia Earhart of his had just nailed the weather by eyeballing it.

He fired up. They taxied out. DC ran up the engine, diligently reading aloud each item on the Pre-takeoff Checklist, then taxied up to the hold short line.

"Short field takeoff," she announced.

DC looked at her in surprise. Most examiners allowed a normal takeoff and landing or two for the examinee to settle in before moving on to the trickier stuff. "Short field?" he repeated.

She turned slowly to him, her neutral gaze saying it all.

Finally she said, "Most every operation around here is out of short strips with mountains on each end, so you might as well get used to it. I do them all the time myself, regardless. Just to keep sharp."

He pursed his lips and nodded. "Good point. Okay, short field it is." He keyed the mike. "Juneau Tower, SEAS Trainer One ready for takeoff. Request Special VFR, westbound for . . . ," he turned to her and whispered, "what was the place?"

"Chichagof."

"Chichagof Island practice area."

"SEAS Trainer One, Special VFR approved, maintain one mile visibility and clear of clouds at all times. Wind two six zero at six, cleared for takeoff."

DC contemplated his first-ever "Special VFR" clearance to flirt with *cumulogranite*, in unfamiliar territory, in a strange plane on a high performance takeoff, all while a check airman breathed down his neck. *Not the easiest career I've picked*, he thought with dismay.

Taking a deep breath, he lined up, pressed down on the toe brakes and pushed the power to max. He released the brakes. The plane lurched forward. As they accelerated, he jiggled the rudders with his feet to keep straight. Not quite used to the new feel of the Cessna 207, he overcorrected slightly, and the plane slalomed down the runway. By the time he dampened the oscillations, he'd blown past liftoff speed. "Shit," he muttered, yanking the plane into the air. He struggled to find the exact nose pitch for the best angle of climb speed, but could only get the craft within a mediocre five knots. By the time they passed the end of the two mile long runway, his altimeter read a paltry 400 feet.

"Level off at one thousand," Innes said.

The cloud base rapidly approached. DC nosed over early to avoid shooting into the clouds. His premature move caused him to level one hundred feet too low. "Dammit!" he exclaimed, and eased the plane up to 1,000.

They cruised southwest over Lynn Canal, then crossed Admiralty Island through Funter Pass. Once out over a wide ocean channel, Ms. Innes told him to make a steep turn.

All around them, fog closed in. He lost sight of land ahead, then to the sides. As he rolled into the turn, he realized the fog hid the way back as well. With no solid reference point, he lost all depth perception. He felt like a ship adrift, hundreds of miles from shore. In a heartbeat, he mused, another airplane could come streaking through that fog, and seconds later they would all be laying on the frozen ocean floor in a heap of twisted metal, never to be found. His heart beat faster; he panted.

"*I said roll out!*" Innes exclaimed.

DC obeyed. He realized then that he'd drifted into a tight spiral and dropped over one hundred feet. He once again pulled back to altitude.

Innes stared at him, arms crossed. "Is there any reason we should continue?" she asked.

DC slowed his breathing and forced himself to relax. "Ma'am, this is all just so new to me. Just give me another chance. I won't let you down."

After a long moment she said, "Second time: steep turn, to the left, 720."

In college, DC had excelled at instrument flying. Relying on his training, he forced himself to ignore the disaster outside and concentrate on scanning the altimeter, attitude and airspeed indicators. This time he pulled off the maneuver, keeping the altitude within a stellar 20 feet. Check Airman Innes seemed unimpressed.

Once they found a patch of better weather, she put him through ninety minutes of stalls, emergencies, engine failures and, back at Juneau Airport, touch and goes.

When he finally touched down on his last landing, a two-bouncer, he felt like he'd sweated off two pounds.

DC taxied in, shut down, peeled from his seat and meekly followed her into the terminal.

Once in her office, Innes dropped her glasses to the desk and sat. She rubbed her eyes as if weary.

DC slumped in a chair. *Sunk for sure*, he thought.

"Well, DC," she began, "I'll cut you a little slack for being new to the plane, but that's no excuse. Let's just hope you get a better feel before your line check. And watch that speed on final. You keep getting slow like that, a *Taku* wind is gonna raise up and swat you out of the sky."

"Yes, ma'am." He felt like a schoolboy being scolded by a marm.

"And memorize that owner's manual. Tonight."

"Definitely."

Holly allowed a thin smile. "Just relax. You'll come around. I know the weather here's a bit different than in Phoenix. It takes some getting used to."

DC looked up. She seemed to have read his mind.

"Just know your limits and don't ever, ever push them. Think of an 'air turn back' due to weather as an honor, not a black mark. As you gain experience, your abilities will increase. And remember the rules: always stay at least 500 feet above the ground, and keep two miles minimum visibility. Don't let these fools around here talk you into anything less. Because people die when they push it."

She didn't need to lecture him about that. The day's flight had seen six miles visibility; he couldn't fathom flying in anything less. DC recited to her the pilots' mantra.

"There are old pilots and bold pilots, but no old, bold pilots."

With a thin smile of acknowledgement, she said, "Words to live by."

She stood. DC quickly stood with her, knowing the torture session was finally over.

She walked him to her door. "We'll see you tomorrow for some route familiarization."

"Yes, Ms. Innes. Thank you."

She opened the door and shook his hand. "Welcome aboard."

DC rushed out.

Jake, Ralph and a few other pilots stood at the far end of the room, grinning as DC emerged from the office. In no mood to socialize, DC made straight for the door.

"Mr. Whitakker," Innes barked.

"Yes, Holly?" Whitakker replied.

"It's, 'Ms. Innes', please. You and Mr. Olafsen in my office. Now." Without waiting for his reaction, she walked into her room.

"Yez, Mizz Innes," Ralph mock-groveled, shuffling over like a subservient plantation slave. The others snickered.

"Let me know if she gets out the whips," a pilot called after them.

Over his shoulder, Ralph said, "Her cat o' nine tails are exquisitely arousing."

Bristling, Holly ignored all the snide remarks.

The two entered and shut the door. Ralph plopped in a seat. Jake stood, hands in pockets.

Holly stood behind her desk. Hands propped on the table, she faced them.

"What the hell do you two think you're doing?"

"Why, whatever do you mean, Mizz Innes?" Ralph asked, eyes wide in false innocence. She opened her mouth to speak, then stopped.

Spying the pilots outside moving discretely toward her office window, she reached up, yanked the drapes down over the glass and turned back.

"Would you please call me by my—"

"Oh, cut the formal crap, lady," Ralph said.

"The door's closed, Holly," Jake added, "you're not fooling anyone here."

"Okay, *Crash*, if you prefer that childish nickname. What I want to know is why? Why do you so blatantly flaunt the rules? That boy had enough on his mind without violating Federal Aviation Regulations regarding alcohol and flying. If Inspector Bruner had caught him busting the F.A.R.'s, he could have suspended our whole operation. Hell, as a designated Check Airman, *I'm* supposed to turn him in."

"Did you smell alcohol on his breath?" Jake asked.

Holly sat and closed her eyes. "No," she answered softly.

"Did he slur his speech or stagger?"

"No," she answered, louder.

"Did you see him consume alcohol within eight hours of flying?"

"Mercifully, I did not attend your drunkfest last night. No."

"Then you had no'Probable Cause'."

Innes's jaw dropped. "*Probable Cause*? That kid had a hangover the size of Denali."

'That's no 'kid,' Holly. He's only a few years younger than you."

"DC's got to learn to perform under duress," Ralph added. "A pilot's never one hundred percent every minute he flies."

"Of course not, but he should always *strive* to be his best. And you two are teaching him to screw the rules. That could lead to an accident."

"Rules are made for idiots," Ralph said.

"Holly, you can't legislate common sense," Jake added. "The only things that lead to accidents are stupidity and bad luck."

"Hmph, that coming from a veteran of how many accidents?" she countered. "And you think flying half drunk isn't stupid?"

Jake said, “You said yourself he wasn’t drunk, just hung over. We complied with the *spirit* of the law. Legally, you were the ’Pilot in Command’.”

“Gentlemen, regardless of who’s P.I.C., it narrows the margin of safety. And as a designated Check Airman, I must inform you—”

Ralph threw his hands in the air. “Oh, for chrissake. The only reason you’re behind that desk and we’re in front of it is because we want to push throttles, not papers. You’ve got five years of bush flying. Between Crash and me, we got decades. So if you want to play control freak, go ahead. But not on my ship.”

Shaking her head, she said, “Just stop it, okay? Stop the nonsense. Before things get out of hand and I’m forced to get . . . formal.”

Ralph stood and screwed his cap on his head. “Lady, you need to get laid. I’d oblige, but I don’t think Misty would be too keen on it. You think, Crash?” Without waiting for dismissal, Ralph spun and left.

Holly looked at Jake with incredulous eyes. “And you wonder why I don’t join you for happy hours. Your sense of humor is straight out of high school locker rooms.”

“I apologize for my friend,” Jake said in a conciliatory tone. “He’s a master of the parting shot. And a little rough around the edges.”

“Ha! Ya *think*?”

“Hey, what do you expect from a hillbilly Army grunt?”

Holly sat. “I expect a professional, that’s what.”

Jake leaned over her desk. “Look, in Alaska, the only law that matters is the law of the land. You learn what works and what doesn’t. Rules are just . . . *guidelines*.”

She stared at him evenly, his words bouncing off her skin. “I think we’re done here,” she said coolly.

Jake looked at her a moment, shrugged, and turned to go. At the door he hesitated, and turned back. “You ever heard of Joe Crosson’s Blue Sky Outfit?” he asked.

Holly creased her brows. “No,” she said guardedly.

“Crosson was one of the pioneer aviators in Alaska. He helped Pan Am establish the first scheduled Alaska air service, right here in Juneau. But his business was ruled by federal bureaucrats three thousand miles away. Arbitrary rules kept his Electras and Lodestars grounded in all but perfect weather, while the local bush operators flew circles around him. Needless to say, his venture failed.” After a moment’s pause, he added, “If you go around loading your plane down with regulations, Holly, pretty soon you're too heavy to get off the ground."

Holly looked away, contemplating his words.

Before leaving, Jake said, "You know, you're pretty cute when you're angry."

"*Out!*" she exclaimed. He scooted.

She blew a lock of dark hair from her eyes; her lower lip stretched tight in frustration. Her battle with the male ego seemed futile. And Alaskan bush pilot egos were the worst.

But once the door was closed, she couldn't help but chuckle at his compliment.

CHAPTER 8: Veronica Onassis Redding

The day her husband backhanded her into the china cabinet was not the day she left him. Nor was it the time he bragged to her of the many waitresses on his truck route impatiently awaiting his services. Nor the day he forced her to bare her breasts in front of his buddies to show off his prized property. Not even the time he threw his plate of roast turkey back at her for being too cold, sending her to the emergency room for eight stitches to the forehead. Afterward, she apologized to him for being so clumsy and inattentive to his needs, and he forgave her by mounting her briefly until getting off.

For Veronica Redding to leave her loving husband, it nearly took suicide.

Ever since she was a kid, Veronica dreamed of flying. She would sit on her father's shoulders and stick her arms out to each side, blonde locks flying and lips *Brrr*-ing as he trotted through the park. When she was five, he took her on a small plane tour over their home town of Los Angeles.

Veronica was awestruck. All those cars below looked like toy matchboxes, the people like ants. The thrill of accelerating and pulling away from the earth's gravity, like an angel flying to heaven. And, perhaps most thrilling of all, the powerful aircraft responded so obediently to the pilot's commands. It was nothing short of magic. She trembled with delight when, after the flight, the grey-haired pilot pinned a pair of plastic wings to her blouse.

Little did Daddy know, from that day on the hook was set. Veronica was determined to become a pilot.

Later, Sergeant Robert Redding, U.S. Army, realized how serious his daughter was of the fool notion. He sat her down on his knee and explained.

He said, "Honey, girls don't become pilots. All pilots come from the Air Force or the Army or Navy. There is no such thing as an airline *aviatrix*."

"But what about Amelia Earhart, Daddy? She did it," she said.

He laughed. "Sure, and look what happened. Her dingy, female sense of direction got herself lost at sea."

At high school, guidance counselors, male and female alike, also urged her to reconsider her crazy dream and instead become something more palatable with society. Say, a homemaker or a nurse.

But their "sage advice" clashed head-on with her dream, and she would have nothing of it.

One night at the dinner table, the Sergeant learned of the counsellors' talk and his daughter's disappointment. He said, "Look, if you really want to fly, why not become a stewardess?"

Mother lay a hand on hers. "Your father's right, dear. Who knows? Maybe you could find a rich husband that way, maybe even a real pilot."

Shaking her head, she said, "I don't wanna marry a pilot. I want to *be* a pilot."

He slammed his fork down. "Enough of this nonsense," her father snapped.

"Now, Sam," her mother interjected. "Let's not—"

"She'll do what I tell her to do," he said.

"Yes, sir," Mother said meekly.

Veronica threw her fork down. "I'll do what I want, goddamnit!" She bit her lip, too late to catch the slip.

Crimson-faced, the Sergeant raised up, his shadow eclipsing her small frame. He slapped her so hard she fell to the floor.

"Go to your room," he boomed, "and don't come out till you stop talking your idiotic little girl nonsense."

Veronica sat at her vanity mirror, eyeing the welt as it grew and colored on the side of her face. Out of the corner of her eye, she spotted the plastic wings pinned to the wooden frame.

Perhaps Daddy was right, she thought. Girls, especially stupid ones like little Veronica Redding, didn't have the capacity to become pilots. She blushed in shame. She yanked the wings off, tossed them in the bottom drawer and mumbled, "Might as well try to be an astronaut."

She became despondent, lost, a plane without a rudder. Her grades dropped. Each night she came home late, in deliberate defiance of her father's authority. He spanked her, whipped her, grounded her; she would sneak out again. Each confrontation drove the wedge further between the two. After her high school graduation party, she didn't come home until late the next day, still drunk.

"You're impossible, young lady," her father screamed between belt straps. "What you need is boot camp. First thing Monday morning, we're taking you to the recruiters and you're joining the Army. Teach you some discipline. Hah! Try telling *them* you want to be a pilot."

That Monday, Veronica snuck out early, withdrew her life savings from the bank, and left. Plastic wings pinned to her backpack, she stuck a thumb out on the interstate.

She was seventeen, but a very naive and sheltered seventeen. She was heartbroken, scared, lonely. And strangely relieved.

Liberated, somehow. She could go anywhere, do anything, be anyone. Her destiny lay in the power of her own tiny hands. Remembering her silly old dream, she chuckled. "Hell, I could even become an *aviatrix*," she mumbled with a roll of the eyes. But she knew she was too poor and too stupid. Daddy had made sure she knew that.

In a truck stop between Tulsa and Oklahoma City, her plans—and her life—derailed.

His name was John Bolt, and like his namesake, he struck her like lightning. He was tall, handsome, suave and worldly. He had traveled all over the States in his rig, and he made it sound as exciting as a flying circus.

Spellbound, she lost herself in his endless, dark brown eyes. From beneath a crop of slick black hair, they blazed at her with enthusiasm.

With one comment, he hooked her. He said, "Drivin' a big rig's like bein' captain of an airplane."

Bolt bought the starving, wide-eyed girl a slice of lemon meringue pie and reeled her in. He said, "You're your own boss. You take orders from nobody. And you can go damn well wherever you please." He sat back and crossed his arms. "Hell, it ain't no big thing. Why a cute little missy like you could do it."

Drive an eighteen-wheeler! So maybe it wasn't an airplane, she thought, but it seemed the closest she'd ever get. That night she left with him.

In the same night, she learned to drive a big rig and please a man.

The next two months were pure bliss. Everything seemed so *right*. In Reno, days after her eighteenth birthday, Miss Veronica Redding became Mrs. John Bolt. His next road trip became their honeymoon, after which he moved her into his small Ulysses, Kansas trailer.

She called her parents to tell them the good news. Against her mother's pleas, the Sergeant hung up on her. Abandoned, all she had left was her new husband.

But Mr. Bolt soon tired of the new Mrs. Bolt. He began leaving her at home on trips. And when he returned, his home never seemed to be in the order he liked. She could do nothing right by him. The young bride's cooking was atrocious, he told her, and any decision on her part turned into disaster. He made sure she knew, both physically and mentally, that he had married a worthless mess.

For six years she endured his abuse. She couldn't remember a world without John Bolt. Each time he left on a trip, she dreaded his return yet longed for it, never knowing whether he would walk through the door bearing flowers or fists. She filled the void of his absence with cigarettes and alcohol and food. Over the years, she loaded her thin frame down with pounds of physical and emotional baggage.

His trips became longer. Days went by without a phone call. Finally, after two weeks away without a word, he called to tell her he'd picked up yet another run.

"When will you come home?" she asked him, her voice pleading, her words slurred by vodka.

"Come home to what?" he snapped. "A fat, drunken pig in a stye? I'll be back sometime next week, if I feel like it. Hell, I may never feel like it." He hung up.

She flew into a blind rage. Minutes later, she sat crumpled on the floor in a pile of shattered dishes, broken ceramic statuettes and smashed bottles of booze. Through the alcoholic fog and the raining tears, she realized that, upon seeing the mess, he would kill her. Or worse, leave her for good.

Might as well spare him the pain, she thought.

She crawled through the rubble to John's gun cabinet. With trembling fist, she pounded the glass until it shattered. She did not feel her sliced palm. When she retracted her hand, it held an ancient Colt .45 handgun, loaded.

She put it to her head.

Everything went dark.

She was an angel now, her spirit flying away from her dead, battered human carcass, up through the roof and into the heavens. She looked down and saw John Bolt. He yelled at her to come back down, fists shaking above his head in rage. But from way up here, her husband's voice sounded comically high. His rig looked like a matchbox, and he like an ant.

She woke up laughing. She had no idea how long she had passed out. Veronica looked at her hand. The glass cuts, while deep, wouldn't be permanent. She stared at the pistol for one long minute. She again lifted it and aimed, this time at a photo hanging on the wall. A photo of John Bolt.

She pulled the trigger.

The rusty hammer jammed. She looked at the gun quizzically. Suddenly, the hammer dropped. A loud explosion ripped through her ears. The kick knocked the pistol from her hand. Once again everything went dark; the bullet had hit the table lamp.

Her mouth, open in astonishment, slowly changed to a faint smile, then a larger one, then a Cheshire grin. The grin turned to a chuckle, then a laugh. She guffawed hysterically, rolling on the floor, her hands wrapped about her stomach.

She picked herself off the floor, walked to the bathroom, and showered for the last time in John Bolt's home. She dressed the wounds on her hand, then dug through her junk drawer.

Finally she found it, buried in the back. Her most prized possession: her plastic wings. She pinned them to her chest.

She wrote him a 'Dear John' letter.

This note, however, read slightly different:

Dear Auntie Em,

Hate you. Hate Kansas. Left for Oz.

Dorothy

In three days she hocked his car, pawned his furniture, cleaned out his bank account and maxed every credit card with cash advance. That done, she took one final look around the wrecked and deserted home.

"*To hell with you*," she said, and left for the farthest place from Kansas she could think of: Alaska.

From Anchorage she called her mother. Her father grabbed the receiver and yelled, "It was unforgivable of you to marry that man without our consent. But even so, a wife should be loyal to her husband under any circumstances. And now you have the gall to call us and blame him for your failure."

This time it was she who hung up.

Divorce was foremost on her mind, but she feared the proceedings would flush her out. To her great relief, she found that her marriage had never existed; there had been a previous Mrs. John Bolt, and still was.

Nevertheless, she knew her life was still in danger. She cut and dyed her California locks and became just another Alaska brunette. But appearance alone was not enough to escape him.

By court order of the State of Alaska, Miss Veronica Onassis Redding became Miss Holly Shannon Innes.

At an abuse crisis center in Fairbanks, Holly Innes began intense therapy. But more than shrink sessions and weight loss regimens were needed to rebuild her.

Her counselor quickly found the key. At Fairbanks International Airport, he enrolled her in flight school.

The change was dramatic and immediate. Her first day of flying did more for her mental recovery than a year of therapy.

After her first solo flight, she wept tears of joy.

The booty snatched from John Bolt paid for lessons. How appropriate, she thought, to use a nightmare to bankroll a dream.

She enrolled in a community college as well. By night she waitressed, by day she took classes and flew.

Mother secretly sent her as much money as she could to help the dream, and in three years' time Holly graduated. Trading her waitress apron for a flight instructor's tie, she went to work at *Tanana* Air Adventures, the same outfit that taught her.

Three years later, she moved to Juneau and joined SEAS.

DC trudged home. The low clouds pressed down on him. Thunder Mountain lay more obscured than ever, the mist hiding all but the first few hundred feet.

Allen was home for lunch. DC walked in and plopped down on their second-hand couch.

Allen stood across from him in the kitchen, spooning Spaghetti-Os from a can and into his mouth. Between scoops, he said, "How'd it go?"

"Don't ask."

"That bad, huh?"

DC nodded. "Barely passed. She's a goddamn perfectionist. With the charm of a python."

"Heh, heh. That's her."

A long hot shower and hot plate of mac and cheese made him feel slightly better. From the small dining table he looked up at Allen, who now lounged on the couch, reading the day's edition of the *Juneau Empire*.

"How 'bout a hike?" DC asked.

"Nah, got another flight in an hour." He stood up and stretched. "I really should be back already in case a charter comes up. That's how you make extra points around here. And, more importantly, extra bucks and flight time."

DC nodded. "I plan on bagging shotgun seat in every float trip they got. You know, learn the routes 'n ropes."

"That's my *cheechacko*!"

DC gazed out the window. "But for today, I thought about looking for that eagle's nest."

Allen laughed. "You set your sights high, don't you? Well, there's a few nice hikes up by Mendenhall Glacier. Just head 'out the road,' as we say around here. You'll find 'em."

"Okay."

"And, DC."

DC looked back. "Yeah?"

"Check out the granite."

A faint smile appeared on his weary face. "Really? I will."

DC threw on a windbreaker and stepped out. He walked north 'out the road', and found the glacier.

The road ended and a muddy trail began, winding up into the forest. He roamed up the meandering path, for how long he didn't know. The harsh city sounds gave way to the quiet crunch of wet pebbles beneath his boots, and the endless hiss of wind through the pines. Sitka spruce, which always looked so small beneath his plane, now towered hundreds of feet above him.

He marveled at how close his new home was to such natural wonders, eons old. Here, man and nature crashed head on. But the result appeared just the opposite. Civilization and wilderness, two entirely different songs, seemed orchestrated into one masterpiece, a symbiotic whole.

Gradually, what sounded at first like the hiss of wind grew louder in his ears. The air grew increasingly damp upon his cheeks. He turned a corner and sucked in his breath. Whitewater burst over a black granite cliff. Thousands of tiny droplets launched into the air, arcing gracefully, suspended for a brief instant before exploding onto the rocks below.

The trail ended at a pool before the falls. Beyond, a sheer granite wall rose vertically into the clouds.

He climbed up boulders and tree trunks, slick and green with moss and mist, to the base of the waterfall. Gingerly he stepped from stone to stone across the stream and reached the rock wall.

His eyes followed the granite face to the top, shrouded in cloud. Somewhere above the cloud layer soared his eagle, tracing a holding pattern above him.

DC tested the rock, searching for a route. His hand slid into a crack and with a grunt he stepped high. But his clumsy hiking boot slipped. DC toppled backward onto the soggy dirt.

He lay there for a moment, stunned. For one panicked instant, he thought himself injured, alone, and far from civilization. DC sat up. After brushing away the dirt, he rubbed his clammy hands together and blew into them. His blood pumped from the effort, but the damp air permeated his skin. A veil of drizzle began to fall. He looked up. The drops caressed his cheeks, tickled his nose and dripped playfully off the bill of his cap.

Fingers of cloud groped their way lower down the slopes. One by one the trees drowned in the mist. Talons of cloud swooped down and swallowed him whole.

"I'll reach you yet, dammit," he whispered to the sky.

* * *

"*Ah, mi amour.*"

"Your hair shines like a palomino's rump at full gallop."

"*Oui, oui, mon ami.*"

"Your perfume is the scent of cowhide as it sizzles from the brand."

"*Je vous aime.*"

"Your voice is the sound of a piglet squealin' for its momma's teat."

"*Je vous adore.*"

Dusty puckered. The sensuous French beauty placed a sensuous French kiss on his lips.

"Eluk, quit lickin' his face."

The words clanged like a cowbell in Dusty's ears. He jerked awake, spitting dog saliva from his lips.

Eluk trotted away, tail wagging.

Kneeling over him with a proffered coffee, Jake Whitakker said, "You know, Dusty, between snores I swear you speak French."

Propping himself on one elbow, he gulped the warm, welcome liquid. Wiping his mouth with the back of his hand, he said, "Funny, I never learned a lick of French. Sounds damned sexy when Suzette whispers it in my ears, though. For all I know she could be telling me I just stepped in cow shit."

From his sleeping bag, Dusty looked around their campsite on Pleasant Island. Through the tree line, he spotted a splash of yellow paint, right where he had landed his Super Cub on the tiny beach the night before. Jake's Beaver float plane sat high and dry on the beach, awaiting the next high tide to depart.

Laying back in his sleeping bag for a moment, he enjoyed the morning peace. The fog muffled the sounds of the forest. Over the soft rustle of boughs and crackling fire, Dusty heard the waves lapping against the shore. Low tide now, by the sound of it.

He inhaled deeply. His lungs filled with a crisp charge of early morning air mixed with the scent of pine, ocean, campfire and coffee. His breath drifted away in a lazy puff of mist. The chill massaged his cheeks, damp with dew like the meadow around him.

Sitting up, he was immediately awarded with a throbbing pain that shot through his back muscles. He winced.

"You're getting soft, Dusty," Jake said, thrusting a steaming plate of Dinty Moore stew in his lap.

"Just morning stiffness," Dusty replied between gulps. "Afraid over the years I've developed quite an affinity for my wife and feather bed. But getting out like this reminds me of growing up. Out under the Texas stars, sleeping with the longhorns."

"Think I'd rather sleep with your wife."

"Careful, Jake, my rifle's loaded."

"Get up, old man, the brave beasts await."

Dusty polished off the stew, then unrolled his tattered leather jacket, his makeshift pillow for the night, and donned it. He rose from his sleeping bag and stretched, turned and urinated.

"Hope this ain't the ladies room," he quipped.

"That's what I like about this place, Dusty," Jake replied. "There ain't no ladies' room."

Dusty turned and eyed Jake, who sat cross-legged by the camp fire inspecting his rifle. Faint flickers of firelight burned through the morning twilight and danced on the younger pilot's cheeks. They set his eyes aglow with the thrill of the hunt.

"Well, what's the plan of attack?" Dusty asked, sighting his own gear and checking the aim.

Kneeling down, Jake took a stick and drew a crude map of Pleasant Island in the dirt. He finished by poking at their location.

"Okay, we're here on the western tip. The Knob's a couple miles southeast of here, tallest point on the island. Good visibility when the fog lifts. South of that's a pond where the Roosevelt herd goes for their morning coffee."

Dusty nodded. "Sounds perfect."

"I'll circle around the pond," Jake continued, "and flush 'em toward you from the east."

Dusty eyed the trees. "Easterly breeze this morning. Good."

Jake gazed into the fire a moment, then looked to his partner.

"Sun's already up. We'd better get humping."

Dusty glanced at his watch: 3:30 a.m. "We got about five hours before my first flight," he announced. "The *cheechako's* route check."

"That DC kid?" Jake asked. "How's he doing?"

"Well, despite your *initiation* the other night, for which I got a ration of cowpie from You-know-who, I think he's doing fine. He's a good stick. Green as hell, but he'll season. If he toughs it out, I'd like to groom him for floats."

Jake raised a brow. "Holly know about this?"

Dusty snorted. "Not a chance. But sneak him aboard your float trips when there's room. I'd like to get him up to speed."

"You got it, boss."

They quickly broke camp. After rinsing the plates in the surf, Jake threw the gear into the back of the Beaver.

The two turned and gazed out over the smooth waters of Icy Passage. Though the fog still hid the opposite shoreline, the glow of the Gustavus Airport beacon swept through the mist in alternating arcs of green and white. Their experienced eyes gauged the visibility.

While Jake seemed content to play guide for the day, both carried rifles just in case. The two experienced hunters moved, quick and silent, through the trees. Dusty strove to keep up with the younger man's breakneck pace. To Dusty's relief, however, Jake seemed to stop more frequently than necessary to check for elk sign.

At the top of the knoll, they split up.

"Let's meet back here oh-seven hundred," Dusty suggested.

Jake nodded. "And if you get a bear in your sights, make sure he's not wearing my florescent orange vest."

Dusty returned fire. "Jake, if I spot any kind of critter with your vest on, I'll know I had too much of your cheap whiskey last night."

For the next several hours, the pilots stalked their prey. While Jake circled the pond, Dusty scrambled up the Knob. He settled into a notch in the rocks that offered him a commanding view toward the east. He set up his gear and waited.

Fully engrossed in his second favorite hobby, Dusty could barely contain his excitement when Jake's movement drove several bulls his way.

Sighting through his scope, Dusty spotted a massive 6x6 elk moving through the trees toward him. Behind the bull grazed several cows. Perfect.

With the steadiest of hands, Dusty aimed and slowly squeezed the trigger.

Click.

Dusty smiled. "Gotcha," he whispered, and advanced the film. He proceeded to snap off a series of telephoto shots that would make Suzette, the girls and grandkids giggle with glee. Several minutes later, he ran out of film. Satisfied, Dusty broke down his gear and sat on the highest rock for a snack.

Jake joined him at the appointed time. "Get any?" he asked.

Dusty nodded with enthusiasm. "Great shots."

"I spotted a few buck myself," Jake said. "Can't wait for fall opening."

Thirty minutes later, the two arrived back at base camp. Dusty helped Jake untie the floating Beaver from the tree branches and spin it around to face out from shore.

Jake glanced at his watch. "Just enough time do a little wiring in the cabin."

"Ain't you finished yet?" Dusty asked.

"Well, it's livable," Jake allowed. "Got four walls and a roof, anyway." He walked up the port float, hopped in and slammed his door shut. Opening the window, he stuck his elbow on the sill. The current slowly started drifting his plane downstream. He called back, "Imagine I hafta get some furniture in before any ladies show up though."

Dusty laughed. He yelled, "Crash, I 'spect the moment you get your damn front door installed, the ladies will be beating it down!"

Jake waved and fired up.

Watching as he lined up and launched, Dusty sauntered back to his Super Cub. He began to roll away the boulders anchoring the Super Cub's balloon tires, then paused. He glanced at his watch.

"Why not?" he asked himself aloud. Grabbing his rod and reel from the back of the Super Cub, he began to partake of his favorite hobby.

Just enough time, he figured, for a few casts.

CHAPTER 9: New Horizons

It was his first true commercial flight for SEAS, an hour-long trip to the Tlingit Village of Kake, and DC could hardly contain his excitement.

Behind his seat, the plane was stuffed like Santa's sleigh full of boxes. Riding shotgun was his lone passenger: Dusty.

Though this was DC's final test flight, the "Line Check," he felt completely at ease with the old man. And anyone other than Ms. Innes in the right seat was fine by him.

The sun blazed from a pure blue sky and every spruce with waterfront property enjoyed a clear view across the Inside Passage. Even the wind had calmed. Tiny thermals nudged them from time to time as the air rose, yawning and stretching, in lazy response to the morning sun. It seemed to DC that the very presence of this great bush pilot sitting next to him had caused the clouds to lift and the turbulence to settle, like a feisty horse suddenly tamed when the wrangler replaces the dude.

After signing off with Juneau Tower, DC slipped off his bulky David Clark headset and hooked it over his neck. The whine of wind and engine blared in his ears. He shouted above the din, "I can't believe this. Yesterday you couldn't see the prop in front of your face."

Dusty laughed. “Well, we always say if you don’t like the weather, just wait a couple hours.”

Rounding Douglas Island, they launched out over the blue green waters of Stephen’s Passage. DC held the 207 steady at one thousand feet.

Dusty pointed across the ocean channel. “Aim for the nearest tip of land there. And you oughta climb a little bit, to keep within gliding distance of shore in case the engine decides to take a vacation.”

DC knew that, as his official check pilot, Dusty couldn’t fly the plane for him. But this was their last flight together, and he could tell the old man felt compelled to impart as much wisdom as possible before letting him out of the nest.

DC eased back on the wheel, the fingertips of his left hand sensing, searching, *learning* the exact pressures required to coax his new craft into a shallow climb. Upon reaching the shoreline, DC banked the plane left and flew south along the coast.

DC glanced down at his lap. In it lay a crisply folded Juneau Sectional, the local aeronautical chart. He scrutinized the colored contours of the map and compared it to the land before him. He pointed to a mountain pass.

“There. That’s the inlet,” he announced.

Dusty smiled. “Very good. Head through the saddle. And keep your eyes peeled. You always see a few black tail deer out here, maybe even a bear or two.”

DC raised a brow. “Grizzlies?”

“Alaskan browns. Technically grizzlies. But these suckers are even bigger, on account of their rich diet of salmon. And *cheechackos*.”

DC shot him a thin-smiled glance.

“Ease ‘er down to 500 feet,” Dusty coaxed. “You fly low enough, they raise up and try to swat you away. Quite a sight.”

“Unless they grab ya.”

Dusty laughed. “Son, if you’re that low, then you got more’n bears to worry about.”

DC dropped back down. The two hundred foot-tall evergreens looked only yards below his landing gear.

Over the pass, the trees gave way to a muskeg bog. From the carpet of sphagnum moss sprouted several dwarf birch, shrubs and a few gnarled, stunted mountain hemlock. They buzzed a U.S. Forest Service cabin on the southern shore and launched out over the canal formed by Admiralty Island and the Glass Peninsula.

Dusty said, "This is a nice shortcut southbound, but the weather can trap you right here. Then again," he added with a grin, "it's a great excuse to land on a sand bar till the weather clears." Dusty pantomimed casting a fishing rod.

Matching his boss's grin, DC peered at a fork in the canal ahead. Even without referring to his chart, he could tell the western route was best. The channel stretched for miles to the south, while the other inlet dead-ended into a mountain.

Dusty pointed to it. "That's called Fool's Inlet, for obvious reasons. You'll find box canyons like that all around Alaska, and more'n one has got a pilot splattered in the middle." He stuck out a downturned thumb. "Bring'er lower."

DC glanced questioningly at his boss. Dusty nodded. "But Ms. Innes said —"

Dusty held up a hand. "I know what she said, DC. '500 feet minimum.' And she's right. But up here in Alaska, Mother Nature's got her own set of rules. You've got to learn to fly—well, *creatively*. Think outside the box. Some day, it'll save you. The sky will fall and you'll be reading the altimeter in tens, not hundreds, of feet."

DC shuddered at the thought. Like most pilots, he loved to buzz the cornfields when no one was looking. But those were safely flat. He reluctantly edged lower. The pines, drifting so peacefully by a few moments ago, now seemed to race beneath him.

"Lower," Dusty urged. "Hug the shoreline. And slow up. If you're in the soup, the last thing you want to do is blast along at cruise speed."

DC recalled his disorientation in the fog on his check ride. Staring at the instrument panel, he concentrated on keeping the plane level.

Dusty tapped the windshield in front of them. "Outside, son. Your mind has to be out there, always watching for what's popping out of the fog next. It could be a canyon, a mountain, or another plane."

DC didn't like that thought at all. He said, "How can I look at the sectional to navigate that way? Do I just wander around lost?"

Dusty shook his head. "You'll get to know the land like the back of your hand. Every curve, island, glacier. It's amazing how fast you learn it all when your life depends on it."

With guts tightening, DC slowed and sank. He now looked *up* at the tops of the trees. He felt he could almost count the cones on each spruce.

Dusty watched the young pilot intensely. "Don't focus on any one object," he advised. "Just keep your eyes moving. Otherwise you'll get vertigo and spiral in."

His boss was doing little to ease his mind. DC forced himself to relax. He did, but wondered if he could when it really hit the fan.

Concentrating on the wild road ahead, DC barely had time to process the radical thoughts his boss was imparting. It seemed that, up here, everything he'd ever learned about flying had been turned on its head.

"Good enough," Dusty announced. "Clean up and climb. We'll take the direct route." DC shoved the throttle forward and flipped the flap switch up. Passing through five hundred feet, he relaxed. The low altitude, so strange to him only minutes ago, now felt remarkably high.

He climbed to 5,500'. The drab greens and tans of his sectional chart paled to the magnificent view out the window. Forest islands stretched for miles, isolated by equally massive motes of ocean. Ripples in the water sparkled so brightly it seemed a thousand footlights lit his winged ballet. In the hundreds of square miles before him, try as he might, DC couldn't see one plane, nor wake of a ship. Not a single sign of man.

Dusty smiled at him. "Best office view in the world."

Approaching Pybus Bay, DC started down. After crossing Frederick Sound, he tracked the coast of Kupreanof Island to the runway. A thick stand of pine lined the coast. But beyond, he saw, huge checkerboard swaths of Kupreanof's ancient forest had been mowed away, clear-cut for Japan's voracious lumber market. The barren land reminded him of a graveyard, each tree stump serving as its own gravestone. Even the great land of Alaska, DC realized with sadness, wasn't big enough to fend off man's inevitable onslaught.

DC lined up for landing on Runway Ten. "Should we buzz the strip for bears first?" he asked.

Dusty laughed. "I like to sneak up and take 'em by surprise." He peered ahead at the gravel runway. "Looks clear. They're probably having lunch at the garbage dump."

DC touched down softly, and the plane rumbled across the gravel. Pebbles ricocheted off the aluminum wings with a *tink! tink!* To keep the prop clear of the rough surface, he held the nose high. The action obscured his view ahead like a taildragger of old. Gazing out his side window to maintain direction, he caught a flash of movement through the trees. A black bear retreated to the woods, its snout curled in a silent squeal.

DC shook his head. "Wild," he muttered.

The sounds of civilization faded away, and all that remained to betray man's presence was the metallic *clink clink* of the aluminum carabiners suspended from their packs. As the ravens and Steller's jays serenaded them with song, so too their man-made trappings wooed adventure. The scent of pine flooded each inhale, the sap sticky on fingers from brush of bough.

DC yanked a stiff sprig from a spruce limb and chewed. The taste lingered bitter and fresh on his tongue. He had already shed his windbreaker and wrapped it about his waist. Sweat dampened the collar of his T-shirt.

Between breaths he said, "I think I'm already used to the cold."

Allen, shirtless, laughed. "Cold? DC, it's in the sixties."

As they hiked, DC looked up at the sky through the trees. Partly cloudy, but nothing grey or ominous. Yet.

He shook his head. "I don't know if I'd rather have the bad weather on my days off or when I'm working."

"Don't worry," Allen answered. "You'll get both."

DC swatted in vain at a swarm of tiny black gnats bent on exploring his eyes and mouth. "I thought the Alaska state bird was supposed to be the mosquito, but they're nothing compared to these damn things."

"Those're *no-see-ums*. Mosquitoes usually aren't too bad in the Southeast. And they're nice and big and slow. I must say, I do take great pleasure in squishing their pesky little bodies."

"You know, I read somewhere they got the largest penis-to-body ratio of any species."

"Hmph. All the more reason to kill 'em."

They rounded the corner and the waterfall thundered into view. The pair tiptoed across the slick rocks and dropped their packs at the base of the cliff.

Allen kneeled to open his pack. "I've wanted to do this since I moved here."

"What do you think it is?" DC asked.

Gazing skyward, Allen sized up the rock face. "Can't see past that overhang. But what I can see looks like a Five-Ten or so."

"That's what I figured. Too tough for me to lead."

Allen shook his head. "Self-fulfilled prophesy, DC. Say it's too hard and it is."

DC bowed. "Nevertheless, I believe I shall yield to your prowess, sir."

Without further word, the old weekend college ritual began. The two dug into their packs. Up from the ratty bags rose a cloud of climber's chalk mixed with the odor of shoe sweat. The musty smell made DC's heart pound with anticipation. While he uncoiled a purple nylon rope from his pack, Allen strapped to his shoulder a bandoleer of climbing gear: carabiners, cams, quick draws and stoppers. After donning their harnesses, the two replaced their bulky hiking boots with soft rubber climbing shoes. Dye-run and sweat-stained, the footwear looked like thrift store tennies.

As Allen tied into the rope, DC slipped part of the line through the clip on his harness.

"On belay?" Allen asked.

"Belay on," DC answered.

Allen nodded. "Climbing, Mr. Alva."

"Climb on, Mr. Foley."

* * *

Peering up the route, Allen stepped up to the wall. His fingers played across the rock, reading each subtle nuance in the texture as a blind man reads Braille. Finally, left index finger hooking a tiny pocket down low, Allen stepped waist high to an inch-wide ledge. Needles of pain shot through his toes and fingers as the granite dug in. His breath quickened. His nose filled with the familiar odor of dust and chalk.

Careful not to upset his tenuous balance, Allen wedged a cam in a crack, then clipped the piece to the rope. Slowly, methodically, he pressed on. Every few yards he placed a new piece of protection.

With each step, DC paid out more rope.

Up the rock face Allen glided, in a slow, graceful poetry of motion, a vertical ballet more skill than strength, like a cat stalking a bird.

Thirty feet up, Allen stopped and caught his breath. His feet rested on a centimeter-wide "ledge," the fingers of his left hand curled around a side-pull for balance. With the free hand he mopped his soggy brow.

"How's it look?" DC called from below.

Allen leaned out for a better view. "Ten feet to the overhang. It looks like an easy pull over the top if I can get to it. But it's damn thin in between."

"Protection?" DC asked.

Allen swallowed. "Really exposed here." His toes began to burn from the strain. With a forced smile, he glanced down at DC and said, "Go for the gusto or stay the fuck at home!"

Stepping off the sanctity of the ledge, he "smeared" the toe of his shoe directly onto the smooth rock face. The soft rubber stuck. Up came his other foot to a high nub. Stepping up, he searched above for the next move, but found nothing. He stopped.

Trapped in the tenuous position, his reserve strength quickly waned.

"Keep moving," DC yelled.

Allen glanced down. Six feet above his last anchor meant a twelve foot fall. *If* the piece held. The thought paralyzed him.

He panted. He banged the rock with his head in frustration.

"Hang in there," DC encouraged him. "You got this."

Allen's chest heaved, his breath coming in gales now. As the pain sapped the last of his strength away, his legs began to shake. The vibration edged his feet from their tenuous hold. His fingers slowly uncurled from their grip.

"*Falling!*" he shouted.

Allen pealed off the rock. DC clamped down on the rope. The line sprang taut. The impact slammed Allen into the rock and launched DC several feet into the air. The two hung a moment, suspended by the equilibrium of their weights.

Allen dangled from his harness, swaying before the rock. A profound sense of failure welled up within him. He stifled a curse. In its place, he let out a blood-curdling *Woo-hoo!*

"That's what it's about, baby," he cried.

"Hmph," DC said, "I thought it was about succeeding."

"That's your problem, DC," Allen said lightly, stepping back onto the rock. "You've got to *learn* to *fall.* If you don't, the fear alone will paralyze you."

"Learn to fall, hmm?" DC asked skeptically. "You want another try, maestro?"

Allen shook his head. "I'm spent. You're going to have to finish it."

DC slowly payed out the rope and lowered Allen to the ground.

The two switched positions.

* * *

"On belay?" DC asked.

"Belay on."

"Climbing."

"Climb on."

DC peered up the route. His heart beat faster. The memory of Allen's fall replayed in his mind.

A bird squawked high above. He looked up, expecting to see his eagle. But all that circled was a raven.

"Come on, stop daydreaming," Allen said.

As he climbed, DC strived to imitate Allen's moves. After several long minutes, he reached Allen's fall point. He paused, panting, searching for a way up. Adrenaline rushed through his veins so strongly it made his own legs shake.

The sky darkened, and his arch enemy came to his rescue; rain began to pour. Never before had he been so relieved to see it fall.

"Shit," Allen mumbled, lowering him down. "There goes the day."

"Bummer," DC said, his insincerity poorly concealed.

CHAPTER 10: Cheechacko

DC and several other airplane drivers sat chatting in the pilot "lounge," killing time between trips. His first day on line had been a slow one; several hours of waiting had produced nothing. The reason, as usual, was weather.

Just as with the rest of the country, the government designers of Juneau Airport had diligently studied reams of historical weather data in order to place the field in a prime location. But, as with nearly every other airport in the country, said designers managed to locate the runway in the exact worst spot. Furthermore, placed precisely at the atmospheric cauldron of ocean moisture, coastal mountain lifting action, glacial *Taku* winds and, worst of all, at the entrance to the wind tunnel called Gastineau Channel, Juneau Airport was a perfect, rain-soaked example of said government logic.

Today, however, was one of the rare days that proved the designers right. Weather was fair around Juneau Airport, but nasty up and down the Channel. Several flights were delayed, and two more had turned back enroute. As a result, Dusty was only sending the veterans out. The only *cheechacko* gone was Allen, on a short Hoonah round trip.

Between pilot banter, DC diligently memorized his passenger briefing announcement, scribbled on a note card in his palm.

"Trip up," Dusty called out to them. Dusty sauntered out to the pilots and handed DC a trip manifest. "Another Hoonah turn," he announced. "Weather should hold between here and there. Allen's inbound, and he says it's good. Take the *Soapy Smith*. Full plane out and two pax back." DC jumped up, tingling with anticipation, and dread, at his first trip alone in this strange new land.

"No problem," he answered with a forced air of casual confidence.

Dusty lingered. Within earshot of the others, he said, "By the way, you'll be bringing back a lovely young Tlingit couple, Mr. and Mrs. Horvath." The other pilots stirred.

"The Horvaths," DC repeated. "Sure thing." He turned to walk out to the plane.

"Oh, and DC," Dusty called to him. "Pick up a couple seat belt extenders from storage. Never know when you're gonna need 'em." Several pilots snickered.

"Hey, DC," Ralph added, "don't forget to check your weight and balance figures." The others chuckled, and one lost it.

"Uh yeah, will do, Ralph," DC replied, wondering if the misfit had ever bothered to crunch a W&B calc since his last checkride.

At the pilot's dispatch desk, DC ran a quick hand calculation of his six passengers and baggage and noted that the crosshairs of weight and balance fell squarely inside the envelope. He shrugged. *Whatever*, he said to himself.

A local rain cell had passed over the field, dropping the temperature a few degrees. DC zipped his virgin leather jacket to his neck and donned a SEAS' ball cap. As he wheeled the cartload of baggage out to his bird, he inhaled deeply the fresh Alaskan air. He eyed the slopes of Douglas Island to the southeast to gauge the cloud base, as Ms. Innes had. A soft layer of cotton cloud blanketed the mountain around midpoint giving him, he figured, a 1,500' base. Plenty, he knew, but still low enough to feel claustrophobic now that he was truly solo. Aside from the local shower, visibility seemed to be improving out west, he saw with relief.

Baggage loaded, he inhaled deeply, pumping up his chest with pure air and confidence, and marched inside for his passengers.

As the automatic glass doors of the terminal slid open, he spotted them, a mix of Tlingit locals and government workers, huddled near the window and looking at him with unsure eyes.

"Flight Twenty Three for Hoonah, ready for boarding," he announced.

"You're too young to fly!" a Tlingit lady blurted.

DC's chest deflated. Not even the veteran passengers of Alaska seemed to accept him. Slowly a broad grin grew across his face, replacing his deer-in-headlights stare. He replied, "Well, they say if I make it through this flight, they'll give me my license."

The passengers laughed, and their tension drained away along with his. As they followed him out, the biggest man said to the lady, "No need to worry, Wilma. These little things are far safer than a car."

"So I've heard, George."

As he led them out to the *Smith*, they chatted away in forced casualness about how safe air travel was, building up their own fragile confidence, as DC had often heard passengers do.

He loaded them, back seats to front, the smallest in the single rear seat, and progressively larger on forward. The largest male he intended to stick in the front seat beside him.

With each passenger, the plane's tail sank lower, the shiny metal shock absorber of the nose strut inching higher. The fifth passenger stepped aboard and into the final rear seat.

DC turned to his "copilot," the one named George. "Okay, you're last to—oh, *shit!*"

The entire plane rocked back on its main gear like a horse rearing on its hind legs. The tail hit the tarmac with a *clunk!*

One woman shrieked inside; two passengers laughed nervously. His copilot turned to him with a quizzical look.

DC ran to the back of the plane and met Dusty, running from the terminal. The two pilots gently lifted the tail. The plane, its center of gravity only fractions of an inch behind the main gear, lifted easily back and settled on its nose.

"Get aboard," Dusty called to the last passenger. After a moment's hesitation the man eased uneasily in. Dusty turned to DC. "Should be okay now."

"I did the weight and balance figures," DC said defensively. "We should be fine."

"Don't worry, you are."

DC jabbed a thumb at the packed cabin. "Was this what you guys were joking about?"

Dusty shook his head. "No. Just make sure you load a front seat passenger first from now on."

DC hopped in.

Dusty poked his head into the cabin. "No problem folks, the plane's fine. Just a little tricky to load at first, that's all."

A few replied with nervous nods. Dusty trotted off.

DC took a big breath. "Uh, okay, well, now that the exciting part's over, we're ready to go. My name's DC, and first we have to go over a few rules." With all the commotion, his well-rehearsed preflight briefing flew out the window. He stumbled through it, finally reading his briefing card verbatim.

"Young man, you *have* done this before, right?" the lady asked from behind.

George turned to her. "Now Wilma, don't insult him. There's lotsa young guys out here flying these days. I for one would rather fly with someone that's less prone to heart attacks. I bet he's got hundreds of these trips under his belt." He hesitated, turned to DC. "Right?"

DC pushed the fuel mixture control in. "Yeah. Well, I normally fly another plane," he explained lamely.

He thumbed the fuel pump rocker switch. A high pitched squeal reached their ears as the pump shot avgas through the lines to the injectors.

"It's similar to this plane, but an RG—'Retractable Gear'—and a bit faster." Falling back on his old habits from the hot desert, he held the switch for several long seconds.

He flipped open the side window and yelled out front, "Clear prop!" After a moment's hesitation, he cranked the ignition.

With a whine, the ignition turned the crankshaft. The propeller spun. And spun. But the engine failed to catch.

He stopped cranking, confused. A couple nervous chuckles drifted up front. He frowned and turned to the passengers.

"Sorry folks, not my day today. I'm gonna have to let the starter cool off." They sat for several long, awkward minutes in deafening silence. On the back of his neck, he could feel the skeptical stares from his audience. How he longed, at times like this, for the sanctity of an airline cockpit and its locked door. Even a commuter plane would at least give him a curtain between flight crew and passengers.

"Forget to wind the rubber band?" one passenger quipped.

"I don't think anyone fed the hamsters today," DC said with a forced smile. "They're having trouble turning the treadmill." That bought him a few laughs.

Allen taxied in from his Hoonah flight, a full load of passengers weighing his tail down as well. All eyes followed the plane as Allen pulled up next to them, shut down and hopped out. As each passenger maneuvered their way through the plane's small exit, Allen held out a helping hand.

DC's eyes bulged as he spotted a small wad of green slip into Allen's palm from each passenger. Sighing, he punched the rocker switch and shot another squirt of fuel.

He cranked again. And again. Try as he might, the stubborn pistons refused to light. With each attempt, the pitch of the whine lowered like a dying car battery.

Allen ambled over. DC leaned his head out the open cockpit window.

"Any suggestions?" DC asked. Ears perked, the passengers stared in anticipation at the two pilots.

"Got any gas?" Allen asked with a smirk. One passenger snorted.

"I may be dumb but I'm not stupid," DC replied.

"How much did you prime?" Allen asked.

"The usual," DC replied.

Leaning closer, Allen whispered, "DC, this ain't the desert. There's no vapor lock to purge."

DC closed his eyes and knocked his head against the headrest. "Shit. Of course. Flooded."

"Need a hand prop?"

"Let's hope not. But at this rate, I probably will."

DC waited a few more agonizing minutes while the excess fuel drained from the manifold. Allen lingered in the background, in case he needed a helping hand prop.

He didn't. One turn of the key vaporized the 100 octane in each of the Continental IO540's six cylinders, and spun the prop. With the engine idling smoothly, DC took a deep mental breath. He flashed a thumb's up to Allen, then donned his headset and called for taxi clearance.

After the required engine "run up" check at the end of the runway, he keyed the mike. "Juneau Tower, SEAS flight Two Seven, ready for takeoff."

"SEAS Two Seven, cleared for takeoff," came the reply through his headset.

DC lined up on the centerline and added full power.

Rotation, and the *cheechacko* took wing on his virgin flight.

* * *

Takeoff went a little smoother, he was glad to see. Eyeing the clocklike spin of the altimeter, he nosed over to level off at one thousand feet. He nailed the altitude, bringing a secret smile to his lips.

Leaning over the controls, he peered up at the cloud deck. About five hundred feet above, he figured. Though it was the legal minimum distance, in the back of his mind a few synapses worried that at any moment a Boeing 737 on approach to Juneau could come plunging out of the clouds and turn his bird into one big bug splat.

Juneau Tower, of course, had made sure that would not happen. "SEAS Two Seven," the controller's voice crackled through his headset, "leaving the airport traffic area, no reported traffic inbound, frequency change approved."

Glancing at the folded sectional chart in his lap, he set course for the Funter Gap, and twisted the radio dial to 122.9, the common traffic frequency.

As he crossed over Thunder Bay and into the open waters of Chatham Strait, visibility dropped. DC glanced up and down the channel. Socked in. The muscles in his glutes tightened involuntarily. Eyes narrowed, he aimed for the north shore of Chichagof, just east of Hoonah's dirt strip. Though not along his route of flight, he dialed in Sister's Island VOR, the navigation beacon in the middle of Icy Strait. Somehow, the radio beam put him more at ease in this strange new land.

Out of the mist, the shoreline floated toward him. He relaxed. Shreds of *scud* clouds lingered by the mountaintops, and he picked his way around them, over town and into the strip.

Touch down was, as one of his passengers euphemistically put it, *firm*. A hail of gravel shot from the tires and ricocheted off the aluminum fuselage like rain on a tin roof. The cabin broke out in applause.

DC's mouth twitched sideways in dismay; passengers only applauded when they were relieved to be alive.

Amidst a round of handshakes and a chorus of "Good landing"—which, he knew, only came with a lousy one—the passengers departed. He looked at his empty palm, wondering how Allen had managed to steal those tips from his passengers.

But at least the dreaded first flight was over.

And then came his return flight, with Mr. and Mrs. Horvath.

Lovely couple, DC recalled Dusty saying. They were nice enough, all right. But each barely fit into an entire row, let alone a single seat. Stuffing them into the small cabin reminded him of the biblical passage about passing a camel through the eye of a needle. Their tendency to sweat and fart at the slightest effort became only too apparent when he pushed and shoved their various body parts through the small doorway. As the two fumbled with their seat belts, DC realized they needed the extenders. He shook his head. Now he knew what the pilots had been snickering about.

It was always an awkward situation for him. He held up an extender. "Um, Mr. Horvath, it might be more comfortable if you—"

Without hesitation, the man grabbed the belt and wrapped it around himself. Mrs. Horvath required not one extender but two.

Back in the Hoonah "terminal," a one room wooden shack, DC ran a quick weight and balance calculation. Room to spare, he saw, but not by much. After loading a few light cargo boxes in the nose, he hopped in and fired up. Mercifully, the Continental caught on his first try. He taxied out. Glancing back at his portly passengers one last time, he instinctively wheeled the trim setting further nose down.

The flight back, he was relieved to see, went smoothly.

Until landing, that is. DC had set up his approach perfectly, speed and altitude on target all the way down final and "over the numbers" at the end of the runway. He eased the plane into a soft flare, trading speed to level off and inch his tires softly down onto the pavement.

But a sudden wind shift turned his intended "greaser" into another bouncer. DC frowned; skills aside, a soft landing always required a bit of luck. The same was true for all pilots, he knew, from the most seasoned airline captain to the greenest student. And no matter how fantastic a job a pilot did, how crisp his radio work, how accurate his navigation, passengers always judged their pilot solely by the touchdown.

Taxiing in, DC spotted a ragtag line of pilots standing under the awning of the terminal. As the prop slowed to a stop, the rain hit. Park brake set, DC hopped out and struggled to pry his passengers out of the cabin.

Two bulky bags in tow, he led the waddling passengers inside. As he passed his snickering coworkers, DC glared from beneath his dripping ball cap as if to say, "Thanks a helluva lot."

They nodded in reply, and Ralph greeted DC's passengers with a formal, "Hello, Mr. Horvath. Hello, Mrs. Horvath. My you look pretty today."

The two passengers beamed at all the polite attention.

Standing aside, DC allowed the Horvaths to enter through the sliding glass doors and into the dry terminal.

As he stepped in behind them, the young pilot's sour mood vanished. For there, standing before him, jean jacket damp, black hair glistening with raindrops, smiling her dazzling smile at him, was Tonya.

He started to say her name, but stopped. She wasn't looking at him, but at his passengers.

Stupid, he thought. She didn't even know him. *Yet*, he corrected himself.

"Auntie! Uncle!" she exclaimed, wrapping her arms around each of the Horvaths. "Did you have a nice flight?" They mumbled something, but he didn't hear. He puffed up his chest and flashed his winningest smile, well aware that her first real impression of him would be that of a rain-soaked porter.

"It was a safe flight, Miss. I flew them back myself. Just a routine flight," he replied, a little too loudly.

She turned to him. Whether her smile was one of politeness or bemusement he couldn't tell. She eyed him up and down. "I'm sure it was. You seem quite capable."

He blushed, suddenly feeling stark naked. He dropped a bag and held out his hand. "The name's Daniel Alva." After a moment's puzzled hesitation, she shook it. He asked, "And you are?"

"Tonya Hunter."

In DC's clammy palm, her hand felt like a log fire. She took it away and reached for the bags.

He pulled them away from her grasp. "I'll get them. It's not a problem, really."

She waved her hand in dismissal. "I'm sure you're too busy."

"I've got time."

She eyed him. "Oh, if it's a tip you want—"

He cocked his head. "Don't insult me." At least from her, the only tip he wanted was . . . he stifled the thought.

"Well. If you insist. Auntie, Uncle, my truck's parked right at the curb." She whirled around. The Horvaths each took one of her arms and the three inched out. DC brought up the rear. Once curbside, Tonya raced around to the driver's seat to warm up her aged Toyota truck.

DC took the opportunity to do a little recon. He pointed at her. "Well, you two seem to have a fine niece. I'm sure you're very proud of her."

The two paused, looked at each other, then him.

"Ahem," Mrs. Horvath replied stiffly. "Yes, we are proud."

Mr. Horvath leaned forward and whispered to him, "Her parents are both Eagle-Bear Clan, you know."

"Harry!" Mrs. Horvath scolded.

"Oh, well, that's nice," DC answered, unsure what the man had meant. Some kind of esoteric clan gossip, it seemed. DC cleared his throat. "So, umm . . . when are you two flying out again? Maybe I'll be your pilot."

Mr. Horvath stared ahead. "Day after tomorrow."

Tonya hopped out and helped them to the truck.

This should be interesting, DC thought as he hefted the bags over the back railing and into the bed. As expected, Harry took up more than half the cab. To DC's surprise, Myrna climbed up and sat in the truck bed, head resting against the cab, face passive and seemingly oblivious to the rain. The image recalled to him the Pima and Navajo back in Arizona.

Tonya shut the passenger door and turned to DC. "Well, thank you, uh, what was your name?"

"Daniel. Friends call me DC."

"Oh, DC. You're Allen's new roommate. Well, we appreciate your help." She began to dig into her purse but stopped. "Oh, sorry, no tip." She held out her hand instead. DC grabbed it and pulled it quickly to his lips.

"All my pleasure, Tonya," he replied.

She giggled softly. "You pilots. Always so dashing," she said, pulling her hand away. The smile vanished. "Well, it was nice meeting you," she finished, with all the charm of a dead halibut. She stepped around him and walked toward the driver's door.

"Hey, wait," he called. "Maybe we could—"

"It's a small town, DC," she said over her shoulder. "We'll run into each other."

"Wait! Um, you work at the Red Dog, right?"

Truck door open, she paused. "Very observant," she commented. After what seemed to him like a moment's reflection, she said, "Tell you what. I'll try to get off early tonight. Meet you at the Salty Sourdough at ten for a Chinook, on me. Consider it your tip."

"Deal. I'll be the one wearing the pink carnation in his tux."

"Plaid shirts and roses work better in this town." She held up a finger. "Don't tell your roommate, please. I'm afraid he's the jealous type."

"Oh, you spoil the party."

She leaned against the truck cab. "Listen, I'd hate to see anyone get hurt. I don't play games."

Aunt Myrna, sitting passively in the truck bed and seemingly oblivious to their conversation, raised her brow slightly. To DC, the reaction spoke volumes. But in what language, he wasn't sure.

"See you tonight, *cheechacko*," Tonya finished. And with that, she was gone. His heart panged with the slam of her door. With the rev of her engine, his libido roared.

A faint echo of another thought nagged at the back of his mind. Feminine words, shouting in whisper.

But Stephanie's voice, thousands of miles and hundreds of years away, back in a strange land called Phoenix, was drowned out by the chugging of an old red truck.

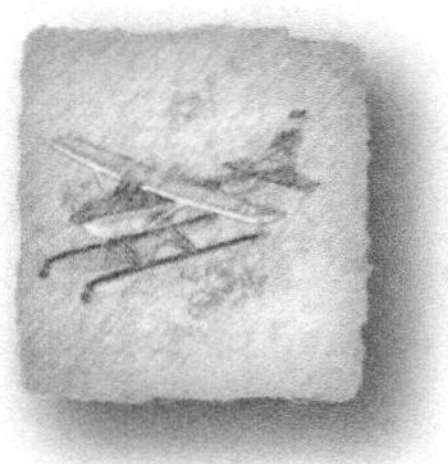

"What a day," DC exclaimed, slamming the apartment door. Several old aeronautical charts, tacked to the wall as decor, rustled in its wake. Throwing his jacket on the coffee table, DC plopped onto the threadbare, green plaid couch and lay back, leg dangling over the side.

Allen emerged from his room, an empty Heineken in hand. Tossing the spent bottle into the trash, he grabbed two fresh ones from the refrigerator. He walked over and handed DC one.

"Here's to your first day," Allen said. The two clinked bottles.

"Thank you, sir." As they drank, DC caught a glimpse of the wall clock. "Seven thirty," he exclaimed. "Is it really that late?" After glancing at his watch, he looked through the window behind the couch. Daylight bright as noon streamed in through the curtains.

Allen sat in a chair beside him. "That's how it goes around here. You work and work and have all this energy, and time just melts away. So, how was it?"

DC stared into the distance. He reviewed his flights in his mind, and the clouds he'd dodged all day. *Scary as shit*, was the thought that ran through his mind. He shrugged. "Not bad. Umm . . . how was the weather today? Compared to average, I mean?"

Allen smiled. "A little intimidating, was it?"

DC gulped a swig of beer. "I didn't say that."

"About average I guess. It's always going up and down like that. Mother Nature can't ever seem to make up her mind. But don't worry, she'll give you *lots* worse than today."

"Can't wait," DC replied with a distinct lack of enthusiasm. *Just get me through this summer*, he thought. He leaned toward Allen, beer arm extended. "Here's to our first step to the majors," he said.

"Amen." They drank.

Allen drew from his pocket a wad of bills and started to count.

DC's eyes bulged. "Holy shit, you made that?"

"Yeah."

"Maybe we don't need the majors."

Allen chuckled. "It ain't that great. How much you make?"

"Nothing. Nothin' at all. All cargo and po' folk."

Allen smiled. "You're the junior puke now. You get the shit detail. And the Horvaths, I heard."

DC sat back and smiled wide. "Yep. And they can fly on my plane any time."

"Really?" Allen sat forward, eyeing DC through raised brows. "Why, pray tell? Those old farts suddenly start tipping?"

DC drained another gulp that nearly emptied the bottle. With a satisfied *ahh* he sat the bottle deliberately on the coffee table.

"Don't have to. I'll fly them any day. As long as their niece picks 'em up."

Allen raised his brows. "Oh?" He smiled broadly. "She a fox?"

"Slightly. She's Tonya."

Though Allen's smile remained fixed, his cheeks seemed to darken. He blinked. "Their niece?"

"What, do I gotta draw you a chart?"

Allen sat back. He stared at the floor. "No, I just—it's just a surprise, that's all."

"I get first dibs on all Horvath flights."

Allen's fist tightened on his bottle. He looked up. "Listen, DC, I'm not sure that's such a good idea."

DC crossed his legs and threw an elbow over the back of the couch. "Jealous, Romeo?"

Eyes narrowed, Allen stared hard at him. "No. You just don't understand her."

"And you do?" Draining the last of his beer, he raised it to the air for emphasis. "You said you couldn't snag her. Step aside. It's my turn."

Before Allen could answer, DC retreated to his room for a shower.

* * *

"Your turn, hm?" Allen mumbled as he walked to the bus stop, cigarette dangling from his lips. "Well, let the best man win."

Once at the Red Dog, he took his customary table in the back, downstairs. He leaned his chair against the wall. The bartender had furnished his Chinook and two shots of Stoli, and he'd drained half the brew between the bar and the chair. A dark cloud seemed to hover above him.

The evening crowd consisted, as always, of rowdy tourists who fancied themselves prospectors in an 1880s saloon. He tuned them out.

Bladder already filled with a Chinook from the Salty Sourdough, he contemplated a trip to the head. But then he spotted her legs, descending the stairs. *Hell*, he thought, even before seeing the legs he'd known those tennis shoes, so damned sexy simply because they graced her feet.

She spotted him, or so he first thought. But several long minutes passed by before she acknowledged his presence with an exaggerated double take. She smiled formally and glided over.

"Hello, Allen," she said, voice oozing with deliberate, syrupy innocence.

He answered evenly, "Hello, Tonya."

"Where you been?"

"You should know. I thought we were meeting at the Salty Sourdough tonight at eight for a drink."

She cocked her head and floated a sympathetic smile down upon him. "Oh, I'm sorry. Didn't I tell you? Mona's sick and I, uh, had to cover."

"You could've called."

"Oh. Well, I lost your number, or something. What was it again?" She pulled the pencil from her ear and poised it above her order pad, forehead wrinkled as if in concentration.

After a pause he said, "Three-oh-three-eight."

She giggled. "For a good time, call."

That made him smile. "Now, no phone sex till You-know-who's on the other end, all right? Remember I've got a new roommate, now." He watched her face for a reaction.

She looked up, eyes seeming to brighten a shade. "Oh, yeah, DC. I met him when Auntie and Uncle came in today. He flew them over." Body twisting as if to a tune in her head, she added, "He asked me out to dinner, you know."

He raised his brows. "Oh really? He hadn't mentioned it." He returned to his beer. "Thought you said you didn't date pilots."

"I don't. They're too . . . flighty." She giggled at her pun. "But then again, he's got a cute butt." She leaned forward and brushed a lock of hair from his eyes. "And rules are made to be broken." Before he could react, she straightened and said, "Want another one?"

"Sure."

She spun and left, left him to simmer.

In a few minutes she returned. Without word he paid, leaving her the customary two dollar tip.

She looked at him a moment then bent down and stared deeply into his eyes, free hand resting lightly on the back of his neck. "Don't worry, lover. I haven't accepted. Yet."

Allen shrugged, trying his best to seem indifferent. "It's a free country. And, as you're so fond of reminding me, we're—"

"Just friends."

"Right."

She ran a finger lightly down the bridge of his nose. The sensation sent shock waves clear down to his rump. "And don't forget our agreement," she finished.

"I promised, didn't I?"

"Since there's nothing to tell, anyway. Right?"

He ran thumb and finger across his mouth. "My lips are sealed."

She straightened back up. "Because, you know, rumors just buzz around this little town like your little airplanes."

Allen sighed. "I know, Tonya."

"Maybe we can get together for espresso next week? I'll call you."

Allen waved a resigned hand in the air. "Sure."

She left him to brood, and brood he did. For the next several minutes, he pretended not to watch her tip-maximizing sway and flirtatious manners as she worked the tourists. To his surprise, he spied her clocking out and ducking out the back door. He glanced at his watch: 10 p.m. Far earlier than normal.

She hadn't even bothered to say good-bye. He stared at his beer, watching the bubbles expand and accelerate as they rose to the top of the dark amber liquid. *Women!* So many conflicting signals.

But this one he knew. Knew better than she knew herself. And yet he felt powerless to stay away. A moth to flame? He wondered.

"Got that straight," he spoke aloud, then drained his Chinook and stood, steadying himself on the wooden chair back. He passed through the crowd and out the swinging doors.

*   *   *

The door flew open. Arm in arm, two figures stumbled into the dark room. DC groped for the wall switch, found it, and flicked the lights on. Tonya shrieked in mock embarrassment and flicked it back off.

"Looks like Allen's still out," he said.

"Saw him at the Red Dog tonight," Tonya replied.

"Hmph. It's a safe bet he'll close the place," DC mumbled, an edge of annoyance in his voice.

"He always does." She wrapped her arms around his neck. "So when the cat's away . . ."

She pulled him to the living room floor. DC offered little resistance. The two wrestled playfully. Tonya wound up on top, straddling DC's waist as he lay on his back. Her eyes burned into him with passion, or perhaps, he thought vaguely, alcohol-induced lust.

She bent down to kiss him. In his enthusiasm, he reached up and bashed his teeth into hers. He tasted his own blood, trickling from a split in his lips. She laughed.

"Oh, fuck it," he said. The two locked lips.

Reaching beneath the front of his shirt, Tonya raked her nails down his chest. DC yelped and pushed her off, rolling her onto her back and straddling her.

"Damn, you're gonna kill me girl," he exclaimed, wondering if she'd drawn more blood. But, fumbling beneath her blouse, he quickly forgot his pain.

For several minutes the two rolled and struggled, fought and groped, caressed and devoured. Jackets and jeans flew off, landing crumpled on furniture and floor.

Last one on the bottom, Tonya once again pushed him away and rolled up on hands and knees. Dark hair ruffled, unbuttoned shirt dangling tantalizingly over her black bra, she flashed a devilish grin and wagged a beckoning finger at him. Kneeling, DC faced her. He could barely keep his tongue in his mouth.

He sprang. She squealed. The two tumbled again.

The phone rang. After the fourth ring, the blare registered in the young man's brain.

"Crap," he said. "I'd better get it."

He fumbled for the receiver on the end table above him. Giggling, Tonya pulled him back.

"C'mon! It might be Allen." He struggled away, crawled up to sit on the couch and picked up. She grabbed the receiver and wrestled him for it. Finally he managed to yank it away and hold it to his ear. His mind miles away, he squeaked out a quick, "Hello."

"DC?"

"Yeah," he answered absentmindedly, stealing a quick kiss from his date, who'd crawled up on his lap. "Who's this?"

After a pause came the reply. "This is your girlfriend. Remember me?"

DC's eyes grew wide. He stood bolt upright, knocking Tonya to the ground on her rump.

He gulped. "Stephanie—of course! I—I—How are you?"

"Feeling rather neglected, actually," came the reply.

"Sorry, uh, I've been really busy. They fly us day and night around here."

Tonya recovered, leaned forward and tickled his legs. "Stephanie, hmm?" she cooed. "Ooh, competition!"

He tried in vain to brush her away. Holding his hand over the receiver he whispered, "Knock it off."

She grinned. "Make me." Her nails tickled their way up his calves. His legs twitched involuntarily as he sat back down.

Tonya continued her assault, finally digging her nails into his thighs.

DC stifled a yelp. Into the receiver he said, "What's up?"

"You tell me," came the reply.

"Well, I—I'm getting lots of flying time. The other guys are really cool. And it's beautiful up here. You should see it."

"Is that an invitation?"

"Um, yeah. Sure." He hoped he sounded sincere.

Tonya worked her way back onto his lap and, putting her arms on his shoulders, began nibbling on his free ear.

Stephanie said, "Finals are over soon. Maybe I could—"

"Yeah that'd be great," DC answered, suddenly finding it impossible to concentrate. "Um, could I call you back? I'm kinda busy."

"DC, is there someone else there?"

"Uh, yeah. Allen's here. I think."

"You know what I mean."

DC gulped. "Well, I—well—yeah."

After a pause that seemed an eternity, she said, "I see."

The next sound he heard was a *click*.

DC replaced the receiver and, eyes closed, ran his hands over his face. "Shit."

Tonya sat back and eyed him. "Girlfriend?"

DC rubbed his eyes. "Well, yeah, kinda. But we sorta broke up when I moved up here."

"Kinda. Sorta," Tonya repeated. "Does she know this?" DC sighed deeply. But before he could answer, she did for him. "She does now."

DC pulled away. "I really should call her back."

With a squeeze of his thigh, she kissed him and said, "What's the point?"

DC struggled to sort his thoughts out, but the girl on his lap forced different ones in. Stephanie seemed so far away, so long ago. Inevitably he succumbed to the here and now. The giggles soon turned to moans.

Eyes wide open and staring at the ceiling, Allen lay silent in his bed.

* * *

"Bastard," Stephanie blurted between sniffles. She grabbed another tissue on the kitchen table beside her chair and blew.

Standing behind her, Linda massaged her shoulders reassuringly. "Don't worry, Stephanie. There are other fishes—"

"Oh, God, don't start that crap," Stephanie replied. She took a swig of her Corona and plopped it back on the table. "We practically lived together for a year. A year! Isn't there such a thing as commitment in this world any more?"

Linda shrugged. "Well, you two did agree to see others."

Stephanie snorted. "Didn't waste any time, did he? Truth is, he wanted it, I didn't. I could've waited." She threw up a hand in resignation. "But, I said to myself, 'If you love something, set it free'." She hung her head. "And look where it got me."

Linda stopped massaging, sat and faced her. "It seems to me, there are only two things you can do."

Stephanie looked up. "Oh?"

"Option A, which I *highly* endorse, find a stud at the bar tonight and pork his brains out."

Stephanie rolled her eyes. "Oh, pa-*lease*. Is sex your answer to everything?"

Linda held out a hand, palm up. "At least you'll get a little revenge. Who knows? Maybe even find true love." She grinned mischievously. "Or at least true lust."

Stephanie shook her head. "I'm almost afraid to ask, but what's option B?"

"Well, if you don't want to dump him . . . fly up there and steal him back. That is, if you think he's worth the fight."

"Are you kidding? Just throw on a backpack and show up on his doorstep?"

"Why not? He did invite you up there."

"Only because he had to."

"At least you'll find out what's going on. Maybe it's not as bad as you think."

Stephanie threw up her hands in frustration. "DC had a girl in his apartment, for Christ's sake. What do you think they were doing?"

"Steph, how many times have the guys stopped by here for a beer and a video?"

"Linda, I could hear her giggling. Sounded like she was—well, I don't even want to say what it sounded like."

Linda grabbed her friend's shoulder and shook it. "Then sneak up there and steal him back. Chalk one up for the jilted females."

For a long time Stephanie stared at the phone. Finally, she looked up at her friend and replied, "*To hell with it.*"

*   *   *

Wow.

That was all he could think.

Wow.

What a night!

Tonya was everywhere he looked.

On her hands and knees, half naked, beckoning to him. An angel and a devil, all wrapped in one sexy package. And, *oh*, that naughty grin! Like a wild animal. Passionate, playful, teasing, daring. He never imagined such a simple expression could be so . . . *erotic*. There was no other word for it.

She'd been more excited, more aroused, more passionate than anyone he'd ever been with, and yet—

How could she stop?

Right in the middle of it all. Just push away, button up and leave. Not mad, not upset, not even confused. Just . . . *switched off*.

Like a light.

And then that kiss at the door. Blown back to him from six feet away. The most erotic kiss in history.

How could she just turn it all off and leave?

How?

"—I say again, SEAS Forty-two, cleared for takeoff!"

DC jumped in his seat.

"Uh, SEAS Forty-two, roger," he replied.

CHAPTER 11: Poachers and Other Pests

His clients knew him as a retired City of San Francisco homicide detective. In reality, the closest the private dick had ever come to wearing a badge and a piece was his old night security guard job. His trade skills he perfected by watching reruns of *Magnum, P.I.*; his body he honed on a diet of pepperoni pizza, Pabst Blue Ribbon and Twinkies. At 5'7", 260 pounds of solid lard, sporting horn rim glasses and a toupee that looked scraped from the shower basin, Raymond Humes, Private Investigator, hardly fit the part.

But *Mercenary Detective Quarterly* didn't care about his looks or credentials, as long as he paid his advertising bills on time. And pay he did, for that magazine alone generated nearly all of his clients.

His office consisted of a P.O. box and phone line. Most clients contacted him from out of state, so rarely met him face to face. But he could talk tough on the phone, and that was enough to put beer on the table. To put food on it took his real job: accountant.

Like most P.I.'s, the majority of his cases consisted of following wayward spouses. Occasionally a customer would need a rough-up job, and he gleefully complied by hiring local muscle. But he always took credit. Humes rarely did a break-in job personally, either; he could barely squeeze through a front door, let alone a busted window. And any witness would have little trouble spotting him in a lineup.

Tonight, however, he had made an exception. He liked the tough guy he'd come to know over the phone, and the man had made it simple and quick. Humes was always cautious about bringing up shady business, but his client had suggested it flat out. And he respected that.

So much in common did Raymond Humes have with his client—their love for guns, violence and tough talk—inevitably the two had hit it off. But then, most of the men who called in response to his *Mercenary Detective Quarterly* ad fit the same profile as his customer, Mr. John Bolt.

Humes quietly entered his motel room and shut the door. He left the light off. Had anyone seen Humes pull up, they would have thought it odd that the man did not turn on the light, but this never occurred to him. Leaving the light off seemed to him what a sharp detective like Magnum would do.

For a long moment he leaned against the rough wooden trim, his heart still pounding from the adrenaline. The motel's flashing neon sign penetrated the moth-ridden curtains and cast a dull red glow across the dull brown room. But for the continual swoosh of cars on I-10, the room remained silent.

He groped toward the phone on the night stand, stubbing his toe on a chair as he did. Cursing, Humes sat on the edge of the bed. The mattress creaked in protest. He glanced at the time: 1:17 a.m. He dialed.

"Bolt," the man on the other line croaked.

"Humes here. Sorry it's so late, but you told me to call soon as I—"

"Get to the point, Humes."

"She's changed her name."

"That *bitch!* I should've known. Nine years I been looking. Nine years! She broke my heart, you know."

"Yeah, and you're breakin' mine, John. I'm sure you'll forgive her for all the dough she ripped off of you."

"Take it out of her hide, more like," Bolt answered. "Any problems?"

Humes massaged his newly sore toe. "Clean job. Those old farts, they could sleep through a hurricane."

"I shoulda had you shoot 'em. They wouldn't tell me where she moved." Bolt paused. "Anybody see you?"

"Look, pal, I'm a pro."

"Okay. What is it? Her name?"

Humes inhaled with pride at his success. "Holly Shannon Innes."

"And where does Holly Fucking Innes live?"

Humes shifted uneasily on the bed. He cleared his throat. "I, uh, couldn't find out, exactly."

"You couldn't find out exactly?" Bolt repeated. "You found her letters, didn't you? I told you where to look."

"They were all dated a coupla years ago. There weren't no current stuff."

Bolt snorted. His voice kicked up an octave. "You're an ex-cop for Christ's sake. Don't you know what search and *seizure* means? She could be in Timbuktu by now."

"Near enough."

"Oh? So where's the old address?"

Humes swallowed. "Fairbanks. That's in—"

"I took geography. What the hell's she doing up there?"

Humes grinned. "It's been my experience they always follow a man. Or a woman. I hear up in Alaska they're kinda different."

He imagined his client reddening at the implication. "Look, I only had time to glance at a couple letters. But I got a lead. She mentioned something about working at a place called *Tanana* Air Adventures, whatever that is."

"Figures. Stupid bitch always had this crazy notion she was gonna learn to fly." Bolt snorted. "Hell, she couldn't even shift my rig without shreddin' the gears."

Humes cradled the receiver with his shoulder and reached for a pad and pencil on the night stand. Pencil poised, he asked, "Any idea what kind of work she'd be doing there?"

"Hmm. She couldn't even cook toast without burning it. Gotta be a secretary or something. Probably bangin' one of them pilots on the side, for free flight lessons. And if that's true, I'd pay big bucks to clip his wings too."

Humes stirred. "Look, we don't even know if she's still there."

"You're right." After a moment's silence, Bolt said, "You gotta break back in the house. Find out where she is now."

"Hey, buddy, I'm good, but I ain't stupid."

Humes heard a long sigh in reply.

"All right, Humes, good job. You're off the case. Bonus check's in the mail tomorrow. Looks like I'd better start packin' my snowshoes."

Smiling, Humes hung up. "Hell hath no fury like a trucker scorned," he said to himself.

The morning had been slow and wet, and DC's next flight wasn't for another three hours. At home for an afternoon lunch, he sat hunched forward on the couch, elbows on knees and staring blankly at the TV. Absentmindedly shoveling another spoonful of a half-heated Cup '0 Noodles into his mouth, DC tried to concentrate on the Andy Griffith rerun. He didn't even realize the set was on mute.

The dark sky cast a dreary hue through the window and across the unlit living room. Rain drummed on the rooftop. Its beating filled his ears and sounded to him like the lonely drone of a plane lost in the wilderness. As depressed as it made him, he was glad to see the front was passing while he was safely on the ground. He'd learned, in the short few weeks, that a wet morning usually made for a dry afternoon, and vice-versa. He hoped the same would be true for his next flight.

He also hoped for something else. He kept glancing at the phone, expecting, willing, *daring* it to ring.

He shook his head. How could he be so stupid? Get greedy, date two women, lose both.

Still, he couldn't get Tonya out of his mind. The image of her sitting cross-legged, half naked on his living room floor, wild-eyed and laughing, was seared into his brain and stirred his desire like nothing he'd ever known. He caught himself reaching for the receiver to dial once more. He pulled back.

Even Allen seemed distant. He'd ignored DC's suggestion of an impromptu lunchtime poker game, and instead gulped down his stew and raced back out the door. The man's Haines charter wasn't for another hour. Well, at least he wasn't off for yet another drinking binge . . . *yet*, DC thought with a scowl.

The phone rang. He jumped, spilling soup down his leg. He cursed, brushing the hot liquid from his jeans. He picked up the phone.

"DC?" a female voice answered.

He resisted the urged to shout her name. "Tonya," he replied, voice as casual as he could muster. "Hello."

"Crummy day, huh?"

"Yeah. We're hardly flying at all today." His mind raced for something to say, but came up blank. "Um, so what's up?"

"Oh, nothing. But I got the message that you called, so I just wanted to say a quick hello."

Called? Nearly twice a day for three weeks! He took a breath. "Want to grab a movie or something tonight? I could probably borrow a canoe to get downtown."

She laughed. "Not today. I've got plans."

DC slumped. "Oh." When a woman said "plans," he always heard "date". "Well, when can I see you again?" he blurted. He winced, wondering if he sounded desperate. No doubt about *that*, he thought.

"Hmm. Well, I might have time tomorrow morning for coffee." Her voice sounded annoyingly noncommittal, almost reluctant.

DC sighed. "I'll probably have to work." Unsure what else to say, he allowed an awkward moment of silence to creep in. So much he had wanted to say to her and now his mind drew a blank. "Well, I'll call you tomorrow if I can get free. Bye."

"DC?"

"Yeah?"

"I had fun the other night," she said, her singsong voice betraying a hint of mischief.

DC chuckled and relaxed. "Me too. Can't wait to do it again."

He hung up. Phone in the cradle, he smacked his forehead with the palm of his hand. "Talk to her, you idiot," he growled.

On the TV, Barney gesticulated frantically in explanation to an agitated and defiant Thelma Lou.

Staring at the pathetic scene, DC mumbled, "Romeo you ain't."

* * *

Jake Whitakker squinted through the fog. Fingers of cloud groped from the overcast and graced his wingtips. Up ahead lay the mountain cut, barely passable.

Frowning, Jake slowed. Not worth risking his butt to pick up his least favorite clients, Mack and Mike Doyle, dropped off by Ralph a few days earlier for yet another high dollar fishing trip. Jake had Allen talked into taking the flight, but Dusty overruled him. The weather was turning sour and required a more experienced hand. Besides, Dusty said with a sinister grin, the Doyles always requested the legendary *Crash* Whitakker.

Jake glanced at his copilot, Eluk, and grinned a sinister grin of his own. At least his faithful Malamute stood ready to ruin Mack's day.

Through the fog Jake found the designated pickup spot, a secluded lake hidden in the scud. He touched down, taxied to the far end, cut the engine and hopped out onto the float. He timed the jump, and turned the Beaver around before scraping beach.

Jake spotted Mack Doyle emerging from the trees. For the first time in history, it seemed to Jake, the man actually smiled and waved.

Mack shouted, "About time they sent a real pilot to get us. Was afraid you'd palm off one-a your wet nose kids on us. And that Ralph guy gets on my nerves."

Doyle sauntered forward, coffee mug in hand, camouflage rain poncho flapping in the drizzle. Under the burden of their combined gear, little brother Mike staggered behind him.

Without a word, Jake turned and opened the passenger door. Eluk bounded out, down the float past his master and with a happy yelp pounced on Mack. The man staggered back by the blow, cursing, and once again spilling his coffee.

"Damn your dog! This is the last time we pay you guys to fly your mutt around."

"I go, he goes." Jake said, grabbing the man's bags and hauling them to the back. He turned and pointed. "And don't build your damn fires so close to the trees."

"Hey, in case you ain't noticed, pal, it's raining." Mack sat on a locker box and sipped his coffee.

Jake shook his head. "Un uhh, not this time, buddy. Both of you grab a load. Weather's closing in fast, and I don't intend to spend the night snuggling in a tent with you two."

Mack motioned at his brother to get the gear. Reluctantly, Mike grabbed two locker boxes and toted them across the beach.

Eluk trotted beside him. The dog sniffed the boxes, pawed at them and whimpered.

"Get away," Mike whispered, kicking in vain at the Malamute.

Peering back over his shoulder, Jake raised a brow. "What's in those?"

With a glance back at his brother, Mike said, "Uh, cutthroat trout, mostly. Some Dollys. You know, the usual."

"Hmph," was all Jake said. Eluk loved to hunt, but couldn't care less about fish. Jake grabbed another load, including Mack's rifle. He took a furtive sniff at the barrel. The smell of burnt gunpowder invaded his nostrils. "Been hunting?"

Mack shook his head. "Target practice. That's still legal, ain't it? Besides, never know when you're gonna run across a crazed bear or something."

Jake stared evenly at the man. "It's been my experience that bears only turn crazy when provoked."

Mack returned the stare. "Well I don't intend to find out."

* * *

On the return leg from his cannery run, DC found himself racing his Cessna 207 into Juneau field ahead of a rain squall. Upon landing, he breathed a sigh of relief and taxied in. Cutting the fuel mixture, he sat for a moment. The piston's roar gave way to the sound of sporadic rain drops on the canopy. Within minutes the drizzle turned to deluge.

He looked toward the terminal, expecting a ramper to run out to help him unload his plane. But no one showed up. He frowned, turned up the collar on his jacket, and jumped out into the torrent. Hurriedly, he tossed the boxes onto a nearby dolly.

Someone tapped his shoulder. DC jumped. He turned to find a man smiling at him from beneath a hooded rain jacket. Something about his cotton candy smile reeked of insincerity. The man's salt and pepper hair, pencil mustache and crisp tie remained bone dry beneath his Gortex wear. Tucked beneath one arm was a shiny, fold-up, aluminum notebook clipboard.

Uh oh, DC thought.

"Good afternoon, young man," the gentleman said. "I'm Inspector Frederick Bruner, Federal Aviation Administration."

FAA. DC cringed at the acronym.

Bruner held out a hand. Reluctantly, he shook it.

"I'm the Principal Operations Inspector for SEAS," Bruner said. "I'm not catching you at an inconvenient time, am I?"

What do you think, nimrod? DC thought, thoroughly soaked. But that line didn't seem to be the best tack to take with a Fed. He shook his head. Raindrops flew from his nose as he did.

"Good," Bruner answered. "Then may I see your commercial pilot's license and current medical certificate? And I'd like to take a little gander at the seat configuration log for this aircraft if you don't mind."

"Sure." DC fumbled for his wallet. *Great,* he thought. Ramp checked in the middle of a rain squall. He held out the documents.

Bruner snatched the papers and eyed them like a Nazi border guard. He attached them to his aluminum clipboard. From inside the hinged notebook, he slid out a brand new, homemade, cross-indexed, laser-printed, *Pilot Inspection and Line Check Form.*

Hood shielding the papers from the rain, Bruner meticulously transcribed the license numbers and dates onto his form.

Shifting uneasily in the rain, DC felt like a motorist stopped by a traffic cop.

"Um, sir," DC said, "do you mind if we step under the wing and out of the rain? You're getting my tickets wet."

Bruner's head snapped up, eyes narrowed, frowning. Then his facial muscles relaxed, and the cotton candy smile returned. "Of course." But the man remained motionless while he jotted down the license numbers.

Finally, Bruner handed the documents back. "Just a routine check, Daniel. I just like to welcome all the new pilots. Sorry it's taken me so long to get to you." He pointed across the ramp.

"If you ever need anything, just come by my office. I'm there for you any time. Twenty four-seven."

DC forced a smile. "Thank you, sir."

Bruner jabbed a thumb at the plane. "By the way, don't you normally tie down after a flight?"

DC shifted from one foot to the other. "Oh, yes sir. Always. Hadn't quite got to it. I was just trying to beat the rain and unload—"

Bruner held up a hand. "No problem. But you never know when a squall might push your plane into another."

Maybe in a hurricane, DC thought. "Good point, sir."

Bruner pointed back at the open cargo bin. "And you might check that cargo strap. It's a little frayed."

DC peered back into the cargo hold. A solid nylon line dangled from the roof. He leaned toward the plane and squinted. Several tiny strands showed microscopic signs of wear. He'd rappelled off webbing far more ragged than that.

"Yes, sir," he answered. "Thank you for pointing it out. I—I don't think I would have caught that without your vigilance," he finished, a hint of sarcasm creeping into his reply.

Bruner nodded. "Well, you can't be too safe. Just last month we lost a guy from that very situation. Strap broke on rotation, and his whole load of frozen fish slid aft." Bruner held a palm high, mimicking an airplane climbing. "Pitched the nose up and he stalled in." He wrenched the palm down then snapped his fingers. "Killed instantly."

"I'll be sure to tell my Chief Pilot."

Bruner chuckled. "I know Dusty. We go way back. It's a small world up here, you know." Bruner scribbled more notes on his form. DC tried in vain to glimpse them. "We'll have to go for a flight together one of these days."

"Looking forward to it." DC imagined he'd rather fly through a thunderstorm. Or with Ms. Innes. Or through a thunderstorm with Ms. Innes.

Finally, the Inspector looked up. With a flourish, he slid the form back inside and flipped the notebook shut. "Welcome to Juneau, Mr. Alva."

"Thank you, sir."

Bruner strutted off.

DC turned away. Running a tie chain through the wing strut, he mumbled the pilot's old joke, "I'm from the FAA and I'm here to help you."

The guy had acted nice enough, he thought. But Bruner's cotton candy smile sent through DC an arctic chill.

* * *

Dusty heard a knock and looked up from his paperwork. The sandy-haired man entered the office, not waiting for an invitation.

Dusty stood respectfully. He held out his hand.

"Afternoon, Inspector Bruner." He shook hands with the Fed. Normally the Chief Pilot would be on a first-name basis with his company's Principal

Operations Inspector, but Dusty had learned long ago that it took formality to grace this man's ego.

Bruner's smile set off warning bells in Dusty's head. Sitting back down, Dusty gestured toward a chair. "Been 'out the road' lately? I hear the cutthroat's jumpin' into the frying pan over at Eagle River."

Bruner held up a palm and remained standing. "Thanks, Dusty, this will only take a minute."

Dusty folded his hands across his slightly rotund belly. "What's on your mind, Inspector?"

Bruner shrugged. "Just had a friendly, informal chat with your new boy."

Dusty's stomach tightened. Despite the man's espousing to the contrary, nothing with Bruner was friendly nor informal. "DC?" Bruner nodded. Dusty said warily, "Good pilot. A little green, but who isn't at first?"

"Well, that's what concerns me." Bruner made a show of whipping his clipboard from beneath his arm and flipping it open. He ran his stubby pencil over the pad as if in review. "Now, I'm only saying this in the interest of *safety*, mind you, but I do think you need to watch him. He seems a little, well, sloppy."

Dusty raised his brows. "Oh?"

"Yes." Bruner jutted his pencil at Dusty. "And of course that reflects upon your operation. Now, I'm not going to bother chasing such minor infractions, but you and I know little mistakes can lead to big holes in the ground." Bruner tapped each item with the pencil as he read. "I'd recommend some remedial training on cargo netting awareness, aircraft vigilance and post-flight ground securing." Bruner looked up, suddenly all cotton candy smile again. "That sort of thing."

Dusty paused, letting his anger wane. "Is that all?"

Bruner nodded. "For now. I'll be keeping my eyes open though. I suggest you do the same."

"Always do, Inspector. Always do."

* * *

Grim faced, Allen tossed in the last notch of flaps and slowed to touchdown speed. The dark cloud still hung over him, but this time the source lay sleeping in the cargo hold behind him. On short final, Allen cracked open his side window. He leaned toward the crack and inhaled deeply. The fresh outside air replaced the stench brought on by his slumbering passengers.

After touchdown, Juneau Tower informally signed him off.

"Three Kilo Alpha, taxi to parking. Good day."

"Good day," Allen replied, then slipped his David Clarks down around his neck. The engine's drone filled his ears.

He heard a groan in back. One was waking now. He glanced behind, but all he could see through the front cage was a massive tangle of black fur.

As he pulled into his parking space, a small procession of people ran up to meet him. *Odd*, he thought, but then again so were his passengers. He shut down and slid out. The group, comprised of several rampers and other airline personnel, stopped a respectful distance away, buzzing excitedly.

Two others continued forward, a bearded man with a dark brown ponytail, and a Native Alaskan woman. Both wore identical brown jackets sporting the blue green breast patch of the Alaska Department of Fish and Game.

The man spoke. "Hi, Allen. Greg Mastis, ADF&G. You flew me in from the bush a few weeks back."

Allen shook the man's hand. "I remember, Greg. Hi."

Greg held an introductory hand toward his partner. "This is Dr. Stella Rittenauer, our resident vet."

The two traded handshakes.

"How're your passengers, Mr. Foley?" Dr. Rittenauer asked.

He glanced back at the ship. "Better than I would be under the circumstances."

Allen opened the cargo doors to reveal three plastic and steel cages the size of large steamer trunks. The two officers peered inside.

"One was growling a minute ago," Allen added.

Dr. Rittenauer nodded. "Tranquilizers are probably wearing off about now."

Allen motioned to a ramper, who dutifully wheeled up a dolly. With great care, the four unloaded each cage onto the dolly. With that, the crowd grew bolder and moved forward. One other man stepped forward and spoke.

"Sirs, Ma'am, I'm Bob Breyson, *Juneau Empire*. Can you tell us what happened, exactly?"

Without looking back, Mastis replied, "Poacher shot and killed a sow for her claws, leaving these three cubs orphaned."

The reporter cocked his head. "Claws?"

"Trophies."

"I see. Can't the bears fend for themselves?"

Mastis shook his head. "Probably too young."

Inspecting the precious cargo, Dr. Rittenauer added, "Not quite sixteen months, I'd say. They're well over 100 pounds each now, so it looks like they were already loading up for winter. But they could still starve before October hibernation."

The reporter stopped writing and stared at the cubs. "So the poacher essentially killed four bears," he mused aloud. He looked to Mastis. "Grizzlies?"

Peering into a cage, Mastis corrected him. "If you mean brown bear, no. Common black."

"How'd you catch'em?"

"Easy. Cubs this age stay right by their mother. They don't know what else to do."

"Where will they go? A zoo?"

"If we're lucky. As their name implies, they're pretty common."

"And if not?"

Unloading complete, Mastis leaned on a cage and looked at the reporter for the first time. He stared hard into the man's eyes. "They'll be sent to our facility in Petersburg and destroyed."

With that the crowd fell silent. With the doctor's help, the ramper pushed the dolly toward the terminal. The crowd parted to let them through.

Watching the cubs recede, the reporter said, "Wouldn't it be more humane to raise them awhile then release them into the wild again?"

Mastis held up his hands in resignation. "Look. You raise them, they just remain dependent. Release them, and they're exposed to starvation. *Maybe* they'd forage enough food to make it to October hibernation and survive. But I doubt it." He shrugged. "So which is more cruel?"

"I see your point. Thanks for your time." The reporter left.

Mastis looked at Allen. "Thanks again for your help," he said.

The officer turned to go.

Allen grabbed Greg's sleeve and pulled him around. Allen nodded his head toward the cage. "Where and when?"

"In a meadow a half mile off Haines Highway, just south of Chilkoot. We estimate about forty-eight hours ago."

Allen released his grip. "Good luck."

Mastis nodded. "Yeah. Take it easy."

CHAPTER 12: Pilot Egos

"Fish, fish fish," DC grumbled, crinkling his nose. "Sickening, stinking, fucking fish!" He hefted another forty pound crate. Across the box read the words, *Excursion Inlet Cannery—Alaska's Finest.* A drop of salmon slime oozed out of a hole in the box and onto his hand. He grimaced, tossed the cargo into the aft bin of his Cessna 207, and wiped his hand across his jeans. "Your place smells like something Eluk would make on the carpet."

Ratcho looked at DC and laughed. The young Tlingit's long black mane bobbed beneath his hair net as he did. "Thanks a lot. I'll try not to take it personally. Don't worry, *cheechako*. You'll get used to the smell."

DC stopped loading and cocked a head. "Not you, too, Ratcho. Everyone calls me that damn name."

"Hey, man, wear it as a badge of honor. Know why I slave at this cannery, my friend? 'Cause my dream's to scrape enough money to go to college in Seattle." He pointed to DC. "At least you've been there."

"Seattle? Yeah, sure, I'm an expert. Saw the airport from my window seat."

"Not just Seattle, I mean the Outside. The Lower Forty-Eight. All those hungry states that buy this shit from us."

DC leaned on a stack of boxes. "Since my first flight, nearly all Dusty's assigned me has been fish runs."

Ratcho nodded. "Hmm. And fish don't tip."

"Well, yeah. That too."

"Gotcha." He handed DC another box from the pallet. "Look, DC, I got a tip for you. I've seen you guys come and go, and the ones that stay get pick of the litter. I can't remember the last time Crash did a run out here. At least, not since our gal Sally dumped a crate of halibut over his head. You stay long enough, you'll get a chance to pick those tourists' pockets."

DC cringed at the thought of an entire year fighting storms in Alaska's skies. He'd been blessed with fairly clear weather so far, but knew sooner or later the clouds would close in on him. He forced the dread thought away. To Ratcho, he shrugged.

"Not that it matters whether I fly tourists. Allen rakes the bucks from them like a titty dancer, and I can't get squat."

Ratcho furled his black brows and imitated playing a miniature violin with his finger and thumb.

DC laughed. "Yeah, yeah, I know. Alaska's a harsh land and nobody loves a sniveler."

"Allen Foley's got his tricks. You'll figure them out."

DC patted the Cessna's diagonal strut. "At least I'll be trading this baby in at the end of the summer for a float, or maybe even a twin. I hope."

Ratcho handed DC another box. "Good luck."

"Thanks."

Back in the Juneau pilot lounge, DC thumbed through back issues of *Flying* and *Alaska* magazines and killed the time chatting with the other pilots. Finally the Chief Pilot's door opened.

"Trips up," Dusty called. He pointed to the grey-bearded man across from DC. "Sam, you're next. Scheduled Kake run or a Hoonah turn. Which do you want?"

Sam yawned, stood, stretched. "Hoonah."

Dusty smiled. "Horvaths." DC perked up.

Sam frowned. "Shit. Kake then. It's longer, anyway."

Dusty looked around the room. "Anyone want to take the—"

"I'll get it," DC shouted. The other pilots chuckled.

Sam shook his head. "I know you want off fish detail, kid, but—geez, the Horvaths?"

DC shrugged. "Hey, I just want to fly. Besides, they're nice people." He too stood and stretched. "You know, just good to get out of the terminal."

With a knowing chuckle, Dusty handed him the paperwork.

Outside, DC pushed the cargo dolly at top speed across the ramp to his aircraft. He plowed straight through the rain puddles, the cart's wheels splattering mud across his jeans.

"Ralph," he called. "Help me load all this shit."

Ralph Olafsen secured the last line on his Beaver and sauntered over. "Why the rush, Cap'n *Cheech*?"

"I gotta get this loaded in time to greet my passengers. The Horvaths."

Ralph raised a brow. "Oh? Why so cozy with them?"

"Ever seen their niece that drives 'em to the airport?"

Ralph nodded knowingly. "Ahh. I s'pose if I was a single pup twenty years my junior, I'd get my panties in a bind over that one, too. Go on, I'll get this. You run off and do your stuff."

"Thanks a ton, Ralph."

"How many pax you got going?"

"Two, I guess. Dusty just said the Horvaths."

"Well, I'd better not load any extra cargo. You can only carry so many beached whales in one airplane."

DC frowned. "Hey, come on. Be nice."

Ralph put his hands on his hips. "Oh, my, but lust has a way of dulling the sense of humor."

"Sorry. I just think they're, uh, pleasant people, that's all."

Ralph shooed him away with a downturned hand. "Be gone, little one."

DC ran off. Inside, he spotted the Horvaths waddling through the front doors, Tonya's red truck pulling away behind them. DC slumped, then shrugged it off and trotted over to help the two passengers to the waiting area.

Hands outstretched, he said, "Great to see you Mr. and Mrs. Horvath. Here, let me help you." After an eternity, DC managed to seat the elderly couple in the waiting area. That done, he picked up their bags and said, "Once I get these loaded and the paperwork done, I'll be back to pick you up for Hoonah."

"Hoonah?" Mrs. Horvath asked. "We're off to Kake. Clan business."

DC set the bags back down. "I was told you were off to Hoonah."

"Oh, not us."

"Well, who then?"

"Me."

DC's spine tingled at the voice. He whirled around. "Tonya!"

She smiled at him. "Hello, DC."

"I thought you'd left."

She shrugged. "Just parking the truck. Didn't you know I was going to Hoonah?"

"You? I was told two Horvaths for Hoonah."

She crossed her arms and shook her head. "Oh. That lady in Reservations, what's her name? Paula. She hears the name Horvath and immediately books a charter for two to Hoonah, no matter what I tell her."

DC snickered. "Sort of like Pavlov's Dog. Surprised when you told her two for Kake, she didn't start salivating." They shared a laugh. DC held up a finger. "Excuse me a moment, won't you?"

She nodded, and he ran back into the office to grab his flight manifest. After a moment's thought, he made a quick side trip to Dusty's office to ask of the old man a very important request. Back in the boarding area, he held out his arm.

"Ready?"

Grabbing his bicep, Tonya smiled wide. "I'm always ready."

Her words gave DC a lump in his throat so large he couldn't reply.

Through the loading doors, Sam entered the terminal. He called, "All aboard for Flight 2386, scheduled service to Kake."

DC smiled wide as he passed. "Your passengers are over there. Myrna and Harry Horvath."

Sam slumped. "Kake," he mumbled. "All the way to Kake."

"Enjoy the company," DC said, patting the sulking pilot on the back as he escorted his prize passenger outside.

Once inside the plane, with the Tlingit beauty seated next to him, DC found it tough to concentrate. He felt as if a spotlight shined on his every move. He imagined Check Airman Holly Innes riding with him. His throat went dry.

DC swallowed, then plodded through the safety briefing. Several times, her attentive brown eyes made him stumble over the lines. She giggled. Rolling his eyes, he fired up the engine.

"Okay," he announced, "today you're my copilot. Push this lever down."

Tonya hesitated, looking to him with wide eyes. "You sure? That's not, like, the ejector seat or something, is it?"

"Never know till you try."

"Right." With a tentative hand she pushed the lever down, then yanked her hand back as if shocked. A hum filled the cockpit. She looked outside, then squealed with delight to see the flaps lowering into takeoff position.

"See?" DC said. "That's not so hard."

He began to don his headset, then paused. Easier to flirt with his copilot without the bulky thing on his head. He turned up the overhead speaker, keyed the mike and called for taxi. From the ceiling, the two heard the ground controller clear them to the active runway.

Once in the air and out of the airport traffic area, DC eyed the weather. As he'd hoped, it had improved considerably. With a sly grin, he banked right.

His copilot tapped him on the shoulder. "Hey, *cheechacko*," she said with an edge of skepticism, "Hoonah's the other way."

Eyes narrowed in mischief, DC said, "Dusty cleared me to take a little detour. You in a rush?"

With a tentative shake of her head, Tonya sat back.

DC climbed steeply, S-turning around the thin, broken cloud layer. He reached the top of Eagle Glacier, nosed over and leveled off above the western end of the Juneau Icefield. He stole a glance at his passenger.

Like a child handed a new toy, Tonya gazed in wonder at the sight.

A brilliant white blanket of snow, shining in the late night sun, spread out before them for hundreds of miles. Jagged brown peaks dotted the crystalline meadow. Pure blue sky lay overhead. Hardly a ripple of turbulence disturbed their path.

Hoping to dazzle her, DC switched to tour guide mode. He banked east toward a striking shaft of distant peaks and said, "That's Devil's Paw, elevation eight thousand, five hundred and—"

Tonya lay a finger on his lips. "Shh. Don't spoil the magic."

He cast an appreciative glance at her, then banked lazily away from the rocky cliffs. He slowed the plane, trimmed for hands-off, and sat back. The plane cruised across the endless sky, content to cut its own straight course.

He slipped an arm around her. She nuzzled her cheek to his shoulder.

After a quick glance outside, DC took his hand off the control yoke and turned toward her. With deep brown eyes she gazed back up at him.

He kissed her. He worked his lips across her cheek, her ear, then nibbled on her neck. The loud drone of the engine seemed to fade away, and all he heard was her sigh.

Encouraged, he continued.

He felt a hand unbuttoning his shirt. A bead of sweat trickled from his armpit, tickling him unmercifully as it worked its way slowly down his side.

He returned his lips to hers. Though he kept glancing at the instruments and outside for other traffic, his mind was already a hundred miles ahead.

Now it was her turn. She ran her tongue down his neck, under his shirt to his belly button, then back up again.

The sensation was incredible. The vibration of the engine ran through his buttocks and down to his toes and magnified what she was doing to him.

Without warning, she bit his nipple.

Yelping, he instinctively smacked her. He started to apologize, but she just smiled her devious smile and attacked his lips with hers.

The two began to grope each other frantically, an awkward entanglement of arms and hands and fingers in the cramped cockpit.

Tonya pulled back. Smile now thoroughly wicked, she leaned back against the doorframe and tugged at her shorts.

A faint memory of college days echoed in DC's mind, an image in the back of his old Mustang, with his new blonde haired, green-eyed girlfriend Stephanie. He pushed the ancient memory away.

Staring into his eyes, she raised her knees above the dashboard and swiftly, deftly slipped the shorts over her shoes and off. A flimsy pair of panties hid her treasure from his gaze. She slid her leg across his lap.

Her foot hooked the yoke. The plane banked and dove. Tonya squealed. Reaching around her waist, DC righted the craft. She giggled with delight as the g-force pressed her back down in the seat.

The two wasted no time returning to the job at hand. After several more awkward attempts, with one arm encircling his neck, she finally managed to straddle him.

The two lovers floated across the vast, surreal landscape.

* * *

The two young pilots lounged at the Red Dog's downstairs bar, sipping Chinooks. One sat hunched over the bar, motionless, while the other could barely stand still.

DC bobbed to the rhythm of the house band, now going through a drawn out version of *Born to be Wild.* He scanned the room, searching for what he didn't know; Tonya was still back in Hoonah.

And so was his mind. He had yet to come down from that fantastic flight.

Allen stared into his beer, brooding more than usual. Occasionally, he glanced up at the wall mirror behind the bar.

Finally, he elbowed DC. "Knock it off, man."

DC turned. "What's eatin' you, Allen?"

Allen drained his beer and motioned for another. "Shit."

"Yeah, like what?"

"Just . . . shit."

DC suddenly wondered if *shit* meant his little side trip with Tonya. He hadn't dared tell the man. Only Dusty had known, but their tardy arrival into Hoonah—and, perhaps, their flushed expressions—could have raised a few eyebrows. And word traveled fast in the small community.

He gazed at his partner. Tonya was right, he thought. Allen was jealous. With an edge of worry in his voice, DC said, "Hey, if we get a break tomorrow, let's bang out that climb."

Allen drank a long gulp and stared into the mirror.

"Sure," in a tone that sounded anything but.

DC spotted some of the SEAS crew upstairs. He tapped Allen on the shoulder and pointed. "There's Ralph and Crash. Let's go say hi."

Allen grabbed his shirt sleeve and pulled him back to the bar.

"Wait till we're summoned."

"What?" DC looked again and realized the two upstairs wore the same dark expressions as Allen. Bent forward across the table, the men conversed in obviously hushed tones. After a minute, the two sat back. Ralph glanced downstairs and nodded.

DC and Allen both caught the cue and headed upstairs. The two pilots joined their comrades.

Staring at Allen, Ralph tilted his head to Jake. "Tell him."

Sitting, Allen leaned forward over the table. "I flew three black bear cubs in from Haines today. Greg Mastis, an ADF&G guy, picked them up here."

"I know Greg," Jake said. "Worked with him a bit. Good man in a bar, too. Go on."

Jake's face seemed to darken even more. After a long pause, he asked, "Gall bladder?"

Allen shook his head. "Intact, he said. Musta been a hunter from the Outside." To DC, he whispered, "Bear gall bladders are considered aphrodesiacs in Asia. They're wiping out tigers and rhinos for that bullshit, too."

"Jesus," DC breathed.

Jake stared at the table and nodded. "Gotta be the Doyles. Gotta be. Eluk was going apeshit over their game boxes." He pounded his fist on the table, sloshing beer out of two mugs. "Goddamnit, I knew I shoulda looked in 'em. Then we'd have evidence."

Allen leaned over to DC and whispered, "Crash used to be a game warden. To him, poachers are about six notches below horse thieves."

Ralph said, "I left a message with Greg to join us for a beer. Maybe he got something on them."

DC sat with the others in silence, letting the band do the talking for awhile. A few minutes later, DC looked up to see a man tap Jake's shoulder.

Jake nodded at the man, then to the others, he said, "Everyone, this is Greg Mastis, Alaska F&G."

Mastis greeted the men at the table. He took a seat by Jake and explained the story. Along with Allen, DC listened respectfully as the sourdoughs discussed the problem.

Finally, Mastis spread out his hands. "There's nothing I can do. Word from on high is it's not *cost effective* to ship 'em to a zoo on the Outside," he said glumly. He swallowed. "The cubs will have to be destroyed."

"Shit," Jake grumbled. "What about evidence?"

Mastis shrugged. "Well, we got a couple boot prints, and slugs from a rifle."

"Same caliber as Mack Doyle's, I'll wager," said Jake.

Mastis continued. "And *maybe* we could get knife signatures to match Mack or his brother's blade, and ballistics to go with his pop gun. But you're talking more forensics and tech work than some homicides these days."

Jake jabbed a finger at Mastis. "This will make front page of the *Empire* tomorrow. It'll stir a nest of hornets in this town."

DC and Allen traded looks.

Mastis shook his head. "Won't matter. The DPS Wildlife Troopers can't go confiscating his weapons to test them without Probable Cause to support a warrant in the first place."

Jake shook his head. "So four bears die, and the shithead walks with another trophy to compensate for his small dick."

Mastis nodded. "That about sums it up."

Ralph scratched his neck. "Look, I don't know about all this cop crapola, but I've seen my share of *Dirty Harry* flicks. Far as I can see, we got motive, method, and opportunity. Opportunity: the guys were in the neighborhood. Method: idiots shoot at anything that moves. Motive: they're assholes." Ralph sat back. "I rest my case."

The two younger pilots snickered.

Mastis sighed. "Wish it were that easy, Ralph. I'd like Mack's nuts for tassels on my hat. It's not the first time I've had run-ins with those two. But there's nothing we can do without evidence. Nothing."

A grin slowly spread across Ralph's face. "Oh, ye of little faith."

The other pilots looked to the prankster.

Ralph's eyes sparkled. "Dirty Harry's got his bag o' dirty tricks spread wide open."

DC leaned across the table. "What do you have in mind?"

Ralph held up a finger. "Silence, little one! Divinity speaketh in my mind." Eyes closed and head swaying like a Swami at a seance, he said, "Yes, yes . . . it's coming to me now."

Mastis raised his hands. "I've heard of some of your stunts, and I don't think I want to know any more. I'm outta here."

Ralph snapped to, half stood and pressed the ADF&G man back down into his seat. "Oh, but the Lord calls you to do His work."

Mastis stared back. "Oh, Jesus," he squeaked.

DC and Allen grinned.

Ralph placed his palms dramatically on the table, sat upright and looked around the table at each man. "My friends, I have seen the light. We shall all partake of a most divine retribution." He shook a triumphant fist in the air and exclaimed, 'Vengeance is mine!' so sayeth the Lord." A few bar patrons glanced at him quizzically. To Greg he said, "This one, Master Mastis, you'll be telling to your grandpups."

The trooper sighed. "Let's hear it."

DC and the others leaned forward, enraptured.

"What, my young disciple, will it take to get our flock released to the wild?" Ralph asked.

Mastis rolled his eyes. "Look, I told you. Without spending a fortune of the taxpayers' dime on feeding them before hibernation, they wouldn't stand a chance. They'd just get—"

"And the lamb lay down with the lion. They'll take their chances. A more appropriate and humane fate for creatures of the wild, I should think. Besides, they'll have their feast, tax free. Can it be done?"

Mastis grimaced. "I might be able to pull it off, if I can get a couple nods from the right people." He looked at Ralph. "No one at the department is thrilled with the alternative."

Ralph turned to Jake. 'The Doyles have a run scheduled in a couple weeks, don't they?"

Jake nodded. "I always check, so I can be busy doing something else."

Ralph lay a hand on Jake's shoulder. "My friend, this flight you'll want. When?"

Jake squinted into space for a moment, thinking. "Friday afternoon the twentieth, I believe. To their cabin."

Ralph pointed at Mastis. "Book the cubs for early morning on the twentieth, at the latest. And we'll hand you your *Probable Cause* on a platter."

Mastis nodded.

Ralph scanned the faces around the table. "My friends, we shall give our cubs a party the likes of which the animal kingdom has never seen." He raised his glass. "I hereby declare this mission, *Operation Dirty Harry*."

"Hear, hear," DC exclaimed. For the first time that night, Allen smiled.

Like Musketeers crossing their swords in salute, the co-conspirators raised their beers.

* * *

The next week, Ralph Olafsen donned his faded bomber jacket, shoved his Tweetie Bird cap on backward and shuffled out to the ramp. He couldn't help but smile. In another week, after all assets were in place, he would pull off his greatest—and most deserving—practical joke on one Mack Doyle and his little henchman. So eager was he that he could hardly concentrate on the job at hand.

A young ramper dutifully followed him across the tarmac, pushing a dolly overloaded with luggage and tackle boxes. Ralph glanced back and shook his head. Typical. Three weekend fishermen from the Outside, packing enough gear for a polar expedition.

At the top of the pilot heap, Ralph could have long ago moved on to the larger, two-pilot, multiengine commuter airlines, and finally to the majors. But Ralph always chose to fly alone, VFR, and in a simple, single engine Beaver amphib.

Now *that* was flying, he thought. Those dickless airliner boys, long on academics and short on sky smarts, might condescendingly label his beloved amphib a "classic," but he called it real. A work of elegant art and solid engineering from simpler times, back when the skies were truly free.

Those times were before his time, he knew. And perhaps he'd not been born with a silk scarf and goggles like Crash. But once the flying bug took . . . .*Let the hot shots fly the newest turbine mods*, he thought, tossing the first bag into the cargo hold. *I'll take a good, old fashioned radial any day*

"Good morning, Mr. Olafsen."

Ralph winced. The voice grated upon his ears like floats on the rocks.

"Mornin', Chief," Ralph said, turning in time to see Inspector Bruner wince himself.

"It's *Inspector Bruner*, please. May I see your pilot's license and current medical certificate, Mr. Olafsen?"

"But officer, the light was yellow."

Bruner cocked his head as if to say, *Please.*

Ralph twisted his ball cap forward. From atop the bill, Tweetie smiled gaily down on the Inspector. "Okay, Chief, here's the deal. You show me yours, and I'll show you mine."

Bruner inhaled and straightened. "You've seen my Inspector's certificate."

"And you've seen my ticket, a dozen times. But Big Brother's official game book states that you hafta show me your badge before I surrender mine."

"I know what the FAR's state," the inspector snapped. He pulled the identification wallet from his breast pocket, then flashed it out and back like a TV cop.

Ralph held up a hand. "Not so fast, there. Hand it over."

"I cannot surrender my 110A identifica—"

"What do I look like, a raghead terrorist? You don't get mine less'n I get to see yours first."

Reluctantly, the Inspector held up the I.D. card. Eyes squinting, Ralph leaned forward and studied the badge as if under a microscope. Imitating the man's habits, he pulled out a dogeared notebook from his inner jacket pocket and diligently scribbled down his license number.

Bruner squirmed before him.

With a flourish, Ralph popped a period on the end of his notes and pocketed the book. "Much obliged, Chief."

Ralph looked up at the clouds. Hanging low over the Cut and points north and west. Looked like a shot over Horse and Colt Islands might be the best departure route to Admiralty today.

"Well?" the Inspector demanded.

"Hm? Oh, yeah. Gotta whip out mine." Ralph patted his pockets as if searching for lost cigarettes. Finally, he dug his tattered pilot's license and medical certificate from his back pocket, a wad of chewing gum squished between them. He handed them over. "Want my Playboy Key Club card, too?"

Bruner frowned. "Thank you, no, Mr. Olafsen." Bruner clipped each document to his board and transcribed the numbers and dates onto his homemade, cross-indexed, laser-printed, *Pilot Inspection and Line Check Form.*

Ralph studied him. "You know, Chief," he said, "a little sense of humor makes for a much better ride 'round the carousel."

Nostrils flaring, Bruner checked off a few boxes on his form then glanced up. "In my business, Mister, seriousness begets safety." Bruner handed Ralph's certificates back. "Perhaps you should think about that."

Ralph slid the tickets back into his hip pocket.

"Ahh. I see. And do I have the pleasure of the Inspector's company on our flight today?"

"You do indeed."

Under the Inspector's watchful eye, Ralph and the ramper loaded up. With the practice of thousands of flights, Ralph shifted bags and boxes for the ideal fit and center of gravity. That done, he hopped off the float and sauntered in to the terminal to collect his passengers.

Bruner remained. Brows raised, he watched Ralph's exit, then turned and looked questioningly at the ramper. Wide-eyed, the man jumped back in the plane and, with trembling hands, tossed the cargo netting over the load and cinched it down tightly. The inspector nodded approval.

Ralph returned and motioned the passengers to their seats. But Bruner remained outside.

One foot in the cockpit, Ralph looked back at the man. "Well, you comin' or ain't ya?"

Bruner stood his ground. "Where are your weight and balance calculations?"

Ralph sighed. "On the dispatch printer inside." He removed his cap and scratched his head. "At least, I think that's where they keep 'em."

Bruner's eyes bugged. "You didn't look?"

Ralph waved a frustrated hand at his plane. "Inspector, you fly these things long enough, they become a part of you. You *feel* if it's sick. You *feel* if it's overweight or out of c.g. I don't need a computer to tell me when my fly's open." He glanced at his Mickey Mouse watch. "We're past departure time. Come on if you're going."

"Well . . . where's your fuel slip? How do you know exactly how much gas the fueler put on your aircraft?"

Ralph shrugged. "On file inside with the rest, I guess. We're late, Chief. All aboard."

The inspector remained motionless, one foot planted on the float. He gestured to the airplane.

"Aren't you going to preflight?"

"Already did."

"But you left the shadow of the airplane. Anything could have happened to the machine while you were away. Don't you always reinspect—"

"Short of your sabotage, Inspector, which I think even you are not fool enough to do, nothing's happened to my bird. I'd know. Now are you coming or not?"

Bruner made a show of crossing his arms. "I refuse to fly in an unsafe airplane. Either you reinspect it, or—"

"Goddamnit, Chief! I play your little Gestapo game every week. Now you're interfering in my company's right to air commerce, something strictly forbidden by your precious rule book. If you're not coming along, then get the hell away from my machine. Eluk!"

The Malamute, dutifully waiting across the ramp, took the cue and sprinted to the plane. He jumped past Bruner and into the front seat, formerly the Inspector's seat.

Bruner jabbed a finger at the dog. "Now just a damn minute, Mr. Olafsen. That canine is unrestrained cargo. He either goes into a cage in back, or you seat belt him—"

"*What?* Now you want me to strap in a goddamn *dog?*"

Bruner raised his head in indignation. "*All* airplane cargo must remain secure during—"

"Mister, your sense of safety is straight out of Never Never Land. You need a good belt at the Red Dog, get a little common sense knocked into you. Maybe *then* we can go for a ride."

Neck veins bulging, Bruner shouted, "Olafsen, you are a hazard to the flying public. I'll have your license revoked before you can—"

"See you at the court martial, Peter Pan. *Clear Prop!*" Ralph slammed the door and keyed the magneto switch.

At the first twitch of the propeller, Bruner leapt backward off the float.

Ralph goosed the engine. The plane pulled away.

Bruner staggered in the gale. His clipboard flew from his hand, scattering laser-printed papers across the ramp. Fist shaking, Bruner yelled. But his shouts were drowned in the prop wash, words falling harmless as rain against the fuselage.

Mouths agape, Ralph's stunned passengers watched as the screaming inspector receded behind them.

CHAPTER 13: Frederick Austin Bruner

He swaggered down the flight line.

He was only twenty-six, but older than most of his ground crew. The war was on, and nobody liked it back home. Fewer liked it here.

But he did. Here, he was in his element. Here, men saluted him. Here, halfway around the world in Viet Nam, he couldn't hear Dad berating him, scorning his failures. So what if he could never throw a spiral or toss a curve ball? And was a B in algebra or physics really all that bad, anyway? It was good enough to land him a commission in the Air Force, and that's all he cared about.

The Navy was for pansies. But of course he'd never say that to Dad's face, not to Captain Howard Bruner, USN. And now he was his family's newest generation of that respected title.

Captain Bruner, that's what his men called him here. OK, maybe the title wasn't as lofty in the Air Force as it was in the Navy. Nevertheless, they still saluted him and stood aside with genuine respect as he strode by, he and his silver polished bars, toward his A-7D Corsair. Besides, this was just the beginning. Next step, Major. Then, Light Colonel. Then, perhaps with a few successful sorties, a couple kills and a heroic feat thrown in here and there for a medal or two, full-on Bird Colonel. Wouldn't Dad be proud. And jealous.

His crew chief was just buttoning up a lower access panel as Captain Bruner reached his machine. The chief spun around, stood at attention and saluted. As always, Bruner spied a mild contempt in the chief's eyes.

Bruner's lips tightened. It was lonely at the top. They hated you. But they respected you, and stayed in line; that's what discipline was all about. And discipline begat loyalty. Not the other way around like some of those cowboy officers would have you believe. Discipline was the key to order, and order was the key to success.

He'd learned that back in his single digit years. When Buddy chased an errant ball out into the street, he'd yanked his hand from his father's and ran after the dog. Too late, his father yelled for him to stop. Too late, he reached the dog. He'd nearly become a statistic himself. That breech of discipline earned him a good whipping and a month of grounding. He cried for three days over Buddy. But never again did he disobey the Captain.

"She's all buttoned up and ready for action, Sir!" the crew chief bellowed.

Bruner nodded. "Good work. But tuck in your shirt, Sergeant."

"Yes, Sir," the chief replied, with notably less conviction.

Captain Frederick Austin Bruner climbed up the cockpit ladder and hopped into the seat. He inhaled deeply. Burnt oil, sweat-soaked seat, dusty panel, all the scents of glory danced in his nostrils. True, he'd yet to take on so much as small arms fire, but each sortie brought to him a sense of victory.

He wiped the sweat from his palms and donned his gloves.

The crew chief pulled the ladder away and signaled, "All clear." Bruner returned a "thumbs up," then twirled his index finger: spinning turbine.

The ground power unit spooled the fan blades and his adrenaline. Soon the hum turned to roar as the burner can kicked in and ignited a whirlwind of fire in his turbine.

The ground crew cleared off. With a nod to his wingman, he taxied out.

Perhaps today would be the big day he'd longed for. And feared. Hot fire, a sky fight, dodge a few SA-2 SAM antiaircraft missiles and come home a hero. A hero to the Captain.

At the end of the runway, he traded another thumbs-up with his wingman. "Skull Three Flight, ready for takeoff," he said, using their call sign for the mission.

"Skull Three Flight, cleared for takeoff," came the tower's reply. He cobbed the throttle, and 14,250 pounds of thrust answered from the Allison TF41-A-1 turbofan engine.

Today's mission for the 354th Tactical Fighter Wing, Korat RTAFB: air support for a ground raid. Flying in a "Fluid Four" formation, his AN/APQ-126 terrain-following radar showed the way.

His squadron could see the smoke from the firefight long before arrival, could hear the frantic chatter on air-to-ground radio channel. Strike Team One took point, and he and his wingman circled in search of MIG's and SAM sites. Bruner banked left, along the GI's scrimmage line.

From the corner of his eye, he caught sight of two distinct fireballs. He turned to look. In a volley of SA-2 missiles, Team One disintegrated. He gasped.

Suddenly his antimissile radar lit up, a Lock-on squeal erupting in his ears. He banked hard and climbed, putting himself between the missile and the sun, grunting as the g-force drained the blood from his brain. As the threat closed, he popped his anti-RADAR chaff and flares, banked hard left and dove for the hills. The missile took the bait and chased his decoys, exploding far behind.

Sobered, he dove and stuck to the earth. A glance right: wingman still there.

"Skull Three, up to bat," he heard the squadron leader call to him. "Primary target's that SA-2 sight, Sector Seven. Skull Five, bat clean up with a strafing run."

"Skull Three, maneuvering," he called, setting up his attack run.

Sweat trickled into his eyes. He blinked. He gritted hard, his discipline overshadowing his fear, and his anger at the loss of comrades. Just one more ridgeline and—there. He rolled wings level and shoved the throttle to full military power. Full-speed attack.

The threat receiver once again screeched its warning of inbounds. He had to trust the physics; too fast a closure rate, and too narrow an intercept for the missiles to react. But Lady Luck always played the final card. He breathed deep, and fought back the urge to let the ordnance fly too early.

The SA-2's flew by. Taking a deep breath, he mashed the fire button with his thumb.

"Fox, fox, fox!" he cried. Two air-to-ground rockets launched toward the Primary.

"I'm hit! Ejecting!" screamed a voice over the radio.

Captain Bruner pulled up, the g-force yanking his heart into his stomach. A flash reflected off the hills and a second later the percussion nudged him forward. A secondary flash confirmed it. A direct hit. The SA-2 site was history.

"Skull Three good run, repeat, good run," he announced with pride and not a little relief.

He allowed a quick smile to his wingman.

Not there. Only then did his brain register the words *Eject!* he'd heard over the radio. He glanced back in time to see his wingman's plane crash into the trees. Just above hovered the chute from his ejection seat. He pulled tight around, protecting him.

"Skull Three, my wingman's down. Repeat, down," he strived to say in his coolest voice. "Good eject."

He watched the pilot, seat and chute, flop into the tall canopy of jungle.

"Call coordinates for pickup," Team Leader announced. Captain Bruner did so, noting with sinking heart that his man was on the wrong side of the scrimmage line.

"All right, we're done here," his leader called. "Skull Flights return to base."

"But we've got a man down," Bruner protested. "He needs cover."

"Those coordinates are inside the Cambodian border, Skull Three. You know they're strictly off-limits to us, man down or no. Ground units are advancing on that sector."

Captain Bruner eyed the *gooks* on the ground, closing in on the downed pilot. "But the enemy's moving in," he protested.

"Bug out now, Mister. That's an order."

Bruner's stomach tied itself in knots. More sweat filled his eyes. Or were they tears? How could they just leave him?

Then it hit him.

This was it. This was his big moment. He could already see the parades. Disobey the order, return and save the buddy. Courage above and beyond the call. Medal of Honor on a platter.

He dried his eyes, took a deep breath and keyed the mike.

"I've got plenty fuel and ammo. I'm staying," he announced.

"Negative, repeat negative. Bug out now," the leader called.

The man's baritone voice sent shivers down his spine, sounding like Dad and nearly willing his Corsair to retreat on its own.

"Just one strafing run and I'm out," he called. It would be his glory run, the one they wrote songs about. He was already in his sweeping turn, 20 mm M61 Vulcan nose cannon blazing. A series of small explosions on the ground told him he'd hit something.

Bullets from a ZSU-24 AAA gun exploded through his canopy; a shard of plexiglass stung his cheek. The cockpit filled with the roar of wind and engine.

AAA'd by the gooks. He swore. Too hot, with no one left to protect him. Pulling out of the turn, he fled. He glanced below at his wingman's chute, dangling helplessly in the trees.

An easy target for the *gook*s on the ground.

The flight home was the longest of his life.

His red-faced Wing Commander dressed him up, down and sideways.

The Colonel told him, in no uncertain terms, that he either resign his commission, or the Air Force would do it for him—dishonorably.

No medals for Captain Bruner. No honor, no glory. No parades. Only the smoking ruins of his once high flying career. A failure to Captain Bruner, Senior.

And the wingman he abandoned was never found.

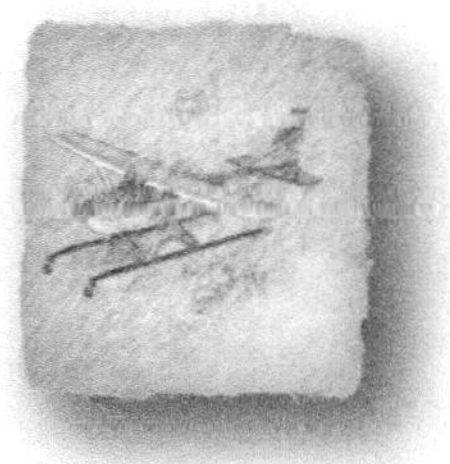

"Enter," Dusty barked.

But the man who'd knocked was already in the room and in his face.

"This is the last straw!" he screamed.

Dusty leaned back in his chair and said calmly, "What can I do for you, Inspector?"

Bruner paced before Dusty's desk like a bear stalking salmon. His hands gesticulated wildly as he spouted.

"What insolence! What arrogance! What callous contempt for authority. *And* the rules, I might add."

Oh, shit, Dusty thought. "Whitakker or Olafsen?"

"Ralph Olafsen. At least Whitakker will give me the time of day without telling me to consult the town sun dial."

Dusty folded his arms. "Okay, let's hear it."

Leaning on his knuckles across Dusty's table, Bruner yelled, "For starters, Mr. Tucker, he—"

Dusty held up a hand, palm out. "For starters, Inspector, I suggest you sit down, take a deep breath and collect your thoughts." He gestured to the chair before his desk.

Bruner blinked, straightened, and sat. After a moment, he began again, this time at normal volume. But the anger in his voice remained.

"Your man Ralph is a hazard to air navigation. No discipline. No respect for regulations. He's sloppy, complacent, a menace to safety." With pointed index finger, he said, "Mark my words, Mr. Tucker, his blatant disregard for even *rudimentary*, accepted aeronautical procedures will one day kill him. And, I daresay, his passengers."

Dusty recrossed his hands. "If you're going to make accusations against one of the best bush pilots I've ever known, Inspector Bruner, you'd better be more specific than that."

Bruner counted off with his fingers. "One. Failure to calculate weight and balance. Two. Failure to comply with basic preflight procedures. Three. Failure to adequately secure passengers and cargo. Not to mention making physical threats to my well being," he finished.

Dusty's mouth opened a fraction. "He threatened you?"

Bruner paused a beat. "Well, in so many words. Said something about knocking me senseless, or something."

If the situation hadn't been so grave, Dusty would have laughed. "Sir, I can assure you that Ralph Olafsen poses no threat to you, nor have I ever known him to make such threats to anyone." Dusty held out his hands in a gesture of placation. "Ralph's a hard man to understand, Inspector. I'm sure it's just a genuine misunderstanding. Please don't let his incongruous ways color your perception of his abilities."

Bruner straightened, as if insulted. "Sticks and stones, Mr. Tucker. I'd never let any such remark color my professional opinion of a pilot's abilities."

Dusty felt the truth was otherwise. Suddenly eager for the conversation to end, he gave a nod of finality. "Glad to hear it, sir. I'll give him some remedial training as soon as he returns from his trip." Standing, he tried to force the conversation into a lighter tone. "Don't worry, inspector, I'll work this problem out."

Bruner folded his hands around his stomach and leaned back, a slight smile betraying his thoughts. "I'm afraid it's too late for that. I'm taking an Emergency Action on Mr. Olafsen's license, pending further investigation."

Dusty's heart went cold. "I assure you Inspector, that won't be necessary."

Bruner waved a hand. "It's already done. Upon his return, Mr. Olafsen is grounded."

"Whoa, slow down there, pardner," Dusty exclaimed. It was his turn to lean over the table. "I don't believe this warrants such drastic measures. If you can be more specific, I can train him back to your *high* standards." He couldn't help but let a little sarcasm ooze into his final words.

Bruner sat up, seemingly eager to play his trump card. "Mr. Tucker, I now consider SEAS on probation."

Dusty slammed a fist to the table. "Now just a damned minute, Bruner! You can't let an isolated incident—"

"Isolated? More and more I'm finding your pilots trained to substandard levels, Mr. Tucker. Between you and me, I'd like to see a little—no, a *lot* of shaping up around here. Starting with training your pilots in standardization of basic pilot procedures."

Such as how to properly kiss the local Fed's ass, Dusty thought with contempt as the man took leave.

* * *

Looking across the table, Holly Innes shook her head. "Congratulations, Ralph. Your big mouth finally caught up with you."

Both Dusty and Jake winced but remained silent, preferring the two foes to duke it out amongst themselves.

In the staff office—*The Ring*, as it had come to be known—the gloves always came off.

Ralph Olafsen looked up from his chair, opposite Holly at the far end of the conference table. "Oh, how you've longed to utter those words, *Capitan* Innes. You must have practiced them all afternoon in the mirror." He grasped the edge of the table. "But don't bury me so fast. We Vikings have weathered worst storms than this."

Holly narrowed her eyes. "I didn't bury you, Ralph. Bruner did. Had I the opportunity, I would have simply suspended you for some remedial training. At least it would look good to the Feds. But it's gone *way* past that."

Ralph looked up. "What do you mean?" He had figured Bruner would do something, but no one had dared tell him what.

All eyes turned to Dusty. The Chief Pilot cocked his head in sympathy, dreading to deliver the blow. "He pulled your license, Ralph. You're grounded pending further investigation."

Ralph jumped up. "What! That bastard can't do that. Not without due process. That's the frickin' constitution!"

Dusty said softly, "On an *Emergency Action* he can."

Jake, sitting between Holly and Ralph, said, "You must have really yanked his chain, Buddy. Dusty says he's never seen Bruner so pissed."

Dusty nodded. "Be lucky you're not heading to the slammer. The Inspector said you threatened to assault him."

Ralph's mouth dropped open. "What? Oh, Christ's fire. I said he needed a good belt at the Red Dog."

Dusty nodded understanding. "Figured it was something like that. Regardless, Ralph, you really ought to think twice before you speak. Especially to a man who holds your career in his hands."

"But—oh, man." Ralph screwed his cap on his head as the revelation hit him. "Misty and I can't go back to living in a bus," he protested.

Holly snorted. Leaning back and crossing her arms, she said, "You should've thought of that before you opened your trap—"

Dusty held up a hand, too late.

Ralph retorted, "More than a belt, Bruner needs a romp in the hay. What do you say, Holly? You need it, he needs it. Maybe lying on your back will keep him off ours."

Holly's face turned crimson. "You bastard! I could sue you for that, if I thought it would do any good. And now your antics got the whole company on probation. You don't need remedial, you need a psychiatrist."

"And you need a—"

"Knock it off, both of you!" Dusty boomed in his Texas foreman voice. "This is getting us nowhere. Holly, you're a goddamned Check Airman. Keep your comments professional."

Eyes lowered, Holly said, "Yes, sir."

"And Ralph, you just shut your yap for once. You're still on the payroll through all this. But it's time for a vacation."

Ralph stared at the table, speechless. For a long moment, silence filled the room. Dusty spread out his hands, palms up. "Look, I hate this too, Ralph; you're one of our best, and you know it. Give me your tickets and I'll keep 'em in my safe, far away from Bruner."

Ralph stood slowly, in no hurry to give away the one thing that put bread on his plate. Digging them from his back pocket, he tossed the ragged, priceless documents on the table.

Dusty slipped them into his shirt pocket. "Things should go fast on this. The Feds take an Emergency Action seriously, especially when property is taken." Dusty looked to Jake, and motioned with his eyes. Jake took the cue and escorted his grounded friend out the door.

Shuffling away, Ralph mumbled, "What the hell? What the hell?"

Jake sympathized. "This just ain't the Last Frontier any more, bud. The sky's filled with rules now. Even way up here."

"And we got to smile as we bend over," Ralph added.

"And we got to smile as we bend over," Jake repeated.

Holly stood and closed the door. She turned to Dusty. "I'm sorry for the outburst." She thumbed over her shoulder at the door. "But that man knows exactly how to get under my skin."

Dusty turned his attention to straightening papers. "You had every right, Holly. His talent for that is why we're in this mess."

Hands on the table, Holly leaned forward. "Is that all? Then why are we on probation? There must be more to it than this isolated incident."

Dusty hesitated. "Well, I didn't plan on bothering to tell you, but there's another incident that sort of warmed him up to all this."

"DC?"

Dusty looked up. "How'd you know?"

"Educated guess. The inspector makes a point of meeting the new pilots, and DC's as green as they come."

"Yeah, well, anyway. Bruner's a perfectionist. He lives to make mountains out of molehills. He just doesn't get it that, up here, his ironclad rules simply can't apply. He rambled on about DC's minor infractions. And I do mean minor, Holly."

"Such as?"

Dusty shrugged. He waved a hand at his papers. "It was nothing. Ridiculous stuff. Things none of us pay attention to. Frayed cargo netting, and not tying down the aircraft immediately after parking. I figured Bruner just wanted to hear himself talk. I assured him I'd do what I could, then forgot about it." Dusty stopped shuffling papers and gazed across the desk. "Guess I should have given DC some remedial, if for nothing more than to appease the Inspector."

Holly straightened and crossed her arms to her chest. "Dusty, he's not just any inspector, he's our Principal Operations Inspector. He has to be seen by his superiors to be doing things. So when he says jump, we don't ask why, we just do." She gazed absentmindedly at the Alaska aeronautical chart adorning the far wall. "Maybe I should ride with DC again."

Dusty shook his head. "What good would it do now?"

"*We'll* be seen to be doing something."

Dusty sighed. "Then I'll do it."

* * *

DC looked up from his magazine as Jake escorted Ralph, slump-shouldered and shuffling like an octogenarian, across the terminal and out the front door. After a minute, Whitakker returned.

DC caught the bush pilot's eye. "Hey, Crash. What's up with—"

"Trip up," Dusty called from behind. He pointed to DC. "You and me are going for a little ride. To Skagway."

Jumping up and joining his boss, DC rubbed his forehead. "Oh, shit. What did I do?"

Strolling back to the office, Dusty smiled. "Nothing, nothing. We just want to keep ol' Inspector Bruner happy."

"What, he thinks I'm a screw-up?"

Dusty shook his head. "He's just being his usual hardball self."

After grabbing the paperwork, the two ambled through Op's and out to the flight line.

"Thought this was Ralph's trip today," DC remarked.

"Not anymore."

As the two walked side by side across the ramp, DC looked quizzically at his boss.

Patting DC on the back, Dusty whispered, "We'll talk enroute."

As he preflighted his bird, DC became keenly aware of Dusty's gaze.

As the old man helped him load the freight, Dusty announced, "Pop quiz." He pointed to the cargo straps. "See that webbing?" DC nodded. "What do you do with it?"

DC turned a skeptical eye to the man. "Is this a trick question?"

"Nope."

"Tie down your cargo with it."

"Outstanding. And what do you do when it's frayed?"

DC rolled his eyes. "Oh, geez. Is that what this is about?"

Dusty shrugged. "Basically."

"Okay. Replace it."

"*Magna cum laude*, my boy."

"Well, if that's the worst Inspector Bruner can tag me for, guess I'm doing pretty good."

Dusty shook DC's shoulder reassuringly. "You are, *cheechacko*. He's a stickler for detail, on the ground and in the air. He likes to think he knows more than you." Dusty gently turned the young pilot to face him. "But don't let him, or anyone, get to you. You know how to fly, DC. Just do your job and don't feed the wild animals any scraps."

DC regarded his boss's face. "Like Ralph did?"

Dusty nodded. "Very perceptive. I'm afraid the only thing greater than Ralph's flying skills is his mouth."

"I've noticed. Don't tell me he did that to Bruner?"

"Among other things. Let's ride."

"This gonna be a checkride?" DC asked.

Dusty nodded. "Officially, yes. But I figure we'll just have a little fun playing over the Juneau Icefield on the way to Skagway. Get you a little more familiar with the *tourista* routes. Ever done steep turns over a glacier?"

DC smiled broadly. "That's the kind of checkride I like."

"Hello, gentlemen," a voice called from behind. The two SEAS pilots cringed, recognizing the false-friendly voice. They turned.

"Hello, Inspector," Dusty replied evenly. "I was just giving Mr. Alva here some additional training, as you recommended. Passing with flying colors so far. We were just about to head up to Skagway and back on another line check."

Bruner nodded. "Glad to hear it. But that won't be necessary. I haven't had a chance to ride with the young man myself. Mind if I cut in on this dance?"

Dusty's gaze went cold, and he gave the inspector a long, pregnant pause. "As a matter of fact, I do. This is an internal company checkride, Inspector, and I don't exactly appreciate being superseded."

Bruner's smile was all teeth. He lay a hand on Dusty's back. "Come now, old friend. No need for such formality. I just thought a little outside advice might do the young man some good."

Dusty crossed his arms and slid away from the man's hand. "Inspector, that's my job, not yours. Don't you have other flying outfits to keep track of?"

Bruner ignored the question. "It's also my job to keep an eye out for potential trouble spots before they crop up into safety problems. And SEAS seems to be having its fair share."

"Inspector, now you're interfering with my training curriculum. This is bordering on harassment."

Bruner's smile vanished. "I hardly think so."

CHAPTER 14: Best Laid Flight Plans

The fifty minute flight to Skagway seemed to DC like a nonstop to Australia.

Inspector Bruner sat in silence beside him, arms crossed, clipboard and *Pilot Inspection and Line Check Form* in lap, a frown pasted on his otherwise stone-faced mug. His eyes followed DC's every move, as if expecting the young pilot to hit some hidden Eject button.

Check Airman Innes times ten, DC thought with dismay.

Once at cruise, Bruner began to drill the pilot on his airplane's numbers.

The grilling, DC thought with annoyance, distracted the Pilot in Command from his primary flying duties, and was therefore technically illegal.

Even so, Bruner never could trip him up. Check Airman Innes' demand that he memorize the operator's manual forward and backward, he realized with relief, had paid off.

Finally the Fed fell silent. After that, little was spoken.

DC made a few lame attempts at conversation, but Bruner's answers remained short and clipped. Worse, he constantly jotted notes on his little form, driving the young pilot crazy with curiosity. DC almost wished the man would continue with the Twenty Questions, or even bark out criticisms like a drill sergeant. At least that way he'd know where Bruner stood.

A dozen heart-pounding minutes of agony later, DC took a deep breath and thought, *fuck it*. Before long, he nearly forgot the man was next to him and kept busy driving.

The tack paid off. On approach to Skagway, he hugged the mountainside and paralleled the tiny dirt strip. Before reaching the end of the box canyon, he deftly reversed course and swooped in. His touchdown, he was glad to see, even earned him a begrudging mumble of "Nice landing" from the Fed.

Back in Juneau, all Bruner mentioned to him were a few items so minor that even the Inspector couldn't find fault. Still, his notebook scribbles seemed to take up nearly half a pad. DC wondered if the comments would find their way back to his employer. Or worse, to Oklahoma City and FAA headquarters.

As he watched the Inspector walk away, DC let out a sigh that shook his entire body. Maybe now the guy would stay off his back for awhile.

But, he wondered, what the hell had happened to poor Ralph?

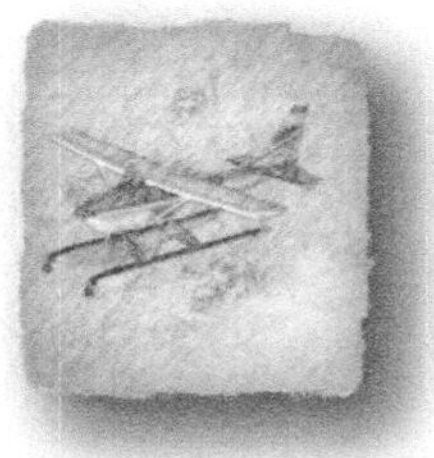

"Calm down, people," Dusty shouted, holding up a hand. He stood behind the dispatcher's long metallic table at the head of the SEAS office. Holly sat next to him. Most of the staff were long gone, but nearly all of SEAS' two dozen pilots had lingered behind to hear the scoop. The rumors of Ralph's demise had flown faster than the company's quickest twin. Though nearly 8 p.m., the sun's twilight rays still poured through the office windows, casting a bluish tint across the room.

On a secretary's desk at the opposite end of the room, DC sat with Allen. Both sipped anxiously from their Dr. Peppers. Through the windows, DC watched the last plane taxi up and park. Its driver jumped out and raced into the office.

The cacophony subsided to a low buzz; the quietest anyone could hope for in a room filled with rowdy pilots.

Dusty cleared his throat. "I know y'all aren't on the clock, so I'll keep this short. The rumors getting back to me today have ranged from ridiculous to absurd. So let's get some things straight up front. Ralph's not in the slammer, nor is he up on murder charges. He hasn't so much as touched anyone, let alone spray an M-16 through the FAA building. And Inspector Bruner is very much alive and well."

"Too damn bad," someone grumbled.

Another said, "But I heard Ralph threatened to kill the asshole."

Dusty replied, "That ain't true. It was just a plain old misunderstanding, which the Inspector later agreed might have been a little blown out of proportion."

"A little blown out of proportion?" one pilot repeated. "You forget to sign your middle initial on a c.g. form and the douche pops you for improper paperwork." Several others grunted agreement.

"So what is it then?" another pilot asked. "Did Bruner fine him because he forget to tip his cap to the asshole?"

"I'm afraid it's worse than that." Dusty glanced at the floor for a moment to collect his thoughts, then continued. "Pending further investigation, Ralph is grounded on an Emergency Action."

DC and Allen traded looks. Murmurs of protest rippled through the room.

Holly stood and said, "I know you're all angry about this. But Inspector Bruner has to do his job as best he sees fit, even if we don't agree with it. You've got to give him the respect of his position."

"Respect *this* position, Bruner," another pilot shouted, bending over and grabbing his rump with both hands. The others nodded agreement.

Holly frowned and sat, giving the floor back to her boss.

Dusty leaned forward. "Now, if y'all are done with the eloquent commentaries, here's the story." He outlined the confrontation, and the state of affairs. When finished, all in the audience wore long faces.

Dusty eyed the pilots. In a lower tone he said, "There's one more thing you should know." He looked to Holly.

Holly raised up and looked slowly about the room, reluctant to break the news. Finally she took a deep breath and spoke. "I have just received word from Inspector Bruner that Southeast Alaska Seaplanes is now officially on probation. One or two more incidents, and the Company's ticket could be pulled."

The room erupted. Several pilots jumped up and shouted at once.

"He can't do that!"

"Guy's fuckin' with our lives, man."

"We can fly circles around that clown."

Dusty pounded the table. In his foreman voice he boomed, "Can it!"

The room quieted.

Holly continued in an even tone. "If his charges go any further, and I think they will, we plan on protesting formally. But then, you have to understand, we'll really be under the FAA's microscope. We have nothing to hide, but we have to be on our best behavior."

Dusty held up a finger. "Listen, guys. You should already know this, but remember: if you're at all uncomfortable with anything—weather, airplane, anything at all—don't go. Be prudent, be professional, and be safe."

"And please," Holly added, "be polite. It doesn't cost anything, and it's what we expect from you as professionals anyway."

The meeting ended. The pilots sauntered out in small groups, talking between themselves.

DC and Allen said little on the walk home. Once inside the apartment, Allen grabbed a beer from the refrigerator and offered his friend one. DC waved it off. "Coke, please."

Drinks in hand, the two sat on the ragged couch and thought.

"Is this the way our careers are going to go?" DC mused aloud. "Get this far, only to be blacklisted by the likes of a *chairborne Federali*?

"Potlatch is just a couple months away."

"Potlatch?" DC asked.

"Didn't anybody tell you?" Allen asked. He gestured with his beer. "At the end of the season, one of the charter companies throws a huge feast. Like the Tlingit's traditional hoedowns. We whoop it up in Skagway, get a hangover and our bonus checks the next morning, and migrate south with the rest of the birds." He looked at his friend. "We've come a long way, *cheechacko*."

DC stared at the wall, blank save for the old aeronautical chart. "I've been here less than half a season, and it seems like a year. God, I can't even remember my old life." He looked at Allen. "We still got a long way to go, too. Plenty of time to get busted. Or worse."

Allen stared at the floor. "Well, I . . . got a plan."

DC raised his brows. "Oh?"

"Some of the guys've been talkin', and—well, here." From his hip pocket, Allen pulled out a dog-eared advertisement from *Conde Naste Traveler* magazine. He unfolded the page and handed it to his friend.

DC eyed the ad. The photo of a bikini-clad island girl smiled back. Piña colada in hand, she lay in a hammock strewn between two palm trees. Beyond stretched a sandy beach and tranquil turquoise surf. Through the cloudless sky above flew a twin engine Grumman Mallard seaplane. The caption read, "The Virgins beckon."

DC smirked. "The Virgin Islands, huh?"

Allen chuckled. "Have to admit, the name's got a certain appeal."

Looking back at the photo of girl and plane, DC said, "She's gorgeous."

"Yeah, and the chick's not bad either."

DC laughed. "That's exactly what I meant!"

Allen explained. "To get to the majors we need twin time, right? No guarantee we'll get it up here." He pointed his beer at the ad for emphasis. "So, I figure, why not have a little fun while we're doing it?"

DC sighed. "Seems like a million miles away. I mean, they're all third world countries down there in the Caribbean, aren't they? Pirates, AK-47-toting guerrillas, no electricity. Do they even speakie-English?"

Allen thought a moment. "Dunno." He slapped his friend's arm for emphasis. "And that's the adventure, ain't it?"

Shaking his head, DC handed the ad back. "Just throw on your backpack and go, huh?"

Allen's eyes, sparkling with the thought of a new adventure, drilled into DC's. "Care to join me?" he asked, an edge of challenge in his voice.

"Hah! Just let me get through this summer alive first." DC had intended it as a light-hearted joke, but both realized the statement for what it was. DC's nervous laugh faded.

The two fell silent.

Suddenly, Allen brightened. "There's only one thing we can do."

DC grinned. "Only one solution to this serious problem we are facing."

In unison the two said, "Climb."

DC jabbed a finger at Allen's chest. "Thunder Mountain, noon. Be there."

Allen jabbed a thumb at the door. "To prepare for this strenuous climb, I think a few drinks at Red Dog are in order." He raised his bottle. "I hereby declare this, Emergency Drunk Pilot Night."

DC cast an awkward glance at his friend. "I got, uh, plans."

Allen raised a brow. "Oh?" DC forced a smile in reply. Allen lowered his bottle. "Oh."

A few minutes later, Allen donned his jacket and walked out. "Have fun," he mumbled.

"You too," DC replied with forced enthusiasm, to a closing door.

* * *

He waited at the Salty Sourdough. And waited. And waited. After an hour and a half, the task of peeling the labels from his beer bottles lost its thrill.

Women! So many conflicting signals. After their magical flight together, how could she forget their date? Musta got busy at Red Dog, he thought. Yeah, that had to be it. She'd call him soon. Explain.

He considered meeting up with the SEAS bunch at Red Dog, but only briefly. Morose over the company's woes, the boys would only serve to drag him down further.

Besides, *she* might be there. He wouldn't want her to think—no, that wouldn't be good. He could stay away. But even as he thought it, he felt the inexorable pull. A moth to flame? He wondered.

"Got that straight," he mumbled to himself.

Draining one last drink, DC paid his tab and left.

* * *

At the Red Dog, Allen sat commiserating with several other SEAS' pilots at a second floor table. From it, he had a perfect view of the ground floor. And Tonya. He spoke little. With every frequent gulp of beer he couldn't help but steal a furtive glance at the flirtatious waitress.

But tonight, she was out of uniform. Tonight, she was playing with her friends from Air Chinook. And Tom Zion.

Allen watched it all. The broad smiles, the sly glances, the seemingly innocent brush of elbow across breast. Both were experts at this game.

Allen felt a nudge. "Ain't that right?"

He looked around. "Huh?"

The pilot seated next to him said, "I've always said that it was just a matter of time before the Feds snagged Ralph."

Allen sneered. "Oh. Yeah, you're always saying that, Brendon." He slapped a none-too-friendly palm across the man's back. "Congratulations on your prophesy. You must be proud." He drained his beer and stood.

Brendon grabbed Allen's sleeve and pulled him back down. "Hey, there. No need to get testy. We're all on the same side, pal." He pointed to Allen's empty glass. "Here, I'm buying next round."

Just then, the noise level dropped noticeably. All eyes at the table instinctively turned to the door.

In shuffled Ralph. Jake followed. Remaining obediently outside the swinging doors sat Eluk.

As the wing-clipped pilot made his way through the crowd and upstairs, several hands patted him reassuringly on the back. But most patrons simply chose to stay out of his way.

One pilot offered his seat. Ralph slumped into the chair, not bothering to thank the man. The crowd slowly resumed its cheerful roar, but the pilot table resembled a still life painting. Armed with a quick round of pints from the bar, Jake handed a drink to his friend. Absentmindedly Ralph took it. Jake raised his glass.

"To the best goddamn bush pilot Alaska has ever seen."

"Hear, hear," rang the others with a hoist of their mugs.

Ralph downed half his glass. The table once again fell silent.

"Fuckin' Feds," one pilot spouted. A few grumbled agreement.

Allen leaned across the table, his eyes squinted into devious slits. "Hey, Ralph. Didn't the Lord once say, 'Vengeance is mine'? What goes around comes around. Eh?"

"Oh, no," Jake said emphatically, pulling Ralph back as if to protect him from the thought. "No, no, no. Not this time. Bruner will get his eventually."

But Jake's concern was unfounded; as Ralph looked up, the familiar spark of conspiracy was gone from his pupils.

"Shit." Allen sat back and crossed his arms.

Another hand patted Ralph on the back. Greg Mastis scooted up a chair and joined them, a conspiratorial smile across his bearded mug.

The ADF&G man said, "Good news, guys. I talked them into sending the bears down to Petersburg on SEAS this Friday, like you said. Ralph, looks like you're on for *Dirty Harry*."

Ralph stared blankly, as if the man had spoken Mandarin.

Jake said, "Guess you're the only one in town that ain't heard the story."

"Heard what?"

As Jake filled him in, Greg's smile wilted.

Allen took one more swig of his brew and slammed the mug down. "'*Harry's*' gotta fly. I'll do it."

Jake shook his head. "No, Allen, this could get you busted, too. You got an airline career ahead of you. I'll do it."

For the first time that night, Ralph came out of his self-induced coma. He gripped the table's edge with both hands and pushed back. "No, my friends. If I'm going down, I'm going down with guns blazing.'

Jake held up a cautioning hand. "No way, Ralph. You're grounded. If Bruner got wind, he could flat out toss you in jail. I'll do it."

Nostrils flaring, Ralph stood. His chest, his posture, his whole being ballooned until he took on the proud look of a conquering king. Mug raised in salute, he peered down at his subjects.

"Men, no Viking worthy of his horns would send others to fight his own battle. *Dirty Harry* is on." Ralph turned and marched down the stairs.

"*Hoo boy*, here we go," Jake said, then jumped up and followed.

The others watched as Ralph and Jake weaved their way through the crowd and out the door.

"God help us," Mastis mumbled.

"We're gonna need it," Allen added.

Outside, loyal foot soldier Eluk joined Ralph and Jake and dutifully took point.

CHAPTER 15: Shell Game

The week dragged on.

At home and feeling useless, Ralph struggled daily to make sense of the tragedy befalling him. Besides Misty's comforting massages, his only solace was the knowledge that, with *Dirty Harry*, he'd at least go out with a bang. The other conspirators knew their parts, and could hardly wait to exact revenge.

DC had all but given up on his calls to Stephanie. Moreover, every time he picked up the phone, he wound up calling Tonya instead. But, the elusive Tlingit had once again disappeared.

"Must be too busy," he said to himself, for the hundredth time, it seemed. He hung up. After a long, hot shower, he trudged off to bed.

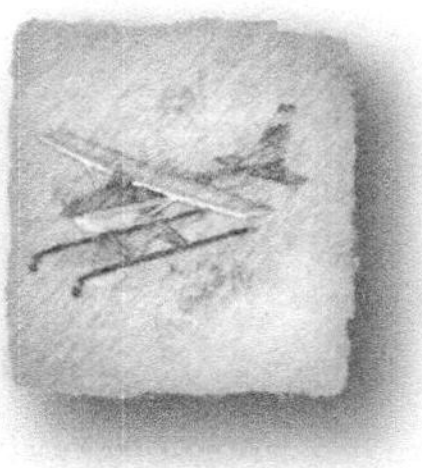

"Mayday, mayday!"

At first, DC thought he was having a nightmare.

Allen pounded on his door. "Wake up, man. We gotta get to the airport, pronto."

DC moaned. Through two slits in his eyelids, he looked at the clock. "Shit, Allen, its five a.m. I don't fly till eight. What's up?"

Allen cracked open the door and held up a newspaper. "*Dirty Harry's* in trouble."

Squinting from across the room, DC read. *Three Little Bears Set Course for Uncertain Future*, touted the *Juneau Empire*.

Beneath the headline read the sub caption, *ADF&G and DPS Wildlife Troopers still searching for clues to poacher identity.*

Allen said, "Listen to this. 'The *Empire* has learned that the *Three Little Bears*, as the cubs have come to be called, are set to be shipped out to Petersburg for destruction on SEAS' Airlines at 6:30 a.m. tomorrow morning'." Allen dropped the paper to his side. "This was last night's edition."

"Jesus," DC exclaimed, jumping up. Shoving a foot into his jeans, he said, "How the hell did they find out?"

"Dunno. But Juneau Airport's gonna be a circus."

Sliding on his work boots, DC added, "Yeah, dancing bears and all."

* * *

Awaiting her flight to Seattle, Stephanie stared out at the runway from the window of Sky Harbor, Terminal Two. Sitting at the very same gate where she'd said good-bye to DC, her mind wandered to what lay ahead. This was either the smartest or the dumbest thing she'd ever done, she thought. Well, she'd know the answer to that soon enough.

* * *

The first sign of trouble came when they spotted the transmission tower from the local news van stretching skyward. Then they heard the chanting. As they rounded the corner on Shell Simmons Drive at full gallop, DC and Allen took in the whole absurd picture.

Outside the gates to the SEAS' ramp, mayhem reigned. With TV news cameras churning away, protesters sported picket signs and chanted, "Free the

Little Three! Free the Little Three!" Like a row of linebackers, security guards blocked the fence, poised to snag any would-be trespassers.

The two pilots threaded their way through the crowd. DC's magnetic card opened the gate, but a guard stopped them inside.

The man checked each pilot's I.D. against the list on his clipboard, then marked off his name. As the guard checked DC, Allen peeked over the man's shoulder and scanned for Ralph's name. No mark appeared next to it.

As they trotted across the ramp, Allen whispered, "Crash must've smuggled Ralph in." Despite the dark overcast, each donned his shades. Discretely, they searched the ramp for signs of Ralph.

Once inside the office, they found Jake alone, staring out the window and sipping coffee.

Sliding up, Allen said, "Ralph and Greg gone already?"

Jake sipped his coffee. "No. They couldn't sneak out before the mob arrived. They're hiding in the fuel house."

Allen nodded. "Where are the cubs?"

Jake nodded to the farthest plane. "Already loaded in Ralph's amphib."

"Any witnesses?" DC asked.

"A couple guys were snapping shots outside the fence. But that was a ways off. Dunno how much they could see."

Allen frowned. "With telephotos? Plenty."

"That's why we couldn't chance Ralph flying out."

Allen lamented, "And now he'll be on the *News at Six*."

Jake nodded. He glanced at his watch. "And 'Holly Her Holy All-Mightiness' is due in thirty."

Allen moaned. "The sooner we get them out of here, the better."

DC turned to Jake. "Any ideas?" he asked.

Jake grimaced. "A few. All suck."

For a moment the three remained silent.

Finally, Jake said, "We need a diversion. A little bit of misdirection."

DC scratched his head. "Hmm. Like the guy that makes you guess which shell the ball's under."

For the first time that morning, Jake grinned. He snapped his fingers. "Yeah. Yeah, exactly." He scratched his stubbled chin, then turned and eyed DC. "How much you weigh?" he asked.

* * *

John Bolt hated planes. No gears, no stick shifts, no visible means of support. But worst of all, no control. Grabbing the boarding pass, Bolt turned away from the gate agent. He scowled. Center seat. Coach. And goddamn connections in Seattle and Juneau. Well, at least he saved some dough on his flight to Fairbanks.

Bolt made his way down the jetway and onto the plane. Trudging down the aisle, he spotted his assigned seat. Sure enough, two men the size of pro wrestlers flanked it. He ran a finger inside the neckline of his K-mart collar, and scanned the rest of the cabin. He spied another empty seat farther back, graced by the presence of a lovely young redhead in the window seat. He smoothed back his hair and strutted down the aisle. Perhaps he could bag two birds with one trip.

But before he reached it, another man coming up the aisle in the opposite direction slid into the seat. The redhead smiled and pecked him on the cheek. Bolt stopped.

"Sir, take your assigned seat please," came a female voice from behind. He turned to see a petite flight attendant staring up at him with a stern look. He frowned. *Damn bitch*, he thought. Reluctantly, he backed up the aisle and wedged himself between the two behemoths.

Bolt felt like a Holstein wedged in the back of his rig and being led to slaughter.

* * *

The three rifled through the warehouse, knocking over crates and boxes and tossing mail bags aside.

"I know I've seen 'em here somewhere," Jake said, shoving a mail cart. "They've been here for years." He bolted upright and shouted, "There! Sky kennels."

The three waded through another pile of boxes and reached them. The square, plastic-and-metal grill cages, DC realized, resembled those used for toting small dogs and cats. But these were much larger. Designed to carry large dogs. Or small bear cubs.

Jake slid the first one out and eyed it triumphantly.

"Perfect," he exclaimed. He blew off a layer of dust from the top. The cloud watered their eyes and filled their nostrils with a musty scent. DC and

Allen coughed. Ignoring the irritation, Jake opened the first cage and stood back. He held an open palm toward the opening. "Sir, your chariot awaits."

DC exchanged looks with Allen. Both pilots eyed Jake questioningly.

With a broad grin, Jake said, "*Cheechacko*, you've been promoted to orphan bear cub. Hop in."

DC's jaw dropped. "Are you shitting me?"

Allen laughed. "Come on, DC. It's for a good cause."

DC reluctantly dropped to his hands and knees and peered in. A dank odor of some unknown animal added to the cacophony in his nose.

"You guys are nuts," he proclaimed, squeezing through the door and into the cage. He looked up through the top opening at the other two pilots, grinning back. "What if they see me?" he asked.

"We'll keep the opening away from them," Jake replied.

Allen patted the top. "But just in case, DC, better give 'em a growl or two."

"Oh, Jesus. I don't even know what a bear cub sounds like."

"And shake the cage a bit, too," Jake added. "Remember, you're being sent to the gallows."

"I can't believe this," DC groused, as Jake slammed the door shut.

Along with two empty kennels and the day's mail, they loaded DC onto a dolly and wheeled him out to the plane. The chants of the protesters grew louder.

"All right, DC," whispered Allen. "You're on."

DC shook the cage as best he could, and tried a low growl.

"Jesus, you sound like a skunk in heat," Jake whispered. "Louder."

DC took a deep breath and roared, kicking the cage simultaneously. The musty smell of the cage threw him into a coughing fit. Muffled by the box walls, it nearly sounded like a wounded animal.

"Not half bad," Allen encouraged.

"Hey, pilots," a protester yelled. "How does it feel to be flying three innocent bear cubs to their deaths?"

"Bite me," Jake yelled back, smirking. "Bite me very much." He turned to Allen. "That oughta make good copy for the *News at Six*."

Out of sight from the crowd, the two hefted DC's sky kennel into the cargo hold.

Jake said, "Now they don't know which cup the ball's under."

Cargo lashed down, the two untied the plane.

Jake hopped in. He deftly pumped the primer with his left hand, as his right flipped the wobble pump and cracked the throttle.

Allen opened the passenger door and leaned in. "Godspeed, man," he said.

Jake winked. "Aye aye. Clear prop."

Allen stepped away. Before closing the door, he looked back at the terminal. His eyes widened. "Holy shit," he exclaimed, pointing. "Traffic twelve o'clock, closing fast!"

Jake looked up to see Holly marching toward them from the terminal. He gave the control yoke a frustrated swat. "*Damn it all*," he cursed. He looked to Allen. "What's your first flight today?"

"Angoon mail run."

Jake hopped out. "Well, now it's the death march to Petersburg."

Allen quickly replaced him. "What are you going to do?"

Jake shook his head. "No clue. I'm wingin' it." Before closing the door, he nodded in the direction of the mob. "Ralph needs some cover. Give them a good blast."

Allen smiled. "With pleasure." Peering over his shoulder and imitating Yogi Bear's voice, he said, "Ready back there, Boo Boo?"

DC muttered, "Growl, motherfuckin' growl. Get me outta here."

"As soon as we get rid of Mr. Ranger Sir, Boo Boo. Clear prop!" Allen flipped up the ignition switch, counted three turns of the prop, then thumbed the magnetos and fired up.

* * *

Upon hearing the engine start, Holly turned her head. Jake trotted up. "Morning," he called, with as much innocent cheer as he could muster.

"That it is, Mr. Whitakker," Holly answered flatly. "Your powers of observation never fail to amaze me."

Jake chuckled. "And I also observe, Miss Innes, that you're looking quite, er, nice, today. New hairdo?"

Holly blinked, touched the ends of her locks unconsciously, and even managed a shy smile. "As a matter of fact, yes. How'd you know?"

Lucky fucking guess, he didn't say. "You may not believe it, but I always notice things like that." He grabbed her shoulder and turned her from the ramp. He walked her back toward the terminal. "Listen, there's something I need to discuss with you. In the office."

She jabbed a thumb over her shoulder. "Who's that?"

"Allen. Gave him my Petersburg run."

"The bears?"

"Yeah."

She glanced back. "Poor things." She shook her head in disgust. "When man mistreats innocent animals . . . ."

"I know. I, uh, didn't have the stomach for it."

Wearing the faintest trace of a smile, she looked up at him. "Or maybe you didn't want your mug villainized on the evening's news?"

"Heh, heh. Cute. But to be honest, I've flown bears around before. And they stink to high heaven." Jake heard Allen gun the plane behind him.

Before Holly could look back, Jake spun to face her, grabbing her shoulders. He glanced at the plane in time to see the prop's blast whip up a cloud of dust and assault the mob at the fence.

Like a kicked anthill, people scattered. Reporters, protesters, guards, all shielded their eyes from the gale. Hats and signs flew, camera tripods toppled, even the TV cameraman turned from the blast to protect his equipment.

Emerging from the fuel shack, shades and jacket hood covering his face, Ralph strolled out to his cub-laden airplane. Similarly disguised, Greg Mastis followed close behind.

Jake looked back into her eyes. He hesitated, noticing for the first time how deep blue they really were. "Um, Holly?" he stammered. "Maybe this isn't the time to say this, but, well, those bears got me thinking about life and all that, and I . . . . What the hell. I think you're a really pretty lady."

She rolled her eyes. "Oh Christ, Jake. I'll never be one of your conquests."

"No, listen. I'm serious about this," he replied, glancing behind her.

Allen taxied out. As the sound of his engine faded, the mob beyond the fence slowly restored order.

Jake gave a sheepish shrug. "I guess I play it up with the others around here, all that macho single guy stuff. But all I really want is . . ." He fumbled for the right words.

A look of bemusement on her face, she arched her brows, inviting him to continue.

"I mean, I'm lonely, Holly. And you must be, too."

"Oh, come on," she said, shrugging him away and marching back to the office.

He ran to catch up with her. Behind, he heard Ralph's engine roar to life.

Holly whirled around. "Now who the hell is *that!*"

Shielding her from view, Jake grabbed her and planted a long, deep kiss on her lips.

Wide-eyed, she struggled to break free. But he held her tight. Slowly, she relaxed. Confident in his success, he loosened his grip. Wriggling free, she hauled back and punched him in the gut.

"Oomph," he cried, doubling over.

She shook a finger at him. "Don't you think for one minute. *One minute!*" She spun and marched into the terminal.

Mouth twisted into a grimace of agony and triumph, Jake turned and gave a discreet 'thumbs up' to Ralph's plane, taxiing out.

Cheshire smile protruding from beneath his hood, Ralph returned the gesture.

* * *

Out of his sky kennel and strapped into the copilot's seat, DC scanned the Petersburg Airport ramp while Allen taxied in. "Looks clear," he announced. "No reporters that I can see."

Allen nodded. "Phase One nearly complete." He parked. The two pilots hopped out.

Petersburg's hunched, aging SEAS agent, draped in well-worn plaid shirt and scraggly white beard, shuffled up and opened the cargo door.

"Hi, Skip," Allen said with a wave.

The old man glanced at him. "Foley." He cast a quizzical gaze at DC, pausing for several long, confused seconds. "And you are?"

"Name's Daniel Alva. Call me DC."

"*Cheechacko*," Allen added. "Uh, out here learning the route."

Not bothering to shake hands, Skip looked back to his clipboard. "Gettin' younger every year," he remarked.

"Or you're getting older," Allen replied.

Skip looked up sharply, with a gaze that reminded DC of a hatchet murderer. Slowly the wild look softened, and a thin smile crept across his lips. "Heh, heh. Could be, sonny. Could be." Methodically, Skip checked off each item listed on his cargo manifest. "Lessee, priority mail, check, standard mail, check. Hmm," he said, scratching his kinked whiskers. "Says here, ADF&G gets three bear cubs."

DC glanced at Allen. "Oh. Um, that must be a misprint."

Allen peered over the Skip's shoulder and pointed to the manifest. "Yep. S'posed to say three bear cub *cages*."

The old man paused again, taking plenty of time to let the point soak in. He said finally, "Don't matter none to me, long as I get paid." He held the clipboard out. "Sign here."

Allen made a scribble that would make a physician proud.

The three loaded the empty cages onto a dolly and wheeled them into the terminal. Inside, a man dressed in ADF&G colors greeted them. DC and Allen stiffened.

Skip said, "Thomas, here's your cargo. Seems a bit of a waste of the taxpayers' money to be flying empty sky kennels all over the countryside."

Thomas the F&G officer stared at the cages, his expression frightfully unreadable to the pilots.

He cleared his throat. "Well, that's big government for you. But, that's the order. Three empty bear cages. Yep."

Skip held out his clipboard. "Sign here."

Thomas jotted his name, then wheeled the dolly around. Over his shoulder, he winked at the boys and said, "My regards to Officer Mastis."

"Yes, sir!" they chorused.

"Enjoy your kennels," DC added.

Behind Skip's back, the two pilots exchanged a discreet *high five*.

* * *

Nestled in the bushes outside the fence of the Petersburg General Aviation ramp, a lone man kneeled by his sturdy but well-worn aluminum case. His job finished, he unscrewed the telephoto lens and placed it in the foam cradle inside. He slipped tripod and camera into their respective cutouts and snapped the lid shut. A smirk appeared on his lips as he stood and brushed his hands.

"Well, well, well. Curiouser and curiouser. The case of the missing Three Little Bears."

* * *

Ralph spied the cabin, hidden just inside the treeline and marked by a dinghy tied ashore.

From 500' up, he circled the lagoon, judging wind and wave. Settling on a northerly approach, he gently touched down. He idled up to the shoreline, hopped out into ankle-deep water and backed the flying boat aground.

Greg Mastis jumped out and helped. Once tied down, the two opened the cargo door. Greg inspected the cages.

"Kids okay?" Ralph asked.

"Hmm. Still lookin' a little groggy, but none the worse for wear." He turned to his pilot and smiled. "Must've been your lousy inflight meal service."

Ralph adjusted his spectacles. "Well, we ran out of peanuts." He gestured to the log cabin. "But I've got something to make up for it."

They hauled the cages, one by one, to the front of the house. Greg walked up the stairs and jiggled the knob. "Jesus, Ralph, they've got it locked." He shook his head in disbelief. "They must be the only assholes in the Alaskan wilderness that lock their cabin."

"Like it's downtown Newark," Ralph said, nodding. "Look under the rock by the mat."

Greg kneeled down, rolled the rock aside and grabbed the key. "Guess Mack figures the wilderness law of helping the lost and starving don't apply to Jersey hotshots."

"Well, today it does. How're the supplies inside?"

Greg held up his hands. "Whoa, Olafsen. This is your horse. I don't intend to add 'Breaking and Entering' to my resume. Being your accomplice is bad enough. The door's locked, and that means I stay out. I'll help you haul them up the stairs, but that's it." He tossed his partner the key and grinned. "But if you have the mind to, *Goldilocks*, feel free."

Hiking up the stairs, Ralph said in high falsetto, "And this cabin is *juuust* right." Though having flown the Doyle brothers to their hunting cabin a dozen times, he thought as he turned the key, he'd never once been invited in. But then, he'd never lost sleep over the fact, either.

Ralph surveyed the room and smiled. Perfect.

Lining the walls between numerous trophy heads were dozens of shelves, bulging with supplies. Mason jars, bags of sugar, flour and cookies were stacked to the beams. Plastic garbage bags concealed from wild animals the scent of some of the more aromatic delectables.

Ralph stepped in and set to work. Whistling the tune to *Winnie the Pooh*, he slid his arm along the shelves. The groceries toppled to the floor. The highest shelf of supplies he left intact. “Think I’ll leave that for my guests,” he said to himself.

Turning to the pile, Ralph ripped open several garbage bags and sprinkled the contents across the floor boards.

“Winnie the Pooh, Winnie the Pooh,” he sang while scattering some Cheerios with his toe, “Chubby little cubby all stuffed with fluff.”

He opened a half-gallon honey jar and poured it over the pile. With a spoon, he flicked the sweet nectar across the walls, the ceiling and support beams. He dropped the jar in the middle of the floor.

“Silly, willy, nilly old bear,” he finished, stepping back.

Licking his hands, he surveyed the room. “A masterpiece,” he concluded with a nod. “A goddamned masterpiece.”

One last task remained. Stepping gingerly around the heaping mess, he made his way over to the gun rack above the door. He lifted off the rifle and checked the chamber. He shook his head.

“*Tisk, tisk.* Leaving a loaded rifle around for the kids to find.”

He ejected each cartridge and replaced them with his own shells, specially modified by Jake for the occasion. He set the gun back in its cradle and stepped out onto the front porch. He spotted Mastis, kneeling by the shoreline.

Ralph cupped his hands and shouted, “Send in the clowns!”

CHAPTER 16: Goldilocks Meets Dirty Harry

"Trip up," Dusty called, holding up a manifest.

DC and the other pilots looked up from their gab session.

Dusty read. "Float trip. A Mr. Mack Doyle, party of two, out here on a supply run. Drop off at their private summer chateau." Dusty looked up at the group and grinned.

"Special request for Mr. Jake Whitakker."

Trading looks with Allen, DC snickered.

Jake stood and returned the grin. "With pleasure," he replied.

With raised brow, Dusty handed him the manifest. "Oh? You *want* to fly the Mack and Mike team? Any reason for this change of heart?"

Jake dismissed the thought with a wave of his hand. "Hey, you gotta feel sorry for poor ol' Mack. He's got it tough. No friends up here. Wife miles away. No one to tuck him in at night but his brother and . . . bears."

DC, Allen and the others suppressed a chuckle.

Dusty eyed Jake skeptically. "Yeah, fishing all summer long. I can hear the violins now."

* * *

John Bolt spotted the hot young blonde at the Seattle gate and sidled up behind her in line. Perhaps he could bag two birds after all, he thought. He checked her out: long hair, pale green eyes, perky tits, hot ass. Probably ditzy as hell. His kind of woman. The chick reached the gate agent, and John edged closer to listen in.

The woman glanced at the girl's ticket. "You're a through-passenger from Phoenix, Stephanie. You're already seated in 11A. Do you mind sitting in an emergency exit row?"

The chick shook her head. "Oh, no, that's fine. Thanks."

"Thank you," the agent replied, handing back her ticket. She turned to Bolt. "May I help you?"

Bolt stepped up. "Yeah. I'd, uh, like to change my seat to an emergency exit row if I can. Aisle seat if you got it." With raised brows the gate agent looked up. Bolt's eyes darted about as he shifted feet. "Yeah, uh, I'm an off-duty pilot, you see, and I don't trust those regular passengers to help out in an emergency, if you know what I mean." He winked.

The gate agent's smile remained fixed. "Wow, I've never seen a pilot with a beard before. And a nonrev flying on a full-fare ticket at that. Guess I should buy a lottery ticket."

What the hell's a nonrev? he thought. But before he could react, she thrust the reissued ticket in his hand. "Here you go, 11C . . . *Captain*."

Bolt smiled at her. "Thanks, honey. You're doing a good job."

He could swear she sneered as she turned from him and barked, "Next!"

At the Juneau Airport Pond, Jake whistled cheerfully while loading the Doyles' excessive cargo onto the float plane. Eluk sat dockside, occasionally sniffing a bag or box before Jake whisked it away into the cargo hold.

Floatplane loaded and preflighted, Jake sat contentedly on the dock, a lazy arm draped around his dog.

Driving the ancient company pickup, a ramper pulled up and dropped the Doyles off next to the plane.

"Glad you could join us," Jake said.

Mack took his cigar out of his mouth and pointed to Eluk. "S'pose he's going too?"

Jake nodded. "I need my copilot."

Taking one last drag, Doyle flicked the stogie into the water. "Well, let's get on with it then." He shuffled resignedly to the door of the plane, his brother shadowing him.

"Sure." Jake slapped his leg, and Eluk hopped up onto the float and into the cabin. He quickly nestled into a comfortable pile of the Doyles' supplies in back.

Frowning, Mack sat in the second row behind the pilot. "You know, he gets hair all over my stuff when he does that," he grumbled halfheartedly. His brother slid into the seat next to Jake.

Priming the fuel pump with his hand, Jake stole a glance at his aft passenger. "Don't worry, he's not lying on your prom dress."

"Hmph," came the reply in back.

Jake looked at him. 'You guys aren't exactly animal lovers, are you?"

"I am," Mike exclaimed.

"Shut up, Mike," Mack growled.

Jake cranked the engine.

Over the roar of the pistons, Mack said, "Sure we love 'em. For breakfast, lunch *and* dinner."

And what goes around comes around, Jake thought.

* * *

Groggy from the tranquilizer, the female cub staggered from her cage and into the room. She sniffed her strange surroundings.

With widened eyes, she let out a roar. She bounded over to join her brothers, already ransacking the pile of human food. At first she sniffed, then licked, then devoured the smorgasbord. Between grunts of pleasure, the three gorged themselves on the goodies. Their state of gastronomic bliss continued until the last crumb was licked from the floor.

Worked into a frenzy over the bounty, the three sniffed the air for more delectables. The scent of honey seemed to beckon from all around. Their keen sense of smell led them to the highest shelf. First one then the other bear stood and pawed at the shelf. Unable to reach, one brother stepped with his forepaws on the first shelf and tried to climb. The board snapped and crashed to the floor. With a roar, the bruin stepped back.

His brother, taller by a few inches, reached the next shelf, with the same disastrous result.

Determined, the sow hopped onto the kitchen table and stood. She leaned toward the top board, only to have the wooden table collapse beneath her weight.

The smaller brother spotted a nearby log pole and began to climb. He shinnied up and pawed at the goodies. Using his hind legs as support, he swiped at the food with his forepaws. His claws dug into the wooden shelf. He lost his grip on the pole and swung away. For a moment, he swayed back and forth like the arm of a grandfather clock.

Shelf, bear and all toppled to the ground, and the feast began anew.

Excited by the treasures, the three cubs began a frantic search of the cabin for more morsels.

Claws and jaws left no cabinet, no door, no piece of furniture untouched.

*   *   *

Putting on his best gameshow host demeanor, Bolt slid into the seat next to her.

With those intoxicating green eyes she looked up at him, flashed a shy smile then returned her gaze back out the window.

As the plane began its takeoff roll, he noticed the pretty young thing tighten her grip on the armrest. He smiled. Perfect opening.

"First time flyer?" he asked.

She looked up. "Actually, no. You'd think I'd be used to it by now. My boyfriend's a pilot."

Bolt cringed inwardly at the word "boyfriend." The committed ones were always quick to slip it in. But hey, that just added spice to the chase.

"Boyfriend, huh? He must really be special if you're flying all the way to Juneau to see him."

The woman groaned. "To be honest, I'm not even sure if we're still together. I caught him with—I mean, I have to be sure about—oh, I don't even know what I'm doing here."

"Sounds like quite a story."

She rolled her sexy green eyes. "Got a few hours?"

Bolt glanced at his watch and beamed. "As a matter of fact, I do."

She laughed. Then started to sniffle.

Bolt took the golden opportunity to offer her his only-slightly-used hanky. What was it about airplane flights that made people spill their guts to total strangers? Same thing with the hitchhikers he'd picked up over the years. By the time they touched down in Alaska, he'd have her crying on his shoulders. Perhaps he could give her a little solace in a hotel room as well. What the hell. He could afford a little side trip to Juneau.

He offered his right hand. For occasions like this, he always used the intro made famous in James Bond films.

"The name's Bolt. John Bolt."

The woman took it and shook. "I'm Stephanie. Stephanie Boulette."

Laying a hand on the young woman's wrist, Bolt narrowed his eyes. "Now, Stephanie," he said in a soothing voice, "tell me all about your stray man."

* * *

Hopping off the float and pulling the Beaver ashore, Jake searched the forest for signs of his comrades. He'd already seen their plane, parked down channel in a well hidden cove. A fake bird call directed his gaze to the bushes to the right of the cabin. He spotted Ralph, sticking an upturned thumb through the bushes. Greg Mastis' head appeared beside him. Jake smiled and gave a faint nod.

"All clear, Mr. Doyle, sir," Jake called back to the airplane. "Can't get your footsies wet now."

Mack stepped out onto the float. "You're just as smartass as that Ralph Olafsen guy. Think with what I pay you guys you'd be a little more sincere about your respect."

"Oh, I have plenty of respect for big game hunters, sir," Jake said in such a menacing and sarcastic way that Mack looked up at him with a suspicious gaze. He stepped ashore, followed, as always, by his little brother. The two ambled toward the cabin.

"Hold on there, boys," Jake said. "You don't pay me enough to sit on your ass while I unload."

With a little more grumbling, Mack complied. Rather, he directed his brother to comply.

Jake opened the cargo hold. Eluk stood, tail wagging and ready to jump out. Jake held up a hand and whispered, "Stay, Boy! Get in front." Jumping forward, Eluk whimpered and lay down, head on paws, eyes drooped in dejection.

Whitakker removed each bag of cargo and handed it to Mike, who dutifully stacked them on shore. Nearing the last load, they heard a high whining sound come from the vicinity of the cabin that made them stop.

Mack gave Jake a puzzled look. Jake met his gaze with seemingly innocent eyes. But beneath the irises ran a trace of the coldest ice.

"You have guests?" Jake asked.

Mack glanced between pilot and cabin several times. After a moments' pause, he walked apprehensively toward the door.

"Hey, Mike, better go help your brother," Jake said.

"Why? He knows how to open a damn door."

"Well, in the woods you never want to leave a man alone."

"Yeah, whatever," Mike said, running to catch up with his brother. Mack produced a key from his pocket, unlocked the cabin and stepped in. Mike followed.

Ralph and Greg emerged from the bushes.

Leaning an elbow on the plane's tail, Jake said to them, "The moment of truth."

A moment later, the three spectators heard a loud roar.

"Jesus Mary and Joseph!" Mack cried.

With a blood-curdling scream, Mike sprinted out of the cabin, across the beach and into the icy water, not stopping until waist deep. There he remained, frozen in shock.

A rifle shot rang in their ears. Mack stumbled backward onto the porch, rifle in hand, tripping on the porch planking and tumbling down the steps. On impact the gun went off again, straight in the air. Coughing up dust, Mack flailed in the dirt like a turtle on its back.

The cubs rushed out, screeching. The last one, the largest bruin, stood on his hind legs and let out one long roar. From his prone position, Mack aimed at the creature and fired. The report sent him scurrying to join his siblings, already escaping into the forest.

The gunshots brought Eluk out of the plane.

"*Heel!*" Jake ordered.

Eluk sat. Spotting the bears, he whimpered, pining to chase, but staying close to his master.

Mack scrambled to his feet. Mouth agape, eyes blazing in terror, he looked at Jake.

Still leaning casually on the tail, Whitakker said with a smirk, "Friends of yours?"

Mack Doyle's eyes slowly filled with recognition. His entire face screwed up until it nearly snarled like the bears, his wrinkled skin turning crimson. He stood hunched over like a troll, eyes drilling holes of hate into Jake's skull. Doyle pointed a shaky finger at the pilot.

"You," he growled. "You did this."

Jake folded his arms. "Actually, you did this to yourself."

"Whitakker, you goddamned mother—" Cocking the rifle, Doyle marched toward Jake.

Jake held up a hand. "Jesus, Doyle!" He cast a nervous glance at Ralph, who nodded reassuringly. Eluk stood and growled.

Doyle raised the gun toward Jake.

Back hunched and hairs bristled, Eluk raced toward the attacker.

"*Eluk!*" Jake yelled, too late.

Switching his aim to the attacking dog, Doyle fired. The blank gave a kick and a flash of flame, but his target remained unscathed. A look of confusion on his face, Doyle fumbled for a reload.

But by then the Malamute was on him. Eluk lunged at the attacker's throat. Doyle turned just in time and the dog caught his shirt collar, ripping the cloth half off his chest. Eluk settled for a pant leg.

Ignoring the dog, Mack charged. Grabbing the rifle by the barrel, he hoisted it high over his head to swing.

Even through the ringing in his ears, Jake could hear the sizzle of burning flesh as the barrel, heated by the three blank shots, burned into Doyle's hands.

Doyle screamed, dropped the gun and fell to his knees, hands hugged to chest.

Jake walked up and grabbed the rifle. He tossed it aside.

Standing over Mack, he said to him, "Children shouldn't play with guns. Especially ones who've been naughty."

Another gun appeared, this one Greg's service revolver, aimed at Mack's head.

"Mackinaw Aloysius Doyle, you are under arrest for attempted murder, assault with a deadly weapon, and about eighty five counts of poaching. You have the right to remain silent. If you waive your right—"

"He doesn't," Jake said, and let fly with a haymaker punch to Mack's jaw that sent the poacher sprawling.

* * *

"Just key the mike there, and I'll tell you what to say," Ralph instructed his "copilot."

Mastis cocked his head in annoyance. "We do use radios in the field, you know."

"Just checking."

Returning to Juneau from their mission, Ralph knew the tower would be open by now. The controllers knew him personally, some were even occasional drinking buddies, and would recognize his voice with the first syllable spoken. But they were officially employees of the FAA as well, and Ralph didn't want them wondering what an unlicensed pilot was doing burning holes through the Alaskan skies.

He just hoped they wouldn't bother training their powerful binoculars on his bird when they heard Mastis' unfamiliar voice.

But then, that was why he'd taken the extra precaution of sitting the F & G man in the left seat—normally the pilot's seat—and he'd thrown the Beaver's control yoke over to the right side where he sat, ostensibly a passenger.

Ralph tucked his head deeper beneath the hood of his jacket.

"Do it," he commanded.

Mastis looked once at his buddy, took a deep breath and held the mike to his lips. He tentatively keyed the mike. After a moments' hesitation he said, "Um, Juneau Tower, SEAS Twenty-Three, over, uh, at Colt's Neck Island, inbound with, er, Information Tango." Letting go of the mike switch he added, "Whatever the hell all that gobbledygook means."

Ralph beamed. "Perfect. Like a goddamned Mynah bird."

* * *

Up in the tower, the controller raised an eyebrow at the unfamiliar voice and its slightly strange delivery, and peered west toward the checkpoint. With his field glasses, he searched for the inbound.

"Sounds like SEAS has another *cheechacko* on the loose," he remarked to his cohort, working Ground Control next to him.

Ground nodded. "Figures. I heard a pilot quit last week."

"Momma Nature beats out another one," Tower remarked, setting his binocs down.

"Yep," Ground replied. "And with Olaphsen's wings clipped, they gotta be getting desperate."

* * *

John Bolt threw his head back and laughed aloud. Grabbing her hand, he said, "That's the funniest joke I've heard in years, Stephanie." It wasn't of course, but it had the desired effect, winning an embarrassed smile from her.

During the flight, Bolt made sure to give her plenty of eye contact. His brown eyes sparkled, nearly as much as his capped ivories. As the minutes passed, he'd edged his personal space ever closer to hers. But she'd kept backing away.

The flight ended before he could make the final sell.

With time to burn before his connecting flight, he tracked her down in Baggage Claim.

Time for desperate measures. Time to play the sympathy card. Standing by her at the rotating baggage carousel, he said, "Unfortunately, I'm also here in search of my long, lost love."

She cast a startled glance at him, then took a step away. "Oh?"

"Yes. You see, my wife left me. She was the love of my life," he said wistfully. "Hmph, she was my life."

Her backpack swung by. She bent to pick it up, but Bolt beat her to it.

As he pulled it aside, he said, "She too ran off with a pilot." He put a finger to his chin. "Say, you don't suppose . . .

Slipping the pack on, she shook her head. "I don't think so. He works for a small charter company here in Juneau. I don't think they fly all the way up to

Fairbanks." Stephanie spun and marched away. Over her shoulder she called, "Thanks again, and good luck."

Before he could reply, she slipped off into the crowd.

Bolt sighed. "Holly Innes, you little bitch," he mumbled to himself, "Why'd you have to pick bumfuck Fairbanks?"

He marched off to his connecting gate.

* * *

Holly climbed the fifty-six wooden steps leading to her single bedroom house, perched midway up Gold Street and overlooking downtown Juneau. When she'd first bought the place, negotiating the stairs had left her breathless. But now the chore hardly elevated her pulse. Besides, she welcomed the exercise after a long day at the office. True, she was home several hours earlier than average, but it had been a particularly brutal day.

As always, Skittles greeted her on the porch with a hungry meow, letting Holly know that he'd failed to bring home a critter for dinner. She picked up the ragged, tabby tom and rubbed his rough coat.

"You love me, don't you, boy?" she cooed. Skittles purred his answer. "You're the only one for me, you sweet thing." Stepping in, she let out a deep sigh.

The nerve of that man! Just planting a kiss on her right there, on the ramp for all to see. With TV cameras rolling, no less. She had replayed the scene in her mind all day.

"Disgusting," she said to herself.

And yet it felt—no, she dared not think it.

As she passed through the living room, she snapped on the TV, tuned to *News at Six*, then set about satisfying her pet's appetite. Skittles rubbed impatiently at her ankles as she poured the dry food into the plastic bowl sitting on the kitchen tile. The cat gobbled away.

That done, she poured the one glass of merlot she allowed herself on occasion. She held the red wine to her lips.

An item on the news caused her to freeze mid-sip. She ran into the living room and stared at the TV.

". . . orphaned cubs, known as the Three Little Bears, were slated for destruction at the Petersburg ADF&G facility," the TV reporter continued.

Holly watched a clip of Jake and Allen pushing the bear cages to the plane. The man continued. "The Three Little Bears took their last known flight this morning aboard a chartered Southeast Alaska Seaplanes aircraft."

Holly narrowed her eyes at the phrase, "last known flight." *Curious choice of words*, she thought.

The reporter recounted the events leading up to the flight as the clip continued. Holly watched as Allen fired up the Cessna, and abruptly swung the aircraft's tail toward the camera. Dust billowed up before the camera, which jiggled for a moment then cut. The next scene showed Allen's plane lifting off the runway.

Following the plane's path westward, the camera panned back across the ramp as well.

Something twitched in the back of Holly's mind. The ramp looked different somehow. But before she could figure it out, the camera zoomed in on the departing plane, then faded to black.

The talking head reappeared. "If all went according to plan, the Three Little Bears have been put to death by now," he ended melodramatically.

Tears welled up in Holly's eyes. Mistreating young, innocent victims was one thing that boiled her blood. She thumbed the tears away, sat down on her couch and took a deep breath.

The reporter's coanchor, a Tlingit woman, turned to him, brows crinkled, as if suddenly being struck by a question. "Any word on the identity of the poacher, Robert?" she asked.

Robert answered, "No, Eve. The guilty party remains at large. Rumors abound as to his identity, but at this time neither ADF&G nor DPS Wildlife Troopers have any conclusive evidence."

Holly stood and turned to leave the room.

Eve said, "I understand there is some question as to whether the cubs actually made it to their destination."

Holly's eyes went wide. "What the—" she blurted, wheeling around and bending so close to the screen that the reporters' faces appeared as a mosaic of colored dots.

"That's correct, Eve. We are attempting to track down an unconfirmed report that the bears never showed up in Petersburg." Robert turned from his coanchor and returned his gaze to the screen. "We'll have more on this story as it develops."

Holly replayed the TV scenes in her mind. Suddenly the alarm bells went off. She stood upright and put a hand to her mouth.

In the camera's second ramp shot, taken only minutes later, Ralph's plane was missing.

* * *

Suzette was off with Betty Lou and Bobbi Sue and their brood for Friday girls' night out, leaving Dusty free. Though he did accompany the pilots to the Red Dog on occasion, Drunk Pilot Night was a game for the younger set. For Dusty Tucker, it was Fishin' Friday. And he'd been looking forward to it all morning.

Yawning, Dusty strolled out of the stuffy office, through the back door and out onto the ramp.

He stopped, stretched, and inhaled the fresh Juneau air.

Fatigue washed away. His nostrils flared as he gulped in the sweet, oxygen-rich air. It surged through his 60-something veins and brought a contented smile to his lips. He looked up toward the heavens, closed his eyes and welcomed the cool, light sprinkle of drizzle upon his face.

It had been a long day. Too long. The job of Chief Pilot kept him shuffling more papers around his desk than airplanes through the skies, and, though he squeezed in an occasional charter here and there, his chance to fly often got lost in the red tape.

And today had been worse than usual. He'd suffered through another bout with Bruner over Ralph's alleged violations, and had to juggle the fleet to cover three weathered-in pilots stuck at outstations. Worst of all, he'd had to complete the paperwork that sent those three bear cubs to their destruction.

Two or three planes were still out on runs, but the dispatcher on duty was competent enough to watch the roost without him.

Besides, the weather in this part of the country seemed friendly enough.

With a practiced and appreciative eye, he studied the grey overcast. Some thought it gloomy and oppressive, but compared to the harsh fluorescent lights of his office, it lifted his spirits in a way that only the great outdoors could.

Papers properly shuffled enough for one day, Dusty was more than ready to slip the surly bonds of earth in his Super Cub, find a remote beach down channel, and drop a lazy line in the water.

And the sandbar off the shore of the Glass Peninsula he'd spotted the day before looked like the perfect place to land a whopper.

In the old days, before they'd grown and got married off, he might have taken a daughter with him. And the grandkids were still too young. So today he flew solo. Just him, his rod and tackle, and his camera.

His bare-panel Cub lacked even a radio to call for clearance to taxi and takeoff, so he had coordinated departure via phone to Juneau Tower minutes earlier. Firing up the plane, he waited for the flashing green *Cleared to taxi* light from the tower.

With a little luck, he'd bring home few good snaps, and maybe even a fresh coho, king or halibut for a late night dinner with Suzette.

CHAPTER 17: Potlatch

Mugs sporting smug smiles, DC and Allen strutted into the Red Dog, parched. A quick trip to the front room bartender solved the problem. For once, they'd even caught the tail end of happy hour.

Chinooks in hand, the two made their way upstairs.

Several patrons along the way stopped their conversations, smiled and nodded. The two bush pilots nodded back, confused; more than a few were total strangers.

Allen noticed the incongruity and mentioned it to DC.

"Seems we're suddenly the center of attention around here."

DC creased his brows.

"You don't think—"

Allen shook his head.

"No way."

Cresting the top of the stairs, they spotted their favorite table, front row center and overlooking the bottom floor. They made their way toward it, but two loggers beat them to it. Allen and DC stopped short. Upon spying the pilots, however, the loggers backed away, placating smiles on their faces. The first man held out a palm in a welcoming gesture.

"It's all yours," he said.

Nodding in thanks and bewilderment, DC and Allen sat.

Allen scratched his head. "Then again . . ."

DC finished the thought for him. "News travels fast in a small town."

John Bolt stood, wavering, as the baggage carousel slowly revolved before him.

Demons danced in his stomach. Sweat dotted his pale skull. With a damp handkerchief he dabbed it away. How, after years of driving the big rigs, and later running wetbacks and drugs to pay off Victoria's debt, could a godddamn airplane turn his stomach upside down?

"Moderate turbulence," the pilot had said over the P.A. in his calm, dry delivery.

More like the fucking Matterhorn roller coaster during an 8.0 earthquake, he thought, still in partial shock.

So preoccupied was he with keeping the last remnants of his inflight dinner down, he hardly noticed his modern glass and steel surroundings. The worldly truck driver had fully expected to find Fairbanks International Airport nothing more than a Quonset hut, or maybe even an igloo.

Wiping a trickle of bile from the side of his mouth, Bolt stowed his hanky and snatched his bags. From his newly purchased Army surplus duffel, he pulled his newly purchased Army surplus arctic parka, and newly purchased Army surplus muffler.

Despite the hot flashes, he donned the parka and wrapped it tightly about his neck. He waddled outside, never hearing the chuckles of others passing by in T-shirts and shorts.

At curbside, he stopped. A sign before him flashed, "Welcome to Fairbanks. Time: 6:45 p.m. Temperature: 64° F." His cheeks reddened slightly. After a furtive glance about, he yanked off his parka and stuffed it back in the duffel.

At least I didn't buy a set of snow shoes, he thought.

Mosquitoes the size of bumble bees buzzed about his head. Cursing, he dropped his bags and swatted in vain at the pests. He lit a cigar. That seemed to keep the damn pests at bay. A little bit.

"Hey, boy," he called to a porter. The man scurried over.

He pointed to his bags and ambled over to the rental car shuttle bus stop.

The porter set the bags at Bolt's feet. "There you are, sir. Enjoy your stay." Bolt turned away and puffed. The porter leaned forward and thrust a hand out, palm up. "I said, enjoy your stay."

Eyes narrowed, Bolt looked sideways at the porter, glanced at his open palm, then stared back in the man's eyes.

The porter dropped his hand. "Have a nice day," he grumbled, and walked away.

* * *

Though the overcast had forced him down below 1,000 feet, Dusty preferred a treetop flight anyway. The drizzle had turned to rain, forcing him to slow the already leisurely cruise speed of his Piper. But that was no big deal. He could still see a couple miles ahead, at least to the next jut of shoreline off the Glass Peninsula.

He leaned forward, squinting through the fog. Sandbar should be coming up soon, he thought. At high tide, his landing field was mostly submerged. But that was still several hours away, giving him lots of room to set the wheelplane down on its balloon tires.

Around the bend the sandbar appeared, a tan-colored strip amidst blue ocean waters. Dusty circled it, searching for rocks, ruts and bears. All clear.

The calm wind was no factor, so he set up an approach over the last bend, angling in on a modified base leg. He swooped over the last of the trees, banked, flared. The balloon tires plopped down with a *thud!*—no room for finesse on a runway shorter than a football field—bounced once, then settled. He hit the brakes. He could have stopped midway down the beach, but he instead added a little power and taxied to the other end of the "runway." He turned around and cut the power.

He popped the door open and hopped out. His ears, ringing with engine noise only moments earlier, were now greeted with a peaceful calm. Just the soothing sound of waves lapping at the beach and the occasional squawk of a bald eagle.

He glanced at his watch: 7:00 p.m. He smiled. Two-plus hours left before the ocean would rally for another advance on his makeshift runway. And the sun wouldn't even set tonight until after 10:30.

Plenty of time.

* * *

Beaming, DC fidgeted in his seat. He pointed to Allen with his beer. "That was great, the way that Fish & Game guy acted, huh?" He gave his buddy's shoulder a playful punch. "Like he's gonna pick up a couple empty cages!"

Allen glanced right and left and said in a low tone, "Not too sure if we should be talking about it here."

DC held up a hand. "Oh, right," he said, making a zipping gesture across his lips. He bent closer to his buddy. "I feel like Mr. Phelps in *Mission Impossible*."

Allen chuckled. "'Your mission, should you decide to accept it," mimicked in a deep voice.

"Is to fly around in a cage making bear growls," DC finished. The two laughed aloud. "Sucks that we can't tell anyone about it."

"Oh, but we'll be tellin' our grandkids," Allen replied.

"Here's to the grandkids!" DC toasted. Glancing downstairs at the front door, he said, "Can't wait to hear how Crash's flight went."

"No kidding, I'm dying." Allen glanced at his watch. "Should be back by now. Be here in a few."

DC searched the room. The missing Tlingit was somewhere, he knew. He finally spotted her, working the upstairs section.

DC nodded toward Tonya. "There she is, Miss Juneau."

Allen glanced behind him. A thin frown creased his lips. "Yeah," he grumbled, so darkly that DC said no more.

With the mission and the girl off the list of topics, DC tried to focus on something else. The two sat for several minutes, chatting about nothing in particular, both minds miles away; each casting furtive glances at a certain alluring waitress. But Tonya never bothered to stop and say hi.

DC said, "Hey, maybe we can get a few hours between flights tomorrow to bang out that climb."

"Huh?" Allen looked up, bewildered. "Oh, yeah."

"Where were you, the Virgins?"

"Hmph, you guessed it," Allen replied.

As DC watched Tonya work the room, he tried to catch her eye. But, while all the other bargoers seemed to notice the two bush pilots, the waitress remained apparently oblivious. DC fought the urge to race over and grab her. Finally, he turned away.

Let her come to me, he thought. Yeah, play it cool. That would be best.

* * *

Bolt grabbed a large coffee and sandwich from the nearby Circle K, picked up a fifth of Wild Turkey at a nearby liquor store, and drove back to the General Aviation section of Fairbanks Airport.

In the *Tanana* Air Adventures' lot he parked, his car facing the entrance.

He held a pair of camouflage binoculars to his eyes. Men and women filed past the windows.

Occasionally he glanced down at the passenger seat where sat his dogeared wedding photo of Veronica Redding, aka Holly Shannon Innes. She sure was a babe back then. So who was the pig in the second photo, the one taken five years later? Hard to believe they were the same woman. Would he even recognize her now? he wondered. And, he suddenly thought with alarm, what if she spotted him first?

Bolt looked at himself in the rear view mirror. He relaxed.

Doubt she'd recognize him. Now a hefty 220 plus, with his logger's beard covering his face, only his deep set brown eyes could give his identity away.

He peered through the field glasses, contemplating what the wench could possibly look like now.

* * *

Eyes squinted in rage, with hair disheveled and dripping in the rain, Holly looked like something Skittles might drag in.

She marched down the street toward the Red Dog.

"Of all the lowdown, double-crossing schemes," she spouted under her breath, "careless, blatant disregard for authority."

The rain seemed to echo her mood, dropping harder and faster with her every step. Sloshing through the puddles, Holly paid no mind. Her focus was on the confrontation ahead.

Ralph would care less, she knew. Her only hope was to knock some sense into Jake. And knock she would.

Her heart beat faster in anticipation. But, she wondered in the back recesses of her mind, what was that damn tingling sensation she felt at confronting Jake?

* * *

Several more SEAS pilots had joined DC and Allen at their table. All traded shop talk, deliberately avoiding the one subject foremost on their minds: *Dirty Harry*.

Allen was in the middle of explaining to DC how tundra formed when they heard a commotion at the front door. Two patrons whistled, a few more applauded, then the entire crowd began to cheer. The SEAS pilots peered down below.

There at the door stood Ralph and Jake. The two gazed around the room with bewildered looks, then, after a quick glance to each other, broke out in enormous grins. They waved to the crowd, tentatively at first, their embarrassment quickly melting. They waded through the crowd, shaking hands like politicians at a rally, and worked their way upstairs.

Trading knowing looks, DC stood with Allen and clapped. By the time the *nouveau* celebrities made it to the table, their hands laden with offered beer mugs, the crowd's cheer had turned into a chant.

"*Speech! Speech! Speech!*" the patrons chorused.

After laying down their burden on the table and shaking the other SEAS pilots' hands, Ralph and Jake turned to the balcony railing. They gazed at the room below like royalty surveying their subjects.

Jake held up a hand. The room settled to a murmur. Hoisting a beer, he shouted, "Here's to Frontier Justice!"

"Hear, hear," the crowd cheered.

A patron shouted, "What did you do with the bears?"

Feigning shock, Jake answered, "We certainly don't know what you're talking about."

"C'mon, guys," another replied. "The whole town's talkin'. What'd you do with 'em?"

Jake opened his mouth to speak, but Ralph beat him to it. "We can neither categorically confirm nor deny that any ursine hijacking occurred at this time."

A few chuckles rippled through the crowd.

"What about the poacher?" another yelled. The crowd went silent in anticipation of the answer.

Jake said, "Well, we're not the ones to ask, of course, but we did hear a rumor that the bears feasted on the supplies of a certain Outsider's cabin. And in the process destroyed the place."

The crowd broke into laughter, then applause.

Shouting over the noise, Ralph added, "And that very gentleman and his brother were arrested for poaching, and assault on," he gestured to his companion, "yours truly."

The crowd erupted in cheers.

Allen said to DC, "Here's to *Dirty Harry*."

"Yow-*za*!" DC replied, clinking mugs with his friend.

Ralph held up a hand. "People, please return to your merriment. We are but humble travelers seeking an elixir in peace."

To another round of applause, they turned from the balcony and took their seats with the other pilots. In typical quirky eloquence, Ralph told the story to the table of enraptured pilots. He finished with a prolonged and graphic description of Doyle's hands sizzling in the crisp mountain air.

"Holy crap!" DC exclaimed. He and Allen cringed at the description.

Allen asked, "So you found the evidence, then?"

"Yep," Ralph answered, motioning to Jake. "Once Doyle attacked pretty boy, here, it was a simple case of arrest, search and seizure for one Officer Mastis, ADF&G. I believe his exact words were, 'Make my day'."

"He cut 'em a deal right then and there," Jake added. "If they didn't press vandalism and battery charges against Ralphy and me, he wouldn't hand them over to our Wildlife Troopers for attempted murder, assault and poaching. Oh, and, one other thing: never set foot in Alaska again."

"Ha!" DC exclaimed. "He ran them out of the *state*?"

Ralph nodded. "Last we seen them boys, they's swimming down Channel towards Ketchikan. And with Mack's burned paws swelled up big as SCUBA fins, he should have no problem doin' the butterfly all the way to Jersey."

The table of pilots cheered. Ralph added, "And I hear Officer Mastis, ADF&G, is signing a book deal and TV series as we speak."

After a round of toasts, DC and Allen sat back as several patrons crowded in, eager to congratulate the heroes. Charlie wiggled in and placed a tray of drinks before them. "Free all night, gentlemen," he told the table. He pointed to Ralph and Jake. "And you two, all month."

In mock grouse, Ralph said, "Geez, what's a man gotta do around here to get 'em free for life, rescue the Pope?"

Laughing, Charlie moved off.

* * *

John Bolt sat in his car, chain smoking, chain drinking, and watching with intensity the workers of *Tanana* Air Adventures. No Veronica.

He sighed, glanced at his watch, and frowned. Sitting and watching, watching and sitting. This was how Humes and those other private dicks spent their time? There had to be a better way.

A departing airplane caught his eye. His gaze followed its arc across the sky.

How to flush the chick without tipping his hand?

The plane shrank to a dot, and disappeared behind a sign mounted on the *Tanana* building. His irises focused on the sign.

Learn to Fly! it shouted to him in big block letters. A wicked smile crept across his face.

* * *

DC had had enough. The whole place was celebrating, and Tonya hadn't even stopped in to congratulate Ralph and Crash. Or, more to the point, himself. He stood.

"Where are you off to?" Allen asked.

"I'm gonna go say hi to Miss Juneau."

Allen stood and placed a hand on his shoulder. "DC, I don't think that's a good idea."

DC shrugged him off. "Why not?"

"I mean, you don't want to . . . that is, I think you're—"

DC raised his brows, waiting for a reply. "Yes?"

Allen raised a placating hand. "DC, let me level with you. She's not what you think."

Wrong, DC thought. He'd kept the secret from Allen long enough. He thumped him playfully on the chest. "Hah! You don't know what you're talking about. You should have seen her on our date a few weeks ago." With that, he was off.

* * *

Dusty let out a deep sigh. Several strikes but no takers. At times like this he had to remember his old mantra, "The worst day fishing is better than the best day working." Although, he had to admit, his life of flying wasn't too damn bad, either. And what a life he'd had so far. A loving wife, two beautiful daughters, a passel of grandkids and a warm home, all on the edge of America's last frontier.

He took a sweeping gaze at his surroundings. As always at times like these, he reflected on his decision to nix the airline career. As always, he smiled, coming to the same conclusion.

While airline captains might be able to afford an occasional trip out here, he owned a special key to the front door. He returned his gaze to the ocean channel, already reversing its flow. The waterline would be creeping up soon. He eyed the sky. Dark, grey and drizzly, but nothing too nasty. Still plenty of daylight to steer a course home by. His heart panged, longing suddenly, for Suzette. His belly growled, eager for a fresh salmon.

Well, he thought. *Maybe just a few more casts*.

* * *

John Bolt disguised himself, quite convincingly, as an obnoxious sleazeball, and ambled into the *Tanana* Air Adventures building.

"May I help you?" the receptionist asked cheerfully.

Bolt returned the smile.

Glancing at the name plate on her desk, he replied, "Yeah, honey, uh, Donna. I always wanted to learn to fly, you know, and I thought, "Why not?"

"Certainly, sir. How'd you like our $40 introductory flight, Mr. . . . ?"

"Zack, Zack Taylor." Bolt replied, using the name of an old trucker buddy and concealing the nausea he already felt welling up in his guts.

* * *

Holly marched straight up to Jake and slapped him across the cheek. The table of shocked pilots fell silent.

"Dammit, Jake," she barked. "What the hell did you two think you were trying to pull?"

Jake opened his mouth to speak, but thought the better of it, and remained silent.

"You thought you could *charm* me into overlooking a missing plane?"

Jake glanced around the table at his buddies for support. None was offered.

Holly turned to Ralph, jabbing a finger at his chest. "And *you*. What the hell do you think you're doing flying a plane without a license? You were on the *News at Six*, for Christ's sake! What were you thinking?"

Ralph looked dead into her eyes and said, "I was thinking of setting things right."

"Right? Right?" she repeated in confusion. She crinkled her brows. "What's right about jeopardizing your career?"

"I rolled the dice," he said evenly. "I won." He leaned toward her and added, "That is, if no one tattles."

She did a double take at that. "God, sometimes I feel like a damned nanny around here." She turned back to Jake.

Before she could speak, he said, "Those bears were going to be destroyed, Holly. *Killed.* At least now, with their bellies gorged and hibernation approaching, they have a fighting chance."

She replied, somewhat less forcefully, "Well, nevertheless, you two have some *serious* talking to do tomorrow. In the Ring, with Dusty and me."

She wiped a frustrated hand across her forehead, gazed around the room and sighed. "I need a drink," she growled, and headed for the upstairs bar.

In a thick Cuban accent, Ralph said to Jake, "Lucy, you got some 'splainin' to do."

Behind Holly's back, Ralph caught Charlie's eye. He pointed two fingers at Holly and winked: *Doubles, all night.*

* * *

Dusty jogged back to his cub, tossed the gear in the back and strapped in.

Really shouldn't push it like this, he told himself as he fired up.

He eased the power up. The Cub leapt into the air. He nosed over, gained speed, then banked away out to sea.

He set a course back up the channel for home.

* * *

"Hi, gorgeous!"

DC slipped his hands around her waist and squeezed.

Tonya wormed free. "Knock it off, DC," she said tersely. "I'm working." She grabbed several empty bottles off a table, turned away from him and made for the kitchen.

DC followed double-time to catch up. "A simple hello would be nice," he said to her back.

"Hello," she answered flatly, not missing a step.

"I was beginning to wonder if you'd seen me and the guys up there."

"I did."

"Why didn't you stop and say hi?"

She reached the swinging doors, stopped and turned. "In case you haven't noticed, I'm pretty damn busy."

DC reached behind her and threw a hand across the door jamb, blocking her way. "Yeah, I noticed. Too damn busy to return phone calls, too."

She stared hard at him, head cocked in annoyance. Her once fiery brown eyes now seemed glacial cold. After a moment her look softened, and she smiled. "Look, we had fun the other day. But I need some space, okay?"

Space? he thought with surprise. Three agonizingly long weeks wasn't enough? "Sorry. Thought I'd given you plenty."

"Not enough."

"Well, how much do you need?" he asked, immediately regretting it.

She shook her head. "I don't know. I need to sort things out, DC."

He nodded. "Ok," he mumbled, and lowered his arm.

Unexpectedly, she reached a free hand out and caressed his cheek. The feeling sent shivers down his spine.

She pulled her hand away. "I'll call you, okay?"

He swallowed the word *When?*

She pushed through the swinging doors and was gone.

DC watched his vision fade away into the kitchen. The door swung back, narrowly missing his nose.

* * *

Donna gestured toward a seat before her desk and lifted her phone. As the man sat, she smelled alcohol on his breath. Concealing her disgust, she said, "We've got a little daylight left, Mr. Taylor. I'll call for an available flight instructor." After chatting with her cohort on the other end she said, "Max will be up in a few minutes." She hung up and pulled out a form. Pen poised, she said, "Age and occupation?"

She knew right away that the man, one Zack Taylor, was obviously lying through his teeth at her questions, and even paid with a couple wadded up twenties.

As the two waited for the instructor, Taylor's eyes wandered about the place. After a few moments, he remarked, "Yeah, I heard about this place from a gal that works here. Used to, anyway. A secretary, I think. She probably took one or two lessons, too."

Donna's radar went up even further. "Oh? What was her name?"

Bolt stared at her as he answered. "Holly Innes."

Donna's brows raised slightly in recognition. "She no longer works here," she answered evenly.

"Oh, I'm sorry to hear that. I was hoping to catch up with her. One of her best friends just got married, and didn't have her address. Any idea where she lives now?"

Arms crossed, Donna leaned back. "And how do you know Miss Innes?"

"Oh, well, we used to be neighbors down in the States. Back in Kansas."

Donna's fists tightened. *Down in The States*. This phony was too dumb to remember that Alaska was a state, too. And Kansas . . . she'd heard the rumors on that one. "Oh. I didn't know she was from Kansas. How nice." Standing, she motioned behind him. "Mr. Taylor, meet Max, your flight instructor."

Bolt stood, turned and blurted, "You're too young to fly!"

The man chuckled. "I'm twenty-four, sir. Been flying since I was seventeen."

He shifted feet. "Oh, okay. I guess."

The secretary added, "Mr. Taylor is an old friend of Holly Innes." Before Max could reply, she added, "You remember her, don't you? The *secretary* from *Kansas*?" The two workers exchanged knowing glances.

"Oh, yes," Max replied. "I remember, uh, secretary Holly. How is she?"

"Mr. Taylor's lost touch," Donna answered. "With *her*, that is. Perhaps you might know more about her whereabouts."

With Bolt's back turned, she gave Max a conspiratorial wink.

Max nodded deliberately. "Yeah, sure. Let me think about it while I take you for a ride."

* * *

Holly held up a finger to catch the bartender's eye. But before she could order, Charlie delivered to her a rum and Coke.

She looked at him questioningly.

Charlie pointed to the SEAS table. With a broad smile, he said, "You're with the SEAS bunch, right? Free for you all night, ma'am."

She glanced back. "Oh, right," she said, an edge of reluctance in her voice. She gave a wary-eyed glance to the pilots, saluted begrudgingly with her drink, and turned her back to them.

Holding the glass eye level, she hesitated. While she'd never really been an alcoholic back in the day, there certainly had been times when she'd turned to its numbing qualities. She really shouldn't, she thought. But under the circumstances . . .

"Why not? Just one," she finished aloud.

The smooth liquid warmed her throat. She closed her eyes and told herself to relax. She stretched, breathed deep, and took in another mouthful.

A tiny smile crept, ever so carefully, across Holly's lips. She turned to the patron next to her and actually started a conversation with him, something she hadn't done since—hell, she couldn't remember when.

Before long her drink was drained. Another one appeared magically at her elbow.

She found herself thinking, *Why not? Just one more.*

Over the next hour, she would find herself thinking that same thought three more times.

* * *

The clouds, Dusty found, had lowered significantly. The rain showers had increased as well. He hugged the shoreline and squinted ahead.

A tiny patch of light still shone through the pass ahead. Enough, he figured, to slip through. From there it should be smooth sailing.

But as he approached, the rain squall turned sour. Frowning, he banked away and retraced his steps. He peered left across the channel. The ocean faded into the mist not halfway to the other side. No way would he risk getting caught in the middle without a shoreline as a reference. That invited disaster. Though he was rated to fly through the clouds, his minimalist Cub wasn't. And that had always been its appeal.

It was beginning to look like Momma Nature wanted him to camp out tonight. He glanced in the back. There was his sleeping bag, rolled up and waiting.

Dusty sighed. "Well, Suzette, looks like I'll be home for breakfast."

He set about looking for a sandy shore above waterline.

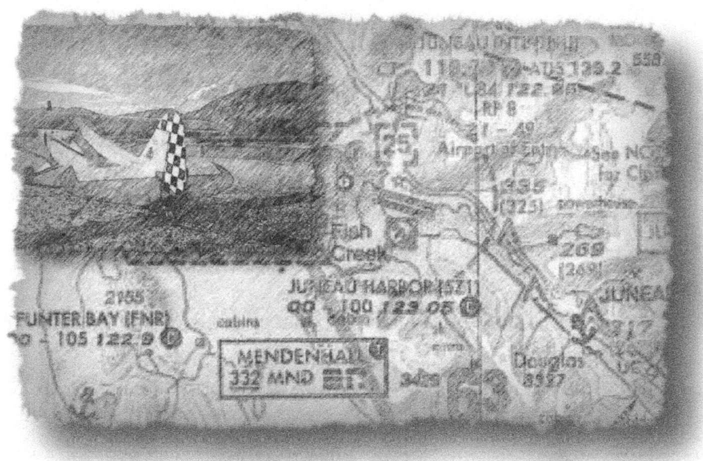

CHAPTER 18: Hazards to Air Navigation

Ralph nudged Jake. "Holly's good and softened up, Crash. Go work your magic."

Snorting, Jake looked up at him, the reluctance plain on his face. "Are you kidding? I ain't pokin' *that* grizzly."

"She's just an orphaned cub now. Go tame her, Marlin Perkins."

Jake stood. Tucking his shirt in and running a quick hand through his hair, he approached her. He stopped a pace away and cast a nervous glance back at Ralph, who nodded reassuringly.

He slid up next to her.

She glanced sideways at him with an *Oh, it's you* look.

He held up a hand in surrender. "Truce, okay? Just let me explain." Head cocked, she eyed him. The anger set her blue irises ablaze, reminding Jake of the sun reflecting off a deep icefield. Cold and beautiful at the same time. He went on. "I'll admit, it was a dirty thing to do. But I had to do something."

She shook her head in disbelief. "Oh, you did something, all right. You used me."

"Look, I couldn't let a damned poacher kill four bears, could I?"

"And you just assumed that I could?" she asked. "Rather than deceiving me, why didn't you just ask?"

"And what would you have said?"

She stared at the bar table. "To tell you the truth, Jake, if I thought it was FAR-legal and safe? Hell yes."

That surprised him. "Well," he stammered, "I couldn't take that chance." He held up his drink for emphasis. "Look, things were moving fast. I just—I did what I thought best at the time."

She jutted her chin toward him. "Best, Jake? Molest me right there on the ramp? With the TV cameras rolling, no less?"

"It was only a kiss."

The two of them turned away to face the bar, their images visible to each other between liquor bottles in the back mirror.

After a long moment, Jake said slowly, "Tell you the truth, Holly, I've been thinking all day about, well, why I did just that."

She looked sideways at him again, eyes narrowed in suspicion. She seemed to do a lot of that lately, he thought.

"And what was your conclusion?" she asked.

He took a deep breath. "Well, Holly. I feel like we—that is, you and I, um. I mean, well . . . ." He looked away.

She threw her head back and laughed. "Crash Whitakker, the legendary ladies' man, tongue tied and shy over a little filly." She grabbed his arm and shook it, her hand lingering on his bicep for a moment. "So, you've finally met your match, eh?"

He chuckled, his grin turning fully sheepish. *Perhaps I have*, he thought. His cheeks felt slightly flushed. Was he blushing? He wondered. The thought itself was enough to turn him a shade deeper.

She reached toward him. He flinched like an abused dog. But she simply chuckled and placed her hand on his cheek. "Risking it all to save three helpless, abused animals. I guess I should give you a medal." She pulled her hand away.

"Better'n a sharp stick in the eye," Jake said.

She laughed again. "Or a punch to the gut!"

They both laughed at that.

Laying an arm on the bar, he beamed a smile bright enough to do a politician proud. "See, I'm not all that bad, once you get to know me."

She stared up at him, shaking her head slightly. "Nor am I, Jake. Nor am I." She glanced at her empty drink, then back up at him.

Her head bobbed a bit too much as she did, Jake saw. He'd seen the sloppy motion many times in the past. As Ralph would say, she was ripe for the pickin'.

What the hell have I started? he wondered. He thought he liked it, but at the same time it scared the hell out of him. He glanced nervously at his buddies. They sat engrossed in their own conversation, having long since lost interest in his conquest.

The bartender set another round before them.

She held up a hand. "I really shouldn't." She held up a finger. "But what's one more, right?" She giggled, apparently at some private joke of hers.

Jake shook his head in disbelief. Holly Innes had actually giggled! This was getting interesting.

Holly gave him a "cheers" with her glass and gulped. Before Jake could take a sip of his, she drained the entire glass and plopped it down.

"Uh, one more, right?" Jake asked.

Wearing a benign smile, Holly blinked in reply.

Two more "one mores" quickly followed.

John Bolt, alias Zack Taylor, staggered back through the doors, a bulging Sic Sac in one hand and with the other dabbing a putrid, soaked hanky at his pale, sweating forehead.

Max caught up to him in the lobby. He patted the suffering man and eased him toward the front door. "Great flight, Mr. Taylor. Don't worry, most people get over air sickness after a few lessons. My business card."

Bolt absentmindedly took the card. With vacant eyes, he held up the barf bag.

With crinkled nose, Max pushed it away with his palm. "No, Mr. Taylor, that's yours to keep as a memento of your flight. Compliments of *Tanana* Air Adventures." He dug into his flight kit. "Here, have another bag for the road."

Bolt took the fresh one and shuffled out the door.

Max and Donna traded looks.

"Have fun?" she asked.

Max nodded. "It's been ages since I've practiced spins."

Her eyes widened. "You didn't?"

"And rolls." The two laughed. "I wanted to show him some loops, but he begged me out of it."

"Tell him anything about Holly?"

"Hell no. If that sonofabitch isn't her long lost, loving husband, then he's his hired thug. Where does she live now, anyway?"

Donna shrugged. "No clue."

"Oh. Well, I'm sure it's not Point Barrow."

Donna put her hand to her mouth. "You didn't?"

Max beamed. "I'll bet he's booking a flight right now."

The two cackled with delight.

* * *

Dusty squinted. Still no sandbars in sight.

Worse, the clouds were darkening as the sun slowly set, making it that much harder to recognize the landscape racing at him through the muck.

With nowhere left to go, he decided to risk landing back on his sandbar. While high tide would soon make it too short for takeoff or landing, a small part should remain dry while he waited it out. He banked his Piper Cub and made for it.

After several long, intense minutes, it floated out of the mist.

Too late, Dusty saw: the advancing water had already covered too much of it. He mentally kicked himself for his error; he should have taken off sooner, or not at all. Rarely did Mother Nature and Father Tide work together in the pilot's favor.

The cockpit suddenly seemed stifling hot. He pulled the air vent knob and stuck his head in front of the cooling stream for a moment. He took a deep breath to calm his mind.

"Okay," he said to himself, "next target."

* * *

Holly lay a hand on his forearm. "Maybe it's jusht the alcohol talking, Jake. But I'm thinking you're looking damned good right now."

Jake pulled away. "Yep. It's the alcohol talking." He glanced back at the pilots' table. All had their backs turned. Looked like he was solo on this one.

Holly grabbed his arm and yanked him so close he blinked. "You know, Ralph was right. I do need to get laid."

"*Hoo, boy*," he muttered.

"What's wrong, Crash 'em up Whitakker, legendary stud pilot? All piston and no prop?"

He eyed her for a long moment. Holly Innes, drunk in a bar and picking *him* up! Now he'd seen everything.

With an exaggerated flair, he set down his drink. "All right, Check Airman Innes, your place or mine?"

"Well, since your cabin's a plane flight away, it'd better be mine, huh?"

"Quite. Uh, why don't you head on downstairs? I'll be right there."

"Of course, my Pied Piper of bear cubs."

Hoping to keep a low profile, Jake crept back up to the table. He lay a hand on Ralph's shoulder, bent to his ear and whispered, "Miss Innes seems to have imbibed a bit too much tonight. I'd better escort her home."

Ralph grinned wide. "Well, now, isn't that—"

Jake held up a hand. "No talk, okay?"

"If you say so, stud muffin."

Halfway down the stairs, Jake caught up just in time to grab an arm as she stumbled. Holly looked up at him, her look of admiration exaggerated by the alcohol.

"My knight has arrived."

"Uh, yeah. Sure thing, *milady*."

Outside, the two bundled up against the rain. Eluk jumped up, wagged his tail, and sniffed at his master's new friend. Jake waved the dog back. "Eluk, you'd better go home with Ralph tonight."

Holly gave the canine a sympathetic pat. "Sorry, Eluk. Skittles wouldn't like you very mush." With a sly grin, she looked into Jake's eyes. "Besides, there's only room for two animals in my bed."

With a dejected look, Eluk sat back under the awning and awaited his surrogate master.

* * *

DC returned to the table, shell shocked. Not bothering to sit, he said, "I don't understand it. Not three weeks ago, I gave her the flight of the century. I had her eating out of my hand."

Allen let out a frustrated sigh. "Other way around, most likely," he mumbled.

DC stiffened, and looked down at his friend. "What did you just say?"

Allen stood up next to him. "She's playing head games with you, Einstein. That's her *modus operandi*, in case you haven't figured it out."

"Head games?" DC repeated, incredulous. He pointed the tip of his beer bottle at Allen. "You can shove your head game up your ass, pal."

"Look. When's the last time you saw her?"

DC hesitated. "On our flight to Hoonah a few weeks ago. But that's only because she's—"

"Uh huh. And when's the last time you talked to her?"

"Well, we haven't really got a chance to."

Allen shook his head sadly. "A lot can happen in three weeks, my friend."

DC slammed his bottle down and crossed his arms. "All right, Allen. Out with it. Just what the fuck are you trying to say?"

Allen swallowed. He stared at the table a moment, then looked up in his friend's eyes. "Look, you told me not to stick my nose in it, so I didn't say anything. But the other night I saw her with . . . ."

"With?"

Through tight lips, Allen said, "Guess."

DC stared hard at his friend. Slowly a look of recognition spread across his face. "T-Tom Zion?"

Allen gave the faintest trace of a nod.

DC's face darkened. "No way," he said finally, his voice wavering. "There is no fucking way that skankbag could—"

Allen jumped up and grabbed him by the scruff of the neck.

"DC, listen. She's just toying with you. Like a cat with a dying mouse."

"Oh, now I'm a goddamned mouse?" His eyes darted between Allen and Tonya, now working below. "You're wrong. They were probably just hanging out with—"

"They were all over each other."

"All over each . . . ?" DC's voice faded.

"Like he'd just returned from the front line."

After a moment, DC's chest filled up. His eyes grew wild with fury. He swatted Allen's hand away and jabbed a finger in front of his nose. "Bullshit. I know what this is. You're jealous. You wanted her, you lost her, and you're fucking jealous." He shoved Allen's chest.

Allen stumbled back a step. He held up his hands in appeasement. "DC, don't do this."

DC advanced. He shoved again. "You made this up. You think just because Tom caught Stephie off guard once, I'd think he could just swoop right in and take Tonya, too."

Allen shook his head. "DC, you're talking crazy."

DC thrust his face close to Allen's. He jabbed a finger in his chest. "Am I? Who spends all his lonely nights here at the Red Dog, peeling off the labels from his beer bottles? Who sits here, night after night, hoping a certain Tlingit waitress pays a little more attention to him than the average customer?"

Allen's jaw clamped shut. He raised his head a fraction. "Maybe it's time you—"

"Don't worry. I am." DC stomped out.

* * *

Getting Holly up the fifty-six wooden steps to her home turned out to be more of a chore than Jake had imagined. He stood at the door, panting, while Holly fumbled with the keys in her purse. Anticipating the classic mistake of the inebriated woman, Jake caught the keys as she dropped them.

Holly hooted, impressed. "My, Jake, you certainly move fasht," she remarked.

"Yes, well. Here we are." He slipped the key into the lock and turned. Opening the door, he said, "Well, my dear, I'll see you tomorrow at work."

She wrapped her arms around his neck. "Now hold on there. You've still gotta checkride ahead of you." She pulled him down and planted her lips on his.

Reluctant at first, Jake soon relaxed and enjoyed her bold advance. Closing his eyes, he let himself get lost in her lust. In the end, however, he pulled away.

"Holly, I don't want you doing anything you're going to regret."

"Nonsense. Get your ass in my house, now. That's an order from your Assishtant Chief Pilot!"

She pulled him inside. Without letting go of his neck, she half spun and kicked the door closed. As she did so, Jake barely managed to hold her up.

* * *

It figured.

The rain was pouring in buckets and he had just missed the bus. DC stood under the bus stop awning, his mind racing with thoughts.

Allen, Tonya, Tom, Stephanie. Was every friend in the world destined to betray him? He snorted and said aloud, "With friends like *that*." He didn't bother to finish the saying.

"What'd you say, buddy?" came a voice from behind. DC turned to eye an old Tlingit man peering from beneath a cardboard box in the alley, dressed in rags and clutching a bottle.

"I said, here," he answered. He pulled a wadded up ten from his pocket and handed it to the man. "Get yourself something warm to eat, okay?"

The man said, "Thanks, *cheechacko*."

Cringing, DC turned back to the street and his troubles.

* * *

A small stretch of sand lay a scant few miles south of the fishing hole, Dusty remembered. Perhaps just long enough to set the Piper Cub down.

He made for it.

Up ahead, another wall of showers barred his way. He grimaced, slowed the craft to a crawl, and pressed on.

Sinking down near treetop level, he concentrated on the shore, keeping just enough distance from the terrain for an emergency turn back. The rain darkened as he entered it, cutting his visibility to less than a mile.

He began to sweat. His breathing quickened to short, rapid gasps. His heart raced, laboring to keep up with his stress. He ignored the sharp pain it caused in his chest.

Another wall of water ahead. He frowned, and banked hard right.

* * *

Fuck. That was all Allen could say to himself. Fuck.

DC, so intelligent, so on top of the world, could be so damned naive. Not to mention egotistical. And now he was taking it out on his best friend.

Then again, Allen admitted to himself, the girl had a way of clawing her way under even a worldly man's skin. Had she ever even been in love? Not that one, he realized. Men fell at her feet like she was Cleopatra. No challenge. The fun was in the power, the teasing, fucking some, then fucking them over. And Tom knew full well he was screwing DC over once again as well. *Birds of a feather*, Allen thought with disgust.

After another shot of courage, this one in the form of tequila, he made a decision. A good, old fashioned wing clipping was in order.

He watched the door for him. He'd show, no question.

And finally, he did. The doors swung open, and Tom Zion glided in. He paused for a moment, framed by the doorway, as if to create a grand entrance for himself.

Flanked by two friends, Tom strode toward the stairs, gaze sweeping the crowd like he owned them. Tonya scurried across the floor to intercept him. After a quick glance around, she gave Tom a kiss so deep that it made Allen nauseous. Tom squeezed her butt cheek then started up the stairs.

Allen drained his sixth pint of the night, slammed it on the table and stood. Someone grabbed his arm to steady him; he shook it off and stepped away. He staggered to the top of the stairs to meet him.

"Evening, Tom," Allen said.

From one step below, Tom looked at him eye to eye. He nodded. "Allen."

"How's it hanging?" he asked.

Tom grinned wide. After an obvious glance back at Tonya, he said, "Right now, it ain't."

"Hmm, tempting. But too small a target." With that, Allen threw a right hook. Startled, Tom flinched away from the punch.

The movement and the alcohol served to fool Allen's aim, and he barely clipped Tom's nose.

With blood trickling from a nostril, Tom clenched his jaw. He popped Allen a quick left-right to the gut and head. Allen toppled backwards.

Over his shoulder, Tom said to his friends, “Damn that felt good.” Turning back, he leaned forward over Allen’s prone body, thrust a finger before his face and hissed, “Foley, you fucking loser. Next time, tell that pussyass friend of yours to fight his own fight.” Stepping around him, Tom strode past.

Allen sat up on an elbow and massaged his rapidly puffing eye.

He looked up to find Ralph staring down at him.

“Maybe it’s time you got home, Ali,” Ralph said.

“Yeah, maybe so,” Allen grunted. He sighed. “Seems the whole world’s against me tonight, Ralph. Mind if I crash at your place?”

“Let me guess. Lovers’ quarrel with DC?”

“Something like that. Come to think of it, it might be a few nights.”

Helping him to his feet, Ralph said, “Misty’s Home for Wayward Pilots is always open, my friend.”

“Thanks.”

He guided Allen gently down the first set of stairs. “You know the way. Tell the Misses I’ll be along shortly. I’ve got a little side trip to make.”

“And so do I,” Allen mumbled under his breath.

* * *

The sky was falling.

Time to set down, anywhere. Now.

The rain surrounded his craft in a thick grey wall. The terrain sailed into view only moments before he could react. At least he knew the land well enough to anticipate the next bend. Up ahead, he recalled, lay a nice low point in the hills, a gap that he could probably squeeze through. The terrain might be different enough to force a change in the fickle weather as well, perhaps lighten it up on the other side. The thought lifted his spirits somewhat, and he allowed himself a long, deep breath. He deftly maneuvered his craft, banking left to cut a path parallel to the coastline.

This close to shore, he could hardly see the forest for the trees rushing by his wingtip.

* * *

Holly planted another kiss on him, this one more lustful than the last. She began to unbutton his shirt. He pulled away and looked around.

"So, this is your house, huh? How about a tour?"

Holly frowned a moment, her lower lip curling into a pout, then did as requested. They found Skittles, unaccustomed to visitors, cowering under the bed. Before Jake could give him an introductory pat, the feline managed to wiggle out of her hands and scurry away once again. That left the two of them standing alone at the foot of her bed, staring at one another.

Holly smiled up at him, and made several obvious glances at the bed.

Jake hesitated. He'd long since admitted to himself how attracted he was to her, but something held him back. Much to his surprise, he realized what it was: respect. A deep, profound respect. When was the last time he could say that about a lover?

Eons ago, he realized, back in a strange land called Akiachak.

Clasping her hands coyly behind her back, Holly said, "Well, what're you waiting for, clearance to land?"

Jake smiled at that. He wrapped his arms around her and pulled her down onto the bed, his lips locking on hers.

All his senses seemed magnified, attuned to his lover. He smelled the alcohol, strong on her breath, tasted it on her lips, increasing, in some animalistic way, his passion. Her thin frame felt light and soft beneath him. Her fingers ruffled his hair, scratched lightly over his back, squeezed his buttocks. All too easily, he saw, he responded *down there*.

Emergency! Emergency! Take evasive action! his brain screamed. Releasing her, he sat up.

She protested with a dissatisfied moan. With closed eyes and dreamy smile, she mumbled, "What's wrong, my love . . . . ." Her voice faded.

Jake looked down at her. Fast asleep. Chuckling, he slipped off her shoes, pulled back the covers and slid her into bed, jeans and all.

He tiptoed through the house and turned off the lights, then joined her. Draping an arm around her waist, he felt the soft warmth of her body, slightly damp with perspiration. Her chest began to rise and fall rhythmically, a light snore escaping her lips.

Jake closed his eyes and quickly fell into a deep, dreamless sleep.

From under the bed, Skittles let out a lonely meow.

* * *

DC raced up the steps through the torrent and fumbled with the lock. Stepping inside, he stripped off his soaked jacket before turning on the lights.

"Hello, DC," a voice said in the darkness.

Startled, he jumped and dropped his keys. But his subconscious instantly recognized the voice.

"Stephanie," he blurted.

He turned on the lights and there she was, sitting in the old easy chair.

"The manager let me in. Hope you don't mind."

Unable to speak, he just shook his head.

"DC. You can close your mouth now."

He did, then smiled. "More like pull it off the floor." Opening his arms wide, he walked over to her. But she didn't budge from the chair, and he was forced to bend over and hug her awkwardly. She replied with a stiff, cold hug.

He pulled away. "It's great to see you," he said.

She looked at him evenly. "Is it?"

He opened his mouth to speak, then thought the better of it. This could get mighty dicey, mighty quick. "Of course," he said finally.

"Hmph. That sounded real convincing." She stared at him a long, agonizing minute. Finally, she sat back. "Well, I must say, I half expected you to walk in with someone else."

DC glanced at the door. "Oh, Allen? He's still back—"

"You know what I mean."

He sighed, then sat down at the edge of the couch, facing her. "All right, Stephanie. You came all this way. What do you want to know?"

She pursed her lips. "Hmm. I'm not sure I want to know anything. How about telling me what you want me to know."

DC thought for a minute. He wasn't sure where to begin. He wasn't even sure what there was to tell. He took a deep breath.

"A little while ago, I met this girl, who—" He stopped. *Who was what?* Even he wasn't sure now.

Stephanie prodded him. "What does she mean to you?"

DC let out a deflating sigh. "I don't know, Steph. I wish I did. I'm not even sure what she thinks of me." He rambled on, lost in troubled thought. "I thought we were doing great. Then all of a sudden—" He stopped again. He could see the hurt in her eyes, knew that she was reading his feelings on his face, and reacting to it. "I'm sorry, Steph. I guess I've developed feelings for her."

Stephanie stared at him for another long, uncomfortable minute. He could see the tears welling up in her eyes. After dabbing at them with a handkerchief, she stood and said, “Well. That’s what I came up here to find out. I guess I have.” Rubbing her eyes, she walked toward his bedroom.

He stood, unsure of her intent.

Over her shoulder, she said, “You get the sofa tonight.”

* * *

The door opened, and a figure stepped out. The low overcast and late setting sun made for a dark twilight, but from the kitchen’s bright light, he could tell it was Tonya. Alone.

She made her way down the alley.

He stepped from the shadows.

She stopped and squinted. “Who—who’s there?” she asked.

Her voice trembled slightly. He liked that. He advanced.

She backed up. In a firmer voice she said, “Stop right there, asshole, or I’ll scream.”

“Leave him alone,” he growled.

After a moment’s hesitation, she said, “Allen?”

From this distance, he could see her face plainly now. Her brown eyes shone from dark sockets, shadows across her pale cheeks making her look Gothic. A night creature, evil and erotic all at once. Her true nature, he thought.

He polished off the bottle and tossed it. It shattered against the wall, the remnants of the whiskey streaming down the brick.

She jumped at the explosion. As he stepped forward into a dim stream of twilight, she frowned.

“Go home and sleep it off, Allen.” She pushed past him, but he grabbed her arm and spun her around.

“You hear me?” he demanded. “Leave him alone.”

She scowled. “I don’t know what you’re—”

His nails dug into her forearms as he shook. “Don’t fuck with me any more, woman! And don’t fuck with him, either. He doesn’t know your kind.”

She sneered. “Hah! And you do?”

"Better than you know." With that he pulled her in. His open mouth pressed over hers. She tried to pull away but he reached around and grabbed her hair.

He bit her lip, then forced his tongue in. She bit back, hard. He yelped and let go.

She pushed him away, but didn't run. Instead, she stared at him with wild eyes, a twisted, triumphant, *daring* grin on her lips.

Tasting blood in his mouth, he wiped it away with the back of a hand. Upon seeing it, black against his pale skin, he clenched his jaw. He yanked her hair again, and shoved her into the shadows.

She whimpered, resisting his advance. He pushed her against the cold, hard brick. He forced his mouth on hers again, this time meeting less resistance. Her trembling lips kissed back, tentatively.

Keeping a firm grip on her hair, with his free hand he lifted her off the ground and pressed against her.

Wrapping her hands around his shoulders, she gazed back at him, eyes ablaze, almost maniacal. This time it was she who pressed her mouth onto his.

With all his passion, all his anger, all his pent up frustration, he kissed back.

All too soon it was over. His knees weakened, forcing him to lower her to the ground.

She pushed him away. He staggered back. Leaning against the wall, she stared at him, eyes and gaze defiant. She stood erect. With an almost whimsical motion, she pushed him aside and paraded past him.

He blinked and fell back, staring at her in disbelief. "Tonya, listen to me," he called after her. "You'll destroy him. You're through with him, hear me? You're through with him, goddamnit."

Gliding away, Tonya laughed. Over her shoulder she called, "I already am, flyboy."

* * *

The sky lightened; Dusty smiled.

That should mean the rain was lifting, the overcast thinning, and the gap large enough to squeeze through.

The bend ahead looked familiar. Just one more cut to the left and. . . *there!*

He banked hard right, up the canyon. The gap was just a few seconds away, he knew.

Something to the left caught his eye. He glanced in time to spot a wall of granite sail by. Strange, he didn't remember any rock cliffs up this pass.

The alarm bells clanged in his head.

"*Dammit!*" he cursed. He cranked the Piper Cub into a hard right bank, nearly standing the plane on its wingtip.

His chest seemed to explode. Pain seared through his heart.

Letting go of the controls, he clutched at his heart.

Suddenly, the engine's roar faded to silence. All became calm. The pain melted away.

The fog returned, shrouding him in a heavenly silver veil.

Through the mist floated his beautiful young bride, radiant in her white wedding gown.

Dusty's whole being filled with a profound peace.

The trees raced up to meet him.

Suzette smiled, cradled his head in her hands, gazed into his eyes and said, "*Au revoir, mon amour.*"

CHAPTER 19: Aftermath

The wreckage was discovered by a passing Beaver out of Petersburg on an early run to Juneau. The weather had lifted considerably from the night before, and the pilot easily spotted the bright yellow fabric of the shattered Piper Cub from several miles away.

Circling the wreckage, the pilot radioed in on 121.5 MHz, the universal emergency frequency.

He reported no sign of survivors.

Nor could he read the aircraft registration number on the plane's crumpled tail.

A Coast Guard search and rescue helicopter was dispatched from Air Station Sitka.

Authorities began a telephone search of airports within range. One of the first calls went to Juneau Tower, who reported logging an outbound Super Cub the night before, destination unknown, and not known to have returned during tower-closed hours.

* * *

With heavy heart, the Juneau ground controller on duty hung up the land line. He lifted his field glasses and searched the ramp. Dusty's tie down space was conspicuously empty.

"Oh, my God," he whispered. Fighting back a tear, he picked up the phone and dialed SEAS operations.

The dispatcher on duty had no knowledge of Dusty's whereabouts, though the Chief Pilot was not due into work for several more hours.

"Well, you'd better call Suzette and check up on him. We've got a report of a downed aircraft fitting the description of his Cub."

"Oh my God," the SEAS' dispatcher replied, echoing the controller's own reaction.

"And Brian," the controller added, "I would be discrete about this. I wouldn't want to alarm anyone until we know the facts."

"Roger that," the dispatcher's voice squeaked.

Several minutes later the man called back; Dusty was indeed overdue. Suzette had not reported him as missing, since he often got weathered in on fishing ventures. Brian had told her that he'd merely had a problem for the Chief Pilot, and to have him phone in immediately if he showed up.

The controller hung up the phone. "Rex, you got the radio for a minute," he said, and stepped outside for a much-needed cigarette. His shaking hands barely managed to light it. Taking a puff, a thought lifted his spirits slightly.

Perhaps Dusty really was weathered in somewhere. Maybe the Piper belonged to some yahoo visiting from the Outside.

But that was a very tenuous maybe.

DC took the chance. Tiptoeing into the bedroom, he bent over Stephanie and pecked her on the cheek.

"Good morning," he greeted with what he hoped sounded like enthusiasm.

Stephanie blinked the sleepers away and looked up at him. He'd forgotten how gorgeous she looked in the morning, just waking up.

"Sleep well?" he asked.

"Not bad," she replied with groggy voice. "I was pretty upset, but exhausted. You?"

He gave her a tired smile. "Hardly a wink." To his relief, she smiled. He said, "Six thirty and all's well." She looked at him in disbelief. Reading her mind, he quipped, "Yeah, I got to sleep in today."

"Sleep in?" she replied. "Wow, I'm impressed. I could never wake you up until I got back from Biology."

He nodded toward the window. "It's that crazy midnight sun out there. And our insane schedule. There are days when we're wheels-up before 5 a.m., and sometimes we don't set the parking brake until Letterman's on."

Fluffing a pillow, she sat up and crossed her arms. "So talk to me, DC."

He sat on the edge of the bed and unconsciously began to stroke her stomach. "Look, I'm chasing my career up here. I can't say whether I'll stay and move up, or do it somewhere else. Either way, it's unfair to keep you on a string."

"What about *her?"* she asked.

"Tonya," he said heavily.

"Tonya," Stephanie repeated. "So, my rival has a name. And you just spoke it like a man obsessed." She looked away. "Game over."

DC looked at the floor, then back into her eyes. He swallowed.

"I don't know, Steph. I don't know."

Stephanie placed a tender hand on his cheek. "Well, DC, I do. I'll be on the next plane out."

DC's eyes widened. "What? But you just got here."

"I found what I came for."

"What's that?"

"Answers." She rested her hand on his shoulder. "You're in love, DC, and it's not with me."

"I—*what?*"

"You're in love with her, not me," she repeated. "And no power in the universe can change your mind."

He shook his head emphatically, and opened his mouth to speak. Instead, he looked away. Was he? No way. Then again, why was he sitting here shunning a woman who'd traveled over a thousand miles for him? "I just—

give me some more time, will you? Time to, uh, sort things out." The phrase gave him a vague sense of *déja vu*. "Look, I've got to run. Just stay here a few days, okay?"

She stared at him a long moment. "Sorry," she said finally.

Ignoring her reply, he said, "There's a key and a map of Juneau for you on the table." He turned to leave.

"DC?"

He turned back. "Yeah?"

"Good bye."

He held his hands up. "Look, just stay here. I'll call you later this morning, between flights. We'll talk some more, okay?"

She crossed her arms. "You've got until ten."

"I hate deadlines."

"You're a pilot. Deal with it."

* * *

Jake awoke to the sharp pain of a knee jabbed into his buttocks.

"Ouch!" he cried. He opened his eyes rolled over to see Holly staring back at him. She lay on her side, her blue eyes burning into him from inches away.

"I can't believe you did this," she said. "You lowdown, dirty, conniving—"

Jake said nothing but threw the covers back.

Upon seeing the two of them fully clothed, Holly stopped her tirade and closed her mouth.

Staring into her eyes, Jake said softly, "I really wish you'd stop hitting me."

Holly looked away. "I—well, I wish you'd stop taking advantage of me," she replied, a little uncertainty creeping into her voice.

"No one used anybody."

"But—"

"But nothing, Holly. You invited me here, remember? Practically threatened to fire me if I didn't. Would have molested me had you not passed out."

"Would have *what?*" She shook her head. "Oh, Jake. You and that big ego of yours."

"Had nothing to do with it." He shook a finger at her. "You were *tanked*, lady, and I wanted to make sure you got safely home and to bed."

"Hmph. Well you sure as hell did that." Sitting upright, she said, "Which begs the question of why you're lying here in my bed. There's a perfectly good couch out there."

"Too short."

"Then there's the floor."

"Too cold and hard."

She folded her arms. "Well, you're a macho outdoors man."

He smiled. "Just a façade. I'm really a pushover for big, warm, feathery beds. Especially when there's a beautiful woman in the deal."

She groaned, but a slight twinkle appeared in her eyes. She grabbed the pillow behind her and hit his head with it. "You old charmer. You never give up, do you?"

He grabbed the pillow and pulled her in, so close that their noses nearly touched. Holly blinked, and tried to pull back. But Jake held her there.

He said, "That's not why I'm here, Holly. And you know it."

Holly stared into his eyes a long moment, then sat back, looking at the far wall as if lost in thought. He edged himself closer and lay a hand across her stomach. Unconsciously she began to stroke it with her nails. Finally, she giggled softly.

"What?" Jake asked.

She giggled some more.

"What is it?"

"I can't help but feel like I'm sleeping with the enemy."

"Men aren't the enemy, Holly. At least not this one."

She looked sideways at him. "I'm not so sure about that."

"You seemed pretty sure last night."

She put a hand to her head. "Oh, God. I can't believe I let myself go like that."

He stroked her belly some more. "Ours is a stressful job. We all need a little release once in awhile."

"But in front of the troops."

"Why not? You're one of us. But don't worry. There were no witnesses to your *amorous* advances."

She jumped out of bed. Over her shoulder, she said, "Oh right. I'm sure Ralph was too absorbed in his rum and Coke to notice a little hanky panky going on between his best friend and his worst enemy." She padded across the floor, peering under the furniture. "Skittles. Here, kitty kitty."

"Give him a little credit, Holly. He may be a prankster but he's no boardinghouse schoolboy. I asked him to keep a lid on it. He won't so much as whisper a veiled comment to you. Or to anyone."

Looking past her through the open bedroom door, he spied something on the floor by the front entrance. It appeared to be a note dropped through the mail slot.

"What's that?" he asked.

She walked over and picked it up. "What the hell?" she murmured. She returned and handed it to him. "What do you make of this?"

He eyed the note. A drawing, scribbled on the back of a Red Dog napkin. A cartoon of two bears in bed, naked but for old-fashioned leather flying caps askew on their heads, satisfied grins on their snouts and smoking cigarettes. Staring suggestively into the female's eyes, the male was saying, *"And this bed is juuust right."*

Jake laughed. "It's from Ralph."

She straightened and crossed her arms. "And what exactly is it supposed to mean?"

He handed it back to her. "It's his way of making peace."

She shook her head in disbelief and began to chuckle. "Ralph never was one to worry about political correctness."

She walked slowly around to her side and slipped back under the covers. Snuggling up to his chest she said, "All of a sudden, I feel like I could use a great, big bear hug."

Jake enthusiastically complied.

A short while later, the two sat contentedly in bed, resembling quite closely Ralph's cartoon.

Then came the phone call.

* * *

With trembling hand, Allen fished out a cigarette.

Misty began to protest, but was stopped by a slight movement of Ralph's index finger. Crying softly, she buried her face in her husband's arms. Ralph closed his eyes, kissed her forehead and stroked her hair.

Allen lit, and pulled a drag deep into his lungs. He gagged, and began a coughing fit. His eyes teared up and turned red, more from the news than the smoke.

Allen looked up from the couch where he was sitting. "He was—he . . . he was the *best*," he finally was able to utter.

Ralph pulled off his glasses and wiped a palm across his eyes. "We couldn't hold a candle to him."

Misty coughed.

Looking up, Allen finally realized his *faux pas*, and took his cigarette out to the second story balcony. Donning his leather jacket, his hand caught in a new rip in the sleeve.

"Dammit," he muttered. *Must've torn it the night before*, he thought.

He leaned against the railing and thought of his boss.

"Couldn't hold a candle to him," he repeated.

And if She could get *him*, he thought, then She could get anyone. To fucking *anyone*.

Gazing out at the low overcast, he trembled, so much that his cigarette slipped from his fingers.

He watched it spin away, and crash and burn in the foliage below.

*   *   *

DC sloshed through the muck to work. Drizzle dripped from his ball cap and rolled down his sleeves, wearing further his previously pristine leather jacket. The air, colder than he'd felt all summer, stung his cheeks. Lost in thought, he hardly noticed the chill.

Stephanie's words replayed in his head. Just like her to toss out an ultimatum. But, he knew, she deserved an answer. He reached the light on Glacier Highway. He stopped, content to wait for the walk signal. Several cars whizzed by, spraying water on his work boots. He gazed indifferently at the soaked shoes.

In love with Tonya? He wondered. How could he know. How does one ever know? He needed more time.

"To sort things out," he heard himself say aloud.

The words startled him. When he'd said it to Steph, what had he really meant?

Adios, that's what. And Tonya had said those exact words to him.

A wave of dizziness hit him. He put a hand on the light pole to steady himself.

Tonya was gone, and—what had Steph said?—no power in the universe would change her mind.

He slapped his forehead with his palm and exclaimed, "You *dumbass!*"

Stephanie was real; Tonya, a fantasy. He knew that now.

The light changed. A man suddenly on a mission, he ran. He had to tell Stephanie. Had to call and tell her now. Before she left him for good. As soon as he got to work, he would call and tell her just that.

But the news awaiting him at the airport made him forget everything.

* * *

Some wept silently. Some whispered in small groups. Some sat motionless, staring out the office window, across the SEAS' ramp and into the woods.

No one noticed that Holly and Jake arrived together, he in the same rumpled clothes from the night before.

All looked to them now for guidance.

Striding into the middle of the room, Holly held up a hand.

"Hold on a minute, people. We still haven't got confirmation that—"

"We just did," a secretary answered solemnly. "The Coast Guard chopper just verified the tail number. No sign of life."

"Damn," Holly whispered, lowering her head.

Jake wrapped a comforting arm around her and pulled her close. She leaned her head against his chest, a little too affectionate for mere coworkers in need of comfort. All noticed the incongruity now, but none cared.

"I . . . I'll be in my office," she said finally. She took a step forward, but Jake held her back.

"Ms. Innes," he said, loud enough for all to hear. He motioned to an open door marked, *Dusty Tucker, Chief Pilot*. "Your place is in there now."

She looked at Jake in surprise, then looked to the other pilots and workers in attendance. No one offered protest. She nodded.

"I guess you're right," she mumbled. Head lowered, she shuffled toward the door. At the threshold, she stopped. Inhaling deeply, she straightened, raised her chin and looked around the room.

In a firm voice, she announced, "This is a shock for all of us. In the interest of safety, I'm canceling all nonessential flights this weekend. If anyone needs more time than that, just let me know." In a softer, almost pleading voice, she said, "For SEAS to survive this, I'm going to need your help. Try to be strong, people. For me, for SEAS, most of all for Dusty. He would want it that way." She nodded to her new office. "Dusty's open door remains open."

Chief Pilot Holly Innes walked in and sat.

After a moments' reflection, she picked up the phone and called Inspector Bruner. A secretary said he was out investigating an accident, and would not be available until late in the day, if then. She thanked her and hung up.

A tap came at the door. She looked up.

Jake said, "If you need us, Ralph and I will be at Dusty's house with Suzette."

Holly closed her eyes. "Thanks."

"Stay strong yourself, Holly."

She looked up at him. "You too."

"Someone should be at the crash site, too," Jake added.

Holly gazed out the window. "I wish we could. But Dusty was off-duty when it happened. That means we're nothing but bystanders."

"But Bruner—"

"Will do his job, and do it right," she said firmly.

Jake nodded, and left.

Holly sat back, hoping her words were true.

* * *

Mud-splattered and rain-soaked, Air Safety Inspector Frederick Bruner eyed the wreckage. The wreckage of a man he had known.

The crash site was so rugged and remote, he and the two medics had to be lowered by helicopter cable. But at least, he thought, he wouldn't have to deal with reporters. Or worse, moronic souvenir-seekers.

The National Transportation Safety Board, as nearly always in the case of a small plane accident in Alaska, had deferred investigation to the nearest FAA Flight Standards District Office. And that meant him. Though not his primary duty, his office was typically short staffed, so he often wound up pulling the gruesome double duty. A more experienced crash investigation team would soon join him, but time was always critical, and he was first on the scene.

Bruner hated this part of his job. And loved it, too. Morbid as hell, but, he had to admit, intensely fascinating. To sift like a homicide detective through the remains of a crashed airplane for clues to its demise. Since the simple aircraft lacked a Flight Data Recorder, or as the media had nicknamed it, the *black box*—bright orange, in reality, for ease of location—Bruner would have to rely solely on physical clues to reconstruct the "crime" scene. He might even discover a previously unknown problem, and therefore prevent a future crash. That was the *real* reason for accident investigation, he knew. And that made all the toil worthwhile.

With a well-chewed Number 2 pencil, Bruner drew a quick sketch on a yellow legal notepad of the impact site. To this he added several notes.

By the swath the plane had cut, it appeared to have struck a tree nearly head on, followed by a quick cartwheel to the granite cliff a few feet beyond. Then the craft had slid further down the mountain until coming to rest at the base of the cliff. Nearly all of the yellow monocoque fabric of the former Piper Super Cub was compacted squarely into the size of a sports car.

At least death had come instantaneously to Dusty—*the pilot*, Bruner corrected himself; he had to think of the man objectively now. Even so, he was glad he wouldn't have to see the body, already airlifted out with the medics *cum* coroners.

A Piper Cub flying at the slowest speed, and the fully-deployed flaps dangling from the twisted wings suggested as much, would still be the equivalent of a car racing down an open highway.

The scenario seemed simple enough. Nearly all air crashes in Southeast Alaska contained as Probable Cause the phrase, *Continued VFR flight into deteriorating weather conditions*, followed by *Controlled flight into terrain.*

Bruner expected this to be no different. But in fairness for his former and very experienced acquaintance, and because the Chief Pilot's outfit came under Bruner's umbrella of scrutiny, he was determined to make sure.

Upon hearing the faint staccato chop of the crash team helicopter, Bruner sat on a boulder and smoked a Camel. He watched them arrive in the same manner, lowered by cable.

Once on the ground, the team hiked up to his vantage point.

Bruner filled them in. Leading the team through the marshy muskeg and thick underbrush to the main area, he said, "All major sections are tagged. Pretty small impact area."

"Trap'n splat?" the team leader asked. Accident investigators, much like doctors, often resorted to gallows humor to cope with the stress.

Bruner nodded. "Looks like it. Weather moved in, he flew up a box canyon, couldn't turn out or climb over. *Cumulogranite.*" Bruner waved a hand ahead, indicating the initial crash site. "Gouge patterns indicate the prop was spinning full power at impact, and paint tics smeared on the glass covers of the engine gauges confirm it. All red-lined."

"Good job," the lead replied. He gave Bruner a pat on the back. "We'll take over from here. Boat should be here for your extraction in an hour or so."

Hiking down the canyon to the beach of the channel inlet, Bruner consulted his homemade, laser-printed, *Accident Investigation Checklist.*

Using the now-stubby pencil, he crossed off each task completed.

One item remained. One that was no doubt going on right then in Juneau.

Perform autopsy on pilot.

* * *

It took awhile for it to soak in, but he finally wept.

Sitting in a chair in the main office, DC buried his head in his hands and let the tears flow. He felt a comforting hand on his back, from whom he didn't know.

Though DC had only known his boss a couple of months, he knew he would never forget the man. Indeed, all the people he came across at SEAS seemed larger than life, superhuman. Indestructible.

Until now.

And what does that make me? he wondered. A damned *cheechacko* who fantasized himself an Alaska bush pilot. Like a kid playing with Dad's loaded gun, oblivious to its true danger.

All the fragile confidence that he'd so carefully cultivated during his short time in Alaska came crashing down, chased away by the demons he'd thought buried.

CHAPTER 20: Pilot Error

Sauntering through the rain, Allen didn't bother to put on his hood.

No need to go into work, he thought. No one would be flying today. No way he could fly straight. And his misery certainly didn't need company.

Besides, DC would be at the airport. Best to give the guy some space, give him a few days to cool off. Now would be a good time to slip into the crash pad, pick up a few things and get out.

Up ahead, the neighborhood liquor store got in his way. By the time he reached the apartment, he realized that his fifth of Jack Daniels was half empty.

"Half full," he corrected himself aloud, a small trickle of whiskey dribbling down his chin as he did. He wiped it away and grinned.

Jack always had a way of brightening his day.

* * *

"I can't believe it," Stephanie spouted, furiously stuffing yesterday's clothes into her backpack. Couldn't believe that a man who'd once lived with her would be so callous as to not even bother with a goodbye phone call, let alone try to stop her. And she'd flown a thousand miles for the chump!

She'd waited until the last possible minute, then packed up. Briefly, she considered staying a few days, salvage the trip with a little sightseeing. But the weather in the Alaska panhandle seemed as dreary as her mood. Besides, she couldn't afford a hotel, and staying in his apartment was out of the question. She'd already been humiliated enough.

She strapped on the backpack. Throwing open the door, she stomped outside and nearly ran over Allen.

Allen stepped back in surprise. "Well, if it isn't the fair maiden Stephanie," he exclaimed. "Come all the way to Alaska for her knight in shining armor."

"Her knight's in the fucking doghouse, Allen. And I'm outta here."

She pressed past him, but he grabbed her shoulder.

"Hold on, Stephie. You just got here. Come back in out of the rain. Too wet and cold for a desert flower like you. Besides, I got something that will warm you up."

She realized then that he was drunk, and raised a hand to slap him for the sexual innuendo. But he merely held up the bottle.

"Whiskey, my girl. Mornin' coffee for us Alaskans."

She turned red, and let out an embarrassed laugh. "Sorry, Allen. I thought you were—My God, where'd you get the shiner?"

He rubbed the bruise. "In my eye, that's where."

"Cute."

"You should see the other guy."

She rolled her eyes. "Yeah, right." She held him at arm's length. "Well anyway, it's nice to see you."

He stepped back into an eloquent, courtly bow, swaying slightly. "And you, too, milady." He stood back up. "Now, please accompany me back into the castle and fill me with your tales of woe while we partake of this fine mead."

She eyed the bottle. "Why the hell not?" she mumbled. Grabbing it from him, she took a swig and choked. Her gag turned into a giggle.

In kingly fashion, Allen offered his arm. She grasped it, and the two strolled inside.

* * *

The Alaska Airlines ticket agent shook her head. Staring at the computer screen, she said, "Not aboard, DC. Sorry."

He turned away, confused. Then why the hell didn't she answer the phone? he wondered. Out sightseeing? Somehow, in her present state of mind, that didn't seem likely. Taking a shower, perhaps.

Allen's absence at the airport worried him, too. Death had a way of putting things into perspective, and their little spat seemed comically petty now. He needed to apologize to him, to set things right between them.

But more than anything, he needed to see Stephanie, needed to hold the one person that could calm his troubled mind.

She would understand.

Stephanie felt herself rapidly approaching Allen's euphoric state.

"You're right, Allen," she said, staring into the bottom of her mug. "Jack and coffee does taste damn good."

"And each cup goes down smoother than the last," he added.

They clinked cups.

She turned sideways on the couch, lay an arm across the back, and faced him. "So anyway, that's how I wound up here," she finished.

"Wow," Allen said, shaking his head in disbelief. "You came all the way up here for a man. I could only dream of finding someone that dedicated."

"Not anymore," she replied. She looked at him, eyes narrowed. "Don't you already know all this?"

Allen looked away. "We don't really talk much anymore. About that, anyway." His grip tightened on his mug. "Not since he fucked—"

"What?" she exclaimed.

"I mean. Oh, shit." He held up a hand. "Sorry. It's not my place to—"

She grabbed his arm and shook it. "Out with it, Allen. Fucked who? Your girlfriend? Is he a damned sex maniac, or what?"

Allen shook his head emphatically. "No. She wasn't my girlfriend. N—not really."

"Who? Tonya?"

He looked up sharply at the name, and his pained expression said it all. She put a hand to her mouth. "Oh my God. You're in love with her too."

"*No!* It was never like that."

"Some women have all the luck," she mumbled, eyes staring at the floor. She looked back up. "Come on, Allen. DC had that same look on his face when I saw him last night."

"We were just going out for awhile. Nothing serious."

"So, you hand DC a job on a silver platter, and he rewards you by sleeping with your woman."

"Not my woman, Stephanie. She's . . . she's a bear that can't be tamed."

"What?" she asked quizzically. With a wave of her hand, she said, "You're drunk."

"No, I mean, she's never been in love with anyone."

"And therein lies the challenge," she said, shaking her head.

"She's nobody's girl," he said. "Certainly not DC's. She dumped him for the same guy that popped me in the eye. Tom Zion."

Stephanie sat back and hooted. "Jesus Christ, *As the World Turns*!"

"More like *As the Prop Turns*," Allen groused.

She took a final swig of coffee and slammed the mug on the table. She wiped a dribble from her lip with a shirt sleeve.

"Tom and Tonya. Sounds like those two tramps deserve each other."

Allen shrugged. "Tom damn well had it coming. As for DC. Well, he's my friend," he finished simply.

She said softly, "Allen, the strong silent one, has a kink in his emotional armor after all. Who would have guessed?" She reached out a sympathetic hand and caressed his cheek. "Not only do you let the girl go, you defend the honor of the man stealing her from you."

His eyes were full of tears, she saw. But from what? Friendship lost? Love lost? It seemed worse than that, but she couldn't tell.

She whispered, "Are you still that dedicated to him?"

He pulled her hand from his cheek and kissed the palm. She caught her breath and tried to pull back, but he held it tight.

"Are you?"

* * *

DC opened the front door and walked in. He spotted Stephanie's backpack by the couch. The door to his room was closed. He peeked through Allen's open door. The bed sheets were ruffled, but no sign of Allen. *Strange*, he thought. Allen hadn't slept there the night before. Then he sniffed the odor of a recently smoked cigarette. He walked over to his room, knocked softly, and opened the door.

"Stephanie?" he called.

The shower was on. But through the bathroom door, he heard a muffled cry. He knocked. "Steph?" he called again. He tried the knob. Unlocked.

He pushed the door open and found her, sitting with head in hands, a towel hugging her body. She looked up. Water streamed down her face. But she had yet to step into the shower.

"Steph?"

She stared at him with a deer-in-headlights look.

"What's wrong?"

"I'm sorry," she whispered.

The hair on his neck prickled. "Where's Allen?" he demanded.

"I'm sorry," she repeated, voice cracking.

DC's face turned crimson. "*Where the fuck is he?*"

"I don't know. He left without saying."

DC stormed out of the room.

"I—we—we were drunk, DC," she called after him.

He slammed the front door.

* * *

He spun him around on the barstool and hit him with all his might. Allen fell to the floor.

Rain dripping from his soaked hide, DC towered over him. "Dusty gets killed, and you're out fucking my *girlfriend*?"

DC advanced. Several patrons grabbed him from behind.

With his jacket sleeve, Allen wiped a trickle of blood from his nose.

"Hey," the burly bartender yelled. "Take it outside, *now!*"

"Damn good idea," DC replied.

Standing, Allen held up a hand in truce and walked to the door. DC nodded agreement, and the others released him. He followed.

Over his shoulder Allen said, "You've got a right to be upset, DC. But it's not what you think."

"Oh, spare me the explanation. Quite convenient, isn't it? Comforting each other in your time of need."

Outside, the two turned the corner into the vacant lot next to the building. DC grabbed him by the shoulders and slammed him against the brick wall. "Our Chief Pilot just crashed, Allen. *Killed!* And all you two can think about is getting even for Tonya."

Allen held up his hands. "DC, it just happened, okay? Nobody planned anything. We were both fucked up. Got drunk. And we . . . we made a bad call."

"*Made a bad call?"* DC sputtered. "You won the *Darwin Awards* with that one, pal." DC threw a left hook to his face. Ready this time, Allen turned with the blow. Grabbing DC by the waist, Allen tossed him over his hips. DC landed on his rump in a puddle of mud.

Allen stood over him and held up a finger. "Now you listen to me, *asshole.* What was it someone said to me earlier this summer? 'You had your chance, step aside. It's my turn'. By *your* rules, my friend, Stephanie was fair game." He lowered his finger, and his voice. "But we stopped before anything happened, DC. Hear me? *She* stopped *me*, alright? Even as much as you've *fucked* her over, she's still dedicated to you. Get that through your goddamned, ego-filled head."

Allen spun and left.

* * *

DC sat up, cold and wet, with mud soaked into his jeans, boots and jacket. He scooped up a handful of the gunk and inspected it.

What the hell was he doing here? he wondered. Turning paradise into a mud hole. He looked up to the sky, half expecting his eagle to drop a load right between his eyes. Instead, rain poured across his cheeks, down his nose and off his chin.

DC let out a long, exhausted sigh.

"Time to clean up," he said finally.

He scrambled to his feet, slipping several times before succeeding.

* * *

She was gone. A note lay on his bed. He sat and read:

Dear DC,

First let me say that I'm sorry. Sorry I ever came up here. But I had to know if it was truly over. I guess it is.

I don't know why I did what I did, maybe for revenge, maybe to convince myself that we were through. But please understand that, in the end, nothing happened. Allen came to his senses first. He stopped us. He's done more for you than you'll ever know. He's a fiercely devoted friend, and you should remember that.

Don't try to contact me. The sooner we drop this, the quicker we can move on. I'm sorry it ended this way. Maybe some time in the future, we can be friends.

Deep down, I'll always love you. Good luck.

Love,

Steph

Several stains on the page marked where she had cried. Now his tears joined them. DC crumpled the letter in his hands.

He trudged to the bathroom for a long, hot shower.

* * *

Eyes wide open and staring at the ceiling, Allen shifted restlessly on Ralph's couch.

The only thing pleasant about the weekend, he thought, was that he would get to stay drunk the whole damn time. But Monday, after the funeral, he would have to face *Her* again. He wondered if he could.

She had beat Dusty out, beat out the best damned pilot he'd ever known. Was that how his illustrious airline career was going to end? Smeared across *cumulogranite*, beat out by Her before he'd even logged a single hour of turboprop time.

Rolling over, he pulled the crumpled paper from his back pocket. He eyed the ad. The beautiful girl and the seaplane smiled back.

He picked up the near-empty bottle from the floor and began to take an unconscious swig. He stopped, looked at it, and set it down.

"To hell with it," he mumbled.

Rifling through his pack, Allen found the list of Caribbean charter airlines. Each already had his resume on file. Glancing at his watch, he did the math. This late hour would mean early morning, V.I. time. Most outfits would be up and running by now.

Clearing his throat, he picked up the phone and set about calling each one.

To his surprise, midway through the list, the former bush pilot landed a new job. All he had to do was show up, and Captain Max Bartoff would hire him to fly twins for Virgin Islands Skyways.

Wow! he thought. Multiengine time at last. Rung Two on the long, rickety ladder to the airline flight deck.

He could already taste the *piña coladas*, feel the sun on his tanned hide, smell the sweet, bikini-clad island girl laying beside him. Paradise.

"How soon can you be here?" the voice on the phone asked.

Allen glanced at the calendar on the wall. One month. One entire goddamn month left to the season, and the bonus check. A ripple of fear raced down his spine. Far too long. Fuck the bonus.

Allen grinned wide. "One week," he replied to his new boss. "Thank you, Captain Bartoff."

* * *

"You're welcome," Captain Maxwell Bartoff replied from four thousand miles away.

Hanging up, Bartoff held his sweaty, bald head in the fan's airstream for a moment, then stared across the cluttered desk at the pilot sitting opposite him.

This damned cramped office, he thought. Made him feel more like a down-on-his-luck Dashiell Hammett gumshoe than a down-on-his-luck Chief Pilot. Some day, he'd have to get the pilots to clean it up for him. That was about all the deadbeats were worth.

"Yeah, I tell you, Clem," Bartoff said. "Those Alaska bush drivers, they're real pilots. You want a job done, they find a way to do it. Unlike you poor, useless slobs."

Eyes half closed, Clem said, "Hey, maybe he'll even be desperate enough to stay around for a couple weeks."

Bartoff ignored the insult. "Which reminds me, you've still got a couple airplanes to wash."

Yawning, Clem stood and turned for the door.

Bartoff rolled up a stack of papers and swatted a fly on his desk. "Hey, Clem," he said. "Why don't you smile once in awhile?"

"About what?" Clem replied.

* * *

Eyes wide open and staring at the ceiling, DC lay silent in his bed.

He recalled Stephanie's familiar sounds, and imagined them coming from Allen's room. He shook the horrible thought away.

Slowly, he became aware of another noise, a soft hiss. He lay motionless for a few minutes, trying to identify the strange sound. Finally, he stood, tossed on jacket and jeans, and crept out to the front room.

The sound led him out the front door. Leaning over the railing and staring into the dark night, he gasped in wonderment.

There, above the mountaintop, dancing amidst a thousand bright stars, shimmered a rainbow curtain of light. He'd heard of the *aurora borealis*, the Northern Lights, but had never seen them.

The curtains shifted, swayed, swelled and played across the stellar landscape. First green, then red, then yellow, then green again. Though on the very verge of his awareness, DC could swear the lights hissed and crackled as they moved.

His heart pounded at the sight.

He shouted back into the apartment, "Allen, get out here! You gotta see—"

He stopped himself. Allen was no longer there. Nor was Stephanie.

How ironic, he thought. His whole world had crashed, and here was Alaska, showing off Her greatest wonders with utter, almost mocking, indifference.

He turned back inside.

* * *

Acting Chief Pilot Holly Innes had been dreading the meeting all day. Just as Dusty had dreaded them in the past, she thought. But there was no way around it. A SEAS pilot had crashed, and she had to answer to the local Aviation Safety Inspector. And she needed answers, too.

Though most government stiffs shunned working Sundays, Bruner, she knew, lived for the job. Besides, under the circumstances . . . .

A soft knock on the open door; Holly looked up to see the Inspector poking his head in, a grim look on his face.

She stood and offered a hand. "Come in, Inspector Bruner."

The two shook hands, eyeing each other for a moment like new sparring partners. They sat.

Bruner began. "First of all, Ms. Innes, let me offer my sincere condolences."

"Thank you," she said softly.

"Dusty was more than a fellow worker, Ma'am. He was my friend."

She unconsciously dabbed a tear from her eye. "He was that to all of us."

"I know what he meant around here."

"So, what's the Probable Cause?" she asked.

He cocked his head and eyed her like a father scolding a child.

"Now you know I'm not at liberty to discuss that. These things take months, sometimes."

"I know, Inspector. But I'm not the media. You can at least give me something."

He leaned forward, as if in a conspiratorial whisper. "Well, between you and me, it looks like a typical *trap n splat*."

Holly cringed. She'd never heard the term, but knew exactly what it meant.

Bruner dropped his file on the desk. "*Cumulogranite*. We're just lucky it happened on his own time."

She gazed at him evenly. "What exactly do you mean?"

Bruner leaned back and began to rock in his chair. "You know that usually means, *Pilot Error*. So, if it had happened on a SEAS flight, and since you *are* on probation, we'd have to look at training, procedures, qualifications and such. Still, I wouldn't mind doing a fine-tooth look-see, just in case. Because, quite frankly Miss Innes, the wolves in Oak City are smelling blood up here."

Only because you set them on us, she didn't say.

Bruner shrugged. "A single problem, and maybe I can save you. But a couple accidents, or even incidents, and your whole ticket could get pulled."

Inwardly she fumed. The nerve of the man, taking credit for saving them while he was the shit-stirrer in the first place. Well, the Inspector lived to cross *i's* and dot *t's*, and if he wanted to run through SEAS' paperwork, she'd bury him in it. She sighed in resignation and waved a hand at the file cabinets. "OK, Inspector Bruner. *Mi casa es su casa.*"

He smiled broadly. "Please, call me Fred."

To Holly, his reaction seemed more gloat than warmth. Her face remained placid. "What about Ralph Olafsen? You've taken one of our best drivers. Now another is gone. You know we're hurting. Do you really feel Ralph is that much of a threat?"

He stared at her evenly. "You know I only operate in the interest of *safety*. If I felt he was safe enough to—"

Holly raised her voice. "He is, Inspector, and you know it."

Bruner sat back and folded his hands to his stomach. "Then no doubt I'll determine that during my investigation."

Holly gazed out the window for a moment to maintain composure. Turning back, she stood and leaned over the desk, hands resting on the edge. How many times had Dusty struck this exact pose with this infuriating man? she wondered.

She said, "Look. Ralph may do things a little less conventionally than we'd like, but he gets the job done. He's experienced, he's smart, and most importantly, Inspector, he's *safe*."

Bruner stood. Half turning for the door, his eyes met hers.

"And for now, he's grounded. Good day, Chief Pilot Innes." With a nod, he walked away. At the door he stopped and said, "I'll see you at the funeral tomorrow."

The term *Dancing on his grave* flashed through Holly's mind.

She fell back in her seat with a *humph*.

Defending Ralph Olafsen! Now wasn't that an ironic turn? Though Ralph did things his own way, she'd always known he was one of the best.

Like Dusty had been. After a quick glance out the window to make sure no one was looking, she dabbed once again at her tear-filled eyes.

The phone rang.

"Innes," she answered.

"I've had enough, Ms. Innes," Allen said. "I quit."

She sat upright. "*What?* Look, Allen, you can't let Dusty's death—"

"It's more than that, Ma'am. *She beat me out.*"

"Allen, we've only got a little over a month left," she pleaded. "Don't forget your end-of-season bonus."

"I'm sorry."

"Allen, you know I'm already down two pilots as it is. Look, give me two weeks. I . . . I'll make sure you get the easy runs. Flightseeing tours and short hauls. And you'll get your bonus, too."

After a long pause, Allen replied, "Two weeks."

"Okay."

She hung up.

And now she was down three float plane drivers. She eyed the pilot scheduling board. After a long minute's thought, she reluctantly hit the intercom button.

"Schedule Jake to give some float training Monday morning, will you?" she said to the secretary. "And put me down to give a checkride afterwards in the same bird. Before the funeral, if possible."

"With whom shall I schedule the checkride?" the secretary asked.

"DC."

CHAPTER 21: Termination Dust

He took his time getting ready. When he finally walked out the door, it was with a daypack loaded with a rain jacket and pb&j sandwich.

A half hour later, he stood motionless before the plunging waterfall, letting the cool mist wash over his face. He eyed the route he and Allen had attempted. As mad as he was at Allen, DC found himself longing to hear the man striding up the trail behind him, climbing gear clinking with his gait. But he wondered if he could even trust the man with his life now. Or trust himself to belay as Allen climbed.

He looked up. Sure enough, his eagle circled high overhead.

He looked back at the rock. Perhaps there was another way. A way to do it solo. He scanned his surroundings.

A thick stand of fallen pines lay to the side. Stepping over a log and into the dense brush, DC propelled himself from branch to branch. He moved quickly up the hill. Tree sap stuck to his hands and smeared his jacket. He ignored it. A branch snapped, and he tumbled into a thicket laced with devil's club.

He found himself on his back, staring at treetops. The thorny bush pricked him through his jeans, and stung his hands and head.

Between the treetops overhead, the eagle continued to circle.

But what he saw beyond surprised him even more. The clouds had lifted to reveal atop the peaks of Thunder Mountain a fresh dusting of snow. The first he'd seen on the ridge line all summer.

Termination Dust, Allen had called it. The death of the summer season.

The end, perhaps, of his time in Alaska.

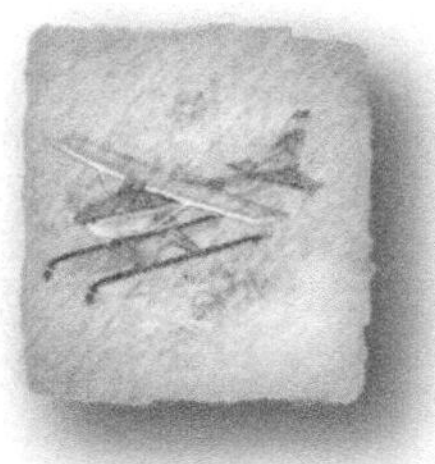

Struggling with his tie in the mirror the next morning, DC contemplated his new job.

He had earned his floatplane rating years earlier. But like a high school course in Swahili, he'd never had the chance to use it. Suddenly the opportunity lay in his hands. All summer long he had bummed rides from the other float pilots, gleaning tips and unofficial time. The night before, the midnight sun had beaten him to bed while he studied the de Havilland Beaver pilot's manual. Like the Cessna 207 manual, he knew it backwards and forwards. He was ready.

But he couldn't help but feel like a warm body being thrown into the cockpit to replace—well, he thought, a cold one. One who's funeral he would attend right after his checkride, no less.

Step up a rung, on the back of his boss. He wondered if bankers and lawyers felt the same remorse as they clawed their way up the corporate ladder.

DC donned his brown leather pilot's jacket, the only coat he had worthy of a funeral, and eyed himself in the mirror one last time. Brushing a fleck of lint away from the shoulder, he realized the jacket had cracked and faded over the past few months. He frowned. Too late to touch it up, or find a replacement.

For no reason he could discern, the jacket recalled to him the first time he'd met Dusty Tucker. The old man had always put him at ease, made him feel worthy of the challenge, but always with hands poised to catch him if he fell.

Now, the safety net was gone.

And, he was alone.

The enormity of the weekend's losses crashed down on him again. He leaned on the sink and let out one long, giant, all-encompassing sob.

With a tissue, he dabbed his eyes and left.

* * *

"Once in the air, flying a floatplane is nothing," Jake yelled over the deep bass rumble of the Beaver's Pratt & Whitney R985 "Wasp Junior" radial engine, as DC banked around the traffic pattern. "It's just a slower version of any plane you've ever flown. Now, reading water and air, that's everything. And once you're on the water and out of the air, all you are is a sailboat."

In DC's youth, Phoenix had never exactly been a sailing Mecca, but he caught the sourdough's drift.

"Unless they're glassy smooth, lakes usually don't take much to read," Jake continued. "But landing on saltwater's a whole new ballgame. And *this* is your holy bible," Jake said, thumping the Tide book on the dash.

Timing was everything, DC found. Practice landing after practice landing, he touched down upon the Juneau float pond in a silvery spray, then taxied the plane fast "on the step" to the dock.

For the first several tries, Jake took over at that point. He then demonstrated the exact moment to cut the motor to glide up to the dock. From there, he had DC practice opening the door, hopping out onto the left float, and stepping onto the dock at walking speed.

After that, it was DC's turn to try it all. Playing it safe the first several times, he cut the engine too soon, got caught short, and had to literally sail the plane into the dock, using elevator, flaps, flight rudder, and even doors as a makeshift mainsail and mizzen. After several successes, however, DC got cocky. On his last try, he cut the engine too late, sending the ground hands scurrying. The craft smacked into the dock with a graceless thud.

After Jake stopped laughing, he endorsed DC's logbook for the checkride.

* * *

Checkride-itis, as always, loomed in the back of DC's mind.

Much to his relief, however, Check Airman Innes seemed uncharacteristically easy on his oral test. And, once in the air, the intimidation he normally felt when flying shotgun with her was curiously missing.

Perhaps they were both too distracted by the events of the weekend, he thought.

A steady, light breeze made for ideal conditions. Like DC's flight with Jake, the checkride with Holly turned out to be as much lesson as test. Just as Dusty had been, Holly seemed compelled to impart to DC as much wisdom as she could in their short time together. And that was fine with him.

Best of all, he felt he could land the floatplane almost anywhere if the weather moved in. The thought gave him no end of relief. But, he also knew, that very sense of invincibility had lured many an Alaska float pilot to his grave.

Instinctively, DC gripped tighter on the yoke.

Holly seemed to read his mind. She said, "A good pilot never gets into situations where he must rely on his superior flying skills to get him out." She finished by quoting the pilots' mantra. "Remember, DC. 'There are old pilots and bold pilots, but no old, bold pilots'."

Never had the words rung so true as up here, he realized.

Smiling, he relaxed. "Words for a pilot to live by, Ma'am."

She returned the smile. "Words for a *bush* pilot to live by."

DC turned his attention to passing the test.

* * *

The small church overflowed with guests. Despite being the Alaska State capital, Juneau still was very much a small town where, it seemed, everyone knew everybody.

And everyone had known Dusty.

Suzette, Bobbi Sue, Betty Lou and the grandkids filled the front row. In the middle of the chapel, most of the SEAS crew filled several rows. Jake sat next to Holly, the two holding hands for support and leaving no doubt as to their new relationship. Ralph and Misty sat next to them, he in uncharacteristically sharp brown smoking jacket, tie and slicked back hair, she in cotton print dress, fresh daisies woven into her light brown and grey braids. Sporting a blue blazer borrowed from Jake, Allen rounded out the row.

DC arrived alone, and sat toward the back.

The funeral was simple. A quick sermon, followed by testimony from several relatives and close friends.

Jake finished it off. Standing before a podium at the head of the crowded room, he said, "There's a saying in our business that goes, 'There are old pilots and bold pilots, but no old, bold pilots'," he said. "But even so, no matter how experienced we may be, no matter how cautious we are, Mother Nature always has the last word. She can beat out the best of us. And three days ago, She did.

"It is a hard but necessary lesson when our best falls. It makes us realize that we are not invincible. So, as we go about our days trying to be heroes, slipping into tiny strips, cheating the weather, pushing the odds, let us remember one thing: *She* is always in charge, and we damn well better remember that. For, if not, She will surely remind us.

"So, today, let us all take the time to remember Dusty Tucker, and his wise lessons in life. But also his lesson in death.

"Be safe, fly straight, and God bless."

* * *

The reception, held at the Tucker household, was nearly as crowded. Suzette found herself surrounded by her daughters and friends, all trying in vain to answer the question foremost on the widow's mind: Why? After all these years, why now?

* * *

After an hour of the necessary socializing, Holly caught Jake's eye.

He slid along side. "Ready to go?" he asked.

She nodded. The two began to weave their way to the front door.

A tap on Jake's shoulder stopped them.

"Good speech, Mr. Whitakker," Inspector Bruner said.

"Thanks, I—"

"Let's just hope you take your own words to heart." Before Jake could react to the implied insult, Bruner turned his attention to Holly. "The preliminary autopsy reports are in."

Glancing around the room, Holly said, "I don't think this is the most appropriate place to discuss that. Care to follow us out?"

He did. Outside, the three walked downhill several houses.

Holly stopped and turned. "Yes?" she prompted.

With a glance around them, Bruner leaned forward and said, "Looks like our man had an *acute myocardial infarction*."

Holly and Jake traded looks.

Jake asked, "And that means what?"

Bruner straightened and thumped his chest. "In layman's terms, a heart attack."

Jake and Holly fell silent, contemplating the last few moments of their friend's life.

Holly took the grim thought a step further. "That would mean the heart attack was the Probable Cause of the accident," she mused aloud.

Bruner shrugged. "It would certainly make SEAS look better."

Under his breath, Jake grumbled, "As if you cared."

Holly raised a subtle finger to silence Jake. "I'm more concerned about Dusty's family right now, Inspector," she said evenly, a slight frown betraying her annoyance.

Bruner held up a cautionary hand. "There might still be contributing factors, mind you. I'm thinking *Continued flight into deteriorating weather* probably got him into trouble in the first place. Even without the bad ticker, he still might have bought it."

"Pure speculation," Jake protested.

Bruner looked Jake dead in the eye. "Perhaps. But it still smells to me like Pilot Error."

"*Pilot Error*," Jake spat. "That's what you live for, isn't it, Bruner? Busting pilots for the *error* of being human." He took a step forward, but a raised arm from Holly barred his way. "It must eat you up inside that you can't pin this on your old 'buddy'. Prove to the world that you're better than him."

"Jake," Holly said, her voice strained with worry.

He ignored her. Jabbing a finger at the Inspector's chest, he said, "But that's your big, dark secret, isn't it? You never could cut it up there in the clouds. What do they call the second rate pilots? Inspectors."

With that, he spun and marched away.

Holly grabbed Bruner's arm, and looked up at him with grave concern. "He doesn't mean it, Inspector. He's just upset."

Through clenched teeth, Bruner mumbled, "I understand."

* * *

"*Jake!*" Holly called after him, running to catch up.

Not missing a step, Jake waved a hand behind him. "Don't even start, Holly."

She raced ahead of him and turned. Putting a hand on his chest, she tried to stop him. "What are you trying to do, take Ralph's place as Federal Enemy Number One?"

He pushed past her and marched down the hill. "That man represents everything I despise."

"He's the key to our survival, Jake," she called after him, struggling to match his frantic pace. "Piss him off, and we might as well pack it up."

"That's *bullshit!* The FAA can't harass us out of business just because we refuse to kiss their ass. That's why we came to Alaska in the first place. To be free. Free from the politics. Free from the red tape. I refuse to let the man wind me in it."

Holly finally caught up with him again. "Well, you can catch more bears with honey."

He shook his head emphatically. "That bear doesn't want honey. He's a carnivore. And he won't be happy till SEAS gets roasted over his fire."

"That's not true, Jake. He wants what we all want. Safety."

With a roll of his eyes, he said, "Ah, yes, safety. The battle cry of the FAA Inspector. And with his pious words, the *Federali* buries us in his rules. But in his blind zeal, he manages to smother the one thing he strives to create. But man doesn't make the rules around here. Alaska does. We fly by *Her* rules, or die."

He continued, his tone slightly softer. "Why do you think we freed the bears, hmm? Because two cocksuckers from the asphalt jungle killed a sow for sport, and the paper pushing *pissants* were going to let them get away with it. This is the bears' land, Holly. Not ours. This is *their* Last Frontier." He stopped, eyes downcast.

She lay a hand on his back. He looked up. She noticed then that his eyes were bloodshot, and filled with tears.

"We're the last bush pilots, Holly. And we're a dying breed. This is *our* Last Frontier, too. We can't . . . we can't let the bureaucrats do it. We can't let them pave it all over," he finished softly.

Jake looked up to the sky. The barest wisp of drizzle alighted upon his face. "Oh, Dusty, I miss your sorry ass. But you died *free*, doing what you damn well pleased, with no one breathing down your neck. I envy you, goddamnit."

His words set off a flurry of tears in her own eyes. She squeezed his shoulders and said softly, "Give you a ride, sailor?"

He looked down at her, the saddest of smiles upon his lips. He ran a hand through her shoulder length hair, and caressed her cheeks. "You're a thing of beauty, you are. Hard and soft all at once. Just like this land that we're in love with." He kissed her. "Take me home. To my cabin. In the woods, where no one can find us."

Holly drove them the short distance to the airport. From there, she flew him home.

To his cabin.

In the woods, where no one could find them.

CHAPTER 22: The Sky Fell

For the next week, Allen and DC did a good job of avoiding each other.

Holly, sensitive to such small company bickerings that cropped up from time to time, did a good job of keeping the two separated as well. Float trips she now tossed DC's way; Allen she confined mostly to wheels. She knew the move could risk flaming their little spat—whatever it may involve—but DC needed to get up to speed in the floats as quickly as possible.

Moreover, Holly had detected in Allen a definite change. He had the far away look in his eyes, like a man stricken with cabin fever. She could only hope that, in his cockpit, he was all there.

It looked like DC would claim the winter job, she mused. But even he appeared a bit gun shy over the accident.

With a month to go, she knew, Mother Nature could still beat them both out.

* * *

Flying three passengers to the fishing village of Elfin Cove on the western shore of Chichagof Island, DC pulled the de Havilland Beaver floatplane off the Juneau Airport pond and into the sky.

The week, while challenging, had proved to be fairly routine. During that time, he'd had only one air turn-back. Allen's turn-back record, he learned through company gossip, stood at four.

Nevertheless, his enthusiasm for float plane flying continued to wrestle with the fears cropping up in his mind.

While Juneau Flight Service Station had provided DC with a textual description of the weather forecast, he, like the others, had grown to take it with a grain of salt. He instead relied on what he saw out the window. And so far, he saw, Juneau was having an exceptionally fine day.

The dry, abbreviated verbiage of his weather printout did little to convince him of the wet cold front racing in from the coast.

A local Tlingit man sat in the copilot seat next to him. In back sat two tourists on a fishing venture.

DC leveled off at 2,000 feet, just beneath the rapidly increasing cloud layer.

Crossing Funter Gap, he noticed the skies over Chichagof appeared lower, and darker than usual. The north route, along the shoreline past Hoonah, was socked in, a solid wall of rain and clouds. Deviating south, he decided to keep to the eastern shoreline of Chichagof a little longer, then cut across the island.

He knew he was taking a risk. If he was forced down over the mountainous island, his precious floats would be useless; he might as well be a brick.

Funny how his perspective changed on what was the biggest threat, depending on whether he had floats or wheels under his butt. Before, in the wheelplanes, the water was deadly. Now it was his friend. And he liked his new friend. Perhaps a little too much, he realized.

The overcast forced him lower, below 1,000 feet above the ground. Though he'd grown used to the strange feeling of buzzing the terrain, it still made for a slightly increased heart rate.

He glanced at his passengers, wondering if they would be worried. He smiled. The two in back peered out the window, a slightly bored look on their faces, and his Tlingit "copilot" was asleep, his head resting against the door frame.

Though he had learned most of the terrain by heart, DC referred to his now dog-eared Sectional folded in his lap. Matching the chart to the curve of land ahead, he searched for an alternate route across the island.

The sky lightened; DC smiled.

"Go for the gusto or stay the fuck at home," he whispered to himself.

Taking a deep breath, he banked the Beaver floatplane west and made for a cut in the mountains.

Just a few more days, became Allen's new mantra. Finding himself suddenly out of favor on the float assignments, he only volunteered for the short, easy wheelplane runs. Even the thought of an hour-long flight to Kake or Petersburg spooked him, especially when he set out across Stephen's Passage between the two islands, where overcast and rain often forced the pilots far lower than gliding distance to shore.

Before each flight, he'd taken to a new ritual. After loading the cargo, he taxied the plane to the fuel pump. Rather than fuel the plane himself as he usually did, however, he let the new line boy gas up while he stood behind the fuel shack and smoked.

The cigarette went a long way to calm his nerves. Therefore, he rationalized, in the eyes of the FAA, it would be a necessary preflight item.

Today had been easy so far, and now he was heading to Haines.

The weather on the previous Skagway trip, on the same route, had been manageable, but now the partly cloudy skies had filled into a rapidly lowering overcast.

Once in the air, he hugged the eastern shore of Lynn Canal, skimming beneath the cloud bases to stay as high as possible. He searched up ahead for an opening to cut over to the western side of the channel.

The overcast pushed him lower.

He glanced at the altimeter: 800 feet. Much lower, and an engine failure mid-channel would catch him too far from shore. He wished again for a set of floats under him.

The rain increased, cutting visibility to five miles. Once, that had been plenty. But now he felt as if he was stumbling blindly.

Dumping all the flaps, he slowed to minimum speed. He relaxed slightly. The curtain of rain seemed a bit more forgiving then.

He found himself wishing for a passenger to talk with, to ease his mind. But all he had was cargo and mail.

The sky lightened; Allen smiled.

He banked the Cessna 207 wheelplane left and headed out over the channel, toward the spit of land south of Haines.

* * *

Lowering a notch of flaps, DC slowed. While light at first, the grey sky had quickly darkened, and seemed to slant straight down to meet the mountaintops. The mist turned to drizzle, cutting visibility across the island to six miles. Still okay, but not exactly infinite.

As he closed in on the pass, the pass closed in on him.

Time to bug out, he decided.

He circled back, and found the pass behind closed as well, a solid wall of rain. He turned back west and met another wall.

His stomach tightened.

"Oh, shit," he mumbled under his breath.

Pulling the power back, he slowed further.

His front passenger stirred at the change. DC glanced at him, inadvertently catching his eye. He turned away, wondering what the man could read in his face. Tension? Fear? He wondered himself what he felt.

The leaden sky pressed down like the slab roof of a tomb, filling him with a claustrophobic sense of dread.

He risked a glance at his altimeter. Five hundred feet and dropping.

She had set the trap and caught him.

A float pilot miles from water and surrounded by squalls.

* * *

Leaning over the controls, Allen squinted through the plexiglass.

Drizzle turned to rain and formed a wall around him. The drops pelted his windshield.

Too late, he realized his mistake. He had panicked, had slowed too much too soon, and given Her time to set a trap.

She'd caught him, mid-channel, a wheelplane far from shore and surrounded by squalls.

* * *

The rain increased.

DC lowered the flaps to full, and slowed to minimum flying speed. Still as fast as a speeding car, he knew. Still plenty of energy to splatter across the nearest *cumulogranite*.

He began to S-turn, searching for a way, any way, around the weather. Foundering, adrift. Trying to swim upstream through a wall of water.

He recalled one of Ralph's first words to him, seemingly prophetic now: "*Are you the eagle, or the salmon?*"

* * *

Wiping the sweat from the ear cushions of his headphones, the engine's roar deafened him. The noise, always so annoying, now seemed the sole beat of life itself. The beat of his own heart pounded like another piston.

The dark cloud base wavered and swayed, a heavy stout floating atop a black-and-tan brew. *If this brew sinks, I'm sunk too*, he thought.

And then it happened.

The sky fell.

The cloud base dropped, sucking the air below into its fold.

Allen pushed forward on the yoke. The plane dove. He led the plummeting ceiling by a mere wingspan. The altimeter needle spun down through five hundred feet.

Four hundred . . three hundred . . the needle spiraled downward.

* * *

DC pressed on through the narrow weather tunnel, squeezed between cloud and ground.

Muskeg, trees, even the air itself retreated into shadows of twilight. A glance out the side window: treetops whizzed by, inches below his floats. A startled eagle took wing.

With a grimace, DC thought, *"Go for the gusto," my ass!* Allen had lived by those words. Until his downfall.

And now here he was, Daniel Christopher Alva, desert *cheechacko*, trying to do the same damn thing. Would this be his downfall, too? he wondered.

* * *

Allen found himself enveloped in a claustrophobic world of black and grey and white. Black sky above. Grey squalls all around. Whitecaps licking at his wheels.

A ship lost at sea.

Sweat streamed down his cheeks. His stomach tightened in knots. He began to hyperventilate.

"God-*dammit!*" he shouted, and rammed the throttle full forward.

The engine surged. Pitching the nose higher, Allen raised the flaps and began to climb. *Into* the overcast.

The clouds enveloped him.

He banked hard right and circled, turning as steeply as he dared to avoid the *cumulogranite*. Eyes glued to the instrument panel, he scanned the artificial horizon and compass as his altimeter slowly crept higher.

Lost in the muck, with no radio navaid to help him.

Flying blind.

* * *

DC looked at his left hand, tight and trembling on the yoke.

Never screw with Mother Nature. Hadn't he learned that lesson? Jesus, what had he been doing all summer?

His throat ran dry. His pulse raced. He began to hyperventilate.

"My family hunts down there," a voice said to him.

Startled, DC turned to his front seat passenger.

"Huh?"

The Tlingit pointed out the window. "My family hunts down there," he repeated lightly.

DC looked at him incredulously. Here they were on the verge of disaster, and the man was sightseeing!

He couldn't believe it. The Alaskan native, so used to living with Her, that She became no threat at all. Was simply part of the tapestry.

Allen, the arrogant bastard, had tried to imitate that attitude. And failed. DC realized now that it had all been a façade.

Arrogance. Cockiness. Inflated ego, easily popped. A pilot's worst enemy.

He pried his fingers away from the yoke and flexed them.

He had gone the opposite extreme. Fear had ruled him. And *that*, he knew, could be just as deadly.

Revelation spilled over him like a *Taku* wind. Fear, properly tempered, could be his *strength*, not his weakness. Confidence, not ego; respect, not fear.

Grasping the wheel lightly this time, he banked the plane momentarily to give the man a better look. The Alaskan pointed out the hunting ground.

Suppressing a laugh, DC nodded. "That's great," DC said, sniffling. With a finger, he wiped a tear from beneath his glasses. "That's just absolutely *great!*"

Confidence within the cockpit, humbleness before *Her* without. That was it. That was the key.

Now he wondered if the lesson had come a little too late.

Taking a deep breath, DC narrowed his eyes, leveled the wings and held his course.

The rain enveloped him. Gritting his teeth, he pressed on.

"Come on, girl," he urged in a whisper. "Help me out, here."

* * *

Allen popped out on top of the overcast.

A thick, smooth layer of clouds stretched to the horizon. Mountain peaks jutted up through the overcast like islands in a vast white ocean. The sun reflected so brightly off the clouds he had to squint.

The beauty of the landscape barely registered.

Allen leveled off. Anger, relief, disgust, euphoria, all coursed through his veins at once. But mostly anger.

"Idiot!" he cursed. How could he be so stupid? He'd panicked. Twice. Mother Nature reserved her most sinister traps for such times. And now, here he was, stuck on top of a solid overcast without the proper nav instruments to guide him safely down again.

Well, he thought, at least he had plenty of fuel, enough for the round trip. He glanced at the fuel gauges. Both tanks read slightly under half full. Creasing his brows, Allen tapped them.

Strange, he thought. Must've been in the soup longer than he realized. Well, half tanks meant about two hours of gas. As quickly as the weather changed around here, that should be plenty.

Triangulating from the surrounding peaks he saw poking above the overcast, he headed for what he guessed to be Haines. Tuning in Sisters' Island VOR, the nearest radio beacon, he crossed referenced the radial to his position on the chart.

Allen dug out a cigarette and lit it. He inhaled deeply.

At least he wasn't lost.

* * *

"C'mon, girl, help me out," DC continued to whisper, peering forward at a wall of water thick as a car wash. "C'mon, c'mon, c'mon."

Finally, She did.

Gradually the showers lightened. The cloud base lifted. The pass appeared before him, wide and inviting.

DC sat back, breathing an enormous sigh of relief.

He pushed the power up, raised the flaps and climbed. Banking north, he made for Elfin Cove.

A few minutes later, the sun broke out of the clouds. Rays of light pierced the misty sky, illuminating his path ahead. And there before him shone a brilliant, full circle rainbow.

Speechless, he pointed out the spectacle to his passengers.

"Stop grinning so wide, son, or you'll hurt yourself," the native said with a chuckle.

All DC could do was grin in reply.

He gazed out the window at the sweeping landscape.

The most beautiful land in the world, he decided. And the most deadly. For those who didn't understand Her.

"*Remember, DC*," he heard Holly saying in his memory, "*there are old pilots and bold pilots, but no old, bold pilots.*"

"Words for a bush pilot to live by," he whispered to himself.

Bush pilot. The phrase sang in his ears.

CHAPTER 23: Crash

Around the bend, Elfin Cove came into view.

DC buzzed the designated water landing area, searching for obstructions. Finding none, he circled, slowed, and set up approach. Still grinning in triumph, he felt like a maestro conducting a symphony.

On short final, DC grabbed the rudder trim control on the ceiling, deliberately making a show of tweaking it. Naturally, the two sets of eyes in back followed his hand movement.

Next to the trim read the words, "*Tips Appreciated.*"

DC alighted his craft softly in the middle of the bay, and timed the engine cut to edge up to the dock with only the slightest nudge.

Once moored, he shook his front seat passenger's hand vigorously, thanking him for a memorable flight.

"Thank you, sir," the Tlingit man replied with a wink. "I'm always happy when SEAS sends me with sourdough. Not one of those *cheechacko* kids."

His tourist passengers readily agreed with the Tlingit, each rewarding him with a handshake loaded with a crisp twenty.

"Gentlemen, it's been my pleasure," the bush pilot answered, pocketing the money and setting about reloading for the solo flight home.

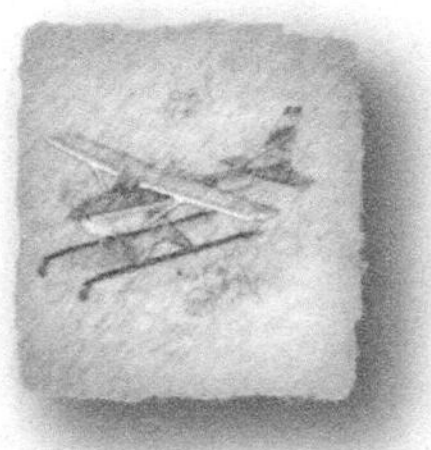

Allen hugged the overcast beneath him.

Up and down the coast he flew, searching in vain for a "sucker hole" to dive through. Twice, he'd flown directly over Haines airport.

His best bet, it appeared, lay a dozen miles south, near Davidson Glacier. He could see the ice fall spilling down into the overcast, and past that point, the clouds seemed to break up.

Allen keyed the mike. "Haines base, *Gastineau King* checking in," he called in the calmest voice he could muster.

"*Gastineau King*, Haines base," the radio crackled in reply.

"Hey, Allen, where you been? We were just about to call you."

"Uh, having a little trouble picking through the weather right now," Allen answered.

"Where are you now?"

"Near Davidson Glacier." He didn't bother to mention he was on the wrong side of the overcast from them.

"Roger that. Keep us posted."

"Will do."

He spotted a break in the clouds several miles ahead. As he closed in, the opening appeared larger. Breathing a sigh of relief, he slowed, in order to make the tightest turn possible.

Banking steeply, he dove through.

Allen spiraled down through the overcast, narrowly missing the clouds as he did. Mercifully, the base ended at 800 feet, and visibility underneath was fair. He'd have to do some more picking, he saw, but at least the bases looked stable. After what he'd been through, he felt he could fly in just about anything.

Turning for Haines, he throttled up. As he did, the engine faltered.

Allen's heart leaped in his throat. Instinctively, he switched fuel tanks. The engine roared back. He checked the fuel gauges.

The left side read slightly under one quarter tank; the right, the one he'd been using, less than an eighth.

"What the?" he muttered.

While it had seemed like hours, there was no way in this short time he could have burned all that fuel. Moreover, the gauges, while reading far lower than expected, still registered *some* gas in them. But even as he thought it, he also remembered that general aviation fuel gauges were notoriously inaccurate.

He had to be leaking fuel. But how? He searched outside around his plane. No fire, no smoke, and therefore no fuel leak in the engine bay. That left the fuel cap. Low pressure on the wing's upper surface, he knew, could suck out Avgas from a poorly-seated fuel cap. Say, one that had been put on by an inexperienced line boy.

Allen slammed the dashboard with his fist.

"*Dammit!*" he cried.

So determined was he to have his lucky cigarette, that he'd neglected to double check the new kid's work.

Allen considered throttling back to the power setting for best range. But if he really was leaking fuel, then time was critical.

Mentally crossing his fingers, he forged ahead.

* * *

Tanks topped and cargo stowed, DC hopped in the float plane and cast off. Taxiing out from the docks, he eyed the weather to the northeast. The cloud bases had lifted, broken up, and only a few spotty showers remained.

Looked like an easy try for the north route up Icy Strait, he decided.

Once in the air, he leveled off at a comfortable 1,500 feet above the Strait. He powered back to cruise speed.

"Just sit back, relax, and enjoy the flight," he said aloud to his imaginary passengers.

He tuned the radio to company frequency. Then, slipping his personal stereo earphones under his bulky headset, he began to jam to a little Bob Marley.

But his celebration of personal triumph was short-lived.

* * *

Too many showers, and too many low overcasts, had forced Allen to deviate too many times. And now he'd backtracked nearly all the way down the canal.

He glanced down at the needle, bouncing just above the 1/8th mark now. Time to stop screwing around.

Haines was still the nearest airport. Banking north back up the canal, Allen forged straight ahead, showers be damned. In a flurry of rain, the visibility vanished, but he no longer cared.

He knew this part of the land well enough to fly it blind, if that was what he had to do.

Though visibility ahead was almost nil, Allen could look straight down and keep the coastline in sight. He searched for possible beaches to set down, and several times considered doing so. But each appeared too short. Besides, now he was only a few miles from Haines.

He called the station.

"Weather's pretty crummy here," the man reported. "Nobody's been in for awhile."

"Well, my friend," Allen answered, "I'm just about *bingo fuel*."

"Uh, what's that? Say again, *Gastineau King*."

"I'm about to run out of gas!" he exclaimed.

"Um, what's your position now?"

* * *

Over the radio, DC heard the familiar voice of his former college friend, now turned asshole. Turning up his tape player, he tried to tune out the chatter.

Until he heard the phrase *Bingo fuel*.

"Jesus!" DC exclaimed, killing his music.

The next words he would remember for the rest of his life.

"Mayday, mayday, I'm going down!" Allen cried over DC's headphones. "Engine failure, south of Davidson Glacier," his voice continued. Then fell silent.

DC's guts churned. Like a jet fighter intercepting a bogie, he banked hard left, north up Lynn Canal, and shoved the throttle full forward. The engine surged. The manifold pressure needle straddled red line.

With trembling voice, he relayed the call to Juneau headquarters.

"SEAS Base, this is *Sitka Shrike*. *Gastineau King* just called 'Mayday'. Engine's failed. South of Davidson. I'm enroute now."

"Say again, who's down? Is that Allen, or DC?" the dispatcher asked.

"Allen," he answered.

Another crash, he thought. First it was Dusty. All he could think of since was, *Who next*? Only in his darkest nightmares had he imagined . . . .

Allen would be down by now. Images flashed through DC's mind of the man dying beneath a smoldering wreck. Instinctively he shoved again on the throttle, already firewalled.

"*Shrike* to *King*," do you read, over," he called.

No reply.

"*King*, this is *Shrike*, come in!"

Static.

Cutting north across the Chilkat Range, he climbed over the rugged, snowcapped mountains. The weather was fine, he saw with relief. On the south side of the peaks, he corrected himself.

Punching through a saddle in the mountains of Glacier Bay, he reached the southern tip of Lynn Canal. Below him lay a solid wall of clouds. Too low to launch a rescue copter, he realized. Let alone a search party.

"*Typical*," he spat under his breath.

For a moment, he circled, unsure what to do.

He peered down the mountain pass, to where the cloud deck met rock. Between the two lay a tiny patch of darkness. A black hole. The tiniest of sucker holes, reserved only for the most desperate. Beyond lay—*what?* he wondered.

She was playing games with him now. Taunting him. Beckoning him. Daring the newest of the bush pilots to join in recklessness his friend Allen.

His friend. Allen. His best goddamned friend in the world.

And right now, the only friend Allen had in the world was him.

DC took a deep breath. And dove.

He plummeted with the retreating terrain, and shot beneath the thick overcast, squeezed between cloud and ground.

The sun vanished. All around turned dark. For a moment, he was blinded.

DC leaned over the controls and squinted through the plexiglass. Slowly, his eyes adjusted. But there wasn't much to see. The amber lenses of his Serengeti sunglasses helped discern shapes, but not by much. He felt as if he were piloting a submarine through a murky underworld.

"Coastline," he mumbled, "got to keep the coastline in sight."

Rain surrounded him. The drops pelted his windshield. Each visual cue, each bulge in the land or curve in the shore floated toward him through the misty curtain like ghosts in a fog-shrouded graveyard. With each passing minute, the terrain popped through the curtain ever closer—visibility dropping fast. Less than a mile, he figured.

"*Dammit*," he cursed, and throttled back.

The drenched air formed fog; all turned murky. The saturated atmosphere phased between the elements of cloud and sky, water and air.

"Holy . . . ." His voice trailed off. His gut churned.

The sky fell.

The cloud base dropped, sucking the air below into its fold.

DC pushed forward on the yoke. The plane dove. He led the plummeting ceiling by a mere wing's breadth.

He glanced at the altimeter. Four hundred and falling.

Illegal as hell, he thought. But satisfying Bruner's arbitrary rules was the least of his worries.

Four hundred . . . three hundred . . . the altimeter spun downward.

At a shade over one hundred feet, DC leveled off, skimming the wave tops. As rough as the tidal seas were now, he saw, his floats would do him little good.

Sweat streamed down his sides. With scant time to react to approaching obstacles, he let his body go into autopilot. He stared ahead, motionless, working the controls subtly, praying to miss any stray fishing boats or forgotten islands.

Gradually the cloud base lifted, and with it visibility.

He hugged the thick overcast, throttling up and climbing ever so gradually.

Finally, like a lighthouse beacon, out of the fog drifted a familiar spit of land.

DC plopped back in his seat and breathed, it seemed, for the first time in ages. His stiff back muscles scolded him with a shot of pain.

Only a few more miles, he figured. He surveyed the terrain, scanning for wreckage.

High tide hid the soft beach. Ocean waves slammed against a rocky shore, backed by a forest wall. Nowhere, he saw, could a pilot glide his plane to safety. Worse, at this low altitude, Allen would have had mere seconds to save himself.

In the back of his mind raced a thousand questions.

Out of the fog came the first answer.

"I've reached the crash," DC radioed to the others, voice pitched high.

He powered back. The rumble of the Wasp Jr. engine softened to a purr.

No fire, he saw with relief. But the feeling quickly died; no movement from survivors, either.

"*Shrike* to *King*, do you read?" he called, for the hundredth time it seemed. "*King*, Come in. At least key the mike, dammit!"

No reply.

Fighting back a tear, he announced, "No sign of life." The words sank in his stomach.

He circled the crash. Out the side window he eyed the wreckage. The broken Cessna looked like a deformed dragonfly alighted on the rocky shore, its nose buried as if rutting for food, its tail hanging half over water.

Still, the crash looked survivable. How Allen had managed to deadstick the fixed-landing gear Cessna and keep the plane somewhat intact was nothing short of brilliance. And blind luck.

Somehow, some way, he had.

He circled lower, and saw how. Allen must have turned immediately for land, and timed the approach to hit water just *before* the beach. The shallow water had kept the plane from flipping, yet slowed it before hitting the rocks.

"Incredible," he whispered.

Still, the impact had been violent. The wings drooped from a busted main spar. The nosewheel had sheared off, and the entire nose section, including the six-cylinder Continental engine, had compressed like an accordion and slammed rearward into the cabin.

And his friend could be pinned—crushed—behind that mass of metal.

He spotted Allen, motionless beneath the shattered cockpit window.

"Jesus," he whispered.

The young bush pilot lay slumped over the control yoke, head resting on the dash board and covered with blood. Suddenly, Allen's head lolled to one side.

"He's alive!" DC exclaimed over the radio. "Looks hurt, bad. Could be trapped. He needs help *now*."

Frantically, he searched for a patch of calm water in which to land.

He eyed the waves near shore: chop the size of Volkswagens. More appropriate for surfboards than floats, he thought with a grimace.

Just up ahead, where the coast took a sharp right turn eastbound, he spotted a stretch of sand long enough, perhaps, for Will Steven's Luscomb taildragger.

He keyed the mike. "I think you can land, Will. How far out are you?"

Will's voice crackled in his earphones. "I just took off from Gustavus. Half-hour at best."

Too long. Though Will's taildragger was the shortest-landing plane of the fleet, it was also the slowest. The other pilots joked that if Will ever had a birdstrike, it would be from *behind*. Now it didn't seem so funny.

"SEAS Base, what about rescue?" he asked.

"CG chopper's launched. ETA thirty minutes."

Looking up, DC eyed the cloud base. Still solid. "I don't know if they can get through," he announced.

"Can you land?" Will asked.

He eyed the whitewater. "I—I'm not sure."

"Negative, *Shrike*," Holly's voice shouted. "Seas are too rough. Continue circling."

But his life's in my hands, he thought.

His hands. He looked at them: white and trembling.

Landing in this weather was hazardous at best.

Landing in this weather could mean two accidents.

Landing in this weather would take all the training and all the experience he'd strived to gain while flying the Alaska bush—which, he realized now, was pitifully little.

If he crashed, his dream of flying for airlines would crash too. Inspector Bruner would hang him by his balls. *If* he survived.

DC swallowed hard.

And made the biggest decision of his life.

CHAPTER 24: Rescue

"Hang on, Allen," DC whispered.

He continued circling, looking for a way, any way, to set down.

He found himself wishing for an amphib, or at least a wheelplane, to cram it onto the small beach. But even wheels and brakes might not stop him short of the trees.

There had to be a way. Had to.

Dusty's words came back to him. "*Fly creatively*," the sourdough had advised the *cheechacko*.

"C'mon," DC urged himself. "Think outside the box, dammit!"

He eyed again the tiny beach ahead. Perhaps with a retractable gear airplane, came the whimsical thought, he could keep the wheels up and belly in.

"Wait a minute," he murmured. He edged up the coast and circled the beach. "Yeah."

He keyed the mike. "I'm gonna try it," he announced over the radio.

"Negative!" Holly shrieked. "Rescue's on the way."

"They'll get here too late," he pleaded.

"There's nothing you can do, DC. Get back to base. That's an order."

"*To hell with it*," he didn't say over the radio.

DC dropped over the wavetops, and buzzed the crash site southbound. Though he could only catch the briefest glimpse, he swore Allen had rolled his head and looked up.

Banking hard left, he circled back, and paralleled the coastline northbound. A quarter mile ahead, the land jutted east. Stretching left and right before him, lining the coast, a thicket of pine trees stood guard.

And past it lay the beach.

Pumping down the flaps, he slowed for landing. He drifted lower.

The line of trees grew bigger.

Though already at minimum safe flying speed, DC eased the nose up even higher. He glanced at his instruments. The airspeed trickled down, knot by precious knot. The stall warning horn assaulted his ears. The smooth airflow above his wings began to burble; the wings shook in protest.

He added more power to fight the craft. The last few inches of throttle he held in reserve.

He aimed at the top of the first tree, flanked forward from the rest, at the east end of the beach. Concentrating on the topmost branch, he again let his body go into autopilot, fighting the aircraft all the way in.

"Just . . . a little farther—*now!*"

He banked the airplane hard left.

DC felt a bump, and thought vaguely that it must have been the treetop hitting a float. Next came the drop, a momentary sensation of freefall as the wings stalled.

Turning in the tightest possible arc, the airplane dropped toward the beach. Adding full power, he pushed the nose lower. The beach filled his window. The engine screamed.

DC yanked back on the control stick. The nose pitched to the sky, suddenly filling the wings with lift. The plane fought the downward trajectory. The g-force drained the blood from his head.

The floats hit with a *Whomp!* His seat rammed into his spine, his chin snapping shut from the impact.

Chopping the power and cutting the fuel, he yanked the flaps up to kill the lift.

And now he was only a passenger. Letting go of the controls, he cut the fuel to the engine and braced.

The floats skidded across the rough beach. His teeth chattered as he bounced over the washboard sand.

A large boulder lay ahead. Unable to swerve, all he could do was watch.

His left float struck, and spun him around. DC was thrown sideways, but his shoulder strap caught him. The right wing tipped and struck the sand, spinning him back.

Wobbling like a top, the plane bounded toward the tree line at the far end of the beach.

Little by little, the oscillations slowed, along with the speed.

A mere fifty yards short of the trees, the plane slid to a halt.

DC sat a for a moment, stunned.

He watched in a trance as the 3-bladed prop wound down, his heart pounding as fast as the *click click click* of the fuel-starved pistons.

The sight of the waves, crashing into the rocks beside him, snapped him to.

He checked his body parts. All there.

Except for a trickle of blood down the side of his head, and probably more than a few bruises, he felt fine.

His headset, thrown off in the impact, lay on the passenger floor. He picked up the hand held mike and called base.

Will Stevens was close enough to relay.

"I'm down, Will," he called. "I'm okay."

"Good job, DC," Will exclaimed. "You're gonna get the medal of honor for this one. Let us know what you find."

DC looked up the coastline at Allen's plane. Suddenly his elation at surviving was replaced with extreme anxiety.

"Roger that, Will."

Snapping off the battery master switch and releasing the belt buckle, DC scrambled over the back rows and reached into the aft cargo hold. He grabbed the Emergency Survival Kit, fire extinguisher and crash axe, and jumped out.

He sprinted up the coastline.

CHAPTER 25: Daniel Christopher Alva

Inspector Bruner strolled up the beach from the crash site, far away from the fumes. He sat on a boulder and lit a Camel. All alone in the woods, the world around him seemed astonishingly peaceful. Above, puffy white clouds drifted silently by, while the ocean, its tide at midcycle, lapped lazily at the shore before him.

He felt alone. Isolated. Stranded.

The NTSB, as always, had deferred the investigation to the FAA. Citing lack of resources—and perhaps, he suspected, because there wasn't a corpse—the FAA in turn had deferred even sending a team, and instead left the investigation solely to him.

Imagine their surprise, he thought, when he got back to report, not one, but *two* downed planes.

Looking left and right along the coast, Bruner eyed the planes, one drooped and sagging like a Dali painting, the other, well, just as surreal. A perfectly normal floatplane, barely scratched, sitting well up the beach, surrounded by trees and a coastline of rock. Upon observing the scene, any rational person would wonder just how in the *hell* it got there.

He had to chuckle at the kid's ingenuity. What was his name? He checked his notes. Daniel Christopher "DC" Alva. The sloppy *cheechacko*. Well, Alva was certainly a hero now. After all, he did save Foley from bleeding to death.

Too bad he'd have to bust the kid for *Careless and Reckless Operation of an Airplane*.

He looked at the Dali plane and shook his head. Foley's landing had been equally brilliant. Nevertheless, the young man was lucky to be in one piece. Several cracked ribs, broken ankle, concussion. Probably a nice little sexy scar across the bridge of his nose to remember it all by. Oak City would yank his Class One Medical certificate of course, till he proved himself medically fit. And as for his pilot's license, well . . .

So, what was Probable Cause shaping up to be for Foley's plane? he asked himself. Fuel leak, that much he knew. But from where, he couldn't tell. Now, balled up on the beach, the Cessna had more leaks than a presidential staff.

Bruner took one last draw from his Camel. Well, *Pilot Error* or not, Allen David Foley now had an official accident under his belt. And *that* would blacklist him from the airlines for sure. Too many perfect pilots out there with perfect records, just waiting to take his place in line.

Dropping the cigarette butt, Bruner buried it deep in the sand with his toe. Not to worry. Foley would fly for hire again. Just not airliners, that's all. The whole state of Alaska was filled with his kind.

Over the peaceful sound of the ocean, Bruner heard a low hum.

He looked south down the channel. A tiny dark speck appeared against the blue and white-dappled background. Rounding the peninsula, the speck grew to a de Havilland Beaver floatplane.

With the tide mid-cycle on this fair day, the floatplane had no trouble skimming to a smooth landing and sailing up to the shoreline near him.

The engine stopped.

Southeast Alaskan Seaplanes' Chief Pilot Holly Innes hopped out. A man sitting beside her followed.

Holly spotted Bruner and waved, then, with her Chief Mechanic's help, pulled the plane well up the beach and secured it to a tree, lest it drift away as the tide returned.

That done, she turned to Bruner. "Good afternoon, Inspector."

He tipped his ball cap. "And to you, Ms. Innes."

Wiping her hands, she said, "Okay if he checks out the Beaver?" Bruner nodded. "Granted. I'm done with it."

The mechanic grabbed a toolbox from the plane, and headed up the beach toward DC's plane.

Bruner called after him, "You'll find a couple dings on the right wingtip, and both floats. Water rudders are a bit bent up. Other than that, not much."

In reply, the mechanic waved over his shoulder as he walked off.

Turning back to Holly, Bruner held up a small pine branch. With a slight edge of sarcasm to his voice, he said, "As a memento, I saved for DC the branch stuck in his left float strut."

Taking it from him, Holly bit her lip. She didn't know how to react to that. With it she pointed to Allen's plane. "Um, how goes the investigation?"

Bruner glanced back at Allen's crash. "Well, I need at least few more hours here. I'm having trouble finding the fuel leak. Starvations are usually straight forward. A guy fuels for three hours, tries to fly four, and *bingo!* Instant death," he finished, snapping his fingers for emphasis.

Holly was not amused. "You know that's not true here, sir," she replied. "Allen Foley had more than enough for a round trip—"

Bruner replied like a professor to a slow student. "*And* that means a fuel leak." Placing a hand gently on her back, he guided her toward the wreck. "I always check for unseated fuel caps first. Both were closed tight. But they often snap shut with the force of impact, so who knows?"

Holly replied, "Well, I just came from the hospital. I asked Allen about that possibility. But, I'm afraid he can't remember anything. Concussion, you know."

Bruner twitched his mouth sideways. "Yes, yes. Quite convenient, these concussions that come at such times."

Holly bridled. "Inspector Bruner, I resent your implication—"

Bruner stopped and turned. "Hold on, girl, I'm not finished. Look," he said, holding up two fingers and counting off, "either he misfueled—ergo, pilot error. Or, we've got a broken fuel line. Ergo, mechanic error. Either way, fault rests on SEAS' shoulders."

Holly thought a moment. "I see."

He scratched the back of his head, as if at a loss. "Frankly, my dear, I'm getting tired of investigating your company's accidents. I don't know how I can keep you open for business any more."

"*What!* Now look, Inspector, Dusty's accident—"

"Was irrelevant, yes. Thank God for that." He swept his hand up and down the coast. "But what do you see here? I see two planes, both of which are now unflyable, both of which were flown by SEAS' pilots on commercial runs."

Red-faced, Holly pointed to the beached float plane. "That bird does *not* have substantial damage. *Ergo*, Inspector," Holly said, mimicking him, "no accident."

"Agreed, Holly. But minor damage means it *is* an incident."

"Strictly up for interpretation."

"In either case, just one look and you know he's up for *Careless and Reckless*."

Holly groaned, and put her hands to her face and rubbed. She looked up. "Inspector Bruner. DC dreams of flying for the majors. He's well on his way, and well worthy of it."

Bruner shook his head. "He *broke* the *rules*, Ms. Innes."

Stomping the ground, Holly turned to face him. "God-*dammit*, man! He exercised his emergency authority as pilot in command to deviate from the rules as necessary to meet that emergency." *There*, she thought. Bash the man over the head with his own rule book.

"My dear," he replied softly, "that only applies to the pilot of an aircraft *already* in trouble."

Holly clamped shut. Turning away, she cast her eyes across the ocean channel, to the peninsula bathed in partly cloudy, late night sun. Each tree cast long shadows across its neighbor, giving the forest a tapestry of dark and light. Cast in random patterns of light, each appeared vastly different from the other, yet remained essentially the same.

All her adult life, she'd seen the world as the inspector had, in simple black and white. No random shades obscuring the truth.

Rigid rules had been her lifeline, strict order her lifejacket, rescuing her from drowning in abuse. Restoring order from chaos.

But, now, the absolute seemed so . . . *relative*. Something Dusty and Jake, even Ralph, had been trying to teach her.

Black and white. Shades of grey. *What was the truth?* she wondered. Certainly not the unbending bind of red tape.

They were right.

"Screw the rules," Holly whispered.

"Excuse me?" Bruner asked.

Holly turned back to him. "I said, *Screw the rules*." It was her turn to sweep her hand about them. "Look at this country, Inspector. It truly is the last frontier, the wildest land left in the world. We came up here to escape the unbending rules. We came up here to *live*, by the laws of Nature, not to wither away in someone else's interpretation of what they think is best for us. Screw the rules, I say."

Bruner's face reddened. He pointed a finger at her. "Young lady, that attitude will get you shut down. If it doesn't kill you first."

Holly ignored his threat. "You ever heard of Joe Crosson's Blue Sky Outfit?"

Bruner creased his brows. "No," he said guardedly.

"Crosson helped Pan Am establish the first scheduled Alaska air service. But the arbitrary rules of federal bureaucrats in Washington kept his fleet grounded in all but perfect weather, while the local bush pilots raked in the business around him. Needless to say, his venture failed."

"And I fail to see your point, Ms. Innes."

Stepping forward, Holly continued. "Let me ask you this, Inspector. *Why* do we have rules, hmm? To ensure *safety* in the cockpit. But, you and I know the realities of living here. Every day, we face situations that the regulations didn't anticipate. Where blindly following the rules could get us killed." She spread her hands before her. "They're just *guidelines*, Inspector." Looking up at him, she finished softly, "Haven't you ever bent the rules to do what was *right*?"

* * *

Bruner looked away. Once, a lifetime ago, in 'Nam . . . .

Holly continued. "DC bent the rules to do what was *right*, Inspector. Now you have a chance to do the same."

Bruner recalled the flight that had ruined his life. Not a day went by that he didn't remember. He'd been drummed out of the service for it. His wingman had died because he bent the rules.

But that wasn't quite right, was it? Disaster befell him because—why? Because he didn't have the balls to *break* the rules, to stay behind and do . . . what was *right*.

He looked to the Chief Pilot.

"I've got to report what I find, Holly," he said defensively.

Holly stared him down. "And what do you find, Inspector? I remind you, you're the principal investigator—the *only* investigator—here. What *you* say is *reality*." She leaned forward. "I see one crash, Inspector. Not two."

Eyeing her, Bruner rubbed his stubbled chin. The reality of it was . . . his reality. DC had bent the rules. Court martial the young man for it, like they'd done to him so long ago? Ruin DC's life—*for going back*?

Bruner straightened, and cleared his throat.

In a loud, clear voice he announced, "I see one crash."

Letting out a long breath of air, Holly smiled. "Thank you, Inspector."

"Don't mention it. Least I could do for a—a *hero*."

"You won't regret it, Inspector." Holly bit her lip. "Um. Now, about Ralph . . ."

Bruner waved a hand in dismissal. "Already done. Charges dropped."

Holly raised a brow. "Oh? Were you going to tell me about this any time soon?"

Bruner turned and walked up the beach toward the crash. Holly fell in step beside him. He said, "Fax came back from Oak City this morning before I left. They said not enough evidence to pursue. And, quite frankly, looking back at the incident, I—well, I had to agree with them." He chuckled. "Oh, and, by the way. Next time Ralph decides to take a litter of bears on a little flightseeing tour?"

Holly's eyes widened to saucers. "Yes?" she squeaked.

"Tell him to make sure there aren't any cameras around."

Holly cracked a grin that extended from ear to ear.

As the two strolled down the beach, she placed a hand on the Inspector's back.

"Freddie," she said, "I think this is the beginning of a beautiful friendship."

* * *

For an entire week, John Bolt had searched Barrow and the surrounding towns. A week of trudging across the tundra, swatting mosquitos the size of magpies, scratching bites the size of golf balls.

He knew he'd been had. No one in this pathetic microdot of a town had ever known, or heard of, or seen a Holly Shannon Innes or a Veronica Redding, nor had they seen anyone vaguely resembling the woman in his photo collection. And now the local authorities were getting curious as to his curiosity.

That damn pimple-faced flight instructor! Ought to return to Fairbanks and clip his wings.

Bolt stared across the barren countryside. He removed the ball cap and swatted at the mosquitos.

Upon spying virgin territory, the insects attacked his balding skull.

Bolt swatted in vain, dancing frantically to avoid the onslaught, to no avail.

"God-*dammit!*" he screamed, throwing his hat to the ground. He sank to his knees, arms flailing about him hysterically, swiping at the demons and clawing at his itching skin. "Get off me, *get off me!*" he cried.

A crowd of curious locals gathered around him.

"What's up with him?" an Inupiat woman asked.

Shrugging, her husband answered, "Looks like *She* beat him out."

* * *

"Allen?"

Through the fog of drugs and delirium, he heard her voice. But what brought him around was her erotic, flowery scent.

Tonya.

He forced his eyes open. Tonya's beautiful dark eyes peered back at him.

He wondered for a moment if he was still dreaming. But his aching body told him otherwise. He tried to sit up, but it seemed every bone had been pounded to pulp. His head felt like a rugby ball.

Fumbling with the electric control, he finally managed to raise the upper half of the bed. "What are you doing here?" he asked, ice in his words.

She gazed into his eyes. "I've been here all along, Allen. Right here, by your side."

He tried to swallow, his mouth cotton dry. "Why?"

"I'm so *stupid*, Allen," she said. "When I heard that you'd crashed, well, I started realizing how I really felt about you. And I thought, *ohmygod*, I'm too late. He's gone. And I never got a chance to—"

"Save it." It was then that he realized she had been holding his hand the whole time. He yanked it away.

"I'm serious, Allen. Believe me," she pleaded. "You fought Tom for me."

"Not for you. For DC. And a woman who wants to be fought over . . . isn't worth fighting for."

"Give me a chance, Allen." She looked back up at him, her deep brown eyes glistening with tears.

He could get lost in there, he knew.

Like he could get lost in the bottom of a whiskey bottle.

Like he could get lost in the clouds and crash.

He crossed his arms and said, "Too late." Leaning forward, he locked his eyes on hers. "*I beat you out.*"

* * *

Emerging from the cigar store and turning up the street toward the hospital, DC inhaled the crisp, fresh Alaskan air. He saw his breath, but hadn't even bothered to put on his jacket. Short sleeves felt just fine. He remembered with amusement how Phoenicians back home practically bundled up in parkas when the mercury hit a "bone-chilling" sixty-five.

He strolled up Egan Street, toward the vacant lot where he and Allen had duked it out. As he approached, he heard a horrid hacking noise. He found Tom Zion in the lot, leaning against the building. Facing the wall, with his head bent low, Zion spewed an endless stream of vomit to the ground.

"Jesus, Tom, you okay?" DC asked.

Zion looked up, his face pasty white, breath foul with whiskey and puke. His eyes were bloodshot, and filled with tears.

"She left me, DC. Left me for that, that *loser!*" Tom turned back to his task.

DC couldn't help but smile. Typical Tonya. Poor Tom. Break out the violins.

With a sympathetic pat on the back, he said, "She beat you out, eh Tom?"

Tom turned back, a baffled sneer on his face. "What the fuck's *that* s'posed to mean?" he asked, spittle dribbling down his chin.

"Nothin'." DC slapped him on the back one last time. "Good luck, *cheechacko*."

DC strolled on.

* * *

He knocked lightly on the door.

"Come in," he heard Allen answer, his voice weak and scratchy.

DC poked his head in. Allen was sitting upright in his hospital bed. To DC's surprise, Tonya stood by his side.

"Oh, I'm sorry," DC stammered, "I can come back later if—"

"She was just leaving," Allen said flatly.

Tonya looked at Allen with what, shockingly, seemed to DC like pleading eyes. By way of reply, Allen jerked his head toward the door. Like a scolded pet, Tonya lowered her head and trudged to the door. DC noticed then that her eyes glistened with tears.

Over her shoulder, she said, "Remember what I said, Allen. I meant it." Turning back, her eyes lit up, and seemed to dry in an instant. She flashed DC a wicked grin. "Hello, DC," she greeted in passing, her words oozing with innuendo. She might as well have said, *Let's do it right here, lover.*

"Tonya," DC said with a cold nod, stepping back to let her pass well clear.

"Congratulations, hero," she whispered in passing. "Come on down to the Red Dog and have a Chinook on me."

DC said nothing but smiled stiffly. She glided out.

Walking over to Allen's bedside, he said, "What the hell was that about?" he asked.

Allen shrugged. "I think they call it, 'Florence Nightingale effect'."

"So you're the one that stole her from Tom? Congratulations. I guess."

Allen snorted. "You can have her."

DC held up a hand. "No thanks. Felt like she shoved me through a spinning prop." Upon closer examination of his friend, DC exclaimed, "Damn, you look like *you* got spit through a prop!"

Allen chuckled weakly. "Feels like it, too." He pointed to the package in DC's hand. "What's that?"

"Oh. A little celebratory box of see-gars." DC leaned over and handed the box to Allen. "Cubans, or something. Better be good. Cost me half a month's salary."

Sniffing a stogie, Allen chuckled. "I oughta crash more often."

"I saw how you pulled it off. Your solution was brilliant."

Allen shook his head in disbelief. "I think I played an entire chess game in my head before I hit."

DC chuckled knowingly. "Me too."

Allen looked up. "I hear that I owe you my life."

DC shrugged. "You'd have done the same."

The two remained silent for an awkward moment.

With a lopsided grin, Allen said, "Hey, let's go bang out that climb."

"Yeah, right. I think you've been doing enough banging around lately."

Allen sighed. "Guess Bruner's gonna fry my ass."

"Mine too, I'll bet." DC sat on the bed near his friend's waist.

Allen looked away, shaking his head in dismay. "Doesn't matter any more. *Fuck* the airlines."

DC raised his brows. "Oh really?"

"They're nothing but a bunch of button pushers."

"Hah! *Very highly paid* button pushers. So what now?" DC asked. "On to the Caribbean? Assuming we still have pilot tickets, of course."

Allen waved a hand in dismissal. "Alaska's my home, DC. I know that now. She beat me out. But She won't beat me out again. I understand Her now."

DC leaned closer. "So do I."

Allen cocked his head. "Oh?"

"I . . . I learned to fall."

"Really?"

DC nodded.

"Me too," Allen said. He thrust a weak fist to the air. "Go for the gusto, or stay the fuck at home!"

DC shook his head. "No, that's not it at all. That's all show. Fake Tom Zion shit. More like, 'confident humility'. Confident in the cockpit, but humble before Her."

Allen pondered that one. "Hmm. Yeah. Exactly."

For a moment the only sound in the room was the steady *beep!* of the medical gizmos around them.

Allen finally said, "So, Holly tells me you bagged the SEAS' winter job. Congratulations."

"Thanks," DC replied. "But I turned it down."

Allen jutted his head forward. "What?"

"The job's yours, Allen. I'll cover for you, until you get back up to flying speed."

Crossing his arms, Allen sat back. "You little *fucker!* Wracking up the brownie points, aren't you?"

DC fake-punched his arm, *very* lightly. "You owe me big time, bubba."

"So what about you?" Allen asked.

DC grinned. "I thought the Virgin Islands sounded nice."

Allen raised his brows, an amused smile spreading across his lips. "Just throw your backpack on and go, huh?"

"Why not? But not before taking a side trip to Phoenix. To try and retrieve a precious little gem I threw away."

Allen's eyes went wide. "Listen, DC. Nothing happened between—"

DC held up a hand. "I know, Allen. Besides, I brought it on myself. The important thing is to get Steph back. If it's not too late."

The nurse poked her head in the door. Catching DC's eye, she tapped her watch.

DC stood. "Well, I'd better git."

Allen held out his hand. "Thanks again."

"Any time." The two shook hands. DC ambled across the room. At the door, he paused. "On second thought, never again."

"Hey, DC," Allen called. "So what are we, the eagle or the salmon?"

DC pursed his lips. After a moment's pause, he said, "It's nice to finally know."

Smiling, Allen sat back. "Good luck, sourdough."

"Don't you mean, *cheechacko*?"

Smiling, Allen shook his head. "Not anymore."

* * *

It took him two hours of steady hiking, but DC finally reached the summit. The whole of Juneau lay spread before him, a modern city perfectly melded with the wilderness surrounding it.

While the rock climb posed its own unique challenge, the goal was the thing, and here he was on top. Funny, he thought, how an easy solution always presented itself when one merely took a step back. Thought outside the box. Flew creatively.

He found the top of the granite face he and Allen had attempted. To his surprise, two rusting bolt anchors had been drilled into the rock; their route had long ago been conquered by others.

Dusty's words came back to him: *"You're always a pioneer if you've never done it before."*

He heard a loud screech. An enormous shadow passed over him. Instinctively he ducked. He looked up to find the eagle—his eagle—circling, close overhead. In its talons dangled a shredded chunk of meat, but whether it was a salmon or something else, he couldn't tell.

Sailing lower, the bird alighted on its nest, not twenty yards away.

The thing was magnificent. The most majestic aviator in all the world, perfectly at home on the ground or in the air. Eyeing him suspiciously, the raptor let out another warning squawk.

Slowly, DC retraced his steps. "Easy there, friend. I don't mean to intrude."

He retreated back down the trail until it seemed to relax. DC crouched, and watched in silent fascination while his eagle fed its young.

"Hmph," he mumbled. "You're not mine, are you? You're Hers."

The sound of a floatplane buzzed in his ears. He looked down.

Ralph's Beaver was just lifting off the Gastineau Channel, loaded, no doubt, with another group of gawking cruise ship tourists for a flightseeing venture over the Juneau Icefield. Crash Whitakker's plane idled behind, awaiting his turn.

DC smiled. He'd miss this place, of course. But there were more steps to take. Other adventures to chase on his climb to the airline flight deck.

Dusty's voice continued in his mind. "The adventure's still out there, son. You just gotta go find it."

Above Eagle Pass, a glint of sunlight on metal caught his eye; an airliner, its contrail streaking far above, arced north toward Anchorage, or Fairbanks. The white rainbow beckoned.

From his new vantage point, the contrail seemed a tad closer.

"Soon enough," whispered Daniel Christopher Alva. "Soon enough."

Glossary of Terms Used in this Book

ADF-Automatic Direction Finder. Onboard radio beacon that points like a bird dog to a broadcast station, including A.M. radio stations.

ADF&G-(Also F&G)Alaska Department of Fish and Game. Basically, Game Wardens.

Airframe & Powerplant License-(also A&P) An aviation mechanic's license.

AGL-(Above Ground Level) Altitude expressed as feet above the ground.

Air Traffic Control (ATC)-Officials on the ground coordinating and directing aircraft movement through the sky between airports, usually with the use of RADAR. Not to be confused with Tower controllers.

Airframe-the structure of an aircraft without the powerplant.

Airspeed Indicator-An instrument or device that measures the airspeed of an aircraft through an air mass, but not its groundspeed.

Altimeter-A cockpit instrument used to measure an aircraft's altitude. *Altimeter Setting*-Current, local barometric pressure adjustment so the altimeter reads accurately.

Amphibian-(Also, *Amphib*) A float plane rigged with retractable wheels for runway landings as well.

ATIS-Automatic Terminal Information Service. Weather and airport information, recorded hourly or as needed, for a specific airport, and continually broadcast on a specific frequency.

Avgas-Aviation fuel.

Chaff and Flares-RADAR countermeasures, launched as decoys from a plane being intercepted by incoming missiles.

Cheechacko-Tenderfoot, greenhorn. From Chinook jargon, originally a reference to someone new to Alaska or the Yukon. *chee* ("new, lately") + *chako* ("to come, arrive.")

Chinook-Mostly used in this book to refer to a brand of beer popular in Juneau in the late 80's, now known as *Alaskan Amber*. Can also refer to a native people of the Pacific Northwest, or winds (not to be confused with Taku winds.)

Center of Gravity (CG)-The longitudinal and lateral point in an aircraft where it is stable; the static balance point.

Controlled Airspace-A generic term including all airspace classes in which ATC services are available.

Conventional Gear-("Taildraggers") Having two main landing wheels at the front and a tail wheel at the rear, as opposed to a "tricycle gear" with two mains and front or nose wheel.

Common Traffic Advisory Frequency (CTAF)-A communications radio frequency for reporting positions while operating to or from an airport without an operating control tower.

Control Tower-("Tower" or "Ground") Officials in charge of a controlled airport, usually from a tower or cab on the field. Using radio commands, a Tower Controller directs aircraft movement, such as clearances to land, takeoff, etc. A Ground Controller directs taxi movement.

Cumulogranite-A pilot's colloquial, morbid reference to mountains hiding in clouds.

Elevator-A horizontal, movable control surface on the tail of an airplane that changes its pitch and therefore, angle of attack.

Empennage-An aircraft's tail group including the rudder, vertical fin, stabilizers and elevators.

Empty weight-the weight of the structure of an aircraft, its powerplant, and all of the fixed equipment.

Eskimo-Indigenous peoples of the circumpolar region, from Siberia to Greenland. Refers to Yupik, and Inuit. A third group, the Aleut, is related.

FAR's-U.S. Federal regulations governing air transportation. *FAR PART 91*-Flight rules pertaining to non-commercial flight operations; *PART 135*-Air Taxi operations; *FAR PART 121*-airline operations.

FBO (Fixed Base Operator)-An airport-based business that parks, services, fuels, and may repair and rent aircraft.

Flight Plan-Data for a specific flight, such as route and fuel, filed with the FAA. Not required, and often not used, for noncommercial or local flights.

Flap-A movable, usually hinged airfoil set in the trailing edge of an aircraft wing, designed to increase lift as the plane slows.

General Aviation-Any aircraft flown by other than major and regional airlines or the military.

Go Around-Aborting or abandoning a landing by climbing out. Usually followed by a return for another landing.

Gross Weight-The total weight of an aircraft when fully loaded.

Ground Speed-The actual speed that an aircraft travels over the ground. Like a boat traveling upriver, a headwind will slow the forward speed, a tailwind increases it.

Gussik-Yupic term meaning caucasion; white man. Derived from "Cossack."

Hangar-A building used for housing and maintaining aircraft.

Headwind–A wind that is blowing in the opposite direction the aircraft is flying, thereby impeding its forward airspeed.

Indicated airspeed-Airspeed as indicated on the airspeed indicator.

Instrument-any device indicating the attitude, altitude, or operation of an aircraft or aircraft part.

IFR (Instrument Flight Rules)-Operation of aircraft primarily by instrument reference, including onboard flight instruments and radio beacons precisely guiding aircraft, often through clouds and low visibility. In general, Alaska bush pilots must avoid IFR conditions and fly VFR.

Knot-(See *Nautical mile.*)

Landing gear-The wheels, floats, skis, and any attachments that support the airplane when it is resting on the ground or water.

Nautical Mile-(Knot) The most common distance measurement in aviation. A nautical mile is equivalent to 1.15 statute (standard U.S.) miles.

NAVAID-"Navigation Aid." Radio beacons to help navigate through clouds.

Navigation/Nav lights-lights on the aircraft consisting of a red light on the left wing, a green light on the right wing, and a white light on the tail.

N-Number-(Tail Number) Federal government aircraft registration numbers. U.S. registered aircraft numbers begin with "N" (example: N737AK).

Nonrev-"Non-revenue" passenger. Airline employees flying standby for little or no fee.

Octane-The rating system of aviation gasoline.

Overload-to apply a load in excess of that for which a device or structure is designed.

Pancake landing-an aircraft landing procedure in which the aircraft is on an even plane with the runway. As the aircraft reduces speed and lift, it drops to the ground in a flat or prone attitude.

Pattern-the flight pattern an aircraft must follow when approaching the airport for landing and when leaving the airport after taking off.

Pilot in Command (PIC)-The pilot responsible for the safe operation of an aircraft.

Pitch-the rotation of an airplane about its lateral axis.

Radial engine-A reciprocating aircraft engine in which all of the cylinders are arranged radially, or spoke-like, around a small crankcase. Also referred to as *round engines*. Example: the de Havilland DHC-2 Beaver's original Pratt & Whitney, R985 Wasp Junior, nine-cylinder radial engine.

Ramp-the apron, tarmac or paved surface around a hangar used for parking aircraft.

Ramper-One who works on the airport tarmac, loading bags, servicing planes, etc.

Rudder-The movable vertical control surface used to rotate the airplane about its vertical axis. The pilot operates the rudder by the movement of the foot pedals in the cockpit.

Scud-Shreds of clouds or rain, often driven by winds.

Scud Running-The bush pilot's technique of flying visually, ducking beneath overcasts, and dodging around clouds and rain showers.

Solo-Flying alone, especially as a beginner. Student pilots are permitted to undertake some flights solo to build experience without a flight instructor on board.

Spin-An uncoordinated stall, which also can be practiced.

Spiral-("Tight Spiral") Increasingly steep turn resulting in loss of altitude.

Stall-Not to be confused with engine operation. Occurs when a plane loses its lift and falls. Pilots train for stall prevention, recognition and recovery. Recovering from a stall requires adding full power and lowering the nose further to regain speed, then pulling back up and climbing out.

Student Pilot-Someone training for a sport or private pilot certificate.

Sourdough-An old timer, especially in Alaska.

Special VFR-An exemption from VFR cloud clearance and visibility requirements, issued by a tower to an aircraft when traffic is light.

Sucker Hole-A tiny break in the clouds, tempting a pilot to squeeze through, only to close up at the last minute.

Tachometer-an instrument that measures the rotating speed of an engine in revolutions per minute (RPM) or in percent of the maximum RPM.

Taku Winds-Strong winds in Southeast Alaska that create severe wind shear and turbulence.

Taxi-To move an airplane on the ground under its own power.

Tlingit-(Also *Tlinkit* or *Linkit*, "People of the Tides.") An indigenous people of the Pacific Northwest coast of America. Different from *Eskimo*.

Touch and Go-Landing an aircraft and then immediately taking off again. A technique to practice takeoffs and landings.

Tower Controller-See Control Tower.

Uncontrolled Airport-An airport without a control tower. Pilots follow traffic pattern procedures and report their positions and intentions using the common traffic advisory frequency (CTAF), often called UNICOM.

Useful load-Weight of the occupants, baggage, usable fuel, and drainable oil. The difference between maximum and empty weight.

Vertigo-When flying, loss of orientation, often in low visibility or when practicing instrument flying techniques.

VFR (Visual Flight Rules)-A defined set of FAA regulations and "rules of the road" covering operation of aircraft primarily by visual reference.

VOR-"VHF Omni Range." A radio beacon, similar to an ADF, but more accurate.

V-speeds-("V_{so}," "V_{ls}," etc. Pronounced, *"Vee-ess-oh," "Vee-el-ess,"* etc.)-Airspeeds, such as stall speeds or minimum flying speeds, that a pilot uses. Often depicted on an airplane's airspeed indicator.

Wildlife Trooper-Alaska Department of Public Safety officer, responsible for enforcing state law in the wilderness.

Also Available from Eric Auxier

There I Wuz! Volumes I-4
Adventures From 3 Decades in the Sky
(Volumes can be read in any order)

"An aviator with a gift for storytelling!"
—Karlene Petitt, Airline Pilot-Author-CNN Correspondent

"The altimeter spins backwards in a blur, like a mad scientist's time travel clock."

By popular demand, feast on a smorgasbord of Cap'n Auxier's *true* aeronautical tales, from such publications as *Airways* Magazine, NYCAviation.com, *Plane & Pilot* and his own blog, Adventures of Cap'n Aux (capnaux.com). Also included are several unpublished works, guest stories from fellow pilot-authors and other gems.

From his first daring forays into the sky as a daring (make that foolish) teen in a hang glider, to his extreme initiation as a young bush pilot in Alaska's volatiles skies; from fighting off hurricanes in the Caribbean to an explosive decompression in a heavy airliner, Mr. Auxier shares tales from over three decades (now four), and 24,000 hours of flying.

Excerpt from Vol. 3: *Aerial Assassins*

by Major Rob Burgon

The gold-tinted canopy of my F-22 Raptor motored closed, isolating me from the noise of the Auxiliary Power Unit (APU) operating just a few feet aft of the cockpit. The cockpit displays are slowly waking up with power from the auxiliary generator—it will only be a few minutes before the powerful Pratt & Whitney F-119 Turbofan engines are roaring to life. I pause for a brief moment to reflect on how lucky I am to be sitting in control of the world's most lethal Air Dominance aircraft. My cerebral moment is interrupted by the voice of my crew chief crackling over the aircraft intercom.

"Alright, sir," says my crew chief, "we're all ready to go down here. I'll clear off when you're ready."

"You're cleared off chief," I reply. "Thanks for the start."

"No problem, sir. Good luck out there, and happy hunting!"

I smile as I check my formation in on our flight discrete frequency. With my three wingmen all on frequency, I call for taxi clearance and work my flight into the line of aircraft flowing towards the two runways of Nellis Air Force Base, Nevada. Over 100 aircraft are participating in today's Large Force Exercise (LFE), and my four-ship is responsible for air-to-air escort of a strike package consisting of B-1 and B-52 bombers, F-15Es, and A-10s. It is a complex mission, and I know I need to be at the top of my game to make sure the mission is safely executed. Even though our aircraft are not loaded with live missiles, the threat of a midair collision lingers in the back of each pilot's mind.

We get airborne, climbing effortlessly into the cloudless, azure sky. En route to the fight airspace, we hop from one controlling agency to another, eventually ending up with our tactical controller, call sign Darkstar. There is no chatter on our flight discrete frequency; each flight member is focused on the mission ahead of us. There will be time for chitchat later as we regale each other with tales of airborne heroism after the mission in the squadron bar.

I check the clock as I turn my four-ship to the west, focusing our tactical sensors in the direction of our objective. Our vulnerability period—the time during which we will be responsible for mission accomplishment (also known as the vul)—is about to kick off.

Utilizing operational communications brevity terms, I ask the controllers onboard the E-3 AWACS to provide a verbal description of the location and number of airborne enemy fighters. The large dome radar on the AWACS turns slowly several miles behind us, painting an electronic picture of the battlespace.

"Raptor 1, Darkstar, picture: six-group wall. North group, bullseye two-eight-zero, fifty, fourteen thousand, hostile, heavy, four contacts…"

The Air Battle Manager proceeds to provide my escort package with a rundown of our airborne threats. Each pilot compares the radio communication to what he sees on his displays. Once Darkstar finishes providing the tactical picture, each pilot goes to work targeting and shooting his assigned group.

The initial volley of shots takes place beyond visual range. Some of the bandits execute a 180-degree turn, called a drag, as a defensive measure against the missiles coming their way. They have no way of knowing if the maneuver will work, and most won't survive the initial shots. I check the position of the strike package, which has started its push towards the target area. I check my flight's weapons and fuel states to find that we still have plenty of both.

In the few quiet seconds following our initial attack, I make a quick radio call to our tactical controllers and my flight, letting them know our status and our next plan of action.

"Darkstar, Raptor 1, weapons green, fuel green. Raptor 1 and 2 reference North CAP, Raptor 3 and 4 reference South CAP."

My four-ship splits up to provide 360-degree coverage of the target area, ensuring it is safe for the strikers to enter and drop their weapons. The geographic location where I will orbit with my wingman is called a Combat Air Patrol, or CAP. Once established in our CAP, high above the strikers, we prioritize our sensors to the enemy airfields nearby only to see a massive launch of hostile aircraft intent on destroying our strikers. The radios erupt with chatter as the tactical controllers alert the pilots of the danger.

My wingman and I go to work in the South CAP targeting and shooting the bandits as they seem to belt feed off the airfield.

It is only a matter of time before I'm out of AIM-120s, the only beyond-visual-range weapon I am carrying. With a closure rate in excess of 1,000 miles per hour, I am quickly approaching visual range with a two-ship of bandits. I push up on my Weapons Select Switch to put an AIM-9 missile in priority.

My only two missiles left—the heat-seeking, short-range AIM-9 missile—is used in the visual area, which requires me to execute a close-range intercept. In the F-22, performing a stern-conversion intercept to the six o'clock position of an unaware bandit is relatively easy. Undetected by the fire control radars of two F-16s simulating a Su-27 Flanker, I saddle up in a Weapon Engagement Zone (WEZ) and fire my last two missiles at the bandits . . .

Code Name: Dodger Missions 1-4

Series Rated a **perfect 4/4 stars** by the Online Book Club

Missions can be read in any order

"One of the best books I've ever read!

More twists and turns than many mysteries. Absolutely in the same league as *Harry Potter*!"

—Online Book Club Official Review—Mission 4

My name's Justin Reed, a fourteen-year-old New York street kid. My mom died in a drowning accident when I was six. Then, when I was 11, my dad was murdered by the evil spy Pharaoh.

CIA Case Officer Bob Cheney discovered the Pharaoh was after me, too, so he took me into protective custody.

The Artful Dodger was my code name, and Bob, code name Fagin, trained me in all sorts of cool spy stuff: advanced self-defense, weapons, surveillance, evasion and survival. "The Company" even taught me how to use some sneaky spy gadgets. But I had other plans.

Escaping CIA custody, I used my old street smarts—and new CIA training—to track down the Pharaoh myself. But, I quickly learned, I was no match for a seasoned killer.

Bob rescued me.

After that, he adopted me. For the first time ever, I finally got to settle down into that quiet, suburban family life, the kind I guess most normal kids get to live.

But fate had "other plans" for me as well.

* * *

Excerpt from Mission 3: Jihadi Hijacking
CODE NAME: DODGER
(Missions can be read in any order)

EurEcono Air, Flight 924
Airbus A321
29,000' MSL over the Mediterranean Sea

It really wasn't my fault this time.

They were going to kill the guy, and I just wasn't going to let that happen.

The first hijacker wore a black headband, and held a Glock 18 automatic pistol in his hand, making him look scary as all get out. He had it aimed at some random guy, who was cowering in his seat six rows ahead of us.

The scumbag was ready to pull the trigger.

We were just about to start down into Tel Aviv when it happened.

The plane was nearly empty, and my adopted dad, Bob, and I had a row to ourselves in Coach. I had my nose pressed to the window, while Bob sat in an aisle seat, reading. He was combing through a stack of documents on his laptop that all said something like, *Consolidated Industries, Inc.* on the letterhead. But, I knew, they were actually some of his insanely boring *Top Secret* intelligence briefs.

Three more dudes in our section jumped out of their seats, wearing ski masks, and shouting. Two waving knives, the other, a Micro Uzi. How they'd smuggled those aboard, I hadn't a clue.

People screamed. A flight attendant fainted, right there in the aisle beside us.

Bob yanked her out of harm's way, just as one of the knife-wielding perps ran up the aisle to the front of our section to join the first guy.

"We are God's beloved soldiers of the World Islamic State Caliphate," the man with the Glock announced. "By His blessing, *WISC* has overcome the cockpit, and are now in command of this vessel."

Around us, passengers gasped. Bob and I traded alarmed glances.

"Cooperate with us and, most of you will not be harmed."

"*Most*?" I whispered to Bob.

With his fingers, he quickly "spoke" to me in ASL, or American Sign Language. It had been over six months since my CIA Communications training, so I was a little rusty.

"Don't move a muscle," he signed. "He's a major terror suspect. I didn't tell you this, because it's classified, but he's been the subject of a worldwide manhunt. We tailed one of his known associates onto this plane, hoping his colleague would lead us to him."

Gazing at him in pure disbelief, I signed back, "Well, I guess your plan worked."

I glanced behind us. The other two terrorists stood guard in the single aisle in our section, eyeing the passengers.

Looking back at Bob, I signed, "We can take 'em."

Bob shot me an alarmed glance. He signed back, "Stand down! We're outgunned, outnumbered, and there may be sleepers," he said, referring to more terrorists that might still be posing as passengers.

The hijacker continued. "If you do not comply with our instructions, you will be killed." He strolled down the aisle toward us, and stopped by a man wearing a Jewish yarmulka. "If you do not believe me, then this will be your fate."

To my horror, he aimed his Glock at the side of the man's head.

So, despite Bob's strict orders to stay seated and shut up, I jumped out and ran up the aisle toward him.

I screamed, "My God, my God! We're all gonna die!" I flailed my arms in the air like I was some kid spazzing out.

The slimeball snapped his head toward me. His eyes went wide.

He glanced back and forth between me and his target, as if unsure what to do next.

Finally, with narrowed eyes, he aimed at me.

All books now available in print, eBook, or audiobook at:

amazon.com/author/ericauxier
or
capnaux.com!

About the Author

Captain Eric Auxier is a pilot by day, writer by night, and kid by choice.

Never one to believe in working for a living, his past list of occupations include: Alaska bush pilot, freelance writer, mural artist, blogger, and pilot for a Caribbean seaplane operation.

He is now a Boeing 777 Captain for a major U.S. airline.

A Columnist for *Airways Magazine*, Mr. Auxier has also contributed to such publications as *Arizona Highways, Plane & Pilot*, and *AOPA Pilot*.

Author of nine books, the award-winning *Code Name: Dodger* is his first novel. In 2013, his second novel, *The Last Bush Pilots*, captured a coveted Top 100 spot on Amazon's Breakthrough Novels—Mainstream Fiction category, and is an aviation techno-thriller inspired by his experience as a young pilot flying the Alaska bush.

He is currently working on *Water and Air*, the long-awaited sequel to *The Last Bush Pilots*.

Mr. Auxier makes his home in Phoenix, Arizona.

CONTACT INFO

Author Email: eric@capnaux.com
Author Blog: capnaux.com
Author Books: amazon.com/author/ericauxier

Made in the USA
Las Vegas, NV
23 February 2022

44432308R00184